"So, I've been thinking of getting into the agency racket . . ."

All the familiar words came out.

"Advertising is just what you put into it. I think if you could find a good, reliable company with a suitable opening I would try it. Have you any other ambitions?"

Shane stopped. He was getting involved.

Janning answered with some diffidence, "I did . . . in a way . . . well, I wanted to be a writer . . . "

He added self-consciously, "I did a lot of poetry at Western – University of Western Ontario – some of it wasn't too bad . . . at least the prof liked it. Oh yes, I also wrote, you know, the Great Canadian Novel, but he said it was junk."

Farewell, Canadian author for the mills of advertising copy!

a novel by HARRY J. BOYLE

THE
GREAT
CANADIAN NOVEL

PaperJacks

A division of General Publishing Co. Limited
Don Mills, Ontario

Published in PaperJacks 1973
Reprinted by arrangement with
Doubleday Canada Limited.

ISBN 0-7737-7044-5
Printed and bound in Canada

To Marian

1

Shane Donovan came out of sleep muzzily. He was relaxed but aware of the gas bubbles giving a sensual pleasure to his buttocks. He was sleepily amused.

"When you can let the old britch snappers go without embarrassment," McAllister had said, "watch out. You're becoming a Mexican. Half the noise you hear at the fiesta isn't firecrackers. It's coming from beans—fried—refried—any way."

Shane lay still. The coarse sheet was beginning to feel warm. He didn't want to stir and whinge the rusty springs of the cot. A noise would bring Marguerita in from the other room, and he was content to look silently at the plastered walls and the rough joists of the ceiling and be alone.

God, what a relief to come awake without a throbbing head! It was actually pleasant in the coolness before the sun began glaring on the town. There was relative calm after another noisy night of roosters crowing, exploding rifles defending chickens from the wild dogs and the yapping of the domesticated ones. The leaves rustled scratchily. People on their way to market left sound trails of high-pitched conversation.

Shane now had only the normal discomfort of a northerner in a Mexican morning. During the first months there was a repulsive morning ritual of headache, nausea, and disgust. Now, because of Marguerita and so many people like Berrendo and something he couldn't identify even yet . . . he almost enjoyed itching and scratching in the way of a native. It wasn't so bad. It was real, and not like the tourists. In the flashy places with the swimming pools they would be waking in the same chilled wombs as millions of others in the international sameness of chain hotels. From Ankara to Bismarck, North Dakota, or from Vancouver to Miami Beach they were comforted by multi-national decorations and service. All neutered. So American and so alien.

But it wasn't like that in the house of Miguel. It was pure Mexican—poor! He felt fleas and sand. The fleas were a fact of life. The sand was always present, a new mist of it even now beginning, stirred up by the hooves of the tiny burros packing bundles of grease wood for the cooking fires of San Miguel.

Felipe had said it:

"Señor Donovan, it is not good to stop drinking tequila. Gringos never die from tequila. Pulque, maybe? Tequila, no. Gringos just get rubbed down by the sand or kicked to death by the fleas. Fleas live on gringos. They make Mexicans healthy."

Felipe was okay. Felipe really was glad when he didn't drink too heavily. Felipe felt responsible for him.

"There are bad Mexicans—and good Mexicans, Señor Donovan. But I have not been in your country, in Canada, so I cannot say—but some are good, I feel, and some are bad. To me you are a guest. In my family, a guest is to be respected."

Donovan ran his tongue around his mouth. It was dry. Not scratchy or sore. Just dry. His body was relaxed. Not aching.

"My body is dead. There is a soul and my soul is alive. That's all. My soul is alive and living in San Miguel." He hadn't thought much about soul. No, that was wrong. In San Miguel he had thought a lot about—soul? Something had triggered him to come around and appreciate days that were interesting—and startling sunsets and coming awake clearly and distinctly in the morning.

Maybe the geography cure had worked. There were those countless times of simply going away from Toronto—to Vancouver or Chicago or Montreal—on an excuse for a day that stretched into a week, and then finally being found in a remote hotel—oh, to hell with it. Coming to Mexico—perhaps it had worked.

Press release. *Shane Donovan alive and well in San Miguel de Allende,* would shock some of them. But the sense—the urge—to move—had it come back again just when he was relaxed? But this was different because he hadn't been drinking. That wasn't really true because he had started again—and, oh hell, it was too confusing to worry. You couldn't overlook wanting to run away—go walk about.

Like now. Get up and walk away—transparent—out past Marguerita—past Felipe's cantina and leave only the husk for Miguel—his landlord. No saint Miguel.

3

"Madre de Dios, who will pay for the funeral of this gringo? He owes me many pesos for the room and tequila."

It would be a lie, but it would give Miguel a reason for selling his stuff. He had already tried to buy the typewriter and radio. With hangovers Shane had often thought of wafting away on his soul and leaving the rotten carcass on the gritty bed in a cell of a room in the Mexican hill town. Now even the thought was cowardly.

"Shane."

She came in, nut brown and padding on the tiles with tiny, slapping sounds of her bare feet. She had tequila. Once it had been a morning ritual. She still persisted in spite of what he told her. A half glass of the water-clear fire to reignite the coals of last night's drinking and take him into a fuzzy day.

"No, goddamit!"

She recoiled. He was sorry.

"Oh, Marguerita—Maggie, love—I'm sorry."

Doe eyes and a smile that trembled until she knew his mood. If he were sick or angry her face would be a light brown mask. Now she was pleased. Child-woman smile.

"Not this morning."

How long would it take her to learn? She didn't want to be wrong in case he changed his mind.

"Come here."

Her tongue was an inquisitive visitor inside his lips until he pushed her gently away.

"Coffee, Maggie. You're a nymph."

He pictured her in the other room fanning the coals. Coffee, he wanted. Coffee she would make. If it had been tequila and it hadn't stayed down, she would watch with pain in her eyes until the coughing and vomiting stopped. That was when he didn't even have to ask for the beer.

She would bring the *cerveza* and he would writhe and sleep

4

and writhe more, coming awake late in the day to shamble across the road to the cantina. She would wait patiently to help shoulder and half-carry him back to his cot after his head had finally come to rest on the table.

When he started working regularly at the typewriter, he would simply reach for her. She was a dusky idol who sensed exorcism in his use of her body, but she didn't object or appear to mind. How could he tell her moods? Did he only imagine there was a faint trace of greater happiness when he drank and was dependent on her? Wonderful, mysterious people! Dignity edged with tragedy.

The breeze came in to rattle and play with the beaded strings in the doorway. It was different. This wasn't the usual sharp heat that increased hour by hour until it baked everything. This was soft and humid.

"Marguerita."

She was at the door of the bedroom almost instantly. He put down the glass. The girl moved towards him while fumbling with the buttons on her dress.

"No—no—coffee."

He pulled on his trousers and slipped his feet into the *espadrilles*.

Shane looked around the room. White plaster that stayed amazingly clean in spite of cooking fires in the other room. The face of Christ on a poster—or was it the anguished, tortured face of a Spaniard impaled there by a Mexican artist with an inherited memory of the agony of his country at the hands of the conquistadores? A crucifix—two gnarled pieces of thornbush on the wall, more evocative of passion than an old master's detail of Christ crucified on Calvary.

He stopped. He was stock-taking. This really must be a different morning. What had the instructor at the school—the Instituto—said? Something about beginning with a day

5

that's different. Marguerita placed the washbasin on the shelf under the mirror with the crack that was a constant reminder of the time he had thrown something, because a monster was crawling on the wall . . .

"You wash."

The water felt good. His beard was long enough to be soft. It had a sensual feel. Marguerita often ran her tiny hands over it, and if he came awake in the night while she was doing that, a strong sexual feeling came to him. He hadn't shaved at first because his hands shook so much. Then as the beard filled out he felt it gave him a new sense of identity.

Marguerita brought him the earthen mug of hot, bitter coffee. He might keep the beard. He had always felt beards were an affectation except on old, primitive men. Perhaps he was really a primitive. It was somehow satisfying.

"Like my beard, Maggie?"

That always made her giggle.

"You are like a padrone."

Shane was surprised at himself. Mornings had become different. Days had been mechanical simulations of days before. Now, each day was different. The crowd in the plaza, a domestic quarrel echoing over ancient walls, the excitement of people preparing for a fiesta or a bullfight, the almost daily semi-pagan rites at the cathedral, artists engrossed in their work on the mountainside, women washing clothes in the stream—and even the daily ritual he had painfully developed at the typewriter.

"Goddamit, Marguerita, I never knew life could be—"

He stopped. That was the one difficulty. There were things you couldn't explain. It was like being with a child. A vocabulary worked to describe an object if it could be seen. But how could you explain about feelings?

There were other mysteries for Marguerita as well. The

manuscript for instance. She watched him silently when he typed. Each typed page was something magical to be stared at as she hunkered on the floor and stared as if sheer concentration would bring interpretation. She cried the day he took the originals to the post office and mailed them to Eric McMaster. She placed the carbon copy in a plastic sack and hung it with her starched Sunday dress from the roof joist.

The day they walked by the river where the tourists never went, he had tried to tell her something. Something important—like a whole life he was finally only beginning to understand.

"Maggie, you will never know how much of you there is in that book. Maybe not you, but I don't think it ever would have happened without you."

It was no use. Yet, feeling her close, he knew there were things he didn't have to explain. They made love in the dry, brittle grass and the remoteness went away. Words on a page would be an eternal mystery. But this girl-woman sensed how he felt at this moment without a word being exchanged. She was a part of a sensual country; she felt.

"Is it going to rain, Maggie—is it really? I can never tell. You can. God, you can tell. Sometimes I think you are part witch, Marguerita—Marguerita." When he poured her name out slowly she smiled with pleasure.

"My name, señor—Marguerita."

She had said it that morning as he came awake on the cot in the house across from the cantina. He was feverish and his head ached. She had gone to bring Felipe. Felipe was a ministering—oh, no angel. Not Felipe.

"It would take a very long time to explain, señor, but you do not listen so good. Take this and you will be better."

That was the beginning of the morning ritual of tequila.

7

The pocked face of the cantina owner relaxed when Shane stopped coughing.

"Good. My cousins bring you from Mexico City. You drink very much and say you must stay away. We know, and Miguel who owns this place says you may stay here. My cousins—how do I say it—they are not saints, but they too have suffered."

They imagined he was in trouble, and accepted him. The rent was twelve dollars—approximately—he was vague about the rate of pesos. Marguerita would work for him—for about the same amount of money—

"But, my money—"

Felipe smiled.

"You drink a lot, señor, but you are no fool. You trust Marguerita."

Marguerita unbuttoned her dress and, putting her hand in the cloth binding her breasts, drew out his wallet. He felt foolish.

Felipe roared with laughter.

"Take it, señor, and see."

The traveller's cheques were intact. Somewhere he had spent about two hundred dollars since leaving New York.

"Marguerita would not let my cousins take more than you promise. She is a very good girl. You have a good woman."

That was eleven months before, and Marguerita was still there as housekeeper, nurse, mistress—faithful and fiercely devoted. As if to break his musing she spoke again.

"Si, Señor Shane. The rains come soon."

From the pocket of the coarse brown shift she was wearing, she brought a packet of dark Mexican cigarettes, lit two and placed one between his lips. His hair was matted, a mop of blond hair tinged with grey. His beard was untrimmed, yel-

8

lowish brown with a darker smear on the chin like a stain. His belly, now slack-skinned, barely rimmed the waistband of his trousers.

He reread the letter. Marguerita pretended to be fussing with the charcoal under the pan, but she was watching him. The letter, like the manuscript, was an object of mystery, and he sensed her fear.

Marguerita rested her hand on his forearm. Shane moved to touch her hair, jet black, fastened with the silver brooch he had bought her in Guanajuato.

"You're a doll, Maggie. Good, God—a doll and so damned much more civilized than . . . than those harpy bitches who pretend—"

The smoke triggered a convulsive cough that spread to his stomach.

"Señor Shane. The tequila."

"No, Marguerita, not today."

She poured it slowly down the drainhole in the tiled floor, and her action had the quality of a ceremonial rite.

"You know, don't you? You know something's up."

Her shoulders barely moved.

"I think you know more about me than anybody. I've lived and worked and married and had children—and known people for years and they don't know me—but you do."

No response.

"When I was a boy on the prairie, the cottonwood leaves would show the white side, and the breeze felt different and no matter how hot it was, we knew it was going to rain. Then my mother made us go and dump the spiders out of the rain barrels and put the barrels out to catch water from the rain spouts of the eaves troughs."

What a change a rain made! Dry prairies that turned green. Dust that turned to mud. Your skin no longer itchy.

9

"Maggie, your coffee is strong enough to galvanize a man into anything. Maybe that's why my stomach feels better. It's galvanized!"

Marguerita smiled as he laughed. Their communication was more sensory than oral.

Shane moved the bench under the skimpy shade of the palm tree in the patio. It would still be cool in Felipe's bar, the big fan stirring the air. Pablo the beggar stared from the doorway, and José, the crippled wood seller, must be inside waiting for his morning treat.

"Here," he said, fumbling for pesos. "Take this and buy Pablo and José a drink."

"I bring you *cerveza*—very cold."

It made him angry. Why couldn't she understand? But he didn't say anything. When Marguerita brought back the moisture-beaded bottle he held it in his hand.

"You seek?"

Shane shook his head.

"You can't say sick."

"Seek—seek."

She said it several times slowly and when he shook his head she went in the small adobe house. A sailor he had been drinking with one night printed *DONOVAN'S REEF* in chalk over the door. With no rain to erase it, the name stayed.

"My reef. Shane Donovan aground."

Miguel's adobe was on the Street of the Goats. There was no need for an address, in the native quarter of San Miguel. It could have been a thousand miles from uptown and the plaza and the ancient cathedral and the tourists and the art students and the writers in search of colour and the film maker—no, people didn't get mail here and if they did, it came in care of Felipe's cantina or Hernandez's Grocery or the Venetian Botica. Shane stayed on because the people accepted him and maintained a conspiracy of silence about his presence.

Routinely, his visa had once been checked by a policeman. It was a six-months' visa about to expire when Felipe reminded him. Apologetically, he explained the need for some money and Shane endorsed a traveller's cheque for twenty American dollars. A week later, he had an extension for six months. He didn't ask for an explanation but Felipe said:

"It is good to have friends—the policeman is a cousin of my wife in Cuernavaca."

Donovan was also hazy about how the arrangement with Marguerita had come about. At first, she swept, cleaned, and made tentative offers of meals. One night she stayed and nursed him. Next day she brought a small handwoven rug, with some trinkets and clothes. At first when people came and drank with him, he was acutely aware of Marguerita, but there were advantages. His money and typewriter would be locked in the small cupboard that was the only piece of furniture apart from the bed and two wooden benches in the bedroom.

"Why do you do that?" he had asked her.

"They steal when you drink. They make crazy like they loco, but they wait until you sleep. Then they steal. They not steal when Marguerita"—she added hesitantly—"stay here."

She had become his woman. He knew she was regarded that way even by the grave little Italian-Mexican apothecary, Roncalli, at the Venetian Botica.

"A good girl, Marguerita," said Roncalli once when Shane had gone in desperation about the tremor pains in his legs. "She lights candles for you every Friday at Immaculata Concepciona."

Strange people! She was his woman, his mistress, lighting candles for his soul.

At first he lived on drinking, occasional food, and on the warmth of Marguerita. No matter where he was she seemed to be able to find him. When his drinking companions deserted him at the *tabuada*, she came to stoke a fire, keeping the wild dogs away until the bus to town came by in the morning.

He was certain it all began with the idea of writing. The trip from New York, he kept reassuring himself, had been deliberate. Putting the money in the bank was a sign of that. He had even enrolled in the Instituto as a writer. But one class left him in a stunned rage. The tousle-haired young instructor's incoherence and clichés were too much to bear.

Two days of drinking in La Cucaracha. Then he talked to a veteran writer by the name of McAllister.

"Get to hell out of this bunch of phonies. Go and write. Write when you're sober. Write when you're drunk. But write and tear your guts out. Find out if you can do it."

He stayed away from the Instituto and even uptown as much as possible. There were two rooms in the house. White, plastered walls. Packed earth floor. An old army cot. The barest of possessions. A few cooking pots and a charcoal stove over which Marguerita worked miracles when he felt like eating.

Now, he had a manuscript. Three hundred and eighty-seven pages. Days of writing when he sat on the edge of a white hot knife with each stroke of the typewriter sending jolts into his mind. Nights of coming awake to listen to the roosters squawking and the dogs barking. Times when he had gone to sit and smoke and stare at the purple dark sky and try to ignore the tremors and pains in his legs. Days when he wanted only oblivion. Times of sandy crawling noises on the black walls when Marguerita clutched him to her naked body trying to coax the devil out of him. A whirly-go-rig of writing and drinking—and of compassion from a girl who could not even write her own name.

Marguerita had made only one tremulous request. It was Christmas and would Señor Shane come with her. It was an ordeal to move with the packed mob to the cathedral. There was an eloquent simplicity in this faith, ornate as some of the externals were. Yet, he was deeply moved by the *posada*, representing the search by Joseph and Mary for a place of refuge until the ninth day, Christmas Eve, when they reached Belén, where Christ was born.

Marguerita sang a strangely sad hymn, more pagan than Christian, as they walked back from the cathedral. He didn't go to the cantina but sat a long time before going to bed. Next morning was when he started trying to write in earnest, without any drinking bouts. There had been hangups, dark depressions and some drinking, but he always managed to come back and go on again—and as he wrote the anger burned out.

Had some release been triggered by the cathedral crowd? Religion? No, it wasn't a religious feeling, unless a recognition of simple human beings had a sanctifying gift. He was reminded of a time as a youngster when there was Midnight Mass in the stark, cold little chapel in Nonsuch. San Miguel was gaudy. But both places were primitive and he smelled the incense and the people—and thus they were alike—and there was joy and peace with the same earthy feeling.

Here there was a sky to watch and people who never hurried. They took days and hours and living and religion as a part of something to be spun out and if death and pain and even starvation were close each day was for living and existing. Each day was a triumph of survival against the odds. A tomorrow was a mystery, so why worry about it.

Today, he would go to the plaza.

13

A haircut and a shave?

A haircut, yes. No shave. A trim. The beard was now a part of Shane Donovan. Marguerita laughed at his squinting in the cracked mirror and brought the small hand mirror he had bought her. It wasn't cloudy. God, he looked wild. He would definitely get it trimmed. Vandyke! His eyes were better. A faint bloodshot tracery. His cheeks were tanned and the veined lines had gone from his nose.

"Maggie, when will the rains come?"

The girl looked at the sky. It was cloudless.

"Two days—three days—a small rain each day—and then big ones. Everything, Señor Shane, will be green and beautiful and we go out in the country, no?"

"Yes."

"You not go away?"

He stood up.

"Not go away. Come on, we're going to the bank."

She cringed back.

"No—no—too many people."

"Too many gringos?"

"Señor Ornandez, not like me very much."

The banker disapproved.

"To hell with Ornandez, you're my woman. Come on."

A fat man on a tiny burro nodded, his eyes raking Marguerita. The policeman sitting on a chair beside the door of the municipal brothel called out something that Shane didn't understand. The girl clutched his arm tighter.

"What did he say?"

"He is a pig. Said there was work there when the gringo goes north."

A dog with a bleeding eye passed. He didn't stop. At one time he would have, but the months had changed him. Blood and suffering were simple elements in this country. That fat

14

old man who ran the emporium of handicrafts beckoned to him. It dawned on Shane. His second visa had only a month to go. The people who protected his anonymity were keenly aware of it.

McAllister had explained it, shrugging his shoulders. "They accept you. They think you are in trouble. I don't think they would have the same attitude if they felt you were just a writer. Remember these people live with pain and trouble. They are simpatico. They know how to cope."

It was stifling in the narrow street. The heat bounced back from the cobblestones and the plastered walls. Along the four sides of the plaza, tourists moved in clusters from shop to shop. From inside the dim, shuttered La Cucaracha bar, a juke box played one of the endless Mexican variations of the Bonanza TV theme. A few people at individual tables in front of the soda fountain nursed plain bottles of brilliant, gaseous drinks.

"I wait over there."

He went in the frosted glass doors of the National Bank of San Miguel. The fat woman tourist muttered "Bum" as he brushed against her enormous straw basket. Her hips were threatening to burst from her pink shorts, and the insides of her legs were like blue-veined parchment.

"Señor Donovan, this way, please—"

Ornandez was the Mexican equivalent of the smug banker anywhere. Dark suit, vest, glittering stickpin—the kind who would look formal in the bath.

"How much money do I have—?"

Ornandez ticked his oiled moustache with the tip of a ringed finger.

"Not thinking of a withdrawal, Señor Donovan?"

Shane laughed.

"Just curious."

Ornandez relaxed.

"Eight thousand and twenty-two dollars—"

He pushed a bit of paper showing the calculation from pesos.

"I want a thousand dollars in cash."

Ornandez's eyes glittered. He knew of Shane's drinking.

"Is that wise?"

"Yes. I have decided."

Ornandez nodded. Shane was enjoying the uncomfortable feeling of the banker. A cheroot gave him something to do until the transaction was concluded.

"Mr. Ornandez, you are a banker, and like a priest or a doctor, you keep the secrets of your clients?"

Ornandez beamed.

"Of course, Señor Donovan. You can depend fully on me. This bank is known for its discretion."

There was a look of naked, sensual curiosity on the banker's face. Shane smiled, well aware of the banker's interest.

"I may be going away for a time and I wish to provide money for Señorita Marguerita."

"Of course, Señor Donovan."

Ornandez was pleased.

"How do you wish to provide it?"

"I thought so much a month."

The banker nodded.

"If I might suggest, and remember I do not wish to intrude. The interest on your balance would be almost seventy dollars a month—a good deal of money here and—when you return, the balance would remain."

It made sense to Shane. But Marguerita would never come to the bank. Roncalli? Yes, Roncalli was an honest man.

"A very good idea, Señor Ornandez, and now—"

He knew he could trust Ornandez. Something in the man

16

had changed and he only learned it when he was leaving. Ornandez stood up to shake his hand formally.

"You are a gentleman, Señor Donovan. You have my word of the best interest of Marguerita. She is a fortunate woman to have known you, señor. If I may at times have seemed—a bit—a trifle—"

He didn't have to finish. Donovan knew how many girls were left each year by gringos. He felt better about Ornandez.

Marguerita was talking to a plump woman with a small child.

"Who was that, Marguerita?" he asked as the woman, whose face seemed almost familiar, nudged the small boy away.

"It is my mother, Señor Donovan."

This was the never-ending mystery of Mexico. Marguerita had been living with him for months, going home only occasionally, and he had never before seen a member of her family. He knew vaguely that the father lived with a second wife and family in Mexico City.

At a store just off the plaza, he bought shoes, socks, underwear, and a ready-made suit of olive drill such as the local landowners wore.

"Now," he said, steering her into the ladies' wear department where a few solid matrons were fingering yard goods, "we must get some clothes for you."

"Are we going away, Señor Shane?"

"Maybe, Maggie."

He had never given any consideration to clothes for her. She had one black, satiny kind of dress with white lace collar and cuffs which she kept stored in tissue paper and which she wore only on feast days or to church. The rest of the time she wore the shift of brown homespun material that faded to a dustier color each time it was washed.

"Do you speak English?" he asked the bosomy woman with

the thin threads of hair on her upper lip. "Good, I want to dress this young lady up completely."

The saleswoman pointed to the privacy afforded by racks of clothes and proceeded to undress Marguerita. Off came the pinned cloth that served as a makeshift brassiere. She had no slip or panties. She was beautifully proportioned and when the salesgirl folded her into a brassiere, it seemed a shame.

"So much money—so much money."

Marguerita kept saying it over and over as he paid the beaming woman.

She sat, not willing to part with her clothes bundle, and watched as the barber cut his hair and trimmed the beard. On the way into the public baths, he caught sight of himself in a mirror. A middle-aged professor who came to lecture to a ladies' group about the wild orchid of Yucatán.

The attendant left them alone in a private part of the bath for a tip. Marguerita was torn as if the experience was part of an illusion which might vanish.

"Shane—Shane."

This girl who had always responded but never with excited passion, seemed suddenly possessed by a fire beyond control. She was both laughing and crying, whispering in one moment, and in the next exclaiming without shyness or restraint.

"Marguerita—I do love you."

He was saying things he had never thought of before. She lay half in the water and half out, her head against his chest. She was a living part of him and no longer merely a part of Miguel's house.

Was this love?

Was it what he had been searching for? Did it come from simplicity and the reality of loving and hating and suffering and being joyful, with tomorrow a mere abstraction never to be considered?

In the restaurant he devoured the *gaspacho* with great chunks of bread. It was tart. On the way back, they rode a rickety taxi because it was an occasion.

"Look, Señor Shane."

She was an excited light-cocoa elf trying on each piece of clothing and taking each off to wrap it in tissue paper, and the hot afternoon wore on and he sat and smoked and watched her.

"I get you a *cerveza.*"

She was so happy she would bring him anything.

"No, Marguerita—I don't want any beer."

It was a lie. He wanted a beer. The desire was unmistakeable. Sip a few beers and let the slow, misty feeling slip in to stifle his resolve. Then move to Felipe's for tequila and talk and fire in his belly—and then he would come awake the next morning and the urge to move on would have passed.

When his thirst got to be a raging thing he went to Hernandez's Grocery and bought mineral water and ice and sipped at it. When night came, Marguerita cooked tortillas and he ate some, but his stomach rejected the food. He was sweating and weak, almost as if he had been drinking. The codeine and aspirin he took put him into a sleep of nightmares.

He woke and the air seemed cooler, but he was shaking and Marguerita came in, and gradually the warmth of her body relaxed him. He was falling in a deep pit and when he came out of it the air was different. It was like the stillness at home in Saskatchewan before a storm. The dogs howling off outside the walls of the old village sounded like coyotes.

A dry drunk! He hadn't believed in such a thing but both McAllister and Dr. Leddy had warned him. McAllister spelled it out.

"Of course, you'll get the same—almost the same symptoms for quite a while after you stop. That's the hell of it. A few drinks will fix them, but then you're right back where you started from. It's going to be tough every three months or so, and that may last for up to two years."

There was something even more difficult. He had failed before, but this time he had to do it without fail.

"Marguerita," he said finally, "I must tell you something—"

Her body moulded to him and he couldn't speak. Perhaps there was no need to tell her. She knew he was going back. She was fierce and tender and close. He felt a mixture of devotion and passion, but he would have felt better if he had been able to express it.

When he finally slept, it was without fever or dreams. When he woke up, she was sitting naked in the doorway, with the beaded curtain streaming down her back. The rain washing down over her body made the beads look like red stripes of wounds from a lash. They were illusions. Only her tears would be real.

Marguerita was soft and tender but life had prepared her for sadness. She had a wisdom beyond her years. She lived, as her people lived, to appreciate to the full the surprise of comfort or happiness, without the torture of expectation.

He would leave and she would marry and bear children and remember him, in the way she remembered her religion. It would be a presence, to be recalled on special occasions with a flickering flame of memory, like the votive lights she lit in the cathedral.

She came back to bed and lay close to him. He felt her breasts on his back. Her lips were touching his neck. It roused him when her hand came like a soft pulse on his loin but he didn't move. It was too late. She was crying silently but it was too late.

When he woke up in the pre-dawn, the dogs were still barking. There were crickets in the room.

"A cricket."

What biological mysteries there were about men and creatures! The crickets had moved in just before the rain. He tried to explain.

"They have to and they don't know why. I have to go back. I don't know why. I have to go back because there is something inside me which says I must go back. I've been here and I must leave but I do not know why. I must."

It had all started that Sunday, when he left Toronto and unknowingly began the trek to this mountain town in Mexico. San Miguel de Allende was another Nonsuch, Saskatchewan, but he couldn't have gone back there. You can't go home again; Thomas Wolfe explored that. Yet now he had to go back.

On that May morning, almost a year before, he had only expected to go to New York for an award. It had been a long time since then, but nothing compared to the few days in New York that stretched into an eternity—or simply a nightmare. It had started as another runaway—no doubt about that now—only he had, for once, a valid excuse—the award—when he left Toronto.

It was strange that now he thought of tiptoeing past Marguerita. He had left Toronto in the same way—unobserved—flitting away!

2

They grouped in the steely functional atmosphere of the Malton International Airport waiting room. In *Airport* Hailey had been right about one thing. New York-bound passengers always seemed impatient. They bunched like nervous sheep near the ramp. It was the Sunday 12:01 plane from Toronto to New York.

"Flight 791 now loading at Gate Seven. All aboard and no smoking, please."

Shane Donovan moved with the crowd down the stairway.

"Hell of a time to be going to New York, isn't it?"

The nervous young man smiled at Shane.

"Better than the late afternoon mob," muttered Shane, going faster to avoid having a seat mate.

"Do you travel much, sir?"

"Quite a bit."

The conversation died in the process of trooping across the tarmac to the plane.

Shane Donovan had the look of an athletic man with too much flesh, although his tailoring partly disguised the extra weight. He was slightly flushed, in the manner of a person unaccustomed to exertion, and he wore sunglasses.

"Good morning, sir."

"Good morning . . . ah . . . Miss Dumonte . . . with an e."

The pretty, angular face smiled.

"Thank you, sir."

The crowd settled thinly in the jet. People took window seats and barricaded their privacy with briefcases on the outside seats.

"Everything okay, Mr. Donovan?"

He was surprised.

"I am flattered . . . but maybe I should be ashamed."

"Oh no, sir, I just remembered you gave me the Chanel."

"Did it work?"

"Pretty well . . ."

She folded his topcoat carefully and as she stretched to place it in the rack he noticed the well-curved outline of her figure.

"That was a bribe from me to you."

"You didn't have to. You didn't really cause any trouble."

Shane winced.

"Well, it was Air Canada's fault. If the plane hadn't been delayed, I wouldn't have been stranded in the bar for so long."

"You were just happy, Mr. Donovan. You should see some of them."

She was off to join her companion stewardess in the ritualistic routines of air travel. Here a bag to be stowed under the seat, a cautionary word against smoking until the aircraft is airborne, a coat to be tucked away, a nervous passenger to be soothed and the flat platters of newspapers and magazines to be proffered as pacifiers.

As they surged into the air he automatically braced his feet against the floor, squirmed in the seat to ease the crotch binding of his underwear and felt in his pocket for aspirin. He had a seething hangover, apparent in the sharp pressure on his head and the touch of bile rolling in his stomach. Toronto was spread out below, caught without any of the glamour of night and revealed as a swirling mass of houses, trees, concrete buildings, and almost deserted streets.

12:08. Mona, Bill, and Rita would just be out unless Monsignor McQuarrie happened to be the one saying Mass at St. Teresa's. Six minutes home. They would find the note:

Mona, dear, have had to rush and catch noon plane for New York. Come and join me. Love. Shane.

She would lift her hat off carefully, holding it on her left index finger, saying absent-mindedly, "Put the kettle on, Rita, please."

"Anything you would like, Mr. Donovan?"

"Well, I could stand a couple of aspirins and a glass of water."

He should have left it at that but had to add, "Getting an award in New York and the office had a celebration last night. Sorry to trouble you."

"You're very welcome, Mr. Donovan."

But she wanted to talk.

"We'll be serving lunch, Mr. Donovan."

"I had breakfast a little while ago . . ."

Breakfast! Two raw eggs in tomato juice with Worcestershire, salt, and pepper. It was cloudless, and the sun flared against a wing, stabbing in the window. His head hurt. His stomach felt acidy. He grimaced.

"Black coffee."

Her smile was impersonal but curious.

"May I ask you something?"

"Sure."

"That shaving lotion? I have to get something for a boy-friend and it's rather intriguing."

"Shaving lotion? Oh . . . oh, I know. It's a cologne for men. They gave us samples to try out, and get a name for it. I splashed it on to cover a multitude of sins."

"It's intriguing."

"Do you like men to wear stuff like that?"

Miss Dumonte wrinkled her face.

"You know something, Mr. Donovan? To be perfectly honest, the best-smelling man I ever remember was my father —old-fashioned shaving soap with a brush, Castile soap, to-bacco—"

Her eyes showed amusement.

"And occasionally whisky."

She flitted off then, leaning over the aisle seat to adjust a seat for a passenger, exposing a knee and remarkable thighs. His erotic interest was natural enough. It was often a by-product of a hangover.

Man scent . . . spoor . . . Tiger Bay . . . Triple O . . . Jackman wanted a name for a new line of men's toiletries. Toiletries? They were more like cosmetics. A half billion dollars in sales of paints, powders, and perfumes to make American and Canadian males more alluring. Call them Man-A-Lure . . . like Man-A-Live. God, but won't we be the scented generation?

J. B. Williams shaving soap. It was a round cake that his father kept in a cracked mug. He could see him with the skin of his face stretched taut between his fingers, the blood vessels coming close to the pink transparency in the wake of his prized King Kutter razor.

The plane lurched sideways and it brought back the discomfort of his inner rawness. Outside the plane there was nothing to look at. A ridged mass of clouds below merely reflected the pitiless sun. The plane pulsed on, steady and monotonous. There was nothing to do but close his eyes and feel the tiny beating behind his eyelids. His hands gripped the armrests. Relaxed, they had a tendency to twitch.

His mind kept running over the night before.

The scene at the Country Club was like a pandemonic beer commercial on television, with people pushing and jostling around someone pounding the piano.

"Boy, it's really something to get a gang like this together without weapons."

They were there to congratulate him on winning the big A.

"Shane, this is the best damned get-together of the business in years."

Joe Tulk was sloshed but there was something in what he said.

"Boy, you sure did it. Make those Yankee bastards sit up and take notice with a Canadian winning."

That was Bill Evers, a transplanted American. Like converts, they were always more fervent.

"Great industry, isn't it?"

Jackman had also said that when he first congratulated him on winning the Hiram Aldred Award. Suggested advertising wasn't such a bad business, in spite of the smart-asses who always wrote about it.

The whole thing wouldn't have been so bad if he hadn't taken such pains to persuade Mona to go with him.

"You go by yourself, Shane . . ."

She said it flatly.

"Mona, I can't go tomorrow night without you. It wouldn't look right. I can't face that crowd without you."

"Oh, Shane! I feel out of place with those people."

He had no difficulty in seeing her. Soft, golden hair paling to a gentle lemonish, drawn into a bun at the back of her head . . . old-fashioned . . . but suiting the broad forehead and the face that had softened as it fleshed with age. Her breasts swelled below the ruby pendant he had bought her in London. It glowed like a globule of deep crimson fire in the hollow of her throat. She was stouter and fuller now . . . hips and breasts . . . but her legs were still as slim and un-marked as when he had met her twenty-seven years before.

Mona was buttoning and unbuttoning a blouse button. It was a sign of agitation and, remembering it, he wondered why he always desired her so ardently when she acted like this. Maybe before they went to the party at the Country Club . . . but it was no use. Encounters, other than in bed behind locked doors, had ceased since Bill, who then was five, had wandered into their room on a Sunday when he was supposed to be asleep.

"Are you hurting Mummy?"

Shane winced.

"It's just so hopeless, Shane. We've been through it . . . time, time and again . . . You say you have to go to a party and you can't go without me and you're not going to drink too much. I think you even believe yourself. I used to. So we go. You look like a little boy making his First Communion . . . all shiny . . . and I relax . . . And you vanish and when you come back you're glowing . . . but in a different way."

Her hands went up helplessly.

"Mona." Shane knew how to talk to her. "Do you think for one minute I'm going to do anything to wreck . . . or jeopardize that affair in New York? Do you really think so?"

She was weakening. She wanted to believe him.

"Well, Shane . . . you know you *have* done some pretty stupid things. If I go . . ."

He walked over slowly and put his hand on her shoulder.

"Mona, dear, you know that it's the first time the Hiram Aldred Medal has come to a Canadian . . . to me . . . and Mona . . ."

He left his hand on her shoulder. It helped with the convincing.

"You and your talk, Shane. All right, I'll go, but it's against my better judgement. Please be careful."

It was Michael Bawlon's fault. Mona said he always blamed somebody else. It was still Bawlon's fault. Why did he come along with that phony bet on the difference between Demerara and Jamaica rum?

"Look, Shane, old cock . . . come along and settle this bloody argument. You're a rum fancier . . ."

It was the main lounge at the Eastwood Country Club. There was a cluster around Mona and T. A. Jackman and his wife Trixie and himself. He was drinking ginger ale. Trixie with the slithery body and the pouty pretence of being a Marilyn Monroe reincarnation had been hip-rubbing him and smiling over her glass. Why in hell did he go to the bar with Bawlon for that silly bet?

It must have been to get away from Trixie. Everyone knew Trixie was poison. A young wife of an aging man is madness . . . and when that man is your *boss!*

Shane recognized it was an excuse. Maybe it was a training for Confession. Somebody called it "devil wrestling"—and he knew he was good at finding reasons that were on the edge of the truth.

"I wanted a drink."

Now, he admitted it, aloud. He had liked being in the congested bar downstairs, sipping the rums and making the announcement, "This is Jamaica . . ." He was right! That called for several rum swizzles. When he went back upstairs, Mona scarcely seemed to notice his absence.

The crowd in the Main Club room simmered down as T. A. Jackman told them he wanted to say something. Trixie leaned over to whisper, "Ah surely do envy Mona tonight."

Mona looked up as she was fumbling with his cigarette lighter. He could feel his face flush. The cigarette lighter clattered to the floor and as he bent over, Trixie beat him to it, coming up slowly with her dress hanging to expose her breasts. She was being provocative and Shane lost his balance and landed on the floor.

There had been a lot of banter and when it straightened out, Mona was standing beside him.

"What's wrong with you?"

"Trixie was trying to show me the tattoo on her navel." It didn't come out the way he intended.

"You've been drinking."

His tongue went sliding like ponies on ice.

"Noss . . . sssh."

"Quiet!"

T.A. was speaking . . . "and I can't help but be proud of the fact that we have an increase of billings of over two million this year . . ."

Someone yelled, "Get in the plug, T.A."

The stringy man waved his hand.

"At Jackman and Bates we never miss."

He beamed at the mingled applause and booing.

"As I was saying when interrupted by a jealous competitor . . ."

It was the so-called hearty rivalry and jesting that always went on at such affairs.

". . . and I am proud of the recognition of one of the brightest jewels in our crown of achievement . . ."

"Twinkle, twinkle, little star," whispered Trixie. He tried to smile, becoming aware that Mona was looking at him. When he dropped his cigarette there was a fussing until he managed to stamp it out.

"Shane, what's the matter?"

"Nothing."

". . . and Shane is typical of the new breed of men who are making an adventure out of advertising. He has experience in daily newspapers and radio broadcasting, but he also has a keen and individual sense of creativity. I must say he has used this with great success. He brought the full impact of his imagination to bear . . . on . . . well just think of his winning the Hiram Aldred Award for creative achievement . . . not alone in Canada . . . just think of it . . ."

Jackman's voice had gone up in intensity ". . . but also in the Yew Ess of . . . Ay . . . and now I say to you . . ."

T.A. was going solemn ". . . he ranks with the great men in the industry . . ."

There was reverence here: "Such men as Lasker . . ."

Shane had tuned out. He didn't want to hear the bag of tricks . . . public relating the industry, it was called . . . God, if he ever said what he felt to Jackman . . .

But he had said it to Jackman! There was the hazy, filmy curtain that kept him from remembering . . . that kept drifting across his mind. He had said it to Jackman in the parking lot afterwards.

The argument . . . no, it was a declamation . . . a drunken declamation . . . God Almighty, what was it? . . . Jesus, for the life of him he couldn't remember what had happened. He didn't want to think about it but it haunted him all the time . . . like in Montreal when he had met Ned in front of the Mount Royal and Ned had laughed about his Polynesian dancing the night before . . . and *he couldn't remember even being in the place* . . .

Jackman had said, "Watch the booze, Shane. You know you can pull my leg like you did tonight, but these boys in New York have no sense of humor . . . absolutely none . . . it's too much of a cutthroat operation there."

That was Jackman's way of passing it off. But when? Whatever had he said? It was no use trying to bury it.

Three o'clock . . . three o'clock . . . Scott Fitzgerald's time of the dark night of the soul and it always being three o'clock and he had come awake on the chesterfield, groping and trying to remember where he was. His hand could tell from the texture of the fabric that he was at home . . . coat on . . . pants on . . . tie strangling.

"Mona?"

"Yes . . ." dully.

Then nothing. He heard a car come slowly down the street and the headlights swathed across the room.

"Are you all right?"

It was her Canadian Martyr Number One voice.

"Yes—in a way."

"You said you wouldn't drink."

"Everybody knows I drink. They'd think I was going high hat on them just over winning the stinking award . . ."

". . . What an answer . . ."

"Well, what's wrong with it?"

"Which would be better? To make an ass of yourself as

you did, or to be high hat . . . and that I don't believe . . . most of that bunch would *envy* you for staying sober."

His thoughts were orderly and precise but when he tried to speak they splashed like dots on a radar screen.

"Will you come to New York with me?"

"I can't help you in New York."

She was standing in a sheer negligee with her figure perfectly outlined by the light from outside.

"God, Mona . . ."

She stepped away when he lurched from the couch.

"I just want to think and get straightened out and get some answers."

He shouldn't have tried that word.

"Why don't you get all the alcohol out of your system first?"

He ignored the point.

"I have to make a speech when I get that award and somehow . . . I know what I say in it is going to determine the rest of my life."

She didn't answer. She didn't understand.

"I don't want to spend the rest of my life at this thing. There was a time I believed in it . . . but now there are more important things to do. I know . . . I know . . . you'll say that this world is only a place of temporary something or other and we'll get our reward in Heaven."

"Don't tell me you're losing your faith?"

"Faith . . . shmaith . . . I don't know. I still believe . . . I guess I do . . . but there are a hell of a lot of things changing. Before I slip off into that void, whatever it is . . . I want to have a feeling that I've left something besides . . . a stained-glass window."

"Here's your coffee, Mr. Donovan."

Shane sat up in the seat. The stewardess was back.

"Thanks."

The Saturday night flashback wouldn't go away. The picture came back like a film reel snapping into focus. Every word and nuance was painfully clear. He had told Jackman off!

"That was a lot of bushwa in there, T.A."

Hands were pulling and pushing at him and grabbing his car keys until they shoved him in the front seat with Mona behind the wheel. They couldn't shut him up.

"Now," soothed Jackman, "too much excitement."

"I'm no goddam little boy . . . I'm a big boy who just got the lollipop for advertising . . . and you didn't tell all those big mens and womens in there what it was for . . . wild flowers in toilet paper . . . wipe your fanny with a pansy . . . and snapdragons for old maids . . . and how about next we dress up the old mail order catalogue or introduce corn cobs again for all those silly bastards who want to live amongst antiques . . . real backwoodsy . . . the way I grew up . . . and maybe you too, T.A. . . . and now the barefoot boy is getting the Pulit—sherr prize . . . that's what you said . . ."

The car started away as he leaned out.

"Doesn't this whole business give you a pain where the wild flowers are going. Think of all those people in there standing around getting drunk on me . . . the Crown Prince of Toilet Tissue . . ."

Mona pressed down on the accelerator and he snapped back in the seat.

Morning . . . this Sunday morning and the sounds of a suburb awakening. That old bastard Henderson fiddling around with a lawn mower . . . a big noisy, backfiring gasoline

34

powered lawn mower when there was only a bald fringe of grass on the lawn. The bells of the church down the street, jangling over and over . . . and the awareness of Mona leaving the bedroom. The smell of coffee . . . tantalizing and sickening at the same time. When he moved his head it felt as if it were cracked.

"Mom, are you ready for church?"

It was Bill calling. Mona answered from the kitchen, in a voice that ripped at Shane with his eyes pressed shut.

"Just a moment, Bill. You get the car out. Is Rita ready?"

Rita answered farther off.

"I'm ready, Mom. Is Dad coming?"

Shane shivered in bed, expecting Mona's answer.

"Your father is resting, I presume."

He had to keep on playing dead, aware that his eyelids were quivering when Mona came to stand and stare at him. It was an infinite relief when the front door banged and he heard the car drive off.

Ten-fifteen. They were going to 10:30 Mass and they would be back at twelve. If he made it, he could go to 11 o'clock Mass at the cathedral.

He remembered the torture of trying to scrub what seemed to be scum from his mouth in the bathroom. The instant coffee jar had slithered to the floor and smashed, and the effort of sweeping up the debris brought on the excruciating headache.

"Mr. Donovan?"

"Yes?"

It was the neat young man in the fashionably tight suit. Shane's glance took in the feathered, unruly black hair and tie pin. My God, somebody better wise him up about that tie pin if he were going to New York on business.

"I'm Byron Janning of Zandorff Construction."

"How do you do?"

"May I sit down?"

"By all means."

"I just want to congratulate you on winning the award. I saw your picture on the CBC news last night."

"Oh. I didn't know."

"It's a great honour to meet you, sir."

Shane had never been able to accept tributes without being embarrassed.

"I see Zandorff is going great guns building in Canada."

That triggered Janning to a flurry of talk.

"Our mission is to get Canadians out of the habit of living in houses. Real estate is too valuable. We have to get them in apartments. You see, a large number of Canadians come from a rural life and they want to own houses and plots of land and it just makes it too complicated in the city."

Shane was scarcely listening. Beehives. Put them into little boxes on stilts and let them eat carbon monoxide and crawl on the streets and come home to their little cubicles and . . . grind them until you have a nation of silly and conforming little people who look alike and talk alike and love alike and listen to gabbering mushmouths on radio and watch muscular idiots on TV going through patented situations and . . . Canada had miles and miles and miles of space and we want to pack the poor bastards up like tins of biscuits in a supermarket.

"Eh . . . sorry, my mind wandered off there."

Janning licked his lips nervously.

"Well, I wanted to ask your advice."

"I don't know if I can be of any help."

"I've been wondering if I shouldn't get into an agency."

He had worked for a suburban newspaper in Toronto. His

wife had been a secretary at the Toronto office of Zandorff. They had needed someone to give handouts to the press and arrange hotel rooms for New York executives and take local zoning authorities out to posh luncheons, and he had been accepted. Now he had a staff of four and his wife was pregnant.

"I don't see the future here. They have an agency that represents them in New York and, incidentally, I'm going down now for a briefing on our new development in connection with the potash in Saskatchewan."

It stirred Shane to ask about their interest in potash.

"Oh, yes, we're building apartments near the big strike." Zandorff apartments piled up on the bald prairie where space was unlimited. He focussed back on Janning.

"So, I've been thinking of getting into the agency racket . . ."

All the familiar words came out.

"Advertising is just what you put into it. I think if you could find a good, reliable company with a suitable opening I would try it. Have you any other ambitions?"

Shane stopped. He was getting involved.

Janning answered with some diffidence, "I did . . . in a way . . . well, I wanted to be a writer . . ."

He added self-consciously, "I did a lot of poetry at Western —University of Western Ontario—some of it wasn't too bad . . . at least the prof liked it. Oh yes, I also wrote, you know, the Great Canadian Novel, but he said it was junk."

Farewell, Canadian author for the mills of advertising copy!

Shane wanted to tell the nervous young man, "Get to hell out of it and go and write your poetry and starve and find a way." He felt guilty as he said instead, "Well, a feel for words is indispensable in this business. We desperately need good copy writers."

37

Janning brightened.

"You think so?"

"Oh, yes. Our senior copy man is J. T. Ludlum."

"Is that so? I read some of his stuff on the editorial page of the *Clarion*."

Good old Joe, bitter and despondent because of a sick wife and seven youngsters, spending each summer vacation desperately searching for a key to financial success in writing poetry. Still rewriting his novel about the English war bride finding Canada, and still having it rejected.

"Well, Byron, you might go and see Joe some time."

Joe would even find significance in the name. Byron! He would take him every day to what he called a "pub where you can smell the workers." Joe worked in the morning and sat in a cloud of tobacco smoke and beer fumes all afternoon staring at copy that he ultimately approved without actually reading.

Shane didn't want to listen any more. He reached down to his attaché case.

"I think I'll go and freshen up."

He felt foolish taking liquor into the john. It was like the old game of running the gauntlet.

"Hello, Louise."

They had used her on the tea account but the sponsor objected to her superstructure.

"Are we selling sex or tea? That dame is all breath and no butt. Put her on for evaporated milk."

He nodded to a Stratford Festival actor he had once had a drinking session with. The actor had a part in an American TV series and one of the Toronto critics had suggested that another great talent was going to America. Talent for what? He remembered fighting him off before the night was over.

There was the old actor who always smiled. Hate to tell him he was used in the newspaper ads for shoes because he looked like a bassett.

He plunged into the little room and clicked the latch. It was a padded cell. He sat down on the toilet and reaching into the briefcase, brought out the bottle of scotch. Mona hadn't known about this one being stashed in the garage.

The whisky tasted hot, but by swallowing and diluting it with saliva, he kept it down. Better than tepid water.

"What a hell of a way to be going to New York."

3

Coming out of the toilet, he heard the pilot's voice filtered through the crackly public address announcing landing and temperatures and—

"Seventy-one in New York. That's high, isn't it, Mr. Donovan?"

Now, he could face his seat companion.

"They're always a few degrees warmer than we are."

They both watched a very stout woman girdle-waddle her way to the washroom.

"I suppose you'll be moving to New York to work after winning the award, Mr. Donovan?"

"No, I don't think so. I'm fifty and I like Canada. I'm not anti-American, but Canada is my home. I think we have a responsibility to work at home—if we can."

"But there are so many opportunities in the States."

"I agree, but we're improving at home. Dammit, when it comes down to one thing—like in my case—the chances come along and you end up by staying—because in spite of the stupidity of our politicians and the buggering about of things like ownership—we are still different from the Americans."

Janning didn't answer. Shane guessed his vehemence had stopped him. Shane closed his eyes and black dots skeltered across the pink, flamed lining of his eyelids. He had to keep his eyes open. He toyed with the idea of going back for another drink.

"Oh, well, who knows? We're making a hell of a fist of it at home. The politicians and businessmen are completely out of touch with Canadians . . . and yet, I'm still a Canadian."

Janning was troubled.

"You know, of course, the only way for promotion in our firm is to go across the line."

Shane had the positiveness of "outer space" drinking . . .

"Listen, don't get taken in. You're a young prefect from Byzantium on his way to make a report to Augustus, but you won't meet Caesar. No, some young executive will meet you at the airport and say the boss is sorry and they'll get you tickets to a play . . . you know"—he was grinning now—"with some of 'your Canadian talent' in it . . . Kate Reid or somebody, and they'll get you a date with a doll who turns out to be a call girl . . . and you'll have a ball until it's time for you to go home and then you'll remember your dear little wife who was a virgin from Kentville . . . or Kitchener . . ."

"She's from Orillia . . ."

Janning said it so intently it stopped Shane.

The plane had bumped to a stop.

"You don't like Americans, Mr. Donovan?"

"Oh, I don't dislike them. It's not that . . ."

He was groping around for words.

"The best . . . the biggest . . . and it's their goddam total disregard for anybody else in the world."

Janning squirmed. Shane ignored him.

"They landed on a virgin continent and raped hell out of her . . . high, wide and handsome, and they're still at it. They pillaged everything and now they're out to pillage the world with their economic empire, and that's the least of it. Let them steal what they want but they're after the hearts of everybody. You know their great American system—land of the free and home of the brave . . . my ass."

He could feel Janning's hand resting gently on his sleeve.

"Sorry, I guess I was a bit loud."

"They've got quite a record of achievement, Mr. Donovan."

Shane shrugged his shoulders.

"No two ways about it, and to be reasonable, Americans . . . well . . . individually, they're fine . . . but as a group I find them hard to take. Pushy, shovy . . . maybe somebody will teach them a lesson. They'll stick their nose into some other country's affairs once too often. In fact they have in Viet Nam."

"I guess we won't lose you to the U.S.A."

The plane was taxiing.

"Sorry, old man," mumbled Donovan, standing up.

But Janning was interested.

"No, I want to know . . ."

"Look," said Shane, reaching for his briefcase, "I'm still tiddly from a hangover and I shouldn't be saying these things. It's just that there's a kind of blackmail that goes on if you have any talent. If they can't entice with the golden carrot they'll find the way."

43

"I wouldn't think . . ."

They were moving down the aisle.

"Listen, the ethic of American business is the most flexible thing in life since they put elastic in bloomers."

They were jamming along then and Shane slipped away from Janning. He was sorry for Janning. He had the hook in his gut and he wouldn't listen to anyone.

New York was gripped by unseasonable warmth and greasy air that smelled and felt like french fried sand. The suburban streets looked like industrialized Appalachia. They marched up to get lost behind the façade of business buildings and apartment blocks lining the way in from the airport. That and cemeteries!

"Be a great city when they stop destroying it," he said to the hunched back of the driver.

The words were flung back at him.

"Sure, but the damn' niggers is goin' to take over before that happens."

The driver glanced up enquiringly at the rear-view mirror.

"You a Canadian?"

"Yes, I am."

"I was up to Montreal one time last year to see my brother. God, it was a long way to walk in that airport. Lots of Frenchmen there."

Defensive bastard! Should ask him if he has a brother in the Mafia—Shane checked himself.

"Where ya goin', mister?"

"The President."

Cars *sup-whupped* by in a steady procession as if all the city dwellers were intent on escape to the country.

"Not many going into the city today."

"Just try it about six tonight and they'll all be comin' back."

The conversation was over. Everything was a mismatch in this part of New York. Rows of houses and factories, shops and apartments and one-way streets and cut offs and everything shabby and needing paint and scabbed signs of every shape and design, as jangling to the eyes as the varied cries of beggars and dealers in an Oriental bazaar were to the ears.

This was New York where people lived and died in simulated perpetual motion. Suddenly the driver leaned out the window screaming at an elderly man driving an aged, black sedan.

"Look, Pops, ya cut in like that—you'll be over in that marble orchard."

It was both disturbing and amusing. The driver pulled his head in like a grumpy turtle, moving back into the shell of the cab, still muttering. They were passing the slotted rows of tombstones of the graveyard; for even in death, New Yorkers were in amazing proximity to one another.

Shane was feeling half guilty. It was sneaky to simply move out when the family was at Mass. Now in the dulling taxi ride he was casting about, in a familiar way, for an excuse. The extravagance of tombstones made him think of Dr. Jim Leddy. The nerve of the bastard! He had merely gone for a checkup.

"My fine bucko, you're pitching for a membership in the Graveyard League."

"Jim, what the hell are you talking about? I just came here because Mona had some fool notion I might be—well, she thought I needed a checkup."

The blunt Dubliner didn't mince words.

"I guess she has more sense than you have, old cock."

"What do you mean?"

"I mean simply that you're blowing your health all to hell by drinking too damned much."

"Is this by personal observation or by diagnosis?" answered Shane caustically, because he remembered the week before when they both had to take taxis when the club closed.

The doctor roared.

"A bit of both . . . but look here, my Canadian imitation of an Irishman . . . and my friend . . . there's a hell of a difference in the way we drink. I still drink happy . . . and you drink mad. The day I start to guzzle as if I had to drown something inside myself I'll get worried and I hope to hell I have enough sense to stop."

"Doc, why do you say that?"

The doctor's eyelids closed as he match-puffed his pipe.

Shane remembered it all. The secretary talking on the telephone in the outer office . . . the words maddeningly close to being recognizable . . . a sink tap dripping . . . the spring in the chair scrunging in protest as Leddy rocked . . .

"You didn't come to me for flattery, Shane. You want the truth. You're that kind of man. You're scared. Why? Why does your wife seem like a crosspatch so much of the time . . . your kids probably rejecting you . . . and why are you so unhappy when you can't seem to find out a simple reason for being unhappy . . . you're a success, boyo . . . a real success . . . but it's Scotch and Success on the rocks . . . when you order a drink."

"You're quite a wordcoiner. You should be in advertising."

The shivery feeling on his spine, like a drip of icy water.

"Not on your life, Shane. Now listen, I don't know but I'll bet you . . . and it's an educated guess . . . you've just had a few brushes with the D.T.'s . . ."

"You're out of your mind, Doc."

"Am I? . . . hold up your right hand . . . straight out."

No matter how hard he tried, Shane couldn't keep it from shaking.

"And another thing . . . you didn't sleep last night."

"Something I ate before I went to bed last night . . ."

"You had a few belts this morning, too . . ."

"It helps."

"Are you hiding liquor at home—at the office?"

"No . . ."

He hadn't been very convincing.

"Well, you know how it is when your wife has this idea . . ."

Leddy nodded.

"Afraid to get caught without it?"

"It's just that . . ." he had started but there didn't seem to be any very convincing reason.

"Look, Shane, don't try to hide it from me. I know. My old father died with a vacant look on his face and he hadn't had a consecutive series of thoughts for five years except for trying to get a drink. He had a wet brain . . . I didn't know what it was . . . but my poor mother said it was the terrible chills he got in his bones when he was with the I.R.A. blowing up English barracks."

Leddy had a wan look on his face.

"God rest his soul . . . and now look, one thing . . . it can happen to you or me, or anyone, and I am scared for myself at times . . . because the craythur is something I like . . . but it's a treacherous bastard to get involved with."

"You're saying I'm a lush."

The doctor looked at him steadily as he answered.

"No, but you're awfully close to it . . . seeing things . . . hearing whispers . . . running sensations on the wallpaper when you try to stay awake to escape . . . nightmares."

Shane started to twitch in an uncontrollable manner.

47

The doctor poured out two drinks, handing one to Shane.

"Go on, take it. You're in no shape for cold turkey."

Shane gulped the drink while Dr. Leddy sipped his.

"So, I'm a lush, Doctor."

"You're on the way. You've got pains and aches in your legs and you drink to kill that. You've started keeping a bottle of vodka in your desk."

It was painful and true. He lit a cigarette, trying to steady his hands as he did so.

"Oh, Shane, I'm not condemning you. It's a hell of a time to be middle-aged. If you're old, you can pretend and if you're young, you can bitch. Our generation is caught . . . we're all successful, but we wonder what the hell happened. My father-in-law is a Canadian . . . working on the same farm his grand-father cleared . . . tough old bastard . . . not much money but guts and determination and the last time I saw him he was clouting hell out of a bull with a stick . . . and he was then seventy-nine . . . and driving a 1949 car."

He went to look out the window.

"Every day I see a procession of men who wonder what the hell hit them. They've got more cars than my family had pots to piss in. Their wives are about as responsive as half-inflated rubber rafts, and they hell around or else marry their work until they get retired or fired and then die because their an-chor is gone. They leave rich and unhappy widows who buy good-looking, useless young bastards who like racing cars . . ."

Shane shook his head.

"You don't sound very optimistic. What does medicine say?"

"Oh, what can we do? Every time I go out in the country or even go into a workman's pub, you'll see old codgers that look like that old bastard who used to sail over the fence on the packages of salts."

48

"Kruschen . . ."

"Yeah, and I often wondered if that little tin spoon in the package was for goosing him and that's why he sailed over the fence."

The doctor said other things as well. He was concerned about middle-aged men who were lost. A legion of lost souls. Not damned in a spiritual sense but lost, without identity.

"Look, Shane, I have one thing. I try to heal people. Sometimes I do. Sometimes I don't. That's what I have to do. But guys like—well, I hate to say this, but you're up a creek without a paddle."

Leddy's words haunted him. Now he opened his briefcase. The liquor rolled down like fire. For a split second he had a wave of nausea but swallowed repeatedly and it passed.

The smothering loneliness of New York came in on him now. There was a confined closeness in the dirty cab with the slippery black leather seat and the litter of cigar and cigarette package wrappers and ashes on the floor.

Shane felt minute in the frantically hurrying place. Mechanized monsters flowed along and went to and fro and flowed off into side lanes and whipped across to other levels, and everything jangled with the constant throb of noise.

"Why do so many New Yorkers look tired?"

The driver shrugged his shoulders.

"People don't sleep enough, I guess."

"Toronto is getting pretty much like here."

The driver wasn't paying attention because he was street hopping now to edge up toward Seventh Avenue and avoid one-way streets. It was April but it seemed like summer. He felt a surge of excitement as the cab pulled before the entrance of the President on 48th Street. It was one of the older hotels undergoing a slow but not startling conversion into modernity. The doorman recognized him.

"Mr. Donovan. Good to see you. Don't you worry about these bags now."

The assistant manager got up from his little glassed-in cubicle to come over and shake his hand.

"Good to see you again."

He escaped registration. There were some places like this left in New York. They were oases of friendliness in the smothering impersonality of the city. Waiters and clerks indicated no resentment at serving—Canadians always seemed to resent serving you.

He walked around waiting for the TV set to warm up. He was shadow-boxing with himself. Inevitably, he was going to take out the bottle. As he flipped the dial he came across an old film . . . commercials . . . commercials for everything from cigarettes to beer to the inevitable detergents. He turned it off.

At times like this, away from them, he felt sorry. Sorry for the resentment built up against Mona . . . and Bill and Rita. There was a smouldering in his twenty-year-old son. They all retreated into insularity when he was drinking.

There were still good times. At Christmas for three days they had captured a good feeling. Christmas night they sat by the fireplace as if all were loath to go to bed. When they finally dragged off to bed he had spoiled it all by taking a drink, one lousy, solitary drink after three days. When he came upstairs Mona had said, not in anger but with a note of resigned hopelessness, "After three days I was beginning to hope."

The time until New Year's was a vague pattern of parties and talking, and Rita had gone to visit a girl friend and Bill had avoided him.

"What is it? What is it?"

He poured a drink, setting it casually on the table without touching it as if it were a display of will power. What caused the feeling of not having any satisfaction? There was the work. It was a matter of peaks and lulls. The peaks were the times when he furiously concentrated on making up for the lulls. Poor Miss Banty. Always defending him!

"Sorry, but Mr. Donovan is busy. He's working on a big campaign and I can't disturb him. You know how it is with creative people."

Creative, hell . . . and sitting in his office and nursing a drink of vodka in the upper drawer and just waiting for the time to go to the Press Club, the Nonentity Club, the Country Club, or the hotel. Sometimes he hid away in a downtown working man's pub, alone and ignored.

There had always been a protective mystique about being an idea man at Jackman and Bates. Old Jackman would look at him with shrewd eyes and say, "Better take it easy, boy. Can't have you wearing yourself out."

Shane poured another drink and realized that the bottle was almost empty.

"Damned stuff mustn't have the same strength."

Shane sat on. He thought about calling Peter O'Hare, who he knew was in New York, but he dismissed it. Once or twice he had an inclination to get up and go down to the lobby for a newspaper. His eyes took in the familiar hotel surroundings. Conventional wallpaper, prints on the wall that looked like Parisian flower gardens and something that resembled the Arc de Triomphe . . . double bed and night tables with large shaded lamps, two chairs, a luggage rack, entrance alcove and clothes closet and the open door of a very large bathroom, which betrayed the fact that this old hotel had been renovated.

He thought of the Commercial Hotel in Clover . . . the old hotel that held such a fascination for him when he was living with his uncle in Ontario. It was odd. Looking back was getting more common with him. It might have something to do with what the doctor had said about men and the menopause. Now that he thought of it he had never been in a room in the village hotel.

But what a contrast with this ornate concrete building that still had vestiges of old-fashioned ornamentation, as opposed to other modern hotels in New York. Four blocks up Seventh Avenue from the President was the slab-sided Americana with its architecture like the dream places in the few magazines he had looked at as a boy. Treasured *Popular Mechanics* used to show sketches of highways and city freeways that looked exactly like the ones coming in from Kennedy . . .

How would the old Commercial look in New York, with the men sitting in the big wooden armchairs on the wooden veranda from early spring to late fall? There was the trough for watering horses and the two hitching posts with the ornamental horse heads cast in iron. Now he could see the fancy pump in the garden beside the hotel and the small balcony over the veranda where some of the ladies used to sit to watch the Twelfth of July parade, the First of July, and the Armistice Day parade. It was roped in by pots of trailing geraniums and petunias.

Shane was slipping into a bittersweet nostalgia. When he got up to walk to the window he staggered a bit, straightened himself and then put on his coat. But the power of remembering was too strong and he sat down on the edge of the chair.

"The settee."

Like an actor he stood up and walked to the double chair and sat on it. In the moment, he could imagine that he was back on the old horsehair settee that sat in the hallway beside the ornate umbrella stand with the large mirror. He had sat there waiting for his uncle. He was forbidden to go in the room marked *LOUNGE* where through a thick veil of smoke he could discern the long counter with the brass rail in front of it and a very red-faced man standing behind it. That would be Ben Miller, the owner who doubled as bartender.

"Ben Miller."

Shane hadn't thought about him or the hotel in years. Now he could picture Mr. Miller with his striped shirt and shiny white collar and the strange bunched-up tie with the glittering stone people said was a real diamond. He wore armbands, and a cigar was always in his mouth; it was never lit and never seemed to vary in length. He moved constantly, either wiping the counter or pouring stuff in glasses.

"Rosie."

It hurt to think of Rosie, because, unreal as she was, she had been one of the principal reasons for his uncle's change of feeling towards him.

Rosie was a long picture of a reclining lady in tights with a rose between her teeth. She was pink and white and pretty and had a garter on her leg above the knee.

How could he know that the Commercial Hotel functioned because there was a general disaffection for the prohibition enforcement of the Canada Temperance Act even amongst the local police, which in effect consisted of one township constable. How could he know that his stern uncle frequented the place but never mentioned it at home?

"Uncle Matt?"

Shane remembered the big man with the squared-off shoulders, the heavy-lined face with the moustache that straggled, and the line of white that showed up in sharp contrast to the tanned and weather-beaten neck when he wore his usual good shirt without a collar for those occasions when he went to the village. Even now he could feel some of the awe and fear he had for this man and could remember how he had blurted out at the supper table, shortly after arriving at the farm home in Eastern Canada, "Uncle Matt, whose picture is that of the girl with the rose in her teeth?"

His uncle had ignored him. His Aunt Olga had started plates moving on the table, which was her means of covering up embarrassment. Uncle Matt had gone on eating. It had never been mentioned, but he knew he had excited a deep-seated resentment that never abated all the time he lived there.

Shane stood up as if to cut off the memory. He was going down to the lobby to buy a newspaper. He knew he was also going to the bar. As he moved around the room he could feel the strings of his own resentment at his uncle. Uncle Matt, the hypocrite! The bloody old hypocrite. Aunt Olga had said nothing. He put Olga from his mind.

The Senate Bar was a dim oasis off the lobby. In the heyday of the President Hotel, it was called the Slave Market, the opinion being that many politicians were bought and sold on the red plush banquettes. Dark wood and wine drapes and Ev, the waggish bartender who continued imitations of a platitudinous senator even after the senator's death.

"Hi, Ev."

"Well, bless me for a prairie flower of sweet innocence, but it fills my deep gratitudinous heart with beneficence to welcome such a distinguished visitor from Northern Climes."

The bartender reached with a practiced hand for the V.O. Shane felt a tap on his shoulder.

"My boy, what are you doing here?"

Thomas Adams Smith, lean and lithe, in what Shane assumed was apparel for the well-dressed New Yorker on a pleasant spring Sunday. British tweed jacket, impeccably draped, with a slash of ascot at the neck of a colored shirt. Without looking, he knew that the outfit would be completed by grey slacks and brown brogues and that on the bar there would be a pair of hand-stitched gloves and a cloth hat with a spray of feather in the band.

"I came a day early."

Tommy ran his index finger on his wisp of silvered moustache.

"And I come on behalf of Waite, Irwin and Tasker to prepare the fatted calf for you—tomorrow."

"Hmmm, that accounts for them saying they would move me tomorrow to a suite."

"My boy, if the conquering award winner is not given the very best of treatment I may be drawn and quartered. Is your wife with you?"

"No—no, she isn't." Shane added hastily: "She may come later in the week."

"Good."

The agency man took the next stool and Ev splashed scotch on ice in a glass.

"You can celebrate a bit on your own if you're so inclined before the better half arrives."

Shane smiled, but changed the subject.

"I don't really need a suite."

"Don't be silly. Take it all in your stride. Be an English nobleman."

"You like the English, Tommy?"

Even as he spoke, he thought how much of an Anglophile TAS really was with his sculptured, greying hair, the tanned face on which the wrinkles appeared to be hand set—and the Sunday, oh-so-English country clothes.

Smith gestured, aware of Shane's look.

"I adore the English. There are two things that keep me from being in England. In the first place, there is the lousy climate. In the second, and this is most important, my father left a good deal of money—which stays with Mater. And she is tough—in other words, this morning when she set off for North Carolina in her ark . . ."

"What?"

"She has a very old Daimler and a very old chauffeur—and after several Bloody Marys this morning here in the hotel—they set out at about six miles per hour to go to Raleigh where she glories each year in the blooming dogwoods."

"She must be some character."

"She is—she is. And now let's be off and welcome you in style to our decadent city."

"Shane," he said later as they settled in a taxicab, "my old mother has done it again. She called me to have breakfast with her—downed more drinks than I did—left absolutely sober and I'm getting gee-squeezeled."

He turned to look at Shane.

"Do you know the remedy?"

Shane, feeling the unmistakable buoyancy, patted him on the knee.

"It's a dreadful thing to get tight on a Sunday."

Smith nodded slowly.

"But a much more dreadful thing to sober up."

They exploded into laughter as the cab moved towards the East Side.

4

In planes or taxis Shane often felt as if moving was the norm of his life. That wasn't true because back of it were those early years of boyhood imprisonment in the dusty dreariness of Nonsuch, Saskatchewan. No matter what he did, part of him was chained to that static and unsophisticated memory. He shared it with an entire generation in North America.

His attitudes were shaped by generations of Anglo-Saxon yeomen, subconsciously aware of their place in society. Only the extremely gifted achieved prominence. Politicians were rascals but with gifts. Artists were dubious and bohemian.

An agrarian background dominated the Donovans, and the Kearneys on the maternal side. There was a mystical hatred of the English, based on legendary stories of the potato famine and associated vaguely with Anglicans and the monarchy. Even royal prejudice was tempered. Now and again there would be a "dacent" one. Like the Prince of Wales, with his seldom-visited ranch in Alberta. From Shane's earliest conceptions he was aware of the resistance to the outside world he yearned for.

"Books are all right for people who understand them, but a little knowledge can be a dangerous thing."

His father opposed books.

"I've seen too many people who got their minds drugged on books."

He constantly reinforced his statements with the story of the Ontario community where he was born, and the man who read books.

"I'm telling you he didn't even do his work. Missed spring seeding one year because he bought a lot of secondhand books. Just sat there in the house—reading. Bloody useless, that's what he was."

Shane's brothers roared with laughter. They lacked an interest in anything outside basic knowledge. Pat was already becoming a motor mechanic. Mike had an obsession for the railroad, in spite of the lesson of his father's occasional work. The railroad was there, a solid fact in rails and ties and station and rolling stock—and there could be nothing else but a prosperous turn-around for it—and the Donovans.

Shane hated the railroad and the way it bound him—and his family. The line ran east and west—shining rails swallowed up by the place where sky and prairie met—and he felt they should walk one way or the other and discover what was behind the place of sky meeting the land. The hope and faith of his father in the railway irritated him.

And there was always the wind! He was affected deeply by the wind. It could be a hot night or a freezing night or a black

58

rainy night when the wind skittered across the flat land—
there never seemed to be anything between the house and
the North Pole but the disturbed wind.

Other things in his memory were tinged with loneliness.
Stooped men were replicas of his father, who had come in
time to walk in a pose of lifting. Lights—a searchlight—or a
stab of a headlight at night on a quiet road would send his
mind back to the transcontinental trains that roared by with
a whooshing disdain for everything along the way. The
murmur increased to a thudding, a pounding, and then they
flicked by like monster speeding snakes, their stabbing search-
lights poking into the black night. And they left a vacuum
that gripped at his heart.

They shrieked in a bitter galling way on frosty nights and
they were sweaty breathy monsters on summer nights . . .
and always in their wake there came the lonely realization
that they were going from some place to some place and
Shane was fixed and alone in a nowhere that was in between
for them and not important enough to make them stop. There
was a difference by day when the pokey freights with their
strings of boxcars nosed along. They seemed like friendly
dachshunds ground-snuffing, and the crews would wave . . .
but even the way freights jiggled the house.

It was a desolate boxy house with rooms like the insides
of crates and on the outside it was painted in the institution-
alized dried blood color affected by the railroad. At night in
the room with his brothers Patrick and Michael, who slept on
in indifference to everything, he would wake with the first
throbbing sound of the distant train. He lay clutching his
breath and the headlight of the train exploded against the
wall like a splotch of pockmarked silver. In the fierce glow, the
face of the Sacred Heart hung for an anguished speck of time,
the hands in supplication over the pierced orb dripping garish

blood. The walls were so thin the lathed ribs showed through the pajama-cloth-striped wallpaper.

He always had to get up after that and silently sneak out to the stoop and relieve himself, in defiance of his mother's orders to go into the back yard.

When his eyes became accustomed to the dark, he could see the stark outline of the water tower with its dangling spout like a useless arm. The tall shafts of the elevators resembled the picture of Inca ruins clipped from a Sunday paper and framed and hung in what served as the dining room, kitchen, and living room. Farther down the track the station snuggled low as if trying to hide, but the jewelled riding lights of the semaphore, marked green for GO said "go by and leave us alone!" In the distance there were a few lights from the village, a broken string of beads scattered on the night cushion of darkness. There was always the soft whimpering sound of a dog or a night creature, and in this instant of being sandwiched between the earth and the crowding sky of heaven, he felt suffocatingly lonely, waiting until Old Peek, the hound, came sniffing at his urine. Then he sneaked as quietly as possible back up the stairs—not easy, because they were only rude things installed by his father to convert the small attic into useable space. Then he would lie awake and try not to listen to the animal sounds of his brothers as they wallowed in sleep, or the turning of his parents in their beds at the other side of the partition, or the mystery of their night fumblings, which made him flame with a burning sensation he didn't understand.

There was a strong and wonderful passion in him when he conquered the night loneliness. It was a protection in a way, to try and deliberately shut out the sounds and the smells . . . the smell of his brothers, of sweat, and of something that always made him think of wet sheep's wool . . . and the outside rigidity of night. He wanted to be a Phoenician. There was something tongue and soul satisfying about just saying that word . . .

"Phoenician . . . galleys of the golden East . . . quinque-reme of Nineveh . . . Hanging Gardens of Babylon . . . Madagascar . . . balsam . . . sweet . . . myrrh . . . frankincense . . ."

Once, when he first experienced the sensation of sex and it left him breathlessly satisfied, he remembered these long hours of the night, when these words had given him a similar form of satisfaction. The words came from Nelly Loomis . . . the teacher . . . a sprung, slat of a woman with curved-in belly and a thrust-out back, and thin long hands with fingers slim enough to comb her stringy, dun-coloured hair, who stood at the windows sometimes and said strange things. "There must be far off places where people are happy and where life brings reality to dreams."

She was the first one he ever heard recite the words and it became like a litany so that he had ended up second best in fights when students said that she was "cracked." It had been silly at least when Sid Boranus said her hair was like "cob webs in the granary." It could have been like that with the sun slanted through a crack glinting on it.

Nelly had been kind. The year they promised to pay him six dollars a month for sweeping out the school at night, which he never received, she had sometimes talked to him.

"What are you going to be, Shane? A politician . . . a priest . . . a lawyer . . . ?"

Once she had broken her own reverie to say, "But whatever you do, get out of this place. Get away before you get caught like everyone else. These awful prairies were never meant for people to live on. Get away. Try writing. You write the best compositions in the school. I think you like words.

Maybe words will help you. Don't let them kill your dreams."

Words!

Words had gotten him away. But words had trapped him. They were traps in his mind . . . haunting and reminding him . . . making him come unstuck at times when he wanted to sit down and pour out wrath and indignation about everything.

Words.

The words he said at breakfast the first time his mother served boiled wheat . . . boiled rolled wheat . . . the cheapest thing on the prairies, piled up in granaries and huge rotting piles on the bald land.

"Boiled wheat. This stuff is for pigs!"

His mother's look at his father was a telegraphy of sorrow and pain. Joe Donovan hadn't said a word. He had just looked at him, and Shane had run away from the breakfast table. His father had already said enough. Shane wondered if he had really hated the wheat as much as what happened the night before.

They had been in the room, huddled in the pale yellow light of the oil lamp which burned the coal-oil filched from the C.P.R. section hut. His father picked up his scribbler, given free by an overall firm in Winnipeg. His father read . . . haltingly, in a slow and irregular way, hurting, sarcastic . . . or bitter . . .

"When I Grow Up, by Shane Donovan."

"No, Dad . . . no . . . please . . . don't, Dad . . ."

He tried to get up but his father caught him by the wrist and made him stay . . . a condemned man made to listen to his own sentence . . . or confession . . .

"When I grow up I want to be a director of the Winnipeg Grain Exchange and have money and write books that will sell, so that I never have to be poor again. I will never wear patched clothes again and never have bleached sacks for shirts. Every day I will have enough to eat with white sugar for breakfast . . . and escape being poor . . ."

He tried to stand up again and his father slashed him once across the face with his hand. In the paralyzed moments that followed, they all sat . . . mother . . . brothers . . . father and himself, frozen. He turned then and ran up the stairs and buried his head in the pillow and when Pat and Mike came to bed they were self-consciously quiet. He had been awake, dry-eyed and hot when he heard his father come up the creaky steps and stop at the door to whisper, "Shane." He hadn't answered. He tried, but the words would not come because his throat was dry and parched as if he had been in a dust storm. His father went slowly to bed.

After that they were grittily conscious of each other. Shane withdrew into his fancies. They centred on the railroad as a means of escape. His father might speak, but only with the formality of a stranger.

"How is school, Shane?"

"Fine."

He had taken to walking. Stroll down the track—hop, skip, and make a landing on the odd tie and then lie in the buffalo grass until you were certain no one was looking and then, half-crouched, make for the skinny cottonwoods and start looking for old tracks that creased the prairies. There were cart tracks, buggy tracks, and wagon tracks, and he used to imagine some followed original Indian tracks.

The idea was to keep moving and circle the town and come back precisely at meal time and avoid the dull, hanging time when his father and his brothers sat waiting for their meal.

To be outside and moving was escape. It had the mystery of bunched, prairie wool and spring primroses and the arched, enormous blue sky that made the prairie an ocean.

When the soft wind blew it combed grass and wheat into waves. When the hard wind blew it brought the choking, stifling dust.

Shane only sensed beauty. At times, things moved him in ways he couldn't understand. His heart pounded in anticipation when a black cloud loomed on the faraway horizon, and he felt rare peace at the sight of nesting ducks on the spring-created pools of water. He wanted, at times desperately, to touch his mother, recalling some distant pink and fleshy moments, but she was grey and tired and rarely spoke. Even when she did, her hand camouflaged her mouth, because missing teeth gave her a haggard, even comic, appearance.

Myrtle had started following him on his walks, and he couldn't escape. At first, he screamed at her. He left her behind for a time but there was no place to escape on the prairies, or even in the coulee.

Myrtle was two years older than himself. Her father was the elevator agent. Her mother had a passion for making wine of all kinds, and then doling it out to visitors. It was simple for Myrtle to appropriate a bottle. They were in the clay-bank hole they called a cave.

"Go on, Shane. I've been hiding this for a month."

Myrtle, an early blossoming girl who bulged without restraint in her faded print dress, had been trying to persuade Shane for a month at least to go along with her to the cave. On this hot July day, he could find no reason to avoid the girl. He had some misgivings about Myrtle with her matted mop of black hair, freckles, and crooked teeth. She breathed hot and heavy when she was close.

"Is it strong?"

"Nah, none of it has too much kick."

It smelled yeasty and his first taste reminded him of mould, but the swallow warmed his stomach.

"Go on, be a man."

He gulped at the liquid. The taste didn't seem to bother him any more. They lay back with their heads against the cool clay side of the hole.

"Some more?"

Shane didn't protest. He was hot and floating and the cotton puff clouds sailed smoothly in the blue sky.

"I'm too hot."

Myrtle shucked her dress over her head. She stood in her cotton pants.

"Why don't you take off your overalls?"

"No underwear."

She slipped out of her panties and reached to help him take off his overalls.

"Wanta kiss me?"

He had a vague impression of gagging on her tongue in his mouth. The lumps of her body were soft and she felt like hot satin. They drank more and hugged each other in a confused way, and he didn't remember much until the rest of the boys found them.

His impressions were uncomfortable. The older lads hustled him out under an aspen and went back to the cave. He wanted to get up and see what all the laughing was about but his legs were rubbery.

It was dark when they walked back. He stumbled a lot, was sick once or twice, and Myrtle was dreamily concerned about him.

"Too bad you couldn't take that stuff," she said before he tottered into the house. "But I'll make it up to you. I'll bet you would be nice. Those guys are too rough. I should tell on them. But I won't."

Shane escaped to serve Mass each morning for Father Cassidy. There weren't many Catholics in the area . . . mostly

Poles and Ukrainians who had been railroad labourers and were now laid off and existing along with the Donovans on the flour, oatmeal, and prunes of the relief office.

In the faint chilled sunlight of early morning, he walked on Main Street, deserted except for an occasional dog, to the weather-beaten frame chapel on the edge of the prairie. Father Cassidy was always late. Shane wondered if he hoped that his lateness would make someone appear to attend Mass. He had an almost hopeless task in the administering of religion to the scattered families, who found little solace in faith while they eked out miserable existences.

Shane set out the vestments. They were purple that day. He filled the water cruet and noticed that the wine cruet was almost full. The sight of it gave him an urgent craving. In the left-hand drawer side of the altar there was a bottle of sacramental wine. A sip or two wouldn't hurt. He hadn't eaten. He wasn't fasting. There just hadn't been anything handy to eat when he got up. He was ravenously hungry. The wine was gently warming.

Shane watched himself carefully, while the old priest was lost in the sacrifice of the Mass. Steady, Shane. There was a reeling rocking motion in him. He had to go back to the sacristy because Father Cassidy had forgotten something. He paused to swig at the sacramental wine bottle again.

Deo gratias!

Respond now.

Move to the gospel side.

Don't trip.

Somehow he had known he had to get through without fainting. The minutes were eternity long.

"In nomine Patris et Filü et Spiritus Sancti . . ."

His throat caught when he muttered Amen.

Father Cassidy seemed curious when he looked down at him.

He didn't normally look at all. It was finally over. Help the old priest. He was unpeeling his cocoon of vestments. Mustn't laugh.

"My boy, it's expensive and there are other reasons you shouldn't . . . but don't touch the wine again."

Then the old priest gave him a dollar.

"Here, I should have given you something long ago for serving Mass so faithfully," the old man said. "It's not much but it's . . ."

He hadn't realized the old priest had even recognized him before. He was just a part of the scene, forced by his mother, and the necessity to avoid his father, to serve Mass.

"That's all right, boy. Get something for yourself."

The morning air had warmed quickly and the breath of wind had a dusty feeling. (This was the part he couldn't understand.) Like an automaton he moved to where the train would stop for water. He wasn't sure which way the train was going. He had a dollar and he knew that lots of men were constantly moving on the trains. The police flushed them out sometimes. He didn't care. He had a dollar. Shane moved down, keeping the water tower and the stock pens between himself and the station.

They wouldn't miss him at home anyhow because he had said he was going to pick berries. The wine left him with a thirst. He was catching water from a leak in the tower in a pail when the train whooshed in. He had often imagined running away. In time it didn't seem even to be escape. It was inevitable.

There was an open boxcar. The fireman on the tender holding the water spout had his back turned. The other trainmen were on the side facing the station. Shane dropped the pail and climbed in the boxcar. It smelled of dry, rotted wood. He lay flat on the floor. Something stirred in a corner.

It must have been his imagination. He eased along the side of the car. There was no more sound from the pile of straw in the corner. He could see it clearly.

There was the clickety-clacking sound of the wheels on the rails and they were off—and the straw was stirring.

"Hey, kid . . . don't let me scare you."

"I thought that was just straw."

"That's what I wanted, kid . . ."

He was a craggy-looking man with clothes that hung limply on his frame. His face was almost black from dirt and age. His hand was a claw as he put it up.

"Got any makin's?"

Shane shook his head.

"Are we going east?"

"We're movin' east, son . . . just movin' east."

He made an elaborate gesture of picking apart cigarette butts and adding them to a small tin. He lit his pipe and leaned back, took a couple of drags and then, tamping the pipe, put it in amongst the rags.

"I'm moving from my Western ranch," he said, "to my Eastern estate. And where are you going, boy?"

He said the first thing that flashed into his mind.

"I'm going to my uncle's in Ontario."

The little man nodded.

"Where does he live?"

"Somewhere near a place called Guelph or north of that."

The sharp owl eyes peered at him.

"I spent two years in Guelph—pen, you know."

Then he cackled with laughter.

"Is your uncle in the calaboose?"

Shane was quick to protest.

"No, he's a farmer. He has a good farm."

Caution told him to stop.

"Well, kid, you stick with that story. Stick with me, and I'll get you to this place . . . what's it called?"

"Handrich."

"That's on Lake Huron. Well, we better switch to the CNR . . . these CPR bulls are real bastards."

It was strange and it was final. Shane was lonely in a strange world of rocks and jagged trees on cold dark lakes that was so different from the prairies. He was afraid of the chattering little man who called himself Julius, and yet he was afraid to be alone.

"Got any money, kid?"

He had lied. There was a defensiveness that made him know he must keep the dollar. They moved into the big freight yard and he followed the man racing and dodging through the flaring lanterns and the yelling men and the scringing sound of rolling wheels on steel tracks and the panting of locomotives like tired buffalo in roundhouses. They were surrounded by noises he had never heard before, and they escaped from policemen in ways that were more like fantasy than anything.

In a scraped-out hole in a hill amongst scrub trees they found, as Julius said, "friends of the road." Here were youngsters not much older than himself and old men and young hard-eyed men and two women bundled in clothes that made them hard to distinguish from men. Here was food cooking in big tins and a society he could never forget. From a battered knapsack Julius produced part of a loaf of bread and some potatoes. It was accepted and dumped in the big tin.

The man stirring the mixture looked hard at Shane.

"Got anythin', kid?"

Julius intervened.

"He's a kid . . . Mike—he'll learn. He's with me."

Shane was frisked quickly . . . a knife . . . piece of string and a stub of a pencil, all carefully given back to him. They missed his dollar because he had put it in the watch fob pocket of the old pants his mother had cut down from a pair of his father's.

"Okay, kid," was the verdict from Mike, "but you gotta learn one thing on the road. Everybody's gotta put in the pot."

Little Julius told him he had walked out of a Vancouver rooming house rather than live off his wife who was working as a dishwasher . . . Julius who had taught him to cadge and beg and sometimes steal . . . Julius who, he learned later, had slipped under the wheels of a freight car in the Windsor yards and had gone with a silly squeal to his death. Julius!

"Soliloquizing, old boy?"

"Tommy, I must be getting old. I was just thinking of when I ran away from home."

Smith patted his knee.

"You're bloody lucky. I had my diapers changed for me until I went to college. Cheer up, old cock, we're here. You'll find something to brighten up a dull Sunday."

They were stopped in front of one of the apartments that clustered on the east side of New York, near the United Nations.

5

Apartment 1-A was a penthouse that smelled like a temple. Protest was postered and proclaimed in the contrasting, somehow similarly sad, eyes of Ché Guevara, Pope John, Mao Tse-tung, and Charlie Brown.

Against a semi-Victorian background of elaborately panelled wood, smothered by white paint, it was a place of Plexiglas, black and white shaggy rugs and blooming confections of overlarge and brilliant artificial flowers. The sculpture was painfully abstract.

The air was full of smoke. Tommy and Shane were ignored in a studied way, in the effete manner of people who work at resisting surprise.

There was one focal point. She was a woman like a dramatic

slim priestess in white slacks and a silk poncho projected by overripe breasts. It was fastened by a silver thong on each side.

"I'm Tina—Tina Bond."

She pecked Tommy's cheek with a kiss.

"You're Shane. I'm so glad you're here."

The toenails of her bare feet were silvered. A streak of light hair flared from above her left eyebrow. The face was ivory, sharply defined. A one-horned devil. Her hand on his wrist was hot . . . but dry.

"I'm flattered, Miss Bond."

"Tina, please . . . You drink a lot . . ."

"I suppose, but . . ."

"They say you drink well, Shane. That's an accomplishment in New York."

She led him by the hand through the designed clutter of the apartment.

"Tommy says you're keen as hell. This is the Tiger."

A man was reclining on a chaise longue covered by a fuzzy white throw. He raised his arms languidly. He was neither young nor old. Corduroy trousers and turtle neck shirt and soft black boots. He acknowledged the introduction with a limp wrist flick, bared his teeth and mockingly purred.

"Pretty pussy, man. But watch out."

Tina leaned closer, "Pay no attention, Shane. It's all part of this crazy thing of New York. This is the mad time between winter and summer. We're still caged."

Women were attracted to Shane. It had taken him some time to realize it. He still remembered gaffes in the face of normal advances.

"You're an attractive man."

She looked him over coolly.

"And you are an attractive woman."

72

She butted a barely smoked cigarette. It was deliberate, and as the garment moved he saw her bare breast.

"With unhidden charm."

She laughed.

"I like you."

He had to look away. She was arousing him. Even her scent was powerful. Musky. Her voice pitched to a lower tone.

"You admire old things?"

Shane had been fingering a scarred wooden butter scoop.

"In a way. You see I was brought up with things like this."

"You're different. Most people in this room would try and pass themselves off as being to the manner born."

"I don't like phonies."

Her long silvered nails traced the lines in the scoop.

"Everything is so phony. I bought this because it has reality. It contrasts terribly, but somehow it's good to know that someone took a knife and carved it out because his wife needed it. Somebody cared."

He thought he detected a subtle change in her voice. A fat young man with enormous sideburns came from the kitchen clutching strips of bacon in his hand. Tina's voice became abruptly harsh.

"For Christ's sake, Eddy, don't spill grease on the rug. It cost me fifty bucks to get it cleaned."

The fat man mumbled an apology, spilling his drink, and moved off.

"You don't seem to like them very much."

The eyes glinted. Sparks. She ignored his question.

"Tommy said you liked Canadian rye."

"Thanks. Who are these people?"

"Sunday bums. Oh, some are okay, but most of them stay bombed all weekend. They start Friday noon at lunch. Go to a party Friday night. Nurse hangovers Saturday. Really flake out Saturday night and then come here on Sunday because Tommy likes to have boozy brunches."

"What about tomorrow?"

"They'll flake out this afternoon between booze and food —or get sick or something, and make it to work on Monday— somehow."

"What do they do?"

She listed rapidly a magazine writer, a musician and his faggot friend, a decorator and his girl friend, two lesbian editors of a magazine of family life, a defrocked priest, and a film writer—and left when Tommy called from the kitchen. The snatches of conversation came to Shane.

"Honest to God, if that pill hasn't worked I'm going to shoot George. Another abortion and there won't be anything left. I've told him I'll be all used up. Maybe that's what the bastard wants."

"Father O'Malley, do you think the Curia is really to blame? Could we have a folk Mass right here?"

"I'm beginning to believe in God. Jason left me for a subway guard and I prayed and prayed, and he came back and said, 'Clarence, I'm never going to leave you again.'"

Humpty Dumpty had fallen asleep, two strips of bacon lying on top of his mound of a stomach. The noise was deafening and Shane was relieved when Tina came back.

"Gets kind of sticky, Shane, if you're not used to it. God, we had a party here one Friday night and fat Eddy was here until the following Tuesday."

Weekend bashes happened in Toronto, too. Men getting together on Saturday morning, milling back and forth from suburban garage to suburban recreation room—boozily friendly and calling wives to pool food for barbecues on Saturday night and then nursing each other's hangovers on Sunday morning. Mona hated them for interfering with the only time the family could be together. She was annoyed when he missed Mass.

Tina was taking rolls from the oven.

"Why do you put up with it?"

Tina shrugged her shoulders.

"Here, try this."

"Delicious. You cook, too?"

Her eyebrows arched as she took the plate from the kitchen. He sat down because for an instant his balance was awry. Tina's scent was disturbing. She came back, picking up the conversation.

"Of course I can cook. Katina from Sault Ste. Marie. I was raised in a restaurant. You know—the Acropolis Gardens."

"Now I know. You look like that widow in Zorba—God, she was something."

She leaned down and kissed him. Full on the lips.

"Please, they stoned her to death, didn't they? Stoning I don't mind, but not that way."

She slipped from his arms.

This was New York and it was Sunday. It was another day of unreality. It had already started. If he relaxed, he would simply be moved along. A leaf on a moving river. But Shane felt a familiar sense. They were phonies, but it was life. You had to know. Experience counted. That was really why he had the answers when the chips were down. Jackman and Bates and the rest of them in the agency didn't really know. They knew the same people—same golf partners—same going home—same old things.

Tommy lurched a little coming in the kitchen.

"Shane. Are you okay? Come on and join the gang. Betty says she's going to seduce that fellow who used to be a priest. God, isn't New York something? Can't have a party now without a former priest. Where's that vodka—orange juice—"

He was messing in the refrigerator.

"I'm getting smashed. Get in on the fun, old boy. Sober up tonight like the rest of us. I live for Sundays."

Tommy was swallowed up by the noise in the other room. Shane made a half-hearted attempt to stand up but his legs were weak. Why fight it? He was an observer! God, it was impossible that the creature Tina—from Krypton or Plankton or whatever the hell that planet was in *Star Trek*—was really Katina—something or other. Now she was back.

"Shane, if you stay near the food, at least have something to eat."

Her fingers dabbed his hand. Melted snowflakes. He was sweating. Reaching for a paper towel, he upset a tray from the edge of the sink. He was mopping up when she came back.

"Shane, don't worry."

She kissed his cheek. Not a snowflake. More like a blossom. Funny but some women could kiss you full on the lips and nothing. Just a touch from this one felt like fire.

"Thanks, Tina. Sorry about the mess."

"Don't worry. These people are boring you."

"Well, I am tired."

Now she didn't bother to move away when he reached for her. His hands were on her bare back and her breasts felt firm against him as he kissed her. She returned the kiss, forceful, warm and full—but something bothered him.

He was tired. Tina sensed it.

"Shane, go in my bedroom and have a rest. These people will leave as soon as Tommy passes out."

The significance of the remark escaped him until he was lying on an enormous round bed in the centre of the room. For a time, he was wide-eyed, but the hum of the air conditioner lulled him.

"Tina?"

The outside light was suffused by the curtains. He sensed her in the room before he saw her at a closet door. She was naked.

"Yes."

"Come here."

"Not so fast, Mr. Donovan."

When she came to the edge of the bed, she was wearing silk. His hand touched her knee, but he made no effort to turn towards her.

"They're all gone, lover."

"Tommy?"

"Asleep in the other room."

There was nothing to say. He was lifeless and inert. The moment had passed. Again, she seemed to sense his condition.

"Are you feeling all right, Shane?"

"Terrible."

"Sunday is a dreadful day."

"It is if you drink too much. I didn't really eat since yesterday."

"Can I get you something?"

"You wouldn't have the makings of a stinger?"

"I can do it. I hid the brandy and crème de menthe. They would have gobbled that as well."

In the half light from the window and a night-table lamp which she turned on, he sipped the drink. She nursed a glass of milk and the conversation was easy. About growing up in the Soo. Waiting on tables and trying to go to school while her father was busy inviting prospective husbands from Greece.

" 'You don't need school. Just a good husband, and babies.' That's what my father said."

Shane had known the experience before. Two strangers, pinioned by circumstances, a flare of thwarted passion and then a sympathetic bond making them exchange intimate memories—which they might or might not regret later.

"Oh, Shane, I shouldn't be talking this way."

"Why not? I'm a good listener."

She hadn't really heard him.

"There was a man. Oh, he was some distant relative from Athens—or maybe one of the islands. I was just too disgusted and he wanted to marry me. He was at least, well, more than twice my age—and fat. I begged my mother, but father was boss, and up until a week before the wedding I cried and screamed and didn't really believe. But father was insistent and the guests were all invited and I said I wouldn't. A seventeen-year-old girl and a forty-year-old bald man with a belly—and, I suspected, a wife back home."

She was bent over, rolling the glass between her hands.

"And did you marry him?"

"No," she said, after a long pause, "I said I wouldn't and my father locked me in my room. Then he took my mother down to the restaurant and gave Gus the key. That son of a bitch came up and raped me. I guess they thought it would clinch the wedding, but I waited until the night before and ran away with a hosiery salesman to Detroit. I went to Chicago for a year, got into a modelling school and came here—for guess what? A hosiery account. Golden Edge. The same kind as poor Hank was selling in northern Michigan."

Then there was the uncertainty of modelling in New York, and the usual routine of working as a salesgirl. She had been auditioned once as a Gleason Girl.

"Turned me down. Said I wasn't American enough. God, when I see them I'm glad I didn't get it. They're zombies to me. It's a funny thing about looks. My boobs are too big, they say, for fashion, and yet every magazine is loaded with melons. My hands and legs are good so I get gloves and hosiery. But it's all the same racket. Photographers and agency types on the make and producers who want to make nudies. The guys who aren't on the make are watchers. They make my flesh creep. So, it's tough."

She stopped and got up to leave.

"Then, I met Tommy. Sweet Tommy with an old bitch of a mother. I really don't know how he puts up with me."

Shane didn't press for an explanation. When she brought him another stinger, he sensed she had looked in on Tommy in the other room.

"Tommy has been good to me. I guess I feel sorry for him. That mother of his has squeezed all the man out of him but— he likes me and I couldn't afford to live like this. For all he gets out of it, I wonder if he isn't being gypped, but he seems happy—and he finds me some work at the agency when it gets tough."

"Isn't it an—well—odd way to live?"

He felt silly for saying it. She moved to the window.

"Everybody in this kind of world lives a strange life. Mine hasn't been exactly natural right from the night father gave me away."

"Do you hate men?"

"I don't hate you."

He felt like a man roped and tied. He wanted to get up and go to her but his body simply wouldn't respond. She came finally and leaned over him. After what seemed a long time, she kissed him. There was a desperate quality in the way her lips and hands roamed over his body but he was helpless.

"Poor Shane. Men and women need each other at times. Even dear old Tommy. I like you. There's something, away deep in me, vibrates over you—you're kinda beat up in a way,

79

but you're still healthier than a lot of those creeps you saw today. You drink too much. We wouldn't help each other now. Maybe only hurt. Sometime—perhaps."

She moved around the room, bunching her words and tossing them out in quick batches. When she stopped talking, Shane felt he had to reach her with words.

"I feel old, beat up—tired. I was fifty last week. Fifty bloody years old—and I'm on a slide down to—to nothing, I guess."

In the dim light, he felt as if he were in a confessional.

"From Sault Ste. Marie, Sioux City, or Saskatchewan we're all from the boondocks. We're all private draftees in an army of frustration. Each of us has a secret dream inside and we can't seem to get it out. I'm supposed to be successful. Most times I feel like a guy on a bloody merry-go-round."

"What do you really want to do?"

"Tell it like it is, as they say. Get something out of myself. Write a play that will bring people in every night to be moved —or a book—I guess maybe a book."

"Why don't you?"

"Want to really know why?"

"Of course."

He sighed.

"I've never really had the guts. No—let me put it this way. I start and I seem to know, but the hellish doubts start about my ability—and a lot of things—oh, not much education— none of my people ever did anything like that—and I give up and go back to the agency—and get money for luxuries and booze to cover up the unhappiness."

"Shane, I'm not sure I understand."

"The hellish part, Tina, is that each of us wants a life that's enjoyable. You know, decent place to live and all, and we scream about it, and then we go to work and become helpless parts of a monster thing that's causing all the trouble."

"I don't get it."

"*I'm the guy who says Canada should be a great place, and all I do is help to make it more like all the things I don't like in the States.*"

The sweat started when he swallowed the remainder of his drink.

"You better take it easy. Here, let me wipe your brow."

He grabbed her by the shoulders and kissed her.

"Now, Shane. Don't be rough. You don't have to."

When his hands eased from her shoulders, she leaned over and kissed him warmly on the lips. She had removed the overgarment and he could feel the softness and curves of her body, and a deep rage welled up in him at his own impotence.

"Wasn't that nicer, Shane?"

His cheeks flamed, and while she leaned over him he refused to make any move which would heighten the embarrassment.

"Sorry, Tina, I've about had it."

She folded a cover over him.

"Don't worry. Just you rest and I'll go and clean up the mess, or at least some of it."

She closed the door gently, and he was tired. When he came out of the sleep, it was abruptly, terrified at the instant of awakening by the strange surroundings. It was almost eleven by the time he dressed. He wanted to find Tina, but the door of the other bedroom was closed. He left quietly and took a taxi to the President.

The hotel suite ordered by Waite, Irwin, and Tasker was enormous. He was exhausted, scarcely noticing the flowers, food, and liquor. He dropped his clothes and crawled into bed. The sleep lasted fitfully until seven. It was mid-evening before he stood fully dressed at the window eating some of the canapés.

The moon away up through the slit afforded by the tops of the buildings was a scarred, cold ball of light. Down below cars were beetles and people were dots. It was almost unnatural. Even the air was tired and heavy.

This was New York, the lonely place. Friendships were fearful, or else as callously impersonal as Tina's Sunday brunch where people chattered about the personal affairs in an impersonal way. They broke chatter only long enough to stare a stranger into silence. Then they went back to their talk, which was largely protestation and anger.

"C'mon, whatcha say?"

"Nuthin', got nuthin' ta say."

"Lissenya, got nuthin' ta say?"

"Whatcha wannme ta say?"

"I didn' ashyatasaynuthin' at all."

"Well, always with the yakk. So I wanna say nuthin', I ain't gonna say nuthin'."

Loneliness spilled and rolled across the city by night. The people movement of day spilled over into the night. These were the ones without homes in the suburbs and Brooklyn and Queens and the Bronx. They existed in pockets wedged amongst stores, factories, hotels, bars, and night clubs. Mask-faced, like extras from a Fellini film, nursing drinks and reading newspapers and ignoring the waves of strangers constantly arriving to sin, to get drunk or to find mythical excitement.

Shane put his drink down and left the room.

"Got any Havana cigars?"

The wrinkled face of the gnome-like attendant scowled.

"Who ya kiddin', bud? You some kinda Commy, or somethin'? We got the best cigars in the Yooessay, but none of them goddamned Castro ones. Waddya want?"

Shane resisted mentioning that he could buy the best cigars in the world, Havana cigars, in Canada. It wasn't worth the effort to argue with the little man.

Nothing was what it seemed. "These cigars are predominantly natural tobacco with non-tobacco ingredients added." Pure, thought Shane, is an adulterated word. He wished he had brought some Havana cigars with him. Fathingham always appreciated them. So would Tommy.

"Tommy has offered several times to send me back home just to look around," Tina had said, "but I think he just wants some decent cigars. He paid for my auditioning in Toronto for the CBC, and warned me to bring back all the—what do you call them—Uppman, I think—cigars I could find. I did okay in the audition until the producer discovered I was a Canadian. He picked a little movie actress from Hollywood. Script girl said it was an excuse to have conferences out there."

Shane sat down in a lobby chair and unwrapped the cigar.

Here were the tired people. Here were the out-of-town visitors who walked all day in confused circles. Now, too exhausted to move, they sat on hoping for something to happen that would justify their trip. Men blinked owlishly and sedate matrons sat exposing more varicosed leg than usual. In tentative conversations they discovered others were from Peoria and Albany and Iron City and were just as tired and lonely. They would sit and talk, imagine famous people walking, and see Mafia nabobs in every chauffeured limousine on Broadway.

Shane took out his address book. Julia Browne? Two years before when she was making her first cigarette commercial, it was plain Aggie Brown.

"Hello . . . Aggie . . . I mean, Julia?"

"Who is this?"

"For the smoke that gives pleasure, not danger . . . try El Ropo?"

For a second, the background sound of music was cut off as she muffled the receiver.

"Who is it?"

"You mean you've forgotten after only a year in the big city?"

"Shane? Is it you?"

"It is, indeed . . . faith and it's me."

He was beginning to feel self-conscious.

"Gosh, how are you, Shane?"

"Fine . . . and you?"

"Not bad . . . are you in town for long?"

The gambit! The stall!

"Oh, all week, just thought I would see how you are."

"That's nice of you. Listen, maybe . . . I mean . . . how long are you here for?"

"All week. I'm getting an award of some kind . . ."

"That advertising award. I know . . . I was so proud when I saw it in the *Times* . . . I said . . . to Bert . . . See, I do know important people."

Now, the awkward pause.

"Well, kid, maybe we can have a drink . . ."

"Sure, can I call you?"

"I'm at the President . . . well, I have to run now . . . but it's good to hear you, Ag . . . Julia . . ."

"Ditto and thanks for calling."

There was nothing to do but join the crowd. He crossed with the lights and was caught in the press of a movie audience swirling from the exits. Air gushed at him, warm and strong-smelling from the open doors . . . the crowd chattering and talking and rupturing from the sidewalk to the street.

Wisps of conversation came to him.

"Jesus H. Christ, seven dollars to see that crap!"

"Herman, for the love of Gawd, stop squawking . . ."

They were gone then, the florid-faced man in the brilliant blue suit and the stout woman with the flowers waving in her hat.

"Come on. Christ, do I need a drink."

"I thought he was going to have her right there on the screen."

"Well, I wouldn't mind . . ."

"Watch it . . . watch it . . . let's go to that theatre place . . . what do they call it?"

"Oh, Gert, that joint is packed and besides they wouldn't even let us in last time."

Shane moved downstream, conscious that it was like swimming in a sea of people. This was the world of clothing stores and restaurants and shops, windows filled with records and curios from the Eastern world and always the mass of recordings, recordings, recordings.

He saw the man in the vivid shirt and the girl with the long tawny hair talking on the side street. When he paused at the window display of books, she was beside him.

"Want a little action?"

Her face was a mask of white slashed by two gashes of green eye shadow. Thin to the point of emaciation, mini-skirted with knees made prominent by dark stockings, the tone of her voice matched the dry strange look.

"What about your boyfriend back there? Will he show up and play injured husband?"

"Smart bastard, ain'tcha?"

She was gone, leaving Shane more alone than ever. Individuals sidled up to men who were walking by themselves. Girls sauntered by with swinging movements of their hips. Two

85

girls were kissing. A boy on the curb with a blood-smeared forehead was crying.

Shane turned back. It was too late to go to the movies. A drink? Must have food. He settled for one of the orange and red vinyl-upholstered ham and egg places. The dusky-toned girls with straight black hair which they fingered as if in wonderment, were sitting with rake-eyed black men in tight suits moulded to lean frames. They obviously dared anyone to answer the flirtatious provocation of the girls.

His body was caught and tired. Sleep would be impossible, or would be a kaleidoscope of dreams and restless turnings. Tina! She had responded, and his helplessness angered him. Like old Ibn Saud who spurned a bullet in his groin to prove his virility with the first woman he saw afterwards. Call her? He finished eating.

Into focus came the woman toying with the coffee cup. Shane looked around. The woman was the centre of attention of the staring black men. One in particular was making a motion of his head. Her hands shook when she took out a package of cigarettes. The man shoved his shoulders back and made an elaborate movement for his lighter, grandstanding for the others. Shane moved on a reflex.

"Light?"

"Yes, please . . ."

He sat down. Hostility poured at him!

"Look, I . . . saw that guy . . ."

"I know, I've been stalling here for half an hour."

"Well, what . . . I mean . . ."

It was an attractive face, an edge too full but still pretty, with lips that were moist and full. Her skin was soft and her hair made him think of someone. When she looked up, her suit coat parted and he could see the veins of the full bust and the blue lace edging a white brassiere.

"I left my girl friend at the subway and for some strange reason I wanted a coffee and I came in here. I didn't expect it would be full of . . . well . . . these are Broadway studs and I suppose you can't blame them . . . and I was . . ."

"Trapped . . ."

"In a way. I don't come out very much like this and, well, New York is changing . . ."

Her voice was deep but still feminine. He thought of Simone Signoret or Madeleine Carroll. When she stopped talking, he said, "I don't know, but I have the blues tonight for some reason or other. I had an unnerving experience today."

"Was it any worse than this?"

"Not really."

They were islanded. It seemed as if every one, except the robot-like cashier, was staring at them.

"Take it easy—"

"Shane. Shane Donovan."

"These men are mean, Shane, and in New York no one cares what happens to you, just as long as they're not involved."

They moved, impaled by the stares, while he paid the checks. When they walked down the street, she clutched his arm.

"They're following. What will we do?"

"I'm at the President. It's just two blocks."

A sauntering policeman glanced at them and vanished into a subway entrance. Now the street was ominously quiet. They skip-hopped across as the light turned red. Without looking back he was aware of the men dodging the advancing traffic as if in pursuit.

Even the lobby was not a refuge. He could see them staring from the doorway. He gave the operator the number of the floor above. As he shepherded her down the fire stairs she laughed.

"Say, are you a detective or something?"

"Oh, no, God, no!"

While he opened the door she said, "I'm Bonnie Baker. Are you an American?"

"Canadian."

"I thought so—"

"Why?"

"I don't know. Something about you. Say, do you own Canada or something?"

She was looking around the suite.

"The American office booked the suite. Advertising. Like a drink?"

"It's pretty late."

"Better wait until those fellows move away."

She moved to look out the window.

"Scotch-on-the-rocks, please. Hard to tell who's down there."

He was conscious of the warm smell of fear. He was tempted to put his arms around her, but moved instead to the serving pantry. When he came out she had turned on the Muzak button of the TV.

"God, how we change! When I was very young, I thought hotels and palaces were alike—very elegant—and very sinful."

"Where I was brought up, the hotel was the place the railroad crews stayed. No one else ever bothered to stay—or wanted to."

It was difficult to keep from thinking of Tina. Once his face flushed.

"Am I embarrassing you?"

"No, something happened tonight—I'm not too proud about—"

"A girl—"

"In a way. One of those cases where there was too much booze involved—"

Bonnie laughed without embarrassment.

"They say it can get in the way." As if catching herself, she added, "I feel better. Any refills?"

They were brought together by danger. Once or twice when her skirt moved above mid-thigh, she tugged at it. When Bonnie looked up to see him watching she laughed.

"These styles are certainly not for girls with a touch too much."

"You shouldn't worry."

"Only twenty pounds."

She was soft. He felt that. Tina was a knife edge of sharp features and leanness that contrasted with her bust. But her breasts were firm and almost of the same firm consistency as the rest of her regimented body. Bonnie would yield to pressure. When he picked up her empty glass, she blushed.

"I don't want to get stiff at this time of the morning."

"It's like the old expression about getting tight on Sunday morning when there's no place to go. All the joints are closed, at least in Toronto."

She responded when he kissed her.

"Lonely people do strange things."

His arousal came out of the dregs of fear and frustration. It had happened before, usually almost shock-like with a passing acquaintance. Once there had been an actress who said angrily, "But don't you damned fool men know we have wants as well." But there were other times when it was merely an arousal by alcohol which could subside just as quickly.

"Are you lonely?"

"Strange tonight. It happens in New York. I was working late. I am with a so-called Señor Fancelli—really Joe Gluckstein—and getting ready for a fashion show. We had a few drinks and he—well, he was difficult."

"You look as if you could cope."

Her smile was sad.

"What terrified me was I almost gave in. He's terrible—and—"

Her gesture was helpless.

"We all get a bit desperate at times. Maybe you should be married."

"Yeh, I guess so."

"Sorry, is that subject taboo?"

"Just painful."

Her hand trembled lighting a cigarette.

"Look, Bonnie . . . I . . ."

She went to the window and said finally: "Oh, it's not a taboo . . . you see, there was a man . . . Mr. It . . . and it was the old story. Married! Started out simply. I met him at a reception . . . he was a magazine editor and we liked each other . . . and then it turned out he was married, kids going to school, wife unhappy and sick a lot . . ."

"America seems to have plenty of divorcees . . ."

Her voice was almost a whisper.

"He was a Catholic and so was his wife . . ."

"Oh, I see . . ."

"Not quite . . . it went on and we broke off and it started again and then finally, he went in the Army . . . didn't have to . . . he was Reserve, but he didn't have to go . . . and he . . . he . . . I guess he ran away from both of us."

"Look, Bonnie . . . sorry it came up . . . I . . ."

There were tears on her cheeks like raindrops, but she didn't bother to wipe them away.

"He died in Korea . . . bloody . . . bloody Korea and now

he's gone from both of us. You're a very nice man, Shane
. . . now it's your turn to go sobby."

He just kissed her. For a long time they stood that way,
their bodies responding as their lips touched.

"Oh, my God."

It was a groan that indicated everything he was feeling.

"I know, Shane, I know . . . there's something like real
pain inside."

"God, Bonnie, love me . . ."

She didn't reply. Her hand stroked the side of his face. She
moved from his arms, going to stand by the window for a moment. There were cigarettes on the little table and he fancied
her hand shook as she lit one, took a puff and as suddenly
squelched it out.

"Do . . . do things like this happen?"

"You mean is it happening to us?"

Her head was inclined on his shoulder. He put his arms
around her gently. He knew she could feel his body and
he stood without pressing closer.

"Shane . . . we're strangers . . . in a way . . . and yet . . .
well . . . I don't mean strange things . . . God I'm babbling."

Shane stroked her hair.

"There's an expression about danger . . . something about
it bringing people close together . . . I . . . oh hell, I'm babbling too . . . I could say a lot of things . . ."

Bonnie pulled away from him, and gently put her finger on
his lips.

"Only one thing. Just answer me one question . . ."

He nodded.

"Do you have any feeling . . . oh, I don't mean love . . .
that would be silly. Do you . . ."

She was staring at him.

"Do you like me at least . . . well, some . . ."

91

He smiled.

"I do, Bonnie. I do . . . there's no line . . . that's what I was going to say . . . I'm not going to make up a line . . . I just . . . feel I want to be close to you . . ."

She kissed him and pulling away asked softly, "Have you a bathrobe or anything . . . Sounds silly . . ."

"Sssh . . . it's behind the door in the bathroom . . ."

His pulse was beating like a hammer as she stopped in the bathroom door.

"Turn off the light. Let's just have the outside light."

It was when her arms reached around his neck that she stopped to say ruefully, "Don't tell me. That's a Catholic medal. God, but I certainly walk into trouble."

It was too late then. It came back to him later when he crept from the bed and went to the bathroom. Her clothes were on the hanger and he stood with his face buried in their feeling and smell. She was asleep when he went back in the room.

How do you explain an incident like meeting Bonnie? But it happened, and it was natural and they didn't spend time conning each other. Who would believe it was anything but the meeting of an out-of-towner and a hooker? Yet Shane knew it wasn't that way. There had been no need for long explanations between them, and some of his loneliness was gone. But there was still a hunger. He drank and smoked through a mood tinged with despair until he was ready for sleep.

6

Shane came sharply from what seemed exhilarated conversation to groping awake in a strange room. Make no sudden movements. Try to get away before the others wake up—that was easier than confrontation.

The door opened. A dark face under a lace cap.

"Excuse me, suh!"

The maid closed the door. The second pillow was disarranged.

"Bonnie?"

No answer. His legs were weak. Lipstick on the bathroom mirror.

384–7888 *after 6.—B.*

He looked around the suite. It was luxury.

"It's not you having it, Shane. It's just that so many always have so little and some have so much. I see it all the time at Fancelli's. The dried-up women and those old fat ones come in and take beauty treatments and try to make out they aren't old. My God, they spend as much on a dog each week as we used to live on when I was a kid."

Bonnie.

She was a pleasant, lonely woman, caught at a job she hated. How would you explain meeting her and what happened? Black studs eyeing her and then her coming to his room.

Bonnie Baker!

That was too cute. Sounded like an old-time singer on the radio. A put-up job. Shane began to sweat. He stormed to the closet in a panic. His wallet was gone. God almighty! His hands were shaking as he sat on the edge of the bed.

What could he say?

The drawer in the night table was slightly open. There it was. His wallet. The money and credit cards were intact.

Now he was assuring himself that he hadn't really mistrusted Bonnie. A bit like Mona! But he knew Mona wouldn't be picked up in a Broadway ham and egg joint. To hell with it. Bonnie is Bonnie. Mona is Mona.

New York and Monday. No, Tuesday. My God, Tuesday. The beer tasted good, Call Fathingham! What difference? There was still plenty of time. Waite, Irwin, and Tasker didn't own him.

But Bonnie! He tried to reconstruct. The place and the black men eyeing her. Hell! Damned if he would let himself feel guilty.

New York was full of people who came from strange places. He was getting confused. He put the beer on the night table and went back to bed.

New York. Alone in New York. Pornographic New York. The ads—the products to make you horny. Fashions are erogenous. A stage-managed and commercial sex show—not for sex—for sales. He had to get going. Make a good day of it and call Mona at night, perfectly sober. But he didn't make any effort to get up.

"Well, old cock, are you drunk or awake?"

He was awake with a start.

"Who the hell?"

"Look, don't have a fit. It's Peter . . . Peter O'Hare."

"Better not turn on that bed light or you'll shatter your eyeballs. Here, put this on."

Naked, sweaty and shivering, Donovan clambered out to put on the bathrobe, half-listening until he heard . . . "Mona must have been desperate to call me."

"Mona called you?"

"Yes, she got my number through the Toronto office."

O'Hare was riffling through telephone slips.

"You're a mighty sound sleeper. A guy called Smith has been calling you all morning."

Shane slumped in a chair.

"Here's another one. Call B. after six. In lipstick, yet. Business acquaintance?"

O'Hare had always been a friend right from Shane's earliest days in Toronto. It was one of the few personal relationships of Shane's where a mutual trust existed. Peter was strong willed, a big man with confidence enough in himself to never be compromised. He had broken a marriage and left several steady jobs for the precarious life of free-lancing because, as he said, he "had to have room to breathe."

Shane was jealous of similar qualities in others. Somehow, he accepted it in O'Hare. That's why he could tell him about Bonnie without hesitation. Peter listened and got up and, taking a bottle of scotch from the table, went to the kitchenette. He came back with two glasses.

"Scotch and milk. Sorry I have no eggs to put in it."

He tipped his glass.

"Here's to romance."

Shane sipped.

"Well, tell me I'm a heel. Goddamit, Peter, I'm fifty years old and—"

"Oh, Shane, for the love of God. Don't ask me for absolution or pity. For fifty I'd say you were not doing too badly at that."

"Dammit, O'Hare, she wasn't that kind of woman. She was in a jam—a real bloody jam—and, well, I think she was lonely. She came up here—and well—you meet her and you'll know what I mean. I—I think she's a pretty nice woman."

O'Hare stretched out his legs, took a swallow from his glass and grinned.

"Shane, you don't have to go into a song and dance for me."

"I know, but the whole thing sounds so—"

O'Hare waved his arms.

"Stop it, man. You're not a flour and feed man from Podunk. You've been around and you bloody well know as I do, that strange things happen—things you can't explain."

Shane nodded.

"I know, so why am I spluttering?"

"That's Turkey Creek, Saskatchewan, speaking. I know. I've got it, too. Nicest girl I ever met I picked up in a bar in Montreal. By God, I actually fell in love with her—but—you know something—I couldn't marry her. You know what happened—I did marry the one everybody said was so wonderful —really good woman—and she was a bloody harpie. So stop explaining—and stop feeling bloody guilty."

"God save us, do we ever escape our upbringing?"

O'Hare shook his head slowly.

"Never completely. Shane, I'm going to tell you something —this is the sexiest and loneliest city in the world. You take a man in New York alone—or a homely, young girl—or one who is just a bit long in the tooth—and they must go almost crazy."

Shane told him about Tina.

"I like Bonnie better. That sounds funny. Bonnie better. Watch out for the other one. They can be dangerous. But Bonnie may be good for you. That's your business, but I'm worried about whatever is eating your behind. Get rid of it. Underneath that slick advertising image, I think you've got some real talent—but you're hooked into the Good Life of TV and all the media crap."

"The hell I am. I'd give this up tomorrow—"

"Stop it. You've been saying that for years but all you do is get better suits and bigger cars—and you drink more—"

O'Hare sat on after the conversation stalled. When Shane finished the scotch and milk, the writer somewhat reluctantly got him another one.

"Are you going to keep on drinking?"

"No, why?"

"Look, Shane. You've gotta stop before it's too late. No, let me finish. You're a smart guy. You're one of the brightest in the business and you still care. That's important. It's what's itching you. Mona knows that and she can't help you."

"She could if she wanted to."

O'Hare shook his head.

"By being like that Greek doll from Fort William, being kept by the phony American Englishman and itching for someone with more power—or something?"

It rankled.

"You don't understand. I—I—well, it's just going by me and there's no satisfaction."

"Is there any satisfaction in *this*? Waking up and not being sure of where you've been—who it was you slept with—"

Shane felt boozy tears. O'Hare sensed them, because he stared at the glass in his hand as he continued:

"You know—rather you probably don't know, but you called Mona last night—probably early this morning."

"Jesus!"

"Oh yes, all about a novel you were going to write—all about some woman who lost her husband or somebody in Korea."

Shane felt something like a hard slap to his stomach.

"Jesus, God help me. That tears it."

When he came back from the bathroom O'Hare was staring out the window. He didn't turn.

"Shane, listen to me. For the love of God get out of this game—even for a year or so—and write. Write until whatever the hell is itching you comes out. Get it done."

"I don't know."

"Now listen." The big man was facing him. "I'm going to tell you something. You can do it. You *can* write—no bloody fear. I know that inside you is a whole package of reactions bound up with the country, your country and people. And you feel so deeply it's tearing you into ribbons. Write it—and you'll have, well—"

He laughed.

"A hell-cracking novel—perhaps the best thing we have at home. The Great Canadian Novel. Everybody talks about it. Try it!"

Shane was silent.

"Now look, fella, only one thing. You've gotta have the

guts to do it. But listen—if you don't—if you don't, I wouldn't give you a nickel for your chances. You'll kill yourself.

"Try it. If the writing doesn't help, something else may. Look at those kids and their communes and experiments. Some of them are nuts, but they're trying, and some are going to make it. You've got to try as well. That's why I've switched. I don't know whether I can hack being a playwright, but by God I'm going to try."

O'Hare was pacing.

"Try for the brass ring. Try writing the—the Great Canadian Novel you talk so well. Try. You're up to your ass in nationalism, and creativity and the Canadian ethos—so write it. If it doesn't work, what the hell. You'll be out of that damned rat race and you can get a franchise for fried chicken —or beat the old wheezer in the white suit and sell French-fried beaver tails—à la Johnny Canuck."

When Shane started to speak he shushed him.

"No bloody arguments. I really should lay off the 'Great' bit. Perhaps that's a bit much. My number is there, so call if you need anything."

He stopped at the door.

"Write, you bastard. Crap or get off the pot. If you decide to go for it, I'll help any way I can. If you don't—well, I'll probably go to your funeral. Stop worrying about success. You just need to do something in place of talking it to death when you're boozed up."

The door slammed. He intended to get dressed but it was easier to ignore O'Hare in half sleep. The telephone rang.

"Shane, it's Tommy."

Shane braced himself against the headboard, trying to make his voice firm. An exchange of pleasantries. Some of the boys would like to meet him for cocktails at five. Good idea to get a rest, would be a busy week.

Exercise was out because the room went whirly every time he bent over. The time was edging along to eleven. Call Tina. The number? It was a game. Couldn't ask Tommy. Try Artists' Registry . . . Model List . . . like the FBI getting their man.

She was sleepy and cross.

"I never get up in time for lunch. Besides, Tommy was cross this morning."

"Why?"

"Darling, I don't know. He's not usually jealous—oh well I can't do anything about it . . . look honey . . . I've got to sleep."

He couldn't fight the general lassitude. In a way, he was trying to forget what O'Hare had said. There was plenty of time. It was only two o'clock. He drifted into a state of semi-sleep and dreaming. The dream was almost haunted.

It always opened the same way. There was a cold, rainy spell and he had been coughing. Julius brought him to the deserted sugar shanty and put him to bed in the bunk on the sweet marsh grass with the dirty blanket and the potato sacks piled over him.

"Here, kid. Take this."

He fed him broth made from a boiled chicken. Shane was feverish and the little man mysteriously produced a syrup of bitter herbs and sugar. There were dreams of home and times when he half imagined that it was his mother beside the rusty, old stove—and once when he was spinning in and out of consciousness he heard a train whistle, but it was going away.

The shack was dusty and smelled of mist. The sweat began finally, and on a morning when the sun was shining he wakened early to see it streaming in the cobwebbed windows.

Julius was asleep on the floor. That day he got up and although he was weak he ate the rabbit stew and didn't argue when the tramp persuaded him to go to his uncle's.

He stood at the gateway of the lane with the single row of elms and watched the bundle of ragged clothes climb the hill. Julius stood for a few minutes in silhouette and then waved quickly in a semi-salute before vanishing over the crest.

Shane walked slowly up the laneway, his black loneliness greater than his fear. He needn't have feared. Uncle Matt and Olga his soft, big, young wife accepted him without recrimination.

"Your mother said she thought you would come in her letter. She wanted to tell the police but your dad wouldn't let her. He always was stubborn."

Matt took the letter from the bureau drawer as if for confirmation, but he never showed it to him. Shane sensed that they had been waiting for him.

Uncle Matt was gaunt and slightly stooped with a thatch of faded corn-tassel hair and cheeks that looked as if they had recently been slabbed by an axe. He sat at the table in the kitchen by the slightly smoking lamp every night after supper. Olga, dark and white-faced, her feet slopping down on the linoleum floor, moved endlessly in the shadows at the edge of the lamplight, doing invisible chores.

"Guess I'll go down to the corner for a minute."

Matt put his steel-rimmed glasses in a case on top of the telephone. He smoothed the bib of his overalls into the cave of his chest and belly, before he went to sit silent amongst the loungers at the corner store. Then Olga pulled a chair beside his.

"You are learning good, Shun?"

There was a tension on that soft, spring night when

she leaned over to look at his book and he felt the weight of her heavy breasts on his back.

There was little talk when the silent Matt was present. When he had gone, as he did every night, they talked. Olga Landruchek, twenty-six, who had married the fifty-five-year-old Ontario bachelor when he had gone west on a harvest excursion.

"I marry him to be a wife. I want to be a wife."

Shane had puzzled over the expression. On a soft night when the air through the screen door was like velvet, he began to understand for the first time.

"Your uncle is good, but he should not marry."

She pressed on his neck and shoulders for a long time. Her hand was hot and clammy on his cheek. In bed he heard her come up the stairway slowly, pause at his door, and then go in the big bedroom. Sleep came when he could no longer stay awake to listen to the bed springs squeaking as she turned restlessly.

He began to find excuses to stay out of the kitchen in the evening. Olga was a heavy-busted, stout-legged girl with a surprisingly attractive face. She wore loose dark blue dresses buttoned irregularly so that no matter where he looked he saw her breasts or bare skin. He was conscious of her bloomers on the clothesline, looking like large, twin pink sausages.

Matt accepted him stoically, and appeared anxious that he go to school.

"You can stay here. Help your aunt and do some chores. Behave yourself. Study hard. Your father and me never had the chance for schooling. You take it."

Shane wondered if there was any conversation at all when he was away. Did they sit and eat at noon without words? The house was still in the middle of the night except for Matt's snores and Olga's muttering moans. She walked sometimes in the early evening down by the swale, a mourner's kind of walk.

Then there was the night of the summer thunderstorm.

"Is big storm?"

The valley was rocked and shattered by thunder. The big drops splattered on the roof of the veranda. She stood inside the screen door staring up at the sky. The lightning outlined her figure. When she put her hands and arms up to the rain she looked like an enormous goddess.

Matt was at the store and would stay there until the storm was over. Shane crept up the stairs to bed. The house quivered and groaned as the wind whipped the branches of the old elm along the eaves.

"Shun?"

The lightning exploded through the window and he saw her standing by the bed. She was naked.

"You are afraid, Shun?"

She cradled him in her arms at first and then almost smothered him. He was locked in an embrace of soft flesh and her hair was spilling all around. Her hands ranged all over his body and her moaning was deafening and as he came into full manhood he heard her shriek above the sound of the storm.

When he woke she was gone. The air had a fresh, humid smell and his pillow had the lemony scent of Castile soap. At first he felt lazy and tired and as he remembered he jumped out of bed, naked, to listen to the noises of the house. His nightshirt was gone. He could hear Shep barking at the cows in the pasture. His door opened slightly and as he made a move to get back to bed Olga's arm left his nightshirt on the chair inside the door. The door closed again.

The nightshirt was sewn where it had been ripped.

He had to stop. That damned childish memory. Why

couldn't he have rid himself of it. Over the years he had re-assured himself that everyone has childhood memories. But it would never go away completely. He couldn't even tell Mona. God knows he tried, but every time he avoided saying it and the effort brought a form of shield down between them.

"Mona, you and I have to take time out to get things back on the rails. This is a different world."

He soliloquized to steady himself as he selected socks from the valise.

"Mona, you stick with the church until it ruins our lives. That jazz about suffering in this life and getting your reward in the next is for the birds. So maybe there is a higher power. Family, I know, is important but—"

Family was a strange word for Shane. There were times when he ached to feel and sense what it meant. At home—no! Perhaps he had really felt it with Uncle Matt and Olga.

Big, soft Olga with her fresh Castiled face and the jet black hair drawn back severely. Olga with the exposed soft flanks milking cows in the barn.

Uncle Matt! Matthew Donovan, slow and stolid and un-speaking. Family? Was it the reason why Matt Donovan paid his tuition to college? There was no explanation. He simply said, "You're going to college. The priest made arrange-ments."

When he said it, Matt was on his way from the corner of the kitchen where his hat hung on a nail to the door. He stopped, arms hanging, shoulders sloped, the swirl of grey hair standing like the topknot of an Indian. He was lumpy, like the big stones turned out when they were excavating the barn foundation.

Olga stood by the stove. Shane had been pretending to read.

"Where, Uncle Matt?"

The old man ignored the question. Jamming his hat on his head he dug in the overall pocket and brought up a hard-rolled pack of bills, dropping it with an accumulation of chaff on the table.

"You take him into Handrich and get him what he needs."

He spoke without looking at his wife, "The priest knows about the school. Maybe that will do him—"

He didn't finish the sentence. They heard the tractor cough into life, its noise fading down the laneway. She moved to pick up the breakfast dishes, and came instead to stand beside him.

"I'm so happy."

When Shane looked at her she had become a different person. She was young.

"Olga—"

Her arms smothered him.

"Shane, get away and go now."

He felt her lips on his forehead, the soft yielding of her body and this time sensed her compassion, in place of the fierce demanding of the first time.

"And you—?"

"Never mind me. Now we go see Father Kelly and get you nice clothes."

Matt and Olga were mysteries to him. He had wanted so hard to understand them on the day they stood, all three of them, on the station platform waiting for the train that would take him to St. Gerald's College in New Gordon.

The stock pens were empty. The water tower was neglected. The agent lined up some cream cans and egg crates on a wagon on the edge of the platform. Chickens squawked in a crate. The drayman leaned against the bay window where the telegraph key chattered. No one said anything. The train whooshed in. Olga took his hand shyly. It made him blush and he turned to his uncle.

"Goodbye and thanks, Uncle Matt."

The old man nodded and walked away without taking his hand.

"You get a good schooling."

Olga said it when she kissed him. But Matt wasn't looking. In the coach with the green plush, he fought to keep back the tears, his flushed face close to the window as the train rolled into the night.

Matt Donovan, an older brother reared in the early Puritan atmosphere of an Irish Catholic home, had become head of the house when his father was killed in an accident. Matt would have been a priest, but he was deprived of education because of duty to his mother, whom he idolized. He made a late grab for manhood when the old woman died, and married Olga.

"He is a good man."

Olga had repeated it like a litany to Shane. A good man who worked until he dropped into sleep from exhaustion. A good man who undressed in the dark. A good man shocked into impotence by the presence of a young wife.

"What I did was very bad. Please to forgive me, Shane."

When she said that, she would stir something at the stove or cross her arms as if to smother her breasts.

St. Gerald's was an escape. A series of ugly red brick buildings caught like an island fortress in the middle of the industrial city.

"What are you in for?"

It was the first question Shane faced.

"What do you mean?"

"What did ya do?"

"Nothing. My uncle sent me."

"To get rid of you."

Red, the Swede, a football fiend from Minnesota, explained.

"Donovan, all of these guys were sent here for some reason. Tony got booted from a Swiss school for skipping classes. That guy with the pimples from Toronto got the maid in trouble. Jimmy's got itchy fingers. Don't leave anything out when he's around."

"What about you, Red?"

"All I want to do is play football. My old man has a drugstore and I gotta make some grades before I can go to pharmacy school. You know how to play football?"

In the world he had known, Shane was used to black-and-white values. They came on each Saturday night when the children were pushed, pulled or cajoled to the little frame church and the confessional.

"Bless me, Father, for I have sinned—"

"A week since my last confession—"

"Took the Lord's name—bad thoughts—"

"I—I—"

The stammering incoherence of trying to explain a fumbling session in the grass with Helen Wildyear who at ten had discovered how to make candy money for a feel.

At St. Gerald's there was a constant war of a different kind against the same instincts. Bells at 4:15, cold showers, chapel, breakfast, and always the bells. Gym practice. Cold showers. More bells, and lights that flashed on in the night.

"Hands out of the covers. Hands out and above. No diddly here."

In the black night, with only the street lamps showing

through the dormitory windows, a bear of a man walked. Brother Andrew. An asthmatic man with squeaking shoes and a rattling rosary who kept a vigil against impurity.

There was an exciting world in books. He read whenever he could, and discovered that not all of the college priests saw the world the same way.

"You are blessed or cursed, as the case may be," said Father Oliver, one day surprising him absorbed in *The Forsyte Saga*. "In some ways this is the most wonderful time of your life. There's adventure and action and a whole world in those books. Bless me, I don't know what a lad of your age can find in Galsworthy. Come along and I'll give you some stuff that will stir your powers."

He found Sherwood Anderson, Zane Grey and others. During long periods in Father Oliver's office, he was even allowed to browse in the priest's sub-rosa copies of *The Iconoclast*. William Cowper Brann, the murdered Texas editor, became a hero.

"Word power is what you need."

The priest's eyes were bright.

"Listen to Father Coughlin. That's how he got his eloquence. I was in seminary with him and he used to spout William Cowper Brann by the hour. Brann was only in his early forties when he was shot on the streets of Waco."

Priests were not all uniformly turned out in black soutanes to battle against sin. Father Oliver had been a steel puddler, so his hands were battered broad and his shoulders strained the black shoulders of the cassock. He had a disdain for what he called "mothered priests."

"They push them into vocations. They're wet behind the ears when they get here to seminary. Then the old priests stuff them full of holy writ and they almost pass out in confessional the first time a woman comes in with a juicy mortal sin."

Forty hours devotions and silence. Fasting and silence. Cold winter mornings and draughty classrooms, and the struggle to keep up a semblance of study when his mind was on the mesas of Arizona. Warmth and sunlight and romance in books. Then at night he would think of Olga. Her body was warm and soft and he woke up screaming several times when he felt himself being smothered.

It was Father Oliver who encouraged him to write.

"Get the demons out of your soul. Put them down on paper. Tear it up afterwards if you like, but get rid of them."

He wrote and wrote, and when the veil of fear was broken he even wrote about things he had tried to forget.

"Donovan, did you write this?"

The rector was an iceberg of a man behind a long table with a bare black oilcloth top. The back of his chair surmounted the grey-blond hair. His eyebrows were transparent. Shane felt he was a man without features.

"I—I don't know, sir—I mean, Father."

There was Brother Andrew in the background, his sour lips curled. He rocked on his big booted feet like an enormous toy.

"This—this *filth* is in your handwriting and Brother Andrew found it in one of your books."

He was lying. Shane knew it had been locked in his small chest. Now the mystery of the broken lock was solved.

"But that was locked up—"

"You admit it is yours."

There could be no argument. This was justice, justified. All in pursuit of purity.

"You will remain in the small anteroom of the chapel today and return to my office tomorrow morning when we have had time to consider your punishment."

One chair in a small room, bare of all furnishings except a *prie-dieu* and a shiny lithograph of the Crucifixion. Outside, there were the noises of playing students. The outside door had been locked but he found a small door that opened on the chapel. It was dim, with pale coloured light suffused by the stained-glass windows. By the light of the flickering sanctuary lamp he made out the figure of Brother Andrew kneeling on the altar steps.

Shane's rage made him want to cry. A timid silent novice brought him a bowl of watery bean soup, a piece of bread, and a glass of water. At first he couldn't eat, but finally it all changed. He was a prisoner in a tower. It was all for love of Olga. He might be confined for years on bread, soup, and water and have to smuggle messages out to her.

"Got yourself in a fix, haven't you?"

Father Oliver stood by the door. His pipe made the small room habitable.

"I—I guess so."

He lipped the pipe stem.

"I feel partially to blame—encouraging your writing, but I don't know how to explain it to the rector. He sets himself up as the real St. George, killing all the dragons of sin. Tell me, lad, if you can, what happened?"

Fitfully at first, staring out the window, Shane told him.

"Oh, Mother of God. She was your aunt."

He added hastily. "By marriage?"

Shane nodded.

"How old are you?"

"Almost seventeen."

The chair groaned as the priest stood up to go to the window beside the boy.

"Don't let this whole affair sour you. There *is* a God but he's hard to understand at times. The world is a suffering place and no one suffers like an innocent." He paused. "And no one can make you suffer like an innocent. I won't be able to make you understand that, but remember there was nothing evil about what you did."

There were sounds from the chapel of afternoon rosary.

"You won't be able to stay because people like the rector and that saintly snoop Andrew won't let you. You won't be able to go back to your uncle's either."

It was an ominous note that made Shane turn and stare at the priest.

"Reverend rector called your uncle. He read him a synopsis, I guess, and your uncle said he didn't want you back."

The priest's face was stoic but sad.

"Brother Andrew is a slow, but not unkind man. He snooped and told the rector. The rector—well—he's like a soldier. Fancies himself a St. Ignatius—duty and all that. He can dismiss it, but poor old Andrew is in there on his knees trying to persuade God he did the right thing."

In a half-whisper he added, "I know you want to write—but be careful. Careful you don't hurt others as well. Careful, too, that writing is a vocation and not simply an escape. Shane, I think you may make it—but it won't be easy. They say that a vocation is a cross to bear. It is, but I don't think it's as hard as carrying the burden of creative instinct. My boy, if that's not hell, it's at least a purgatory."

7

The Club! He hadn't expected it in New York. In Toronto, yes; in Montreal, perhaps even more so. He understood a coterie of Anglophiles trying to keep alive an imitation of what they thought an English club should be. But in New York, it seemed ridiculous!

There were framed photographs of elaborately solemn men, each pinioned by individual votive lights. Flickering tributes to departed gods. The sanctuary had few original ideas. The décor was a copy of the worst of English clubs, without the patina of age. Deep and somewhat scuffed maroon carpeting, the washroom to the left with the sombre mortician-like attendant at a desk on the right.

"Mr. Donovan, you may leave your overclothes in the

cloakroom. Mr. Smith is in Salon C at the head of the stairs
. . . left turning."

Shane had never been a joiner. Once he had made a deposit
for the Knights of Columbus, but after a communion breakfast and a speech by a reactionary chaplain he had given it up.
The Press Club he belonged to. Bitching spot it was, but
with none of the solemn defensiveness of this one.

Young men paid exorbitant entry fees at The Club because
they wanted to advance their careers. Middle-aged men
joined to be shielded from their families. Old men hung on
because it was their only link with the world they had
embraced for so long.

The washroom, tiled, and with a profusion of towels . . .
very comfortable! A place to eat well and reasonably when
you didn't need the nourishment or the low prices. Communications Club? J. L. Fathingham had pressured to get the
name changed from The Club when McLuhan went to Fordham University. The drawings of space satellites looked incongruous in the funeral parlor atmosphere.

This was New York. When he first worked in advertising
this city had seemed as inaccessible as the moon. Man had
conquered the moon and now he was an honoured guest of
the advertising profession.

"Shane, old boy . . . made it okay. I was beginning to
worry."

Now he was back in harness. Some kind of adrenalin
responded.

"Sure, Tommy. You said five."

It was 5:02 by his watch. There were several people in the
room and he saw by the empty glasses that they had been
there for some time.

"Tom S. Jansen of Purity Soaps. More competition than
anyone—"

Jansen was younger. Buttoned-down shirt, brown suit, and golden brown tie.

"It's Tom S.," he smiled. "Just vanity. You did some work in Canada for the detergents—fighting all that pollution propaganda."

They had studied the dossier. Shane was a boxer moving into position. The martini was very dry and he merely sipped it. Tommy explained.

"J.L. will try and drop in later. He's having a drink with Mauser of Federal."

Wilton, of the auto account, was trying him out.

"This is very hush-hush, or as hush-hush as Detroit can be. They're bringing out a new little car and we're getting the push. New name—new appeal. You're a very original man, Shane—what does the great American—sorry—North American public want in a motorcar?"

Wilton was a browned lean man with sun freckles. Not likely he would want help from anyone.

"Holland-Wills. Jason Holland-Wills—on Butterfly Paper Products."

"Damned good to see you, Shane. We must have lunch."

Heavy set, flushed face, slow moving but with eyes like snakes' tongues.

He was being watched. Clothes, shoes, haircut, manner were all check points.

"The public," Shane said slowly, "does it want anything it can articulate?"

"Damned well put," exclaimed Holland-Wills. "It's really what they can be *persuaded* to want. Man doesn't know what he wants until he gets it."

This was an opening.

"I am convinced the public may be growing tired of motorcars. When you come to think of it, travelling by car is really an awkward method of transportation in this day."

Wilton's dismissal of the statement was annoying.

"Balls! America is a nation of car lovers. Men treasure new cars more than even women. Cars are status and everything a man wants. Give him a car with real power—and he's the Lord God Jehovah of his own destiny."

Jansen disagreed. Shane liked him the best.

"You simply can't just say automobiles are here to stay. What was it McLuhan said—something about the dinosaurs never having it so good as just before they became extinct."

The name McLuhan ignited a controversy.

"Doesn't know what he's talking about. Oh, he may have had something on the ball at the beginning, but who pays any attention now?"

"Oh, Pete, you're just afraid he may be right. I think he has something. Cities really are hellish places to live now."

"Of course, McLuhan hasn't been yelling about pollution."

Pete Wilton took things seriously.

"Ahh, I'm sick of all these prophets of doom. It's our culture and that's what we are. Now they're trying to spend millions to take down roadside signs. What for?"

Tommy bristled.

"Aesthetics, old boy. What's the use of driving in a tunnel of signs from coast to coast?"

"Bullshit! The average slob enjoys driving a hell of a lot more when he can see some beer signs and pictures of broads spilling out of their bikinis."

Shane couldn't resist.

"Do *you?*"

Wilton looked at him coldly.

"I don't drive. I fly."

"What about Mauser of Federal Motors?"

"Bastard flies himself. Shane, why do you ask if I like signs on the highway?"

Shane thought there was a twitch in Tommy's eyelid, but he didn't care.

"Because we're talking about the public and I am part of it. I think we all make far too many assumptions about the public. I don't know about the U.S.A., but in Canada we live in Toronto and Montreal and think the rest of the country is like us."

"But surely," said Wilton flushing, "we are mostly products of the rest of the country. We come from other places. You, for instance?"

"Hell, most of us want to forget where we came from. Older men may reminisce about boyhood but middle-aged men want to forget. They like to think they're in the mainstream—they buy surveys that prove they're right. I come from a beat-up, dried-up place in Canada called Saskatchewan, and now it's got potash and oil wells—and even skyscrapers—and Americans—American companies with head offices in New York that say what the people in Saskatchewan will like or not like."

Wilton drained his glass slowly.

"Another country where we're not wanted. Well, never mind that now—but we're really the ones who tell the people what they want and—"

Jansen interrupted. Shane liked him better all the time.

"Qualification. We used to, but it's getting harder and harder all the time. Fads start and we commercialize them."

"Like what?"

"The youth thing. There was a time when youngsters would follow any trend. Now, they start them and we rush like hell to make them appear as ours. But hell, Pete, you and I have been hacking this for ages . . . I'm interested if you know McLuhan, Shane?"

Donovan was scarcely aware of being served a fresh martini.

"Yes, I do, and I must say I subscribe to a great deal of what he says. A new environment is changing us. Our children are changed beyond recognition. It's an electronic world of circuitry—and the world we know is one of wheels."

Holland-Wills chuckled.

"There go your motorcars, Wilton."

Pete went red.

"Nonsense. What would this economy do without automobiles? My God, when Detroit goes slack at the moment it puts the fear of death in even the stock market. McLuhan is one of those flash-in-the-pan guys who make up things the damn-fool newspapers and magazines pick up—and they make a hero out of him."

Shane was warm, but Tommy Smith replied: "Oh, for Christ's sake, Wilton, stop acting as if you were a bloody handmaiden of God. The world could get along without motorcars. Who knows, we may have those little flying thingumajiggies like Dick Tracy."

"A comic strip. That's where you belong, in a goddam comic strip."

The rivalry was potent. These men were not bantering. They played for real. This undertone carried over from the office. Shane decided to plunge in.

"One thing to remember about Marshall McLuhan is that he doesn't argue. He wants to explore with people. Arguing to him is a waste of time."

"Screw that nonsense." Wilton added harshly: "That's for guys with no opinions."

"Oh, Peter, I wouldn't go so far as to say that."

The voice was soft, but with overtones of a command to drop the controversy. It was J. L. Fathingham.

"Mr. Donovan, sorry I was busy today, but I'm glad to see the boys are initiating you into our friendly society."

Fathingham was of that indeterminate age that could be anywhere between fifty and seventy. He was of medium height, bald except for a fringe of grey hair, and with a skin baked to a deep brown by year-round exposure to sun or sunlamp. He dressed in a dark blue suit, polka-dot tie, and white shirt with buttoned down collar. He had heavy lidded eyes, and the slack folds on his neck showed that he had lost weight.

"I am most interested in Dr. McLuhan," he said, waving the waiter away. "Can't always understand him but it *is* a new world. Trouble is, we are not aware of it. What is it he says about a fish?"

"It's a cinch a fish didn't discover water."

"Right, Shane. I don't suppose we'll see the end of motorcars but something will replace them, don't you think so?"

"Well, you can't go on clogging up the roads and polluting the atmosphere and not expect the public to rebel at some point."

Wilton started to speak and then stopped.

"Peter, we have that meeting tomorrow at ten with Federal Motors. It might be a good idea to have Mr. Donovan sit in?"

Wilton was angry. He was afraid of Fathingham, but he was angry. He nodded. Holland-Wills delicately sipped his drink.

"Yes, J.L.," said Wilton finally, "I guess we need help, wherever we can get it."

Two can play that game, thought Donovan.

"It's very kind of you, Mr. Fathingham. I'm sure I won't be able to contribute anything, but perhaps I can learn how your big guns really work in a campaign."

Fathingham had a faint smile. Jansen spoiled the moment.

"I'm very keen on this. I'm going to take a course at Fordham this fall with Father Culkin. He's a friend of McLuhan's."

There was a dry note in Fathingham's voice as he stood up.

"Commendable, Jansen. Sorry, Shane, I can't spend time now as I have a dinner engagement tonight. But we'll see you tomorrow—and remember, we are all at your service."

Wilton beckoned the waiter as soon as Fathingham left.

"By God, all we need now is for Federal to get the wind up about McLuhan. They're running scared at the moment with imports. Now I suppose we'll have to sell cars without wheels —or won't your great prophet argue about that?"

When Shane spoke he had a momentary desire to stop and recall the words but he had gone too far.

"One of the problems of having so much of North American life being directed from New York is the unreality of New York. Your Charlie Wilson said what's good for G.M. is good for America. You say what's good for you is good for everybody—but look what happened to Wilson."

It was dangerous but he went on.

"Industries have come to rely too much on public relations and advertising men. They in turn tell them what they think they want to hear."

The room was deathly still.

"You are saying, in effect," said Wilton, his voice barbed, "we don't know what the hell we're talking about? That's a great thing for a hot shot advertising man who's invading New York to say—or is that a tactic—a technique like McLuhan to get recognition at any cost?"

They were hungry for each other's throats, but he was a new, unknown threat. He had to be put in his place. The group were waiting for an answer. This was the moment.

"Interpret it any way you want. The curse of modern business is what they accuse government of all the time. Big business and big corporations become enclosed, locked away in their own processes and systems. They're so busy with their internal wars and vested interests and bureaucracies that they forget their purpose."

"You're a goddam Communist!"

Wilton said it. Tommy Smith intervened.

"Come on, Pete, that's no way to talk to a guest."

"What the hell do you know about it? You're nothing but a glorified greeter—a glad hander. When the hell did you ever sweat yourself over anything except some dumb model?"

Jansen stared in horror. Holland-Wills seemed to be enjoying the scene. Shane wished he hadn't drunk so much. Smith looked silently at Wilton for a long time as if in scorn, then turned away. Shane found himself saying, "The last refuge of the ugly American is to call everyone who doesn't agree with him a Communist."

Wilton stood up. He walked a trifle unsteadily to the door without saying a word. When the door slammed, Holland-Wills lifted his glass and gestured to the steward.

"I think we all need a double."

Smith smiled thinly.

"Don't take it too badly, Shane, old boy. Pete is in what we euphemistically call a decline. Fathingham is on the spot. Peter hasn't come up with any winning ideas and he probably thinks you're here to take his place."

"I didn't mean to get on his back."

"His back! He hasn't room for you. He has a twenty-seven-year-old wife with a roving eye—up in Westchester with two small children—a cook and a nurse—two children by his first wife at college—alimony payments—a mortgage up to his ass—and well, can I say more? The All-American Boy of today —and he'll go home and she'll have the house half-full of the elite lushes of the neighborhood who'll raise hell until morning—and Peter must come back tomorrow with bright ideas —savvy?"

"I didn't mean to make bad friends."

"I wouldn't worry about it too much. You just happened to put your finger on a vulnerable spot. McLuhan."

Holland-Wills nodded.

"You see, Shane, J.L. is keen on McLuhan. I don't really think he understands what the hell it's all about—and I'll deny that if you repeat it."

There was a ripple of amusement.

"It's progressive. I've read McLuhan and I think he's got something when he says the kids are different and largely because of TV."

"Tell us what Marshall McLuhan is really like, Shane."

Donovan was at ease here. He did know McLuhan. Part of his discomfort at Jackman and Bates was the way they downgraded McLuhanism.

"He's a quiet and unpretentious guy who says we are living in a new electronic environment—an age of circuitry in place of wheels. He *prefers* the old-fashioned world—he's a university teacher at heart and not a revolutionary."

Shane went on: "A lot of people talk about McLuhan but few know what he's saying. For instance, he agrees with Harold Innis that writing or prints are tools that require training and that preserve traditional values. Broadcasting is instant and it doesn't require training for perception. If you accept that the use of a medium over a period of time determines the character of the knowledge to be communicated —*voilà!*—instant interpretation of the medium is the message."

Smith applauded.

"By God, he must have something. When did any of you

guys come up with—global village—medium is the message and so on?"

"Why exclude yourself?"

"I've just been told off. I'm only a glad-hand greeter and connoisseur of dumb models."

Shane laughed.

"I wouldn't say dumb."

The edge was off the tension but Shane had somehow lost the sequence and there were farewells with people leaving and new people being welcomed. There was adrenalin in having an audience. He felt a coasting sensation when they began asking questions about Expo.

Shane was at home here. Expo happened because a man, a Montreal city engineer, Claude Robillard, once spent an afternoon with Antoine de Saint-Exupéry who wrote *Terre des Hommes*. "Man is more important than his machines," was his credo and it was used as the basic theme in Expo '67.

They were interested. Someone ordered scotch in place of martinis. There was food but he didn't bother to eat. The crowd kept changing—Gratz, a film producer, was interested in getting McLuhan for an educational TV series. He was making notes in a flying warm world and arranging a meeting of some kind with Marshall.

Gratz was talking a lot.

"Jesus, I'd like to make some TV with somebody like you and McLuhan. In your country you started out with a broadcasting system that was supposed to be free . . . subsidized and devoted to national understanding and communications. We hear great things here about your documentaries—people like Leiterman and Fox."

Donovan grimaced.

"Both working in the U.S., although they do come back."

"What's wrong?"

"That old camel of commercialism got its head in the tent and took over the tent."

He was off and running on one of his pet subjects. The bottled-up venom he felt for only the ideas of the lowest common denominator surviving in broadcasting tugged him into extravagances.

Somehow they were no longer at The Club. It was one thing to talk to a man like Gratz; he could understand. But talking to the advertising men was useless. He must call Bonnie—or call Tina. Tina Bonnie. Bonnie Tina! O'Hare could use it for a stage name.

They were in a bar and Tommy was talking in a way that seemed out of character.

"There's an awful lot of fakery in this business but there's an awful lot around us. Did we create it, or did it create us?"

Shane looked around at the simulated Hawaiian setting. Bulgy breasted waitresses in grass skirts—plastic pasties. Simulated palm trees. A man with the face of a pugilist and the voice of Brooklyn presiding at the bar, wearing a lei—plastic.

"So it's a myth, Tommy, advertising and all. But surely the public accepts it as such."

"Maybe, but Fathingham doesn't. Get down to real scratching with him and you'll find out he's a true believer in the Great American Dream. Rock-hard Republican—dog eat dog —our bad days started with Roosevelt, and Eisenhower wasn't so bad."

"Of course, Tommy, we idolize Roosevelt—those of us who can remember. Kennedy as well—especially the youngsters."

"Our problem here is we don't know what the youngsters want. J.L. is running scared. This town is full of young ad men running hole-in-the-wall agencies skimming the cream off accounts. His first reaction was to try and buy them off." Tommy exploded. "My God, you should have seen the boss when he came back from one meeting. An outfit called Hickory-Dickory-Dick. Offered them a million dollars and they told him to blow. Offered him a stick of grass and told him he could get just as good ideas if he wanted to blow his mind."

Shane felt that Tommy was telling him all this for a special reason. Yet he felt moved to his own confidence—

"Kids—my son—twenty-one—oh, he's polite and all, but I have a feeling he thinks I'm some kind of high-priced whore."

They were being alcoholically confidential, and Tommy responded:

"My sister's boy, Spencer, is twenty-four—not married but with child and girl, living in the village. Bloody flat with weird furniture—or no furniture—pillows and foam-rubber seats. He makes some kind of living from hand prints—Tina says they're the only real people we know."

"Trouble is we judge them by our standards."

"Right, and it's nonsense. But we have this—plastic world. And . . ."

His voice trailed off, as he leaned over the table.

"So much for dreaming. Shane, J.L. is really interested in you. Confides in me. Well, I'm not out to shiv anyone—and I vote Mama's stock."

Shane grinned.

"A very sensible position of strength."

"When you started that campaign for Sno-Buc, the buccaneer's snowmobile, Fathingham was quite impressed."

Donovan winced.

"That hurt. I had been boozing like a bastard and knew I had to make amends for a week AWOL and knew—well, it was born out of desperation."

The conversation was racing in and out of logical and illogical ideas.

"You hate this business?"

"Tommy, maybe I hate it like you do."

"Oh, not quite. Pete Wilton is not so far off. I'm really a useless kind of twit. Know the right things according to bloody rules—might have made a good foreign service type but mother is married to Newport and Palm Beach and that dying crowd."

Shane had to tell it, or at least part of it.

"It's hard to get over that bloody prairie and no money and your parents drying up like the tumbleweed and maybe rolling off. This awful wanting enough behind you, so you won't end up that way and then being too gutless to try to break free and do what you want to do."

There was more. The dragging routine on the newspaper and the nights of writing. Going to work sandy-eyed. The spurt on the agency and the travelling, and always good food and drink and success. Less writing.

"There didn't seem to be any reason for anything else. Stopped writing, and then woke up one day with a kind of hole in my heart. A book gets published by a friend. So you go out and get blistered."

He was riding high now, forgetting Tommy.

"I went back home once. My father died. Same dreary place."

There were four of them. Mona, Bill, and Rita had never been in Nonsuch before. They had often laughed about the name. A line of false-front stores and scattered houses running from the railroad tracks and the grain elevators to a slough, now amazingly green, but always dry in his memory.

Tom Anstett was the undertaker. The hearse was an old polished Cadillac.

"Bought her second hand in Regina," Tom said while they waited for the casket to be brought out of the church.

"It's a nice one, Tom."

"Took her out on the road the other day, the new highway to Regina, and she really can go."

It was incongruous. Tom Senior, in a badly fitting black suit waiting for his son, Tom Junior, to usher the pallbearers out with the casket, talking about the speed he could get out of a secondhand Cadillac hearse. But it was real as the stories of him running booze across the Montana border in his Model T hearse, and of how with prosperity from whisky rather than from death, he had progressed to a Pierce-Arrow. His son was taking over and death was now more lucrative than whisky on the prairies.

It was impossible but real, as real as the thin-faced woman with the habit of holding her hand to cover up the side of her mouth where the teeth were missing. His mother.

Mona, Bill, and Rita were curious, but not part of the scene. He belonged, but the thin men and women who sat expressionless in the church were no longer a part of him. There were no tears and his brother, still wearing his brakeman's uniform, didn't cry. Between them in the back seat of Tom's Buick, his mother was a bright-eyed dusty bird with straggles of grey hair under the rim of her black felt hat; he seemed to remember her once buying that hat from the mail-order catalogue. She wore a coat, but even in the heat she shivered.

The procession came down the one-sided main street, past the gas pumps, the China Café, now called the Lotus, and as they turned by the elevator to go down the powdered gumbo road he saw two men get up from the hole they were digging by the side of the street and remove their hats.

"They stood there in the heat and the dust, bareheaded, and Tommy, I cried. I knew then that no matter what I had thought of my father or what I felt, he was one up on me.

127

There wouldn't be a goddamned soul take off his hat when *my* funeral passed by."

Tommy put his hand on his arm.

"Steady, old boy. You're not alone. We learn too late. I thought my father was a dreary old bastard with no spunk. I found out he had gone broke, paid off every debt, and made a second fortune, so that when he died he had the respect of every man on Wall Street. I thought because he allowed my mother to play her silly role in all the society doings and put up with my capers at college he was a softy."

Shane scarcely heard him.

"I cried, Tommy. I cried as if I had been waiting all my life for that moment. I couldn't stop. Out on the damned prairie, scrabbly little graveyard on the side of a hill and all those people, including my mother, standing there all dried up—no tears—and I cried and cried, and couldn't stop."

Tommy was silent.

"I felt like a bloody hypocrite."

He had a faint sense of embarrassing Smith.

"When we got back to Winnipeg, I made an excuse to send the others on home. Started drinking in the Fort Garry. It was a bout that lasted—well, the usual thing. Met a girl from a newspaper—in the Press Club, I think—and I'll be goddamned if I didn't go back to Nonsuch. She drove me out there."

Tommy didn't seem surprised.

It was a scene that still filled Shane with a form of horror. Drinking in Peter Hodiak's. Trying to get a room in the Maple Leaf Motel and his brother, his face a mask, but his eyes blazing with hatred.

"Get out, Shane. Get that woman out of here. What are you trying to do? Kill Mother? I don't care for myself, but what you are doing is criminal to Ma. Just get out of town—before I kill you—and don't ever come back."

Tommy had theories.

"There was—maybe still is—something about that place you want to kill. Amazing. Love—hate maybe. Take me. My father hated Englishmen. I don't know why—but I couldn't help but drift towards things English—clothes, and my God, when I bought an English sports car, when they were scarce here—he had a fit. I didn't hate my father, but somehow when we were together, I couldn't help speaking with an English accent. Bloody silly on my part."

Shane scarcely heard him.

"Couldn't forget—can't forget—and when it all comes back, I take it out on my wife. She used to suggest we go West for holidays—but it just makes me bloody mad. Course, I couldn't tell her, but in a place like that they never forget. I can't go back. Yet I—"

They were at a point of confidence and couldn't go on. When he came back from the toilet, Tommy was gone.

Mona! This would be a time to have dinner with Mona. A good dinner with splendid service and wine and then go to the theatre. Once in New York he had tried—but he had spoiled it. Arguments with waiters. Lost theatre tickets. Falling asleep in a theatre.

Why couldn't it work? Now he was feeling good. Time for a good dinner—a show. He was smiling and people stared at him. Why shouldn't he be smiling? They said Wilton was in trouble. Gratz was a guy he must see. Tommy—Tommy had problems, too—but with his money why did he stay and take that crap at the agency?

The pattern was familiar to him. He was going through a let-down after the confrontation with Wilton because he was never quite certain. His success frightened him. The truth was that in an industry where anything beyond mediocrity is often considered a minor miracle, he was quite good. Sometimes, he knew, it was the alcohol that saved him.

How long would it last? Would he join the has-beens in the Press Club, looking for small campaigns, or for a chance to write election speeches. Old timers begging to write a little advertising to keep "their hands in the game." The hands were invariably shaky. If you gave them work they convulsed into drinking or brought in senseless copy.

Shane knew that there is a new sense to New York at night. The air is dirty by day, but it becomes sensual by night, especially to a man alone. His imagination feeds subconsciously on the myths of show girls and luxurious apartments and sin —and he feels he is the only one not participating.

"Quite a place, New York."

The bartender flicked an eye over him.

"Yeah. Guess so."

It was neither rude nor friendly. He moved off . . . 9:30.

In the hotel, Shane went through an exaggerated ritual of mixing a drink. Finally, he began calling numbers.

"Is this 361-2824?"

The answer was cautious.

"Is Miss Fletcher there?"

"You mean Goldie?"

"Yes."

"Oh, she's away. Married, you know."

"Who's this?"

The cackled laughter at hearing the same request hundreds of times.

"Mrs. Goldwosser. I'm the landlady. Is there something I can do for you?"

Obscene, almost. After several tries he gave up. Sipping a

130

drink, fiddling with the TV set, finding Jim Ameche on the radio and finally settling for Muzak. The edge of self-pity.

The bloody, awful uselessness of it. From prairie to Park Avenue, but no fun in it. How to cope? Coping was the word. Go down to the bar and start talking to strangers. That was the way of lonely Americans.

"Stranger here? Oh, Canada? I go up there fishing."

That was always the way of it. They knew Canada for cold air or fishing, or they grew belligerent because Canada traded with Castro.

8

For Shane, mornings were often something to be worried through—and by noon with perseverance and the pressure of work, he could recover, and by five—well that was something else again! And coming awake fully clothed on the chaise longue with all the lights on was—well, you had to cope. Shane tried to hang on to his sleepiness, undress and slip into bed. He was thirsty. Pile clothes, sip the vodka and orange juice. Ease back to sleep—and then the mood slipped and he came wide awake!

His muscles contracted with something like a Charley horse in the calves of both legs. He was tense, spasmic—terrified in an atmosphere of whispering voices. They were sleety impressions like the garbled sounds of other connections when you were talking on the telephone.

Shane had persisted to Dr. Leddy that he was not given to hearing sounds and sights. Sober, he could convince himself they were a fancy. When they came he fought to distract his mind from them. Close eyes—hum. Try and remember other places. Green fields and trout streams—words—songs—half-forgotten advertising ideas—the toiletry line for older men—musk and saddle leather . . .

There was only the half light of New York night coming in the window, but when he lay with his eyes open the patterned traceries shifted around the room. Small objects, like the tiny flowers in the wallpaper, grew larger. The anonymous painting of an English garden had a three dimensional effect. When he closed his eyes the voices increased to the volume of muffled whispering in the coffin room at a wake.

Shane got up and went to the window. Lighting a cigarette and smoking helped. More and more often at times like this he deliberately thought of Nonsuch.

Shane's sober version was of a hard-working section man raising a family in a town called Nonsuch on the prairie. "Used to be a stove polish called Nonsuch," he would laugh, "but there was no polish about our place. Just a little pimple on the flat prairie. Railroad town where the transcontinental trains went scudding through and the mail was tossed off in a bag on a hook on a pole. An occasional freight stopped. There was grain when we didn't have a drought, which was most years."

But he added touches. It had overtones of *Wolf Willow* by Wallace Stegner. The buds in the sloughs in the spring. Flowers that made the slopes look like carpets. Characters in the town around the beer parlor.

"Wonderful place to grow up. Something real about those people."

In the mind-itchy time when the morning clock ran slow, Nonsuch came in different shades. He was in the upper room of the house that hugged the track. The heat was a smothering blanket and his brothers' snores rasped like knives on stiff cloth.

He had some good memories of Father O'Malley. When an evening breeze stirred and he sat beside him on the rectory steps, a gentle Irish voice talked of the old country:

"It was a hard life, Shane. Very hard. Seven of us in the family and my Aunt Kathleen in Boston writing to say how she would put one of us through the school. Tim already in the drink at seventeen and my mother rattling her beads night and morning to save his soul. Pat who wanted a bit of land of his own and had little hope of ever getting it. Bridget panting to be married, and my younger brothers not even with a mind to anything. So they picked me. Not even the brightest."

The Christian Brothers ran their school with iron wills, a touch of the boot and the odd clout. This was discipline and learning. At the evening meal the disciplinarian read the prayer of the day and then dispensed some carefully selected news of the world.

There were stone walls, small rooms, and silent walks in the gardens and on the green slopes down to the sleeve of a bay, but never into Donnymore. That was a world of temptation. Family visits grew more formal each year, until even when Moira was with child and the father skipped to England it all seemed to be happening to strangers.

"I came to the priesthood knowing little of the world. Purity, yes. Knowledge, no. At St. Martin's in Montreal, it was a poor time for me. Confessions were dreadful. They tried me in the Chancellor's office, and sure I could work up no lather over the financial affairs of the bishop, and spent me time reading the books I should have been reading as a boy. I don't know what would have happened if the Bishop of Regina hadn't been so hard up for pastors. Innocence, Shane, is a beautiful tragedy in a world like this."

The talks produced a chance to read, for Father O'Malley had one extravagance, books.

"Books are manna for man's soul. Read what you can—whenever you can."

Synge, Yeats, Chesterton, Belloc, Galsworthy. He read eagerly, even books he didn't understand. But it was all so different when he faced Bernard O'Malley in the confessional.

"Father, I've been bad."

It was stifling hot in the cubicle of a confessional.

"Yes. What kind of bad?"

Stammering, confused, not understanding and yet being in awe of what it all seemed to be.

"At night—in bed—I—I—"

"You abused yourself?"

"Yes."

"How many times?"

"Oh—oh—five."

"Is that all?"

A wall of deadening guilt.

"I wrestled with a girl."

"You did—and how?"

"In the old shed, I—I—"

Prompting now, "Yes—yes?"

"This girl took off—I mean we both took off our clothes and wrestled."

"Is that all you did?"

"Something happened to me."

A silence. The cloistered priest and the innocent boy impaled together.

"Who was it?"

"Sally."

"Hmm."

Again silence.

"You know you shouldn't do that. Did you—I mean—"
Coughing and stammering. "Were you close to each other?"

How could he tell him that the act of ejaculation had terrified them both. Sally, in anger, rushing to put on her dress
and run home; Shane wandering into the slough to wait until
his cheeks cooled.

In his heart there were the deep incisions of Catholic childhood. The rhythm of life from the rote of catechism, to the
Saturday confessional and Sunday Mass, and the fact that
you didn't have to attend school on a holy day. The half-
understood responses and punctuation by prayer of everything from meals to bedtime.

Good and evil. Man is mortal and life is a way station between birth and the portals of either hell or heaven, although
some mysterious deposit of grace might allow you to stop
over in purgatory on your way to Paradise. And all those un-
baptized babies languishing in the steam. Shane thought Hell
was fire and Heaven was a cool evening after a scorching day,
and purgatory steamed. But Father O'Malley was moved
and Father Cassidy only read his breviary. Shane could never
talk to him.

Shane sat up and placed his head against the headboard.
Flip on the TV from the bedside control. My God, there
were movies on four channels at least. Charlie Chan in a foggy
San Francisco. Click. Click. Unctuous announcer for a loan
company. Click. Fred Astaire—must be—dancing. Click. War-
ren William. Must be.

"Sir, I don't have to endure this."

Click.

No escape. Turn on TV and get a line as familiar as that one.

"Mr. Jackman, I don't have to put up with this."

Shane popped that when Coronation Tires cancelled and Jackman was sore because Shane had ruffled the Coronation Tire president at a cocktail party.

T.A.'s Jamaica-walnutty face was impassive.

"You have an alternative."

Ominous hum of air-conditioner, creak of Jackman's chair. Tension pulling—pulling—then, lamely—

"Well, I suppose I have—"

Jackman buzzed his secretary. Donovan felt as if he were drowning in a vacuum.

"Call Fishstein at Coronation and tell him I would like to meet him for lunch at the Queen's Club."

Nothing more was said. Shane felt the knife edge. It hadn't suited Jackman to let him go. He would fix it up by taking Fishstein to the Gentile Club for lunch. Shane knew what had happened, but that wasn't the way he told it at home.

"God, Mona, I let Jackman have it."

Remembering, he wasn't sure she believed him.

"Shane, you shouldn't."

It prolonged martini time before dinner.

"Fishstein wanted that silly slogan for his tires—The Crowning Touch—and when it didn't work he blamed me. Well, I wasn't going to take it."

The reaction from Mona was pessimistically fussy.

"Surely you could explain to Mr. Jackman?"

"T.A. was in one of his tough moods."

She was fussing about the hem lengths of the curtains, and he poured more gin in the cocktail shaker.

"Sometimes I think you expect things to be too easy. After

138

all, you must accept some trouble. Shane, you are paid very well, but when things go wrong—"

"Christ, Mona, you assume I'm wrong."

"Please don't swear. I just know you have a good job—and this home."

"And as long as we have a home near Bayview Avenue and two cars and a place in Muskoka, it doesn't matter if I drag myself to death."

The pyramid of argument. She went to put the dinner on the table to placate the children, who had been sullenly half-listening in the library. He went in a rage to the Press Club without dinner when she asked, "Did you ever think that if you went to confession and communion some time, things might be better for you?"

But in a room that betrayed him with whispering and slithering light patterns, Shane knew he had been afraid. He had to carefully nourish the feeling of being essential—but it was work he could never fully believe in—and he even worried at times about the ethics, but that he had to put away and forget.

He was sober. It was a firm conclusion, and he went to the bathroom, stared out the window and made a drink which he swallowed quickly, going directly to bed.

"A depth charge."

Now he felt better. Just a call. A life line was what he needed in this loneliness. Whoops! My God, a wrong number —a recorded voice—dialled his Toronto number—now call Bonnie.

"Bonnie."

Her voice whispered out of sleep.

"Who is this?"

"Forgotten me?"

"Mr.—sorry—oh, my God, Shane." Worried voice. "Are you all right?"

"You care?"

Nonplussed answer.

"You're a human being, aren't you?"

"Not at the moment."

"My God, it's after four o'clock."

His moments of clarity were passing.

"Sorry—sorry, just—just—I forgot."

"Can I help you?"

"Hunh!"

Groping now, he said, mustering each word so that it stood out by itself. "I—said—Mr. Jackman—I do—not—have—to—stand—for—this."

He woke to a series of what seemed deafening bells in his ears. He was in a great room of enormous brass jars and as he passed each one on his way they rang, exploding in his ears. But they stopped suddenly because there was someone in the room.

"Mr. Donovan, are you all right?"

He was lying foetus fashion on the bed with the telephone receiver in his hand.

"I—I—"

They were utterly and completely strange surroundings.

"I'm—I'm—"

The man in the dark blue uniform took the receiver from his hand.

"Are you the police?"

"No, Mr. Donovan. I'm night security. Your telephone was off the hook."

He was cold. The attendant suggested gently, "You might like to move to the other bed. You seem to have spilled something on this one."

Shame that edged into belligerence. "Too many cocktails, I guess. Must have spilled my drink."

The man tactfully withdrew. This was the Executive Suite of the President Hotel and he was a special guest of Waite, Irwin, and Tasker. Answer the telephone.

"Shane, are you sick?"

It was Bonnie. Solicitous.

"I'm okay. Thanks for worrying about me."

"I didn't know what to do. You were talking and all of a sudden it went, not dead, but I could hear you breathing and I thought maybe something had happened to you."

"No, just too much booze, I guess."

"Did you have a fight with someone?"

"That was an old fight. I still have the scars." He was fumbling for cigarettes. "I mustn't keep you awake."

She seemed very close to him when she laughed. He pictured the soft fleshy patch on the back of her neck, the smell of her perfume—

"Shane, I won't go back to sleep. You were on the line so I had to go down and use the phone in the lobby."

"Oh God, I'm sorry. Talk to me."

"What do you want me to talk about?"

"Oh, anything. Just help to keep the demons away."

Apprehension now.

"Shane, are you spooked? From drinking, I mean."

"Oh, no. Just insomnia."

"My father ended his days with all kinds of things haunting him. D.T.'s something awful. We didn't know really what it was. Ma thought he was faking, and that didn't make it any easier."

"Too morbid. Tell me about your work."

He must keep her talking.

"But Shane, you must be kidding. Don't you remember?"

141

"What?"

She laughed in a self-conscious way.

"I'm working for Peter—your friend O'Hare."

"Peter?"

"Yes, Peter. Today in the room when you said you were okay. You'd been sick and then you took a shower and drank black coffee and—Shane. You *do* remember?"

His answer wasn't convincing.

"Shane, you went to the agency. There was a meeting with Fathingham."

"Oh—" Thudding pain in his belly. Stabbing pain in his head. "I did?"

She was alarmed.

"My God, we let you off at the door. You seemed to be perfectly okay. Shane—"

He was cautious again.

"Oh, Bonnie, it was a session I want to forget. Tough, really. Really tough."

He had to get off the line. Probes like paining fingers raked his mind as he tried to remember what had happened. He tried to talk, but the words would not come. She tried, too, but it wasn't working.

"Bonnie, try and get some sleep. Give my best to O'Hare —he's a smart guy to have you working for him."

"Are you sure you're all right, Shane?"

"Yes, dear, I am, but we both need sleep. Sorry—"

"Don't be sorry, my dear. I just wish there was something I could do for you."

Lost hours are a terrifying phenomenon. At first they can be excused as an accident. Easy to pass over. Then they assume the proportions of lost life. Somewhere, sometime Shane had walked, talked, drank, and even worked—and he had no recollection of it whatsoever.

O'Hare and Bonnie. He had a twinge of resentment. He had to do something. Get moving.

Tina answered the telephone almost as if she had been waiting for the call.

"I'm an insomniac, Shane. I hate the goddam nights. Sure you can feel your way over? I'll leave the door unlatched. The doorman will let you in. Of course I want to talk."

The cabby was complaining, "Used to be ya could sleep inna daytime. Now, it's too goddam noisy and my old lady plays the TV all the goddam day."

The doorman was sleepily unconcerned. Tina's apartment was eerily like a moon habitat with only a night light distorting the shadows of the modernistic furniture. He found her in the big circular bed, covers to her chin, but a bare leg showing. There was no need for conversation.

It was furious demanding exercise, draining him of all energy and leaving him on the uneasy edge of being sick. It seemed to have sparked a whole new strength in Tina. She sat up against the bulwark of pillows smoking. Her breasts were full, with large dark nipples.

"See, I would make a wonderful mother."

Shane wanted a drink. She brought it to him, quite unconscious of her nakedness. Snuggling back into bed she leaned to kiss him.

"What a man! What a man, Shane! My God, you can tear an agency apart in a day. Ruin a man, and then this. What can't you do?"

He discovered the story by degrees. Eased it from her by asking to hear the version she had heard. Obviously, it was Tommy who had told her.

"The way I heard it, you appeared late for the meeting. Very formal. Uptight. Wilton was laying for you, and you knew it. They were all edgy. Except dear Tommy. He said you were different than he had ever seen you before. Thought you were drunk at first, but that obviously wasn't the way."

"Peter Wilton?"

He had no exultation. He had no blood lust. Wilton? What the hell did he do to him? He must have been in trouble anyhow.

Tina was excited.

"The more Peter argued the more Fathingham took up the idea. Then, when Wilton stood up and said he was quitting because he wasn't going to be pushed around by any bush league ad man from Canada—that it was a country of bush farm people—you just said so simply: 'It's a mistake Americans a lot smarter than you make every day.'"

His stomach ached.

She was crawling over him. Her hands and mouth were clutching, teasing and trying to excite him. She whispered the words in his ear that brought on the nausea.

"God, you finally got that pig Wilton. You paid him back for what he did to me."

"What did he do?"

"Bastard reneged on me. Came here every turn around and then gave the Eland TV spots—you know, the jungle lady in the TV spots—to a bitch he picked up in Detroit. You don't have to work, honey. I'll do all the work. God, you give me shivers just touching you."

Tina was relentless, caressing and kissing him, refusing to allow him to relax until she had coaxed his response. Daylight was showing in the windows by the time she dropped off to sleep like some nocturnal creature who automatically turns off in the daytime. Shane dressed and sat in the tiny kitchen nursing vodka and orange juice until he had strength to leave.

When he was leaving he looked in the second bedroom door. Tommy Smith was asleep.

The air in the cab was foul, so he dropped it blocks away from the President and walked. There were men clearing the tables in the sunken plaza at Rockefeller Center. Traffic was a dull roar. There were thousands in a massive office-bound dance. Despite the chill in the air, the girls wore dresses so short they showed the curve where their hips met their legs.

He kept thinking about small things. How many million briefcases containing what? Lunches? Maybe contraceptives? What did they all do at noon hour? All those girls and those men coupling somewhere at noon and then going home to waiting wives and husbands.

It was all sex. Everything was for sex. Movies were all sex. The plays were all sex. The store windows were all full of sex, and the bouncy-breasted girl who bumped into him as he crossed Fifth Avenue was really only wondering how good he would be in bed.

He was in St. Patrick's Cathedral. Why did he come back here? Once a Catholic always a Catholic. Escape? Church was no escape. He went because it appeased Mona. He sat, stood, and kneeled beside her but he might as well be on another planet. It seemed to work except when she became concerned.

"Shane, I hate to mention this—but don't you think it would help with—well, all kinds of things if you made an effort to go to—well, communion?"

He screamed. "What the hell more do you want? I go with you, don't I? The kids go with you, don't they?"

They were all participating in a ritual. Bill, at one time argumentative about all religion. Now silent. By the way he sat in the pew he was obviously a million miles away.

Rita, ecstatic about the convent. Wanting to be a nun. Not

being able to explain it, and suddenly pained by the new freedom of the orders.

"Oh, it's awful. They're making convents just as awful as
living outside."

It was dark and peaceful here. A centre aisle crowd of men
moving up. Two dark-suited men serving as acolytes. English
words.

"I confess to Almighty God—"

"Confiteor Deo—"

Old Father O'Malley. Waking in the morning to the raps
on the thin partition. Lingering for precious moments,
guarded by the animal warmth of a brother on each side.
Raps again. Dashing out of bed and clutching the cold-
stiffened clothes, and trying to dress beside the kitchen stove
that smelled of the coal oil his father used to light it. Then
going out to milk the cow.

Right and wrong. Black and white.

Truth and untruth. Purity and impurity.

Geometrical patterns. You did wrong and you paid. God
was everywhere and he knew everything and self-abuse
brought tingling pleasure but was evil. There was God watching and you had to tell Father O'Malley even if it was God
you offended.

God?

Did those men kneeling in their neat rows of seats, attaché
cases neatly stacked, did they believe? Were these the modern counterparts of the conquistadores, attending Mass and
receiving the blessing before participating in the daily blood
bath?

Yet, there was something. The habit of years came back
every time he sat like this in a church without the discipline
of pleasing Mona. He remembered the emotional satisfaction
of serving Mass, the awe-filled moment of Consecration, the

deep-stirring emotions during Benediction, the faces of communicants at midnight Mass, the haunting dignity of the moment when the priest blessed a casket . . . and the blend of every good and joyous feeling in the world at the moment of First Communion.

Crossing Fifth Avenue he had the uneasy sensation of the pavement moving—shifting—and at times he missed his footing. His room was a refuge. The suite was cleaned. Fresh air. Tomato juice. Orange juice. Coffee and croissants.

He was hungry.

Shane had always sensed inside himself from the time he began working on the *Herald*, that he had an urge for expression. The moods of loneliness and the flights of imagination, and the times when it all coalesced into a pattern at his typewriter were real. It was difficult to explain, and he had searched in the lives of famous artists and writers, and there were no satisfying answers. They had all made up their minds and found a way and he had compromised—but why wouldn't it go away? What kind of goddam foolishness was there that tortured him into thinking he had something to say?

Nonsuch! His parents! What was there to write about? But Stegner had taken the town dump in Whitemud and made it—hell, what would Stegner do with Matt Donovan!

Take the hard-shelled old man and his white, overripe young wife—the form—a real drama to be made, but it conflicted with the gut-stirring drama of what really had happened.

"Mr. Donovan, I am Dr. Grahame in Handrich. You are Shane Donovan, Matt's nephew?"

"Y—yes, Doctor?"

He hadn't seen or heard of his uncle in years.

"Is there anything wrong, Doctor?"

The doctor had a messenger quality voice.

"Matthew is in poor shape. He is an advanced arthritic and his heart is—is not too good."

"I'm sorry, Doctor. Is there anything I can do?"

"Yes. He wants to see you."

"Me? He wants to see me?"

"Yes, and I advise it be soon."

"Oh, yes—well, we were never exactly close. What about Olga—Aunt Olga?"

The doctor paused.

"Your aunt has been gone for some time."

"You mean—dead?"

"No, she went away. Can you come?"

"Yes, Doctor. I'll drive up today."

He didn't take Mona or the kids. He wanted time to think on the drive. Not quite fall, but there was color on bushes and occasional maples and beeches. It was summer but it smelled of fall in the chilly morning, with smoke rising from the houses tucked in the valley pockets between the rolling hills of Ontario.

He sat for almost half an hour in the car before going in the hospital. He had driven past Matt's house—shabby and deserted looking—the neat orchard degenerated into an assortment of distorted and contorted trees. Olga's garden was a mass of weeds.

"Mr. Donovan, here's your nephew."

He was an old bent man sitting in a chair by the window. If his eyes had been removed, the head could have been a skull.

"Uncle Matt."

His uncle uttered a raspy monosyllabic sound. Shane sat down.

"How are you, Uncle Matt?"

The hands lifted, two crippled instruments, and dropped to his knees. All around there was an odor which Shane identified with death. The old man stared out the window. The noise of heels click-clacked in the hallway.

"Is there anything I can do, Uncle Matt?"

The silence of the room came in. It was silence until he became aware of the sweet hot ticking sound of the insects, and the lash-lashing of a sprinkler on the lawn, and the hospital murmurs. There were bits and pieces of music, talk, tears, doors slamming, and muffled footsteps.

This crumpled man with the purple mark on the temple and the black patches under the eye sockets and the squared frame holding his clothes like a rack was his Uncle Matthew. He couldn't speak, or he didn't want to.

The sick man's eyes came back and rested for a moment on him. There was a flicker of something like resentment, but the eyes went back to staring out the window.

It was a bare room with a white iron cot, pale green walls, a folding table—a normal, institutional room with a terrazzo floor and no carpet, two chairs and no pictures and Uncle Matt blending in like a rigid fixture.

Shane was sweating. The old man sat on without speaking. Perhaps if he got up and rang the bell—but there was the same power in those eyes to hold him rigid, as when he had finished his meal and Matt would go on slowly chewing.

"Uncle Matt."

A priest, with a shock of ridged wavy hair entered the room.

"Sorry, Mr. Donovan. I had a call to make. There was an accident on the Base Line Road this morning. One of my parishioners—Joe Malloy—" He tossed the name in the direction of the figure in the chair, and turned back to Shane. "So, I'm a bit late. I promised Matt I would be here before you arrived."

"Can't he speak?"

The priest accepted the chair offered by the nurse.

"He can."

The old man kept staring out the window. There was a rustling sound in his throat and he said finally, with obvious effort, "Drinking?"

The priest's face wrinkled into a semi-smile as if recognizing the force of indignation that forced him to speak.

"Wasn't his fault, Matthew. Two young fellows stole a car from McGee's garage and ran into him."

"Aah."

Matt groaned.

"I'm Father Herman."

They made the usual overtures of men who meet without introduction.

"Matt, have you told your nephew?"

The gaunt head moved slowly in a negative gesture. Father Herman made a motion with his shoulders.

"Shane, your uncle wants to know if you will take over his farm—" He hesitated as if embarrassed. "And work it."

The priest stopped and lit a cigarette with the air of a man who has completed a difficult task.

"Me—me work his farm?"

"Yes, that's what your uncle wants to know."

"I don't understand—"

Father Herman looked to the seated figure for help, but Uncle Matt had not changed his position.

"The lawyer has drawn up the papers and he would sell it to you for a dollar."

The room was hot and stifling. Shane nodded to the priest and they went into the hallway. A man sitting in a chair by an oversized philodendron came to them before Shane could say anything.

"Shane, you won't remember me. Joe Carr. I was with you in high school. I'm Matt's lawyer."

Shane acknowledged the greeting.

"Just what the hell—sorry, Father—what is going on here?"

Carr tried to explain, but the priest was silent.

"Joe, it doesn't wash. I was never close to that old man in there. At the end"—he hesitated—"at the end, he hated me. By the way, where is Olga?"

Carr looked at Father Herman, who nodded.

"She left him and—well—"

"He was very hurt," interposed the priest. "She is living with a man—and—they have children."

"Just left him. She isn't married to this fellow at all."

Shane's rage boiled up in angry surges.

"No go! My God, he must really hate her to try a trick like this. How long have you been here, Father?"

"Only three years."

"I see, well, Joe may not know either, but he sure treated her like a slave. The old bastard went every night—" Shane stopped. "That's past history. I suppose he's made his peace with God and only wants his revenge before he dies." His voice was sarcastic and bitter. "Well, I'm not going to be the patsy for him. And dammit, Joe, you're just as mean if you let him give it to someone else."

Shane's voice attracted the attention of a nurse down the hall. Father Herman's hand rested on his arm in a cautionary way.

"A dying man asks you to do something," he said in a faintly reproving way, "what would you do as his priest or his lawyer?"

"I suppose, but let me tell you one thing. Olga *deserves* that farm—no matter what she's done."

Carr shifted his briefcase.

"Well—I tried—but you know your uncle."

"That's the interesting thing, Joe. I never did know him. In some ways he was good to me—but, I—I won't be used to club Olga. In a way, I'm sorry. I've got to go."

He had a compulsion to cry.

"Will you say goodbye to him?"

Shane nodded to Father Herman and took a step towards the door and stopped. He found he had no more words, and walked away without speaking.

He drove home and merely told Mona that his uncle was sick. When Father Herman called to say his uncle died ten days later, he made one of his infrequent trips to the cathedral downtown at noon hour and found, after lighting a votive candle, that he couldn't pray.

The official-looking letter from Carr and Carr said he had inherited the farm. He replied, typing the letter himself, that he renounced all claim in favour of Olga Donovan and tried to keep it from his mind; but it slipped back on many occasions until he finally told Mona.

She listened, curious at first, and finally expressionless. When she was silent after his explanation, he asked, "Well, what do you think?"

"I think it's strange that you wouldn't mention it at the time and now three years later you want my opinion."

"I can't explain. It just didn't seem right for him—or for me to—well, I couldn't do it."

"But did you condone what that woman did? Leaving her husband and—"

"Husband—I don't think—" Shane stopped. "Let's forget it."

Mona hadn't said any more. It was never referred to again openly but it had never gone away.

He had to stop thinking. He had an appointment with Fathingham. It was a relief.

His legs were a trifle shaky but it would pass. New York in the morning had a strangely attractive feeling. There was a fantastic pull of the mass of people on the move. This was the New York of dreams, magnet-like, that could bring millions and hold millions who lived for the power and the surge and who overlooked the dark seams of hatred and passionate concern—and who made her not American but a city state like Rome.

The building soared. The lobby was a hall for Aztec priests. There were pillars, enormous pillars, fathomless murals and a grave-faced man at a tiny desk—just seemingly tiny because everything else was so enormous. Whooshing elevator and neutered music and people jamming themselves in as if afraid to touch each other.

A lemon girl sat behind a brown desk on a soft, orange rug. Windowless room. A monster green plastic plant in a concrete bucket. Swirls of color behind a frame.

"Did you have an appointment with Mr. Fathingham?"

Each husky syllable was carefully manufactured. Mask face, long eyelashes, astonishing thighs; and as sexless as a 3-D incarnation of an advertisement for a faster car, or a fresher drink.

He was ushered into the presence of Fathingham. J.L. was a gaunt brown heron of a man. His hair was a web of thin grey yarn on a tanned pate. His eyes were out of character. They were pale blue, misplaced by a hawk nose and a thin-lipped mouth. Blue suit, as well-fitting as on a model in the *New York Times Magazine*, dark blue shirt, brown-gold tie and coppery brogues. There was a gleam of very large bronze cuff links. When he stood up and before he buttoned his coat, Shane had a glimpse of a small rotund stomach, but it vanished under the influence of good tailoring.

"Sorry I'm a trifle late but I walked."

"Not at all—glad to see you. This is one of our rare good mornings in New York."

Then, with the slightest edge: "You rather took everyone by storm yesterday."

Shane was back in the ring and Fathingham had feinted.

"You'll have to excuse a simple country boy at loose in the city."

That would hold him.

Fathingham moved to the couch. This was a tactical office and J.L. knew how to use the terrain. The desk was an antique refectory table. The place was profuse with easy chairs, couches, and low tables, all the same orange color as the reception-hall carpet, but his rug was shaggy, soft and moss-green.

"You creative fellows are all alike."

"I'm sorry if I was a bit rough."

"Not at all. It was tough talking, but they needed it. You see, Shane, I've been thinking. What you said about the process being more important than the job struck a bell. A real ding-dong!"

Shane relaxed.

"I hope that I won't sound too solemn if I say that I have, I think, a deep concern in me for what is happening. In Canada we are supposed to be solemn people. That may be it. But I know that I feel at times as if we in the advertising business have a grave responsibility."

J.L. nodded.

"Yes, I share the feeling."

154

He moved to the coffee table and punched a button.

"Miss Danver, hold all calls and let Mr. Holland-Wills see the Greystone people."

J.L. made a ceremony out of lighting a cigarette.

"About Wilton."

"That was too bad."

"No, Shane. Don't blame yourself. Peter is a perfect example of a burnt-out case. Too much. You may not know about his personal problems but he's afraid. Full of it. But he still has ability and Federal will take him in the P.R. department in Detroit." He paused and smiled, somewhat maliciously. "I don't know how his wife will react, but—" He waved his hand as if in dismissal. "That's his problem. Now, as to what you think of us."

"Please, I'd rather forget a lot of that."

"No, Shane, I agree with much of what you said. New York *is* a paradox in America. Maybe in the world. It *is* becoming an uninhabitable place. People here *are* like jungle animals. I've thought of moving the business out—upstate maybe, but goddamit, you can't survive that way either. What do you do?"

Shane paused. An impish thought came to him.

"What do you do?" he said. "First of all, create a climate for younger people."

"I know. We try, but those shaggy-haired young bastards want to play around with lights and nudes and slogans that belittle the products."

Shane shook his head. It hurt and he ached now for a drink. His hands were clammy. A drink would be treacherous.

"Did you ever think it was their way of protest?"

"Sure, protest, but what against?"

"The layers of vested interests of older people—the vested interests of vested vice-presidents who so carefully curb them. Keep their best ideas away from you. Refuse to talk to them."

Fathingham was up and pacing.

"You may be right. That's what my daughter says. She's over at *Time* and she complains about them as well—"

Shane took a deep breath.

"We look at them and say they know all the questions but have no answers. We say they don't want to get inside the system and change it, but I wonder if we let them in. They're not the only ones. People of my age are wondering if the merry-go-round is worth it, but by God, we're afraid to let go the brass ring."

Fathingham opened an enormous ornately carved cabinet.

"Got this in Spain. Belonged to some old abbot or other."

He made a ritual out of producing two extra large martinis.

"Here's luck. It's early in the day, but we must give you some opportunities to relax. Don't usually do this!"

The martini felt delicious.

"Would you like to work in New York, Shane?"

Shane was facing what almost every successful Canadian of his age had to meet, sooner or later.

"Why do you puddle around up there when you could make it in the big-time?"

Here was the mecca of his childhood in his grasp.

But the reality of America was so far from the dream. Two days in New York or Chicago and he felt alien—a foreigner.

"I'm not sure. In my heart I am a Canadian. That's not to say I have anything against Americans or America."

(It was a Canadian characteristic to soft-pedal honest reactions. Why couldn't he simply express what he felt? "I get sick of this country. One of the most beautiful in the world. A powerful country being destroyed by politicians and business people with the instincts of—Attila the Hun.")

He said instead:

"I honestly believe there is a breed of people called Canadians. We have survived, in the face of the wash of superfluous culture, product, and environment of Uncle Sam. Our courts, our speech, and our attitudes are different. We do accept a lot of Americanization, but deep down we are different. We're really only happy in that goddam, big, lonely country."

The older man seemed a trifle taken back.

"Well, it's beautiful and it's still clean."

"Yes, and while much of it is like much of America, it's different to us."

Fathingham smiled.

"I travel a lot in Canada and I think you *are* different. Police are different, and I've relatives in Canada, and—well, it was a shock to me the first time I said something rather innocently about joining the United States. My God, they were shocked. Said, in effect—mind you, politely—no, thank you —very strange, but understandable, I suppose."

This was familiar ground to Shane.

"We are perhaps backward in American terms, but a lot of people feel the lag is good. We should make our own mistakes, and not simply imitate yours. It's hard. Not only businessmen are to blame. Our town and city politicians too often equate success with high rise, expressways, and all those duplicate hot dog stands, chicken shacks and motels and even service stations sprawled along the access ways, so you don't know whether you're in Kansas or Ontario."

"Stupid. When I'm in Canada I look for something different. God, why would anyone drive five hundred miles to go to a chain place, just like all the others?"

"Probably a computer told them."

Fathingham exploded.

"Don't tell me about computers. We've got a million dollars tied up and it couldn't, for instance, come up with a suitable name for a TV show. A bunch of wild-eyed kids come along and slam a series together that knocks ours out—no plot—nothing, and it zooms along. What's happening?"

The martini stirred Shane.

"You know, it's a hell of a thing, when you think about it. I've a friend—a Canadian with the embassy in Washington. He says life there is like in the Middle Ages—people live in apartment buildings that are really castles—moats—well, guards at every entrance. Don't drive downtown by yourself —make sure you know the taxi company, because a cab you hail could be somebody cruising for a pigeon. People are living in prisons."

Fathingham nodded.

"I still detect a form of resentment on the part of Canadians to Americans."

This was tricky ground.

"Not resentment, J.L., I'm sure. A bit, but not enough to matter. Fundamentally, Canadians want to preserve what they have and develop in their own way. We'll make mistakes. Be sure of it. But they'll be our own mistakes."

He was repeating himself, but Fathingham didn't seem to notice.

"What about politics?"

"We're usually on the side of the American politicians who get put down. Roosevelt was a hero to us. The Kennedys—people like Fulbright—and I suspect even Gene McCarthy was closer to our style than America's."

Fathingham smiled.

"Strange, isn't it? The break with my daughter was over McCarthy. I couldn't see a poetry professor as President and she went off on that New England campaign. The Chicago

Democratic Convention convinced her the American system was finished. When he pooped out you would think I was personally to blame." The advertising executive was affected emotionally. He went to look out the window. "I tried. My daughter kept saying I should be doing something for the community—especially the blacks. So I volunteered for one of those Lindsay committees. We met twice and this fuzzy-haired son of a bitch in witch doctor robes kept saying, 'I hate your white guts because you're only here trying to save that white hide of yours.' Called me all kinds of indecencies, including relations with my mother—you know the words."

He shook his head.

"Then, Donovan, when my daughter prodded me, I told her why I gave up and she blamed me for being a quitter. My daughter says we are the pirates of Westchester and Bucks County who take our money, live outside, and let the city rot."

He squared his shoulders.

"Can't do much about that."

Leaning over, he lowered his voice, although they were alone.

"I've a problem. We talk about noble things but let's get back to the mundane. I've got Evans Soaps. Hell of an account. Now, they want to get into men's toiletries. Imagine! The bloody market is crowded and, of course, some have made a killing. You know—Jade East and the Orient—and that Japanese gimmick about Karate—and manly stuff—old saddle boys and sweat—and they want an angle. We've come up with dozens—no go."

"Like what?"

"All copies. All imitations. There's only so many ways you can suggest an aphrodisiac. Let's face it, that's what they

159

suggest. They're all supposed to be some kind of fake Spanish fly. You spray it on and the TV laddies and the slick magazines suggest the smell will set females on fire."

Shane laughed. Fathingham was relaxed, but he was still a predator.

"You are a realist, J.L."

"I'm glad you didn't say moralist. I am in a way, because if you want my honest opinion, I think we've gone sex mad. Everything from Dichter and the male ego in a car to nudity. It's like the smog, it's all over, this sex thing."

"And you don't approve."

"I don't know. My daughter says we exploit women. In a way she's right, but where does that leave me? It's all right to feel that way, but your sensibilities go out the window when you have a four-million-dollar account hanging in the balance."

"That's not hay. What's the problem?"

"An idea. None have been good enough."

"Why?"

"Imitation. No originality. Same old thing, as I said. Tropic breeze to match Jade East. I've heard lime until I can't even stand lime in a gin and tonic. We've been through it until we're getting silly and the sponsor is ready to take off." Fathingham waved his hands. "Well, I hate to admit I'm licked. But, that's the way it works."

Shane felt himself reacting to the challenge. Was it creativity or simply the competitive sense? He had an idea. It had been popping in and out of his subconscious for a long time.

"I really don't want to compete with your creative department—" He trailed out a seemingly reluctant—"but."

Fathingham stood up and stared at him.

"You son of a bitch, I think you've got something on your mind." He clapped his hands. "I'll make you a deal. Ten

160

thousand cash if you can give me a name—an idea—just between us. If you want credit—okay. If you want it private—okay. I'll be goddamned if I'm going to let three former copy boys take a four-million-dollar account away."

Shane was thinking aloud, but conscious of the dramatic possibility.

"J.L., one of the things that fascinates me is the concentration on youth. But who has the money? Older people. Who needs the rutting scent? Guys like us, and I'm damned if I'm going to fight off Japanese bushwhackers."

Fathingham chuckled. Shane continued.

"There must be an appeal to older men. A hell of a lot of younger women respond to older men. More than ever. Look at Onassis—well, advertising is the art of making people believe something can and will happen. Whiter than white! Agreed?"

Fathingham was watching him intently.

Shane's blood was quickening. "Now, J.L., let's forget the young bucks. The advertising world has gone nuts about young people. So they've got purchasing power—but what about the guys who fly first class—the ones with the Continentals—the Eldorados—the Mercedeses—the Imperials—who know how to order—who are marrying younger women—"

He had to build his case. Now was his time to make the graphic point.

"Take the handsome, older man." He paused. "Take Cesar Romero. God, he had more sex appeal than anyone I know and it increases. Sort of like an old lion—not too old—but a guy you don't want to tangle with—been places and seen things. Can go anywhere."

Fathingham was agreeing.

"I see—but old lions stink, don't they?"

"Who knows for sure? Who cares? Think instead of rippling savannah grass . . . that mighty beast looking for danger and that soft, warm lioness lying at his feet—golden soft—"

"I see—I see—great visuals—but—what would you call it? But lions—that's old stuff."

"I agree. Lion was a simple name in the old days to stick on a product—but I have some angles. You don't use the word lion. Some words can be used in two ways and have a lot of implications. Listen, J.L., L-E-O-N-I-N-E Leonine, pertaining to, resembling, or characteristic of a lion."

"How the hell did you know that?"

Shane accepted another martini.

"I looked it up." He didn't add the word also could be used in connection with thirteen popes. That was the sort of thing that could queer an idea on Madison Avenue.

Shane took a pad and printed the word:

L E O N I N E

Then he wrote below it:

LEO

9

"Think of the possibilities. Superimpose lettering over a guy who has the characteristics of a Romero—turned out to the hilt—a sexy-looking young golden woman with him—a golden lioness on a leash—or a pride of lions in the background—and think of what it suggests."

Fathingham picked up the pad and stared at it.

"I'm damned. You know, that's exactly what we're looking for. Nobody is going to see this but Castelli—he's the president. I'll tell you something. Do you know him? You don't. Well, he looks like that himself. A cross between Romero and what J. Carroll Naish used to look like. He'll swallow it. Because he's an aging Don Juan in a way."

"Like the man who bought the billboard because he could see it from his own office."

"No, not really, this is a damned good idea. I'm glad we talked. Not only for this, but because I had a chance to find out more about you. Maybe I see a lot of what I used to be in you. I prided myself on being a very creative guy. Played the piano—you know. I once wanted to write music."

Fathingham put his hand on Shane's shoulder.

"Shane, I'm going to do something—which isn't altruistic, it's business. If this works—and I think it will—it'll put out the fire. I'm going to make it twenty thousand cash from the account—to you. Don't worry—it's not charity."

He added, as if to ward off appreciative words, "It's good. If the rutting old lion thing doesn't work, I'll try the Pope Leo 9 on Castelli—he's a big shot in the K of C at St. Pat's."

The smart old bastard, thought Shane, had let him know he understood the meaning of the word. Twenty thousand dollars. That was one difference between Americans and Canadians. They never hesitated when they needed something. It would never happen in Canada. There would be a flap up of meetings and discussions, over and over, until at the last moment the decision would be made. Damn the Americans, but they were never hesitant about an idea that might work.

Fathingham would bypass his whole agency and go direct to Castelli. Of course, it would work. Castelli, as the agency man explained, was part angel and part mobster. He'd go for it.

9

Women raised hell about whisky and clergymen tried to get youngsters to sign the pledge. The idea was to scare hell out of them before they got the taste of it. But older men expanded on wistful memories of drinking exploits. Booze was manly.

Shane's father told stories of an Irish grandfather settling in pioneer Ontario. It seemed as if the great trees were felled, the stumps pulled and the fields tilled only as a result of brawn and booze. There was a tavern on every corner and whisky was five cents a glass. Men who died from exposure or at a barn framing accident were weaklings who couldn't handle their liquor.

There was praise for drinking men.

"Big Pete McAskill could really hold his liquor."

"Drink an ordinary man under the table."

"I've seen him drink all night and go back to work next day as if nothing had happened."

When Joe Markowski went berserk in the Commercial Hotel in Nonsuch, it took six men to hold him down. All the pupils went by way of Main Street to school the next morning to look at the scene of destruction. The broken window, veranda post askew, a door lying in the street and a shattered mirror inside all bore testimony to strength.

"Gosh, he must be really strong."

Every boy in school was convinced that neither Dempsey nor Tunney would have a chance against Joe Markowski. He outranked Buffalo Bill Cody as a hero, and the magic word was whisky. The fact that Markowski was a barrel-chested, dwarfish man with a gentle nature when sober, and a fiendish temper when drinking, didn't count.

Children, in their astute way, noted the hypocrisy. His father professed scorn for the elevator agent who drank.

"He drinks a quart of whisky a day. One of these days, the company will catch on. Imagine having a man like that in a position like that. They'll catch on."

They didn't catch on. The elevator agent drank his daily quart of whisky and didn't make mistakes—and had a good job, and Shane detected the note of envy in his father, who worked only occasionally.

Everyone knew the Anstetts who ran whisky across the U.S. border. Every week there was a new story about a chase by the R.C.M.P. along a dusty gumboed back road—and of how the big Pierce-Arrows of the bootleggers left them behind—"as if they were sitting still." And next day the Anstetts would be drinking pop and eating raisin pie with ice cream in the China Café.

"Here, kid, buy yourself a treat."

A nickel bought enough licorice to last the afternoon. Once he had been spun breathless down the road, with the tornado-like dust cluster behind the car when the white needle showed 110 miles per hour on the black dial. He had been cuffed into admitting it to his mother and didn't know if that shamed him as much as when he lay hidden in the weeds by the section shanty and heard his father lying.

"They'll never catch the Anstetts. I've been in that car when they were doing a hundred and twenty-five miles an hour. Don't blame them. They're living and the rest of us is dying."

Legends! But he knew there were also legends about himself. He helped retail them when the stories started at drinking sessions—stories of liberating demijohns of cognac from hidden stores during the Normandy offensive—stories of being in Nova Scotia cellars drinking pre '14–'18 war stuff that had been snatched in the running battles between Mounties and Bluenose rumrunners. Then someone would ask Shane about the Quebec trip.

"Oh God, you know, everyone needs a grand gesture once in a lifetime. Four of us at the Laurentien Hotel in Montreal and we had been on it for some time and they wanted to eat and there was only a Murray's restaurant. So they say 'Take us to a good place' and when we got in the cab, I simply say to the driver in French 'Take us to Madame Kerhilu's' and slide a ten-dollar bill along the front seat and we start and soon they get worried—and after a time they catch on that we're going to Quebec City. We stopped almost every place on the road. We had a ball."

He knew that wasn't quite the truth.

Kerhilu's was closed. They ate at the Château Frontenac, squeezed in amongst busloads of blue-tinted women on a garden tour of Quebec. They were from Baton Rouge and were nasty to an Indian guest. When his group resented it they were finally asked to leave—the manager admitting the injustice of it all but afraid of provoking a second War of 1812.

The three-hour trip back was a ghastly affair as their energy ran down and they parted in an argument about the cab fare. Of course, in retrospect it had been a grand affair.

A lot of it Shane could never remember very clearly—except for buying a live, suckling pig from the driver's cousin on the way—and then not having the heart to allow anyone to sacrifice it. He never did discover what happened to it, except that it messed on someone.

But who would really believe the truth about drinking—or the lapses? Now there was the mystery of coming awake in Bonnie's bedroom and wandering out to find her asleep on the couch in her living room and Eric McMaster smoking a cigar. McMaster was an old New York friend, a slim erect man who was a senior editor with one of the big publishing houses. But what was he doing here?

"Good morning, Shane. O'Hare's gone but I thought I would see you home."

O'Hare? There was the hellish confusion of not knowing what had happened after leaving Fathingham's office. Something came to him about O'Hare and meeting Bonnie at the White Horse and McMaster and stories about Dylan Thomas and Brendan Behan.

Bonnie was sleepy but didn't appear angry as she kissed him on the cheek.

"No apologies, dear. You needed the rest. Just don't make too much noise. I don't want to get thrown out of a rent controlled building."

McMaster smiled.

"I seem to have arrived at a point of sobriety. Something that approaches it. What about you, Bonnie?"

Bonnie made a gesture of surrender.

"Me, I'm going to bed to see if I can get a bit of sleep. You two can do what you want—but please lock the door when you leave."

New York was coming awake as they walked uptown. Shane felt a pulsing quality and McMaster seemed to be enjoying the moment.

"Eric, you look positively happy."

"I enjoy New York when it's like this. Used to get up early and walk in the park, but had to give it up. Too dangerous now. The junkies and winos come awake desperate for a touch."

Sanitation trucks were gobbling piles of garbage being sent up from opened doors in the sidewalk. It was too early for office workers but the coffeeshops were doing a brisk business.

"Look at the cats!"

A brace of tawny cats padded down a narrow alleyway.

"Funny, but I never thought of alley cats in New York."

"Shane, there are millions of homeless cats in this city. Without them we'd be navel deep in rats and mice."

Two dusky girls in tight white dresses leaned against a building, shiny handbags dangling from their arms. One smiled tentatively at the men and then turned away as if remembering the time. They were only a half block away when a man driving a shiny old Cadillac picked them up.

"We have cats of all kinds here," observed McMaster. "That's their stud. He'll feed them or give them a fix and take their money and let them sleep for a few hours before sending them back on their prowl."

"Why do they do it? I don't mean, why are they hookers,

Eric, but why do they let some guy take their money—beat them—make slaves out of them? I don't get it."

McMaster had edited a book on prostitution.

"I wasn't keen, but this doctor had done some very good research. Scientific more than anything. One of the things I felt he hadn't covered was the relationship with pimps, so he taped some conversations. Very interesting, because the girls were a lot more intelligent than I had assumed. Touches of what you might call masochism in them. I came to the conclusion—and the doctor, too—that they were looking to be degraded. They knew these chaps were Judas Iscariots, in a sense—taking money from several, telling each they were loyal —though they never heard the word 'love' as I recall. Poor creatures admitted there was no future—and of course, many were hooked on heroin or something—and the pimp was often a pusher, so he saved them trouble."

They were near the President. Someone, a bundle of old clothes, poked amongst a pile of trash, and as they passed it looked up. Grey wiry hair poked out from under a greasy bandana. The face was dirty grey, lined, and the eyes raked them without a trace of expression.

"Join me for breakfast, gentlemen?"

The old woman laughed, in a shrill cackling sound. Shane shivered. McMaster touched his arm.

"We have seen the beginning and the end. The morning has a way of disclosing people and events more clearly. I came by here one morning and there was a dead man lying at the foot of those stairs—just by the door into that stamp place. Do you know, I had a hell of a time getting a policeman to even look at him?"

Shane ordered breakfast in the suite.

Eric McMaster was a slim man with sandy greying hair, a narrow face with occasional freckles, a neat light moustache and pale sharp blue eyes. He moved as if his spine were a solid fused unit. It gave him a certain formality.

"I must say I enjoyed last night. Bonnie is very, very charming." He paused. "Very few women I know could come through a session like that without blowing up in exasperation."

"Bonnie is a quite extraordinary person. She's working for a friend of mine, a Peter O'Hare—hell, you know that."

"O'Hare. Interesting fellow. He kept us in stitches about the quirks of getting a play produced in New York. Hope he keeps some sort of diary. I think it would make an extraordinarily interesting book. You had retired by then for a snooze."

Shane could feel an unreasoning heat.

"Well, he's had the guts to stick it out and not let everything get in his way. That's why he'll make it, I guess."

Eric looked at him more closely.

"Are you going to do that?"

"Oh, hell, if I had the stuff in me to be a writer, I would have done it by now. Time has passed me by, I think."

"You were pretty convinced last night that you could do it. In fact, while I can't say it was my principal reason for staying on—I enjoyed myself in a weird and wonderful way— I must say there's a valid point in your reasoning."

Shane held out his hand.

"Whoa—whoa—I've lost you."

Eric tilted his head.

"Your thesis, Shane, as I remember, is that in this current world—when a man is on the verge of middle age—this world gives him some particular problems."

It was Shane's, but surely it was also the theory of every middle-aged man. A man woke up one day and realized he was seeing the names of contemporaries in the obituary columns, that fall was a reminder of winter. He no longer lived on the knife edge of worry about financial things, but with a reasonable security, and wondered what good the money was to him. There were times when he drove away in a new car aching for the heart-pounding satisfaction that came with the first one he ever bought—even with payments due for eighteen months.

"What is it? Eric, what is this madness that drives a person like me on? I started writing, largely because I was too shy in many ways to say what I wanted to say. No, to be honest that's not the only reason. I also started writing to try and make some money. That was part of it. No doubt."

"And now you really don't need the money. So, you wonder —is it inspiration? Do you have something to say? There's also the matter of revenge—or put it another way: Get back at the world for giving you success—success that didn't pan out the way you expected."

It was post-party camaraderie, and neither wanted to break it up. Eric McMaster explained:

"I guess everyone has something to say about advertising. Spent a few years myself there—cost me a wife and family— so I'm not too keen about it."

Eric McMaster had come out of Virginia with a degree and, as he expressed it, a "lust" for New York and intoxication with Sherwood Anderson, Thomas Wolfe and the whole mythology of O. Henry, Damon Runyon, and Heywood Broun.

"It was exciting. It was damnable. It was thrilling. It was tragic."

"That sounds like the dust jacket for a book or a movie come-on."

"My dear Donovan, I simply was not a writer. I enjoyed New York and I enjoyed talking about writing and I loved parties. You know, I drove William Faulkner back to his hotel and he didn't say a damned word because he was in a pique and just as we got there he said solemnly that all New York women were selfish bitches and would I have a drink with him. I did, and at ten o'clock in the morning, he fell asleep and I went home—and, believe it or not, my wife, who was fed up anyhow, left me and took the children. That's when I should have packed up and gone back to teach in Virginia. My family would have come back—but I kept on in the agency and wrote a book—that sold 399 copies."

"What was wrong with it? I shouldn't put it that way. Lots of good books don't sell."

Eric turned his palms up.

"All words. No heart. I'm just not a writer. But I *am* a good editor. In a way it satisfies me. I'm still a hopeless romantic about writing. I like writers better than anyone. I'm like a lot of people in New York. I play a role. The editor! Gives me access to writers and the theatre and—yet, when I listened to you last night I recognized the old feeling about wanting to write—that bittersweet feeling—half sad—half lonely—"

"God, don't I know it. But when I think about writing it—"

"I have a theory about that. You should write—somehow, you'll never be free until you do."

"But every middle-aged frustrated writer in the world wants to do it. Who's going to publish it?"

"Does it matter?"

"But why do it?"

"Exorcise the devil. Get rid of it. That first book of mine did it. Too many people write for publication. Nowadays, the popular writers are simply good mechanics. So much description of a process for the fact-hungry—so much sex, as explicit as possible, for the dirty-minded—and then cast your characters as close as you can to public figures without libel —and get a whomping publicity budget—and you're on the

173

best-seller list. Then write it again with a new cast of characters and a new setting—and you've got a repeat. Simple."

"There's not much hope in that."

"Well, you have two ways. Be a mechanic, or else sit down and write. But write and forget about publication—and get rid of what's bugging you. Then, it may just turn into one of those quite good books that still come out and still get read by a reasonable amount of people—and you will get the virus out of your soul."

"Meaning, that's what I should do."

McMaster was pouring coffee.

"Don't be offended, old boy, but exhaustion and booze and experience produce manifestations of truth. You have no excuses. I gather you are not suffering financially, so for you, poverty is out. You're inclined to blame your family and your job—but what's to prevent you from going away and trying it?"

"I've done that—"

"But have you gone through a real testing period? I did it —four months in a Cape Cod cottage freezing my butt off in October and November, and drinking and dreaming. But I should have gone through the horror and stuck it out, and then, perhaps, that second book would have been a good one. But, you see, I didn't stay long enough. I hadn't peeled away enough layers."

Shane laughed.

"You aren't really a bohemian."

"I am a product of the manse. Good old Presbyterian and feeling guilty as hell—and not really being able to write about the guilt." He shook his head. "It's not the sins of our fathers that haunt us. It's the moral climate. The kind of prejudice against the mysterious devil people divine in writers and writing. My father was a mechanical Christian—really. Playing

174

a role and not understanding. Emotions were something you concealed, and New York was my escape."

Shane was reluctant to see him go.

"Then, you think I should—well, I'm not certain."

"Donovan, it's not easy, but really, let me put it this way. If you can hang on to your family, do it. A sure way not to do it is to let this demon drive you. I think you have to gamble for a year. You're finished in advertising, whether you like it or not. That's apparent—and you're at a peak, where retirement is a gain. But go and try the writing. Explain if you can to your family—if you can't, go anyhow."

"God, I can't explain. You understand, but most don't. To my wife writing is like making a cabinet—only I'm a lousy cabinetmaker."

"Shane, I'll make you a deal. Write your book—send it to me. I'll give you an honest answer. But *do* something. This kind of living death you're in at the moment is not good enough."

"Death is the word for it. I get up the courage to do something and then I go home and the routine takes over. Hard drive at the office and I'm too tired. I take off a few days and get going and then there's my family—probably an excuse, but—"

McMaster was ready to leave.

"Shane, that girl Bonnie is quite exceptional."

"Yes, I think she is."

"Well, be careful. She hurts easily. It's not my business—but—well, I've said too much."

Shane was in the chair when the maid came in to stare at the unmussed bed. She cleaned the rooms quietly and left him.

The room began to close in. He had to escape. Sleep was impossible. There were ideas to be conceived. How did

Churchill manage? Just keep your attention up and keep moving and have a little food. Write a speech and knock the eyes out of everyone. He had to leave the room.

There was exhilaration outside in the dappled morning. In the sunny spots there was usual warmth, but the cold nipped in the shadows. The breeze slipped down the streets swirling the eternal litter of New York and touching bare legs with chilly fingers.

"I feel good—so good. I can write—I can write—" Hemingway drank and wrote. In this mood he could write. "The words roll on—free." Now they streamed through his mind—freely, without obstruction. There were so many characters and so many ideas.

The sight of food in a restaurant window made him remember it was almost lunch time. Joints of red rare roast beef and sleek pink hams and cold lobsters and shrimps like pink crescents made him turn into a place with an Irish name where it was steaming and somewhat grimy.

The beer was pale golden with beads on the glass, and he looked at it a long time before he drank it.

A crooked sign proclaimed DONING ROOM in glittering letters on a faded blue card. Here, heels were hooked in rails and people nudged close to one another and fannies bulged over stools and there was a clattery rattle of dishes. It was a place where dark dried blue blood blueberry pie slathered out of crusts and the sight of the stewed steak special took away his phantom appetite. He got up and went out, away from the noise and pressure.

The newsstand reeked of crime and vice and lurid covers. He resisted the temptation to buy a newspaper. He wanted to stay detached and away and aloof, and if he bought a newspaper he would have to share with all this mob the same troubles and rumours of troubles and the constant recital of the kind of crime and vice so common to New York.

He watched in the window of the cafeteria and the words formed in his mind:

"The Arcadia . . . place of sweating and faded blondes in bust-swollen smocks and purple-faced countermen and old shambling men who shuffled dirty dishes from tables and restored them to an enamelled whiteness. The Arcadia. Place of the sleepless street walker now at noon trying to use the antiseptic of sun and daylight for some kind of spiritual purpose. It is the place of the man with the red and blue nose and the soggy-ended cigar supping coffee and—and—hell!"

Shane moved dully, wondering why he couldn't think of such phrases when he was sober. Anyhow, they were too purple and pretentious. Shane was wandering on, aware of the windows filled with people eating and the overflowing noise of men and women in bars and taverns and of the subdued sounds that came from cocktail bar doors and of the smell of frying onions and of places with artificial-looking juices of a thousand never-heard-of-before tropical fruits. On an impulse, he hailed a taxi.

"Just drive."

The driver roused a belligerent note.

"Whaddya mean, bud?"

Shane's impulse was to tell him to go to hell but he restrained himself.

"Down to Thirty-fourth. One of the big department stores."

The driver relaxed with a definite destination and they nudged and horned their way downtown. In a vague way, Shane was thinking about buying something for Mona. A forty-cent tip on a sixty-cent ride didn't even elicit a thank you from the driver. He tried to think of something he could send Mona. He caught the nagging voice of a fussy little supervisor:

"Look here, you two, this is no place or time for chit chat . . . Miss O'Connor, your stock is in abominable shape."

Two aging women clerks made mysterious swipes with their hands over the packed counter.

"Doesn't he give ya pain?"

"Some day I'll hit that bastard with a tray of something gooey . . ."

"Who'd do such a job? I'll bet he squats."

Shane walked out, soon finding himself in an unfamiliar part of the city. Once he stood up at a sea food bar and ordered a shrimp cocktail. When it came, he swallowed the six shrimps in their spicy bloody sauce and then ordered a boilermaker from the bartender.

"Quiet today?"

The big man with the smeared apron looked at him suspiciously.

"We get most of our customers in the evening."

He moved down to the end of the bar, propped his foot against a case, and studied his newspaper.

Shane walked idly now as if trying to lose himself. There was a small square where several old women with shawls over their heads presided over outdoor stalls full of metallic-looking flowers of all kinds. They were fakes. Flowers? He must send flowers to Mona. It worked when everything else failed.

He sat down on a bench in the square. A bearded young man with a set of charcoaled canvases lounged across from him, absorbed in a book.

"Now *that* is freedom," thought Shane, "not giving a good hot damn for anything. Free of responsibility, and doing what he wants to do. I've spent a whole lifetime . . . almost fifty years of it . . . being responsible."

"I'll never go back to the bastard."

There were two women on the next bench. Out of the corner of his eye he could see them outlined and he didn't turn. It was like watching birds. If you turned and looked full at them they might fly away. They were thin, nervous-looking women in bright coats, sucking at cigarettes.

"I don't blame you."

"Yah, I knew he was foolin' around but when I found out he brought a woman to our apartment when I was away and stayed overnight . . ."

"Who told ya?"

"Mrs. Jacobs down the hall."

When he looked across the square a girl with a baby in her arms was standing threateningly over the bearded young man.

"Responsibility, hell!"

Shane got up and moved off. He spent the afternoon walking, stopping now and again in dim bars to sit and sip a drink, thinking idly of eating but avoiding it. When he came to St. Patrick's he went in. It was a magnet.

St. Patrick's was one of the places in the world that his mother had often talked about. A cousin had once sent her a postcard from New York and in the dreary dusty little Saskatchewan village the color photo of the Fifth Avenue Cathedral glowed on the world, rivalling a lithograph of St. Peter's.

The old woman coming down the aisle moved toward the side altar and knelt. Shane thought for a minute, and then said softly to himself as he stood up to leave, "An old woman with seamed face in the vise of her shawl caught strangle-wise beneath her chin, fingered with her other time-scarred hand her rosary and murmured into the ear of God."

Shane had an elation at times like this. They were so pronounced that when a shadow of suspicion that he must stop drinking came into his mind, he knew he would miss the times when his detached mind soared into flights of creative fancy. It was the one thing he would like to preserve. Parties were a bore, in a sense, and alcohol was a defence, but in the times of privacy when alcohol worked well for him, he could forget the growing weariness about living in general.

In Rockefeller Plaza he stopped to stare at the fountain.

"Now the morning stream of suburban life, like the reversing falls, turns and starts to flow back into the land of the two-carred and mortgaged love hutches."

He was fighting something. His mouth was dry and a trifle parched, and his hands were shaking. He must have slept in the cathedral. He still felt tired, and he moved along 48th Street towards the President with purpose. If he could just keep this edge on, he might write.

At the entrance of the hotel, he hesitated for a moment. On an impulse he sat down in the lobby. He was sad. He was lonely. The walk and the words. Words were like a binge. "Honeymooners on the elevator—gone to a room for fumbling starts and mistakes." But sitting in the lobby he knew he was haunted by Mona. If he went home and said he hadn't stayed for the awards?

Mona?

He was oblivious to the people in the lobby. It was as if he were suspended in a timeless void.

Shane Donovan and Mona Henry drifted into a relationship that was more comfortable than romantic. He was old-young in his way, extremely lonely, and she was undemanding.

"Do you know many girls, Shane?"

He flushed.

"No, not really."

It was the beginning of what Tennessee Williams in *Cat on a Hot Tin Roof* called mendacity.

"I'll just bet all kinds of girls have wanted you to marry them?"

Mona Henry hadn't been thinking of affairs. It wasn't in her vocabulary. They sat on the bench where the bus line turned, and Toronto seemed soft, with smoky blue light. The sounds of children playing seemed far away. House lights with a beckoning lure in the winey fall air gave off a secure and domestic feeling.

"I—well—I've been pretty busy. I've worked hard to get on and my spare time—I write a lot."

She was a shy girl who kissed him in response but never volunteered an embrace. She always felt warm in his arms, her breasts soft, and her body never tensed. He had never really caressed her.

"Shane, have you ever—well, do you feel lonely in the city?"

The question was perfectly wed to the moment.

"Sometimes, especially now when the days get longer and the lights come on in the houses, and maybe it starts to snow a bit and you look in and see people sitting around a table. You know—like parents and kids and—"

"At boarding school, I was terribly lonesome—even for my aunt—but when I went to visit her—I was lonesome for the school—and then I went in the convent—"

He knew she had no close relatives, but he was surprised by this.

"Gosh, how long were you in there?"

"Nineteen months. At first, it was wonderful with all the girls and the thought of becoming a nun—but then one day I knew I couldn't. I was just running away."

When he put his arm around her, she put her head close.

"Running away from what?"

"Me—fear of never being married—having a home of my own to live and to come back to—but mainly just to be in."

181

Later Shane was often to puzzle over what had happened then. He had said simply, "Would you marry me, Mona?"

It was unpremeditated. Mona Henry was a projection of his childhood and church and family and Father Huggins. She was the reverse of his working days and somehow he had never even thought of going to bed with her. Such a thought would in a way be profane. She was not saintly or sanctified; she was Mona Henry and she was associated with the inner light and warmth of the houses he had been looking at.

She had kissed him with the only trace of full sexuality ever displayed in their relationship. He was to remember it uneasily.

Walking home that night it was easy and comfortable to think of being married. But coming awake in the cold-edged dawn he had other thoughts!

The unending joylessness of his father. "Man's a damned fool to get married in this kind of world!"

His mother pausing at some task where her hands were occupied to use her crooked arm to push back the hair from her forehead. "Such talk in front of the children."

But she never denied it.

Then there was Uncle Matt and Aunt Olga!

He started drinking the morning after the proposal and missed work with an excuse that people accepted. That night he slept with a willing stenographer whose husband was in the navy. She escaped from bed shrilling a question.

"Shane Donovan, do you hate me or something? God, even Bill when he's been to sea for six months doesn't go at me like that."

On the third night he went to tell Mona it was no use. But he couldn't explain. Her relief at seeing him was so overwhelming that he didn't say a word about his doubts.

"Thank God, Shane. I was afraid you weren't going to come back to me."

It was a hysterical scene.

"I was at my wit's end. Father Huggins was so kind. He says he'll marry us. You do still want to marry me?"

Her lips seemed demanding and he felt guilty. Later he realized that what he thought was passion was fear and pride. In the face of it he couldn't say a word of what was troubling him.

In the little church downtown where the Italian mommas lit clustered candles and bobbed around in the gloom in their dark clothes and shawls, he poured it all out to a confessor . . .

"And I want to be good and marry this girl and forget what I have done—and—"

"Three-a Houra—Fadda—three-a—Haila—Maria—anda—maka—confezzion—"

The all-listening priest in the black guardian booth—who giva the same-a-fora venial—fora—mortal sin—did not understand and Shane knelt on saying the Houra Faddas and the Haila Marias over and over again in the hope that God could hear in English even if his earthly representative could not.

The letter from home was on a ruled sheet from a ten-cent tablet. The writing was spidery. It wished them well, hoped God would bless their marriage, and gave details of his father's kidney problem and enclosed five dollars.

He bought a bottle of Seagram's V.O. with the money.

Shane had never allowed himself to think of his marriage as an escape. And once he had raged at a suggestion made by a consultant for the agency that most men married women as mother substitutes.

Now it came back. Booze a bit and break the conventional hold and it all came back to dam up his creative stirrings. He got up and took the elevator to his room. He must forget. Draw the curtains. Pull the blinds. Strip to the buff! Try a drink. Sip a bit. Take the edge off.

He felt lacerated. He wanted to go hermit. Clam up in a shell. Lock himself up in the walls of a hotel room womb. No talk. No fight. No argument.

"It feels comfortable, Mona. It really feels secure."

He had been trying to explain after that first time when he locked himself in a hotel room in Montreal for three days.

"I know you can't or won't understand. But, please, God, try to understand."

"You just do it to torment me."

He tried to find words for it.

"It just gets to be too much. From home to Uncle Matt's— to college—to work—to getting married—and never anything I want to do. I was in a newspaper and then in advertising and—there's no way out."

But Mona couldn't understand.

"What *do* you want to do, Shane—for God's sake, what do you want? Is it being married that stops you?"

Why the hell did he evade the truth?

"I want to take life slow enough to enjoy it. To be able to have some joy in it. To really get a kick out of it—to spend a winter in Spain."

His reasoning only infuriated Mona.

"What's stopping you, may I ask? Who insisted on the cottage in Muskoka?"

She had a telling point.

How could he explain the grey, weather-beaten house in Nonsuch? The battered furniture and a place that was either too hot or too cold?

184

"People just don't pay any attention unless you are success-ful." His father moaned it as a litanical response in a prayer of hopelessness.

Mona finally answered his restlessness with a suggestion.

"Shane, I try to understand what you want, but couldn't we do it by degrees? Take six months off, say a year from now? Go up to the lake, and we can live cheaply."

They went for three months.

"Wettest season in thirty years," the old storekeeper in the resort village chuckled obscenely.

Bill developed tonsillitis. They had an anxious time in a local hospital with an elderly G.P. who told them unequivo-cally that all city people were crazy. The three months were lost sad times.

Mona didn't say anything. In time, every glance became a reproach for the piles of paper he tore up—for all the false starts. His burning anger wasn't helped by her lack of ardor.

"For Christ's sake, can't you at least pretend?"

"What do you want me to do, pretend I'm an animal? Make like a cow in heat and wake up the children?"

He slammed off into the night in the car. A rundown garage served as bootleg headquarters for the area. Here, all night with a guide, a mechanic and a local constable, he bought and drank raw whisky and talked. They listened, imperturb-ably, and put him to bed in a vacant cold and musty cabin at daylight.

Mona went back to the city. For a week he tried to write and drink and break the hellish bond. There were torrents of things to be expressed, but he couldn't capture them.

He made roaring fires in the fireplace and sat down to bring it all into focus, slowly and rationally. Then, when the images began to sort themselves out and there was a rhythm and power in his words, he found he could not get them into order. It just wouldn't work.

He retreated sick and tired and shaky to a silent home. For two weeks he tried to work in his study. It was the ultimate act, as if he must at least demonstrate that the period hadn't been wasted. He didn't drink.

They slept in the same bed as if they were miles apart, waking at the slightest touch. Then he came out of tortured dreams to hear Mona sobbing. Reaching to her, he found she turned into his chest sobbing.

"I'm sorry, Mona. I'm useless, I guess. This summer proves I don't know what I want. Can you forgive me?"

She sobbed then as if he were hurting her physically, finally calming down so that he could define what she was trying to say.

"Shane, I know I'm not the kind of wife you need—but—but—now, it's worse than ever."

"No, it's not. I'll give up this silly idea of writing and go back like a good little boy to the agency."

"But—but, Shane, I'm going to have another baby."

They were actually pleased when he came back to the agency. A bit of joshing about the Great Canadian Novel. Not much. There was too much concern for the Edson account. An American agency with local officers was making a pitch.

"Shane, those goddam carpetbaggers are up to it again. Three people in a Toronto office and they'll throw the slopover of the American production here. Write off. It's dumping!"

Edson's was an old Ontario firm. United Empire Loyalists. Several members of the family in External Affairs. Upper Canada College. Queens University. Protestant and Ontario. General Edson had been prominent during World War I. In

World War II he had been valorous in his demands for conscription.

"Surely *they* couldn't give their account to an American outfit?"

Shane couldn't believe it, but Jackman did.

"Dollar patriots. When there's competition you preach loyalty. 'Buy Canadian, support Canadian business.' When there's a dollar to be saved you preach the new North American concept. 'We're all on the same continent'—'Americans and Canadians are really alike,' 'business is business.'"

Shane felt there was more than that to the Edson story. He rummaged in files and scoured Peterborough and Kingston and found a photo of the original log cabin turned shop. A logo showing the cabin and the new Toronto headquarters and the slogan—"All Canadian for 99 years and growing stronger"—did the trick.

"I'll never get over it," admitted Jackman. "I was certain the general was convinced of the advantages of going with the Americans. How did you do it?"

"Look closely. See that outline of a face. See those buildings. Well, what does a general want—every soldier want? A monument. Now the general has a monument—a family seal as well. Those Anglo-Canadians are all alike. There's one thing America can't give them—titles and duchies. And so, while we can't either, we can give them the next best thing."

It made the agency happy. Mona appeared relaxed, even pleased.

"Maybe this summer was just a preliminary for you, Shane. Now you seem to be really working. If there's any way I can help—"

Her speeches ended with that helpless gesture.

"No, Mona. It seems to be better. You see—"

Then he would try to explain.

"I can't begin to tell you what the drives are inside me. I know I'm lucky. That's a hell of a good job at the agency. I'm always able to come up with answers. We have a nice home—enough money—"

"But that isn't enough. You should have married a smart woman—someone sexy and adventurous—someone who could understand you—"

She cried then. She cried a lot before Rita was born. But the girl did something. It made Mona more settled and easy, but terrified of having another child.

But nothing had really been settled. At times like this he knew he could not live alone, and wondered what would have happened if he had married someone not cluttered up with the same kind of bonds. A free soul? Someone to encourage him to go to Walden—to roam like Whitman—to live in Paris like Hemingway and run the bulls at Pamplona—or write all day with the intense, driving passion of Tom Wolfe and make love to Esther by night. And yet, in the centre of his self-created isolation, with his heart pumping with alcoholic enthusiasm, he knew that none of these relationships had been easy—and in his own hermetic blanketed cell of a bed he could not escape the fear that the inadequacies were within himself.

10

The city room of the *Herald* was a tacky place of small desks, people typing, talking or telephoning and constant confusion swirling around a profane, fat man with red cheeks who wore an eyeshade. He stuffed corrected copy in tubes which sucked them down to the floor below where, after a great rumbling and vibrating, copies of the newspaper appeared.

The people at the desks grabbed the copies and searched out their own work. They complained and muttered about the "sonofabitch" fat man on the desk, marked revisions and kept Shane busy running with the proofs. For this he was paid ten dollars a week. In slack times he carried coffee and cigarettes for the various reporters and editors who seemed to ignore him deliberately.

When a second boy was hired, Shane was put to work gathering material on obituaries, and the fat man with the eye-shade called him "Kid" in place of "Hey you." He learned to type with two fingers and began writing routine obituaries. He was called Donovan, when at fourteen dollars a week he covered the beat of the fire department and minor city hall offices.

When he stopped going to Mass on Sunday, Mrs. Delaney, his landlady, fretted him into it. The habit was easier than wrestling his conscience, and she gave him a better breakfast when he did go.

"I do think there is nothing better than making your peace with the Lord and having a good Sunday breakfast," she would say, shoving an extra egg on his plate.

He soon avoided Sunday dinner. Mrs. Delaney, having acquitted her responsibility to the Lord, beerily celebrated for the rest of the day in an uncorsetted way. Then, over a dinner of soggy potatoes and scorched meat, she recited the qualities of her late husband.

"A good man—a good man, Shane. Not a pillar of the Church—but a faithful man, a man who knew his rights."

Wistfully, she would murmur:

"Oh, how I do miss himself. Especially on a Sunday. We always had a bit of a nap on a Sunday afternoon and he would wake up so refreshed. I did so enjoy Sundays."

This invariably preceded her tottering off to bring in the ice cream, taken from the icebox too soon, so that it slopped like velvet soup in the dish.

When he didn't work on a Sunday, he found excuses to wander in the city. There were strange moods in Toronto on a Sunday which left him uneasily lonely. It made him pore through books with overtones of sex and violence and violent love when he went back to his room. It was a disturbing escape. When it failed, he would go into the cubicle at the office behind the piles of newsprint where the night press crews gambled, and try to write.

Sometimes, trying to prime his creativity, he copied the opening paragraph from a story by Willa Cather or Conrad, and then tried to do it in his own words. It didn't work! His characters were trite and wooden.

When he finally was given a by-line for an amusing piece on a fireman rescuing a cat he carried it for a month in his pocket. The night he mailed it to his mother he was invited to Ed Gould's for a beer.

Ed was a feature writer. The apartment was a helter-skelter arrangement of furniture presided over by Edith, the woman's editor of the rival *Standard*. It was casual and friendly. Ed was a chain-smoking asthmatic man with a paunch on an absurdly thin frame. Edith was metallic in appearance and sounded the same way because of clacking bracelets. Shane came to the uneasy realization that they lived together.

He sensed that he was being accepted in an unspoken but real way. The evening was profane, obscene, and tipsy. He learned of passes and freeloads. A convention was a cinch for a free meal and an occasional bottle. The scandal sheets were always good for a two spot for a tip on a story about the Establishment that a city editor would never let pass, because of advertising pressure or friendship with the publisher. Edith was shocked that he hadn't known about movie passes.

"You want to go to the movies, Shane? Ed, give the lad some passes. We got more passes than money between us."

The movies became his escape. He was a slave to the world of James Cagney, Edward G. Robinson, Clark Gable, Spencer Tracy, and the stars of everything from musicals to

Grand Hotel. It was a place where Mrs. Delaney, Nonsuch and Olga didn't exist. Then he was asked to join the Press Club.

There was a camaraderie in the Press Club. Old-timers played cribbage and drank beer and treated everything irreverently. The world was an easier place in the yawning hours of morning when you walked in the stilted comfort of an alcoholic fog.

Once after three o'clock he entered the hallway of the Delaney home, and sensed that someone was there.

"Oh, Shane, I was worried about you."

Mrs. Delaney was standing in the doorway of the sitting room. She was outlined through her nightgown by the street lamp.

"Oh, I—I was just talking."

Shane raced up the stairs, to undress in the dark and go to bed.

In a rare letter from his mother, the inky words splotched by a nib on a sheet from a school exercise book, he heard the news of his father, locked into a perpetual spine-bent question mark by the "artritis," but, "poor soul is spared the pain." He couldn't feel anything but after sitting in Family Court his copy was vicious. Joe Simpson, the night copy editor, sent it back and said to soften it. Joe was a recluse who worked and lived mysteriously alone with a police dog.

"You're nineteen—almost twenty, Shane, and you're letting the world beat the hell out of you. It will eventually. It does that to all sensitive people, but for Christ's sake, don't rush it. At least, you can write. These other losers just talk about it."

Once, late at night when the city room was quiet except for the duty editor, Simpson beckoned him into a cubicle, poured rye in paper cups with water from the cooler and talked.

"Listen to the way people speak, and watch them, and write. Try reading books—and I mean *reading*—not just for stories but for rhythm and tone—light and shade. And try poetry—read it aloud—and write."

He stressed the writing.

"No one knows where the urge comes from. You can't live with it. You can't live without it. But if you let it slip away without a fair chance, you'll never be happy. When you get to be a certain age, you'll find that's all you'll have to look back on."

His voice caught and he handed a small volume to Shane. *Night Drifting* by Joseph L. Simpson. On the inside flap leaf it read: *To Shane. Don't give up. Joe Simpson.*

Shane had started to worry about Mrs. Delaney.

He accepted beer once or twice. She fussed over him. One night she came to sit on the edge of his bed. Her hair was neat. Her bathrobe was cleanly laundered and she talked, as she smoothed at his covers with her hands.

"God, but it's lonely!"

It was a cry. There were tears on her face and for the first time he realized that she was tortured.

"Shane, I envy those people who can do anything they want and not be bothered by it. I'm—"

She left finally, and he lay in the sweat of chill and cold, curious fear. Next morning, she was asleep on the chesterfield, snoring and sprawled with her clothes bundled up around her waist. On the floor there was an empty whisky bottle.

That day he moved to a house that smelled of garlic. He had a small room that was like a prison cell. The house was a way station for Italian immigrants who arrived from overseas and couldn't speak English. They left in pickup trucks early in the morning, and returned covered with plaster and dirt late at night. Most of them snored. They grinned at him, vanished after a few weeks and were replaced by others.

Shane again fled to the streets, but they were lonely and he couldn't write. There were times when even routine assignments on the paper became difficult. He was lonely. Blue, dark loneliness! He avoided Joe Simpson.

He moved to the Frontier Arms on the strength of a promotion to fifty dollars a week and the chance to write features. War had been declared and staff were hard to get. The hotel, a converted apartment building, housed newspapermen, their wives or girlfriends, CBC artists, a few free-lance writers, call girls, strippers, and a drunken novelist who earned booze and bread money writing scripts for the CBC.

"Shane," Brian Burns would say on a midnight visit to scrounge liquor, "keep up the writing. It's bloody hard but in the long run, nothing else matters."

Thoughts of Julius haunted Shane. He forced himself to write about the cadger joining the Army and becoming a regimental sergeant-major in charge of supplies.

"It's not bad writing but you don't know bugger-all about the Army," commented Burns. "Write about something you know about or else join the Army."

Shane was so furious he spent a weekend writing about Nonsuch. Burns, sober because as he said he "needed booze and bread," read it carefully.

"I can *smell* that prairie place. The bootlegging Chinaman and the old priest co-operating to fool the welfare people. And, boy, can I tell you something. This will sell. I'll give it to my agent and he'll sell it. But don't be fooled. You can write better than that, but you've got to dig inside yourself. Get your feelings out in the open. You're hedging. The words are good. You have style, but there's got to be heart. I'm a whore with words. You don't have to be."

It sold to an obscure syndicate for two hundred dollars, and Shane decided to pay his friends back with a party. The party began with Ed Gould, Joe Simpson, and Brian Burns; soon people he didn't know wandered in. The entire floor came alive. They drank and sang, and he had a faint feeling of dancing with a girl who hugged him very close as a man played an accordion.

Shane came awake in Laverne's room. She was a wardrobe mistress for a burlesque theatre. His head ached and the room smelled close and foul. Laverne, curled up beside him on the bed, was snoring.

"Kid."

She came awake as he searched for cigarettes.

"Yeah?"

She looked tired with pouchy bags under her eyes.

"Give me a cigarette. God, I've got a mouth. See if there's a beer left out there."

In the half light from the little dusty windows they sipped warm beer.

"Shane. That's your name, isn't it? Well, I want to tell you something. Stop wasting your time."

"I'm not wasting my life. I like people like you."

She sat up in bed, covering herself with a blanket.

"I'm just an old dancer. Busted marriage, and a kid almost as old as you in boarding school. I know you. You're scared. That's why you hang out with people like us."

"What's wrong with that?"

"Nothing if you were a Rockefeller—but last night—my God, you had every freeloader in Toronto on your tab. Why?"

"I like people, I guess."

"Oh, come off it. There's something griping you. You drink as if it were going out of style, buy drinks for people and then let that tongue of yours cut their hearts out. A happy guy doesn't do that. Besides, you know why you're here. I brought you up here because that hooker in 1A had her eyes on you. Shane, you nit, all you would need now is to pick something up from that slut."

He moved, quit the *Herald*, and for four months wrote and mailed stories to magazines. *Maclean's* magazine paid him ten dollars for one short item. That was it. In desperation he enlisted, only to be told by the Army doctors he was rejected because of a tricky heart muscle.

"Probably never bother you in your entire life," the medic said, "but it rules you out here."

The brown-eyed CWAC who typed up his card was friendly.

"Come back and see me when you join up," she smiled, as he moved into the undressing area. When he came out her smile was gone.

"Some people have pull, like on newspapers. Too good to fight."

She said it to the girl at the next desk when he loitered. He went out into the bright sunshine, hating the sight of men in uniform. That's what he told Brian, who tolerated him for four days of a protracted drinking bout. His money ran out and he was sick. At that point Brian suggested he straighten up.

"You've had a fling, but that's enough. Don't beat yourself any more. Get cleaned up and eat something. When you feel better, I'll send you over to see Jackman. He needs some writers in his agency."

He was despondent.

"Oh, hell, I think I'll go and work in construction. They're building Army camps."

Burns wouldn't let him.

"Don't be a damned fool. You've got to learn a lot. You go

up and down emotionally like a teeter-totter. Try writing copy. It pays well; and you can keep on at your own stuff. I think you get bombed to escape. Well, take it from an old hand. You can't escape. It catches up, and you have to face that devil sooner or later. But that's enough cheap psychiatric advice—you stir your ass over and see Jackman—and get a job because I have to entertain my girlfriend this week before she leaves."

"She leaves?"

"Yeah, she's in the Wrens and is getting posted to Halifax or maybe overseas. How about that?"

"Doesn't it bother you?"

"You mean, like not being a soldier or something? Not a damned bit. My old man got his at Vimy Ridge—and I have no desire for a hero's grave. I'm a professional coward."

It shocked Shane, but he went to see Jackman.

Thomas Alva Jackman was a small-time newspaperman who shifted from a beat to writing political speeches for a hopeful Prime Minister of Ontario. He inherited the province's tourist advertising as a patronage plum after the election. The agency was formed to handle the business.

"I grew into advertising," he was fond of telling Shane, "and I want class. Want our output to be several cuts above the average. Quality!"

In the crowded office quarters they worked in tandem. Jackman was accessible. Shane enjoyed it. The only fly in the ointment was Alf Bates, a rabbity, aggressive little man.

"I think we're expanding too fast, T.A."

It was the constant reproach of Bates.

"Don't mind him, Shane," Jackman said. "Alf is a kind of ballast. Keeps my feet on the ground."

Jackman had placed his hands over those of Shane and Edna Staples.

"I know who my friends are."

Edna Staples was T.A.'s woman. The real Mrs. Jackman was a shadowy creature no one could really identify. Now and then a shrill complaining voice on the telephone demanded to know the whereabouts of her husband. Office gossip said she was an alcoholic. Certainly, Jackman went home as little as possible.

Shane liked Edna. Old-fashioned, in a sense, with her hair drawn back in a knot. Ivory skin. Business suits and blouses with an emerald pin. T.A. had bought the pin on their one trip together to Mexico. It was her talisman.

He worked and found satisfaction and then he met Tom Huggins. Father Tom of St. Peter's. A gaunt, grey man with a long face who had come to a Catholic vocation by way of the Anglican priesthood.

"Mr. Jackman said you might need some help in your campaign for a downtown recreation place for servicemen."

The study was marked with the untidiness of a person who loves books.

"Mr. Donovan, I need help, period! I have this idea, and I'm afraid I'm not the world's best organizer."

There were conferences in the study, while Shane grew more enthusiastic. There were meetings when plump businessmen nodded their agreement that our "fighting men" should be given their very best.

"Yes, Mr. Abrams," Father Huggins had said, "this is a place for all servicemen and women. Black, white, and yellow. Christian and Jew and Mohammedan if we have them. God didn't place priorities on man. Man made the silly system of priorities. It must be interdenominational."

A warehouse was transformed into Canteen Toronto.

Later, drinking coffee with the priest, Shane said: "You sound different from our old priest at home."

Huggins nodded.

"Faith is a personal thing and as I grow older I am more and more inclined to feel salvation is for anyone with the strength to believe, period. That's not to say I haven't had trouble with the Chancery office over the canteen. I suspect some of them down there still feel I am more Reformation than Catholic."

He never asked Shane about his own church attendance.

Shane was writing copy for propaganda, from recruiting to the wartime control of prices, and could never quite eliminate a sense of guilt about not being in uniform.

"Are you in the services?"

People often asked him, and if they were strangers he would shrug his shoulders and say, "Well, you can't wear a uniform all the time."

The staff tripled. More and more older men and young women were being hired. Shane had never thought of Jackman taking a partner. Edna was the one who told him about Bates.

"T.A. is taking Bates on as partner. He needs someone who is business oriented so he can devote more time to the creative side. You know, of course, he depends on you, and now more than ever."

She looked uncomfortable. He half-heartedly reassured her.

"Sure—sure—I understand."

But he had never really understood why Jackman hadn't told him personally.

He went to the Press Club early that day. He drank heavily, and stayed in his room on the pretext of writing. He was on the verge of sickness when Jackman came to see him.

"You seem to be in bad shape!"

Shane realized he was unshaven and unsteady. The fear of losing his job was a jolt. One hundred and fifty dollars a week. It was a lot of money.

"Mr. Jackman, I've been feeling lousy and dosing myself up—and finally I just gave up—"

The idea came.

"But it's not all wasted. I've been thinking about that English firm—you know, Bristol Associates—the one that has no product but wants to be remembered in Canada."

Jackman responded.

"I hope it's better than Joe Alexander's idea of simply running their name in white on black each week."

Shane was formulating an idea as he talked.

"If I wanted to keep my name in the Canadian market, I would have to give a reason. Now, that reason would have to be associated with the war effort in some way or other."

"Agreed."

"Okay, each week Bristol Associates, says in its advertising —sorry, we're still busy fighting Hitler and we can't give you our regular—you know—but we thought you'd like to know how our regular customers, here in Britain, who also do without—you know—how they are also fighting. Then a yarn about the war—just three or four sentences—sometimes funny. Like the old lady—Scotch—who said when the air raid siren goes she reads the 23rd Psalm—says a wee prayer—takes a drop of whisky—gets into bed and pulls up the covers—and then she tells Hitler to go to hell and she goes to sleep!"

Jackman exploded . . .

"It's great—wonderful—"

Jackman appeared to forget Shane's absence from the office. Bristol bought the idea.

It was a close call. Shane had never quite been able to rationalize his job without admitting he might never have had it if there had been no war. The war would be over. What would happen when the men came back?

At lunch Jackman studied the ash on his cigar.

"I do not meddle in the lives of my employees. But you are closer than an employee. You should be married. Find a nice girl who understands you. It will give you peace of mind."

Shane tried to explain.

"There is a girl, T.A. Maybe it's the thought of marrying that's upsetting me. There are days when I want to—and then I get really—almost frightened."

Jackman laughed.

"Just a bit halter shy. I know what it's like. Father Huggins tells me she is a really nice girl and you'll make a grand couple."

He said it with the air of a potentate dispensing a fair judgement. Marriage hadn't worked for him, but it was perfect for Shane.

The city was a jungle of lonely caged people, filled with rages. The people around were insecure in themselves.

"Had lunch with the old man?"

"Got some big deal working, eh?"

It was fear. Fear was something he knew as well. Fear of doing the wrong thing. Fear of walking into a place where he didn't know anyone. Gut boring fear that evolved through anger to belligerence.

It was lonely. He felt he was barely tolerated at the agency. His friend O'Hare confirmed it.

"They're hacks working at jobs over their heads. They're in those jobs because of the war, and already, even with no victory in sight, they're worrying about what will happen."

O'Hare was pessimistic.

"It will take this country at least a generation to clear these bastards out. The press and broadcasting and maybe even government is clogged—or will be clogged with the rejects."

Shane bristled.

"Like myself."

"Oh, don't be a horse's ass. You know your capacities. No. I mean those toss-penny warehouse sorters and life insurance salesmen who have managed to get in. They'll move along. Dear old vested interest and seniority will see to that. They'll be seniors and their main tasks will be to keep everything as mediocre as possible. For God's sake, don't ever compromise yourself with those twits."

He came to radio because a script writer was incapable of doing what was wanted in a dramatic script for a commercial radio series.

"Those characters don't seem right, Al."

The pudgy florid little man who called himself a poet had a contempt for radio.

"Does it really matter?"

"What the hell do you mean?"

"Well, really, who really listens to radio—I mean, who is there that cares?"

Shane flared.

"Well if that's your attitude, why are you doing it?"

"The fee, old boy. My serious interest is poetry."

"It is, eh? Too bad no one has a serious interest in your poetry."

The writer flushed, but recovered to smile sardonically.

"Shane, I write this crap to make money. If you don't like it, there are plenty of other places that do. Every government department is screaming for it."

Donovan had to restrain himself from tossing the script in the writer's face.

"Okay, we'll pay you for this, and that's that."

Two hours later the producer called for the script. Shane, in all-night vigil, produced the script. He was unsure of technical problems but wrote in a form that he thought would work.

"Say, Mr. Donovan, who wrote this script?"

Donovan was wary.

"Oh, a new fellow called John Ross."

The producer laughed on the telephone.

"It must be one of the good CBC writers—like for *Stage* —slumming, because this is really good."

"He was a little concerned about not knowing enough about the technical side."

"Who cares. It plays beautifully. Get me some more of those and I'll get you a good series."

The excess energy, the worries and fears and frustrations were lost now as he began to spend evenings and weekends writing. He had a radio on constantly. News from overseas, plays, music, and drama, mostly from CBC, gave him a new insight. He began to study scripts by Norman Corwin and Arch Oboler. This form of expression suited him, and he had less desire for boozing companionship.

Father Huggins was a constant listener and friendly critic.

"You are very expressive, and I suggest you are a moralist."

"Hardly."

"Oh, yes, there are signs of—oh, less ordered and tidy than people with long and involved educations—but a searching mind. Perhaps a quest for moral values. A poetic sense—yet, hound of heaven overtones."

At the agency the process bothered him. T.A. was a hawk sitting at the head of the table. His eyes ranged around the table—assessing and perhaps wondering how he had ended up with this assortment of people. Edna was pledged to him, and it was more binding than marriage.

Alfred Bates. Bald and rabbit-toothed. His position was secure because he knew the secrets of figures, and he would keep it that way at all cost.

"People want to get their minds off the war. I suggest we give them glimpses of the pleasant side of things. What they're fighting for."

That was the sum total of Chuck Hanning. Tall and tweedy and an avowed Anglophile, his visions were of lawns rolled for five hundred years, dogs, horses, and gin breakfasts.

"Terrific—terrific! Boy, Shane, you really pack it in. We can do a wonderful job with this."

Hal Wynett took his cue from T.A. What T.A. liked, Hal raved about. If T.A. didn't like it, Hal would shake his head and look gloomy. Hal had no ideas. He was a pilot fish that stayed under the belly of the shark.

After sessions like that Shane roamed the night streets. He had a country boy's fascination for the city by night. There was power here. He was fascinated by the traffic and the clanging streetcars, the people always moving, the restaurants and bars and the sweaty smell of beery people from the doors of pubs. There were the fat houses of Rosedale of another time and place, and the transformed houses where landlords packed in students and office workers and found ways of cheating on wartime rent controls.

There was irony about the way he met Mona Henry. A blind date. He was to keep her occupied because Howie wanted an hour alone in the one room apartment Mona was temporarily sharing with his girlfriend.

"Please, Shane, just keep her busy until twelve-thirty."

Time passed so slowly in the restaurant. The waiter was glowering.

"I must go back, Margaret will be worried."

"Oh, just walk a bit with me. I'm lonely to talk with someone."

His story had fascinated her. She listened without offering arguments or analysis. While they walked along Bloor her hand clutched his arm.

"I've got a good job. It pays well—damned well—for a guy my age. I feel guilty because a lot of the chance came because so many guys are at war—but the job was there—and what I can't figure out is why I get so discouraged."

He told her about Nonsuch and the pattern of his family life. He had made it—but he hadn't studied hard and persevered in the classic way of getting ahead and—

"Maybe that's why I'm upset. I've got the ideas, and all the guys who made it with degrees and business training sit there and look stupid in a crisis and I say I won't help. But something moves me and I let the idea fly and it works, and the funny thing is you've saved their necks and they still hate you . . . or perhaps resent is a better word."

It was the first time he had ever admitted the resentment. There were social games he couldn't play. Alfred Bates had a wife with Old Toronto connections. White, Anglo-Saxon Protestant school and her father had connections in the Tory clubs—and Jackman from Cabbagetown was admitted to the Civitas Club shortly after the partnership.

"Go on, please. It's fascinating. I must say I always thought people who got important jobs were ever so clever."

"Sure, some are, but it's a game to a lot. A guy like me comes in determined to make or break and he finds out he's doing it but not according to the old boy rules. Like doctors keeping Jews or blacks out of medicine—or Orientals. Screen 'em out with tests or trickery, but some guys are just too smart or work so hard they have to let them through. They're the best you can find—but they have to be loners. The old boy club won't have them. They'll never be really admitted."

"Are you bitter?"

"Oh, I don't know. The ones that bother me are the guys who develop the protective armour. Flatter the president, play yes men or engage in paper warfare. God, but they are something. I always believed that this type of person ended up in government but there's just as many or more in private business. I sound bitter, I guess, maybe I am. I don't know. It does me good to talk and you're a good listener."

He had gone to Mona for something he couldn't put into words. Mona was different, and he was lonely. Mona had asked, "What do you really want to do?"

He had told her what he wanted to do. Remembering those times before he had asked her to marry him, he was certain he had explained.

But now, as so often before, he realized that Mona didn't understand his need. He had accepted her listening as understanding.

He would take a shower and call Mona and ask her to bring Bill and Rita down for the awards. That was the maddening part—he had no other answers. Maybe, just maybe, with the money he might persuade her. Oh hell, a shower was more important than anything.

11

Like so many others Shane had come somewhat reluctantly
to realize what being a Canadian meant. His reading and his
education created a dichotomy. There was adventure in
American literature and a dull sense of British indifference
about his education. A teacher reluctantly waded through a
perfunctory list of Canadian poets but came alive when
Browning, Keats, or Shelley was on the menu.

America, Oh America!

It was natural to wallow in Thomas Wolfe after a baptism
in the extravagance of Whitman.

There was dust and hard times in Nonsuch. But he hadn't
stopped to consider or realize that American towns were just
as dreary—because to him they were all Tombstone or Abi-
lene or Dodge City.

There was a stirring inside himself to be a writer—but especially a Canadian writer. He sensed that Mona regarded it as something he must exorcise himself of. Her benedictions on his work were elaborate.

"Now you do what you have to, and I'll see that Bill doesn't disturb you."

Shane tried. God, how he tried. Read something. Write a letter. Pace. Try to dredge from his subconscious the idea that had rattled around when they were discussing the soap account.

"Oh, I don't want to disturb you, but how long do you think you will be?"

"Why?"

"I promised to help at the church and Billy is such a nuisance there and I thought he wouldn't disturb you here—"

The process was so hellish he didn't really mind, so he gave in when his son, tired of playing, wanted to try the typewriter. Later he felt it had been another of Mona's subconscious attempts to break his writing. A psychiatrist suggested all writers' wives were enemies of their husband's work.

"Mona, can I just explain what writing means to me?"

"But, Shane, I know it's important to you. You don't have to explain."

He had to try.

"Mona, it's important that you understand. There's something in me—some goddam thing I have to get out—something to say I need to say and—"

"Shane, it's a world I don't understand. I want to, but I can't. I feel sorry for you—all those people who have the urge, and they end up so disastrously—like—well—"

She floundered then, but he knew the scourge. There were writers who drank, and Gauguin had run off to the South Seas —and Christ, maybe he should cut off an ear.

"Oh, for God's sake, all writers don't end up as nuts—or on dope—or—"

So he had chosen to travel for the agency. It had been easy to convince Jackman that with the war over someone should become reacquainted with the country. Make contacts and see how Canada was adjusting.

At first it was an escape. Jackman called him a roving Canadian ambassador. But some things happened. In a stand of centuries-old trees, in a memorial park on Vancouver Island smelling of damp and rotting wood and age, he had stood in the silence of centuries.

Years—centuries of growing. The woman from the Vancouver office had been watching his face.

"Mr. Donovan, I wish you could see yourself. You're a study."

He knew.

"Hilary, I can't help it. I simply can't. There are times when the feel of this country simply overwhelms me. It's corny."

She hadn't said anything then, but on the ferry back to the mainland from Nanaimo, she put her hand over his resting on the boat rail.

"You're not corny. I feel the same way. When I simply get sick at what the politicians and businessmen are doing to beautiful Vancouver I go over to Long Beach or up to see those wonderful real people in the Caribou . . . or refresh myself with the only dignity left in North America, amongst my Indian friends."

Flying back over the Rockies, he thought of her kissing him at the airport. A slim woman with a natural tan and steady brown eyes.

"Shane, you're too sensitive a man to spend your life in that world. Come out here and get a place where the ocean will talk to you. Write about those things you have inside you."

He had talked a lot. She worked part time for the company and had driven him around. For three days on the island he had discovered a certain tranquility, in the world of coastal Indians, wise and gentle people who deplored the ravages of the lumbering interests.

"You should be writing about places and people like this. This is the real Canada."

It had been so peaceful in Stanley Park. Down below him were the Banff, Jasper, Kootenay, and Yoho parks. Farther on were the Waterton Lakes, but a fellow passenger had spoiled it by pointing out the ugly mess near Crow's Nest Pass where they were tearing out the coal to send to Japan.

He met a large, determined man called John Davidson, a returned expatriate trying to batter with his tongue at the CBC and make them re-realize why they were a state-subsidized communications system.

"Because, Mr. Donovan, if they don't, this country will be lost. It's enormous and it's hard and it needs airlines and railroads and broadcasting to let the tough, hard people know they're in it together. This is a country where you don't take chances or you die. You gotta know about slob ice before you take off in a dory or you gotta know the weather before you drive off across the prairie in the winter. If you don't you may never get where you're going."

He went on: "That Cariboo cowboy shoving a horse to his belly in snow to get a mother and calves out of the snow knows the same feeling as a prairie farmer combining wet wheat before the frost grabs the gumbo."

The big man clasped his hands like a priest giving benediction.

"There are voices in this country that must be heard and

they range from wise, old men who put out in dories from Newfoundland tickles to brawny, young bastards with strange-sounding names blasting at the guts of the rocky earth under Sudbury. The voices come from old radicals in Saskatchewan and from idealistic young teachers living in squalor in Toronto—and we must listen. Why? Because they know and love this country more than they love the treachery of money which pretends internationalism but believes in greed."

Shane had fallen in love with Canadian names, even if the idea came from a Benét poem. He learned a litany of Tatamagouche, Kamloops, Squamish, Shubenacadie, Piapot, Assiniboine, Gatineau, Inuvik, and Trois Pistoles.

"I'm bloody angry," he exclaimed one day to a university teacher turned into a computer-like executive of a timber company busily raping northern Ontario forests, "You were the people who could have taught generations about Samuel de Champlain, D'Iberville, Radisson, Marquette, and Joliet and how they loved this bloody country instead of Wolfe and how he buggered up poor old Montcalm on the Plains of Abraham."

But the smooth man smiled. "Does it really matter? We're all Americans at heart."

It was a close call. They almost lost the account, but the president of the American corporation was a former Canadian and in a sense seemed to feel Shane's impatience.

Once he came home from a meeting in Chicago, determined to find a way to make Canadians feel their essential difference.

"Mona, it's the law. We are people who live by different laws. Chicago is a city that's still controlled by brigands and gamblers and whores, but our West never started that way.

We've got Johnny Chinook and Twelve Foot Davis and Bob Edwards—and that's what we should be pushing."

Mona seemed puzzled. The advertising manager of the soap company was polite but practical.

"Shane, I know how you feel but, look, we can buy spots in syndicated American shows and—hell, you should be talking to the provincial ministers of education about your ideas. We can't afford to be Canadian crusaders."

Afterwards in Montreal, the Chicago man, now Hollywood-oriented, insisted on girls. They had to be French-Canadian.

The Man! From being a too-garishly dressed loud talker from the Midwest he had gone show-biz with a vengeance. Suite at the Ritz-Carlton, and a retinue of assistants including Izzy, a tired-eyed little publicity man who hadn't made it as a screen writer. Izzy was at the Man's beck and call.

"Izzy, get me a couple of French-Canadian pros. No cheap street stuff."

In time Izzy produced two girls with shiny black hair, enamelled false-teeth smiles, black satin skirts that appeared to be painted on their twitching backsides, and brassiere cups sticking out like bumps in their too-frilly blouses.

They sat in the anteroom, smoked cigarettes and looked bored. The suite swirled with people; in the centre of it all the Man kept making long-distance calls. One of the girls demanded of Shane, "When do we go to work?"

The Man, a phone at his ear, laughed, "Tell them to keep the meters running. I'll use them both when I want them."

They were window dressing. Shane was disgusted.

"Why don't you girls go home," he said to them, "I'll get the man to pay you."

The smallest one with the thinnest legs and the most obviously Woolworth bosom, who seemed to be having trouble keeping her teeth in place, looked worried.

"The little man said to stay. Mister, we're hungry."

Shane escorted them to one of the bedrooms and ordered the most expensive meal he could—pâté de foie gras, steak with truffles right through to zabaglione—with Pommard and liqueurs and added 25 percent tip—signing the Man's name.

He left feeling better. The Man, who by now had taken the route of all Hollywood neophytes in trying to "swing a deal" to make a series on the Royal Canadian Mounted Police, was later knocked off by the House Un-American Activities Committee.

There was a full attendance the day young Simpson made his initial appearance at an agency meeting. He had a small account, but it qualified him for the creative meeting. He was feeling important.

"I see Johnny Canuck records as the beginning of a major thing in this country."

Polite interest. Jackman pointed his hawk face. Alf Bates shrugged his shoulders.

"Mr. Simpson, it is an account we took—well, God knows why."

Jackman purred.

"Alf, we took it because there is a movement that way these days. Canadian books—artistic things—and those young fellows rather appealed to me."

Joe Anderson, who represented the Kaloni people simply by placing their American ads in Canadian media, jumped in. His Florida-tanned face was flushed as he leaned over the table.

"I get tired of all this hogwash about Canadianism. Who the hell wants to listen to Canadian records, and for that matter Canadian artists? If they're any good, they go to the United States. Let's face it, we don't have any culture. We're pseudo-Americans."

That flared Katie Randier, half French-Canadian and half Irish.

"Joe, if you're so stuck on Americans, why don't you go there and leave us alone?"

Anderson mumbled. "That's easier said than done."

It raged on while Bill Simpson looked confused.

"Just look at what's happening in America and you'll realize why we want to stay separate."

"Americans are so rude. They're the real imperialists! From the Philippines to the Dominican Republic to Vietnam they're an arrogant bunch of new Romans—and they're falling on their asses and I'm delighted."

"They're not so bad . . . as visitors, but I'd sure hate to live with them."

"My sister says living in Washington is like living in mediaeval time. They're locked up in apartments that are like fortresses with guards and dogs."

"My sister says you mustn't drive in Chicago, even on the hottest days, without the doors locked and windows up."

"Downtown Detroit is a jungle. You feel safe on the Windsor side just looking across the river. I used to go over twice a week but do you know I haven't been in Detroit in five years?"

It was all there, exposed like raw nerve ends thrashing on the boardroom table. The dilemma of twenty-two million people living next door to the most powerful nation in the world. Their country was disregarded by their neighbors except as a source of raw materials (an increasingly important source, as they profligately wasted their own) and they were regarded as the somewhat backward inhabitants of a great space which might some day be useful for *Lebensraum*.

Jackman smiled at Simpson.

"See what you started, Bill? The great dilemma of Canada. Are we a people or not—or are we just pale Americans?"

He used his hands as if demonstrating an open and unresolved problem.

"Shane, you've been quiet!"

"Yes, I was just on Vancouver Island—Port Alberni, Campbell River, Nanaimo—and do you know what people there say? They say—stop selling us short. We are here and we like it and we're not Americans. God Almighty, go out and see the people at Banff—or Edmonton or Brandon—or go down to Truro in Nova Scotia. They think we're nuts with our newspapers and broadcasting talking about identity. Like a woman in Vancouver who said "I was born here—I've stayed here— I am going to stay here—I'm a Canadian—and for damned sure I'm not an American.""

Anderson was sarcastic.

"I wondered how long it would be before your American bias showed."

Jackman intervened.

"A difference of opinion is healthy. Mr Simpson, you might spend some time with Mr. Donovan. He—ah—feels very strongly about these things and, oh, you might talk to Mr. Anderson about the possibility of an American market—he— ah—has had a lot of experience in American marketing."

The message from Mona said they were invited to the Allens' that evening. It marked recognition of his steady period. After a reasonable time of behaviour, he noticed a pickup in invitations accepted by Mona.

It made him angry. He slammed some papers in his briefcase and left.

"Miss Wilkins, I've got some reading to do."

Miss Wilkins fluttered like a bespectacled moth.

It was 4:30 and Shane put his briefcase in the car and walked over to the Frontier Arms. He hadn't been in the place for years. George, the bartender, welcomed him like an old friend.

"Mr. Donovan, where have you been?"

Peter DeLucca, the night editor, was in a corner reading. Marge, the beauty counsellor, who never lasted without a drink to four o'clock, and John London Russell, the bass-voiced free-lance announcer, were nit-picking about the role of women.

Shane was aware at times like these of how much he liked talk for the sake of talk. There were questions about his work, and time went on and he made half-hearted attempts to leave, but someone was always buying a new round of drinks.

"Boy, the times we used to have when you were free, white, and twenty-one—"

"Marge, I'll never forget that time you were out of town and your sister came in the apartment and found me asleep in your bed—"

"God, she was sure I was a fallen woman then—"

Marge was an overripe woman but as he drank she became softly beautiful. Peter DeLucca borrowed five dollars and it was like old times.

"Say, Mr. Donovan, that's a great idea. Can we talk to you some time about it?"

The young television producer had heard some of Shane's radio plays. He had read one of his stories.

It was easy to feel that this was a place of idealism. These were the men and women who persisted against the callousness of men who managed for the sake of management or power, or money—the men who had forgotten how to live.

Big Ed, the burly cartoonist stopped scribbling obscene and offensive things about prominent people to tackle him.

"Donovan, why in Christ's name do you screw away your time in that agency? Why don't you come and work on the paper? We need writers, and not those automated little jerks that get popped out like slices of toast each year from journalism school."

The old hungers came back on Shane.

"That's what I'm going to do. Finish off my debts this year and try some writing for real. I've got a lot to say. Want to write a play."

The dreams spun on and the time went by and people came and went and finally when George closed the bar there was only Marge and himself.

There was still the Café de Paris. It had a license for food and liquor until one. It was jammed. There were more drinks, and food barely tasted. Marge drove him home.

"Are you okay?"

No reproach. Just a sound of care.

"Sure, but I'll have to get my car."

"You don't need your car. Now get going before your wife sees me driving you."

Three o'clock in the morning and he was sitting in his own living room still wearing his overcoat when Mona came down the stairs. He was in the ambiguous world where remorse and guilt were mixed with the swaggering, all-conquering phase of talk and drink. The freedom of people who did what they wanted still affected him.

"Mona, it's no use. I can't go on this way. I feel strangled. Spending all my life trying to cope with bastards like Anderson. I'm dying and I've got to find some way of expression better than by advertising."

Mona was annoyed.

"You never seem to feel for me. Having to call and tell the Allens a lie about you having to work. They knew. I could tell that. Said for me to come over anyhow. I was tempted to—"

"Why didn't you?"

Tears in a flurry.

"Is that what you want? Me to go alone? I can't lie to friends or neighbours any more."

He eased out the door and walked until a passing cab answered his signal.

Marge Lawson lived in a walk-up. It was a renovated house in Rosedale, a section which resisted high rises but not landlords who carved up old mansions for rent.

"Shane—what . . . come in."

Blond hair streaming down . . . heavy make-up in patches. He knew the tiny apartment with the hide-away chesterfield that was always a bed. There was a tiny kitchen and an oversize bathroom with Victorian fixtures, including a pull-chain toilet.

"Did I get you out of bed?"

Marge grinned.

"Hell, no. I couldn't sleep."

There was a glass beside the swivel chair and a still-burning cigarette.

"Couldn't sleep. Jittery. Too much booze, I guess. Want a drink? Got beer or gin."

Marge bunched the pillows against the wall. He sat in the chair. The beer tasted good.

"Get so bloody fed up—Marge, the years go by and I work and it means less and less. Everything in the place I can do—so why don't I go and do something else?"

She was a good listener. He liked Marge, with a feeling of something like sadness for her.

"I should be married to you, Marge."

She grimaced.

"Guys like you never are. Possessions mean nothing to me. A trip to Venice would be more important than a dining-room suite. That's what you guys say you want, but you always end up with girls like the ones in the Johnson wax ads."

"Why?"

"God knows. Maybe it's the old thing about opposites. There's something inside me that kind of aches when I see someone like you—smart as paint—burning up."

"What about you?"

"Hmph. I'm not important. I get by. I was married once. Man with a mother and religion. Jesus God—drove me up a tree. I left. Walked out."

"That takes nerve."

"Maybe. I haven't had regrets. I've been all over—Paris—London—the whole bit—but now it gets lonely at night. You don't know a rich harmless old man who would like to live in Spain?"

She went for more drinks. Her bathrobe was disarranged. Her body was soft.

"Maybe, Marge, my problem is that I haven't had the adventure. I jumped from being a boy to a man and got married and I've got this power of words and urge to write—and not very much to write about."

Marge was sympathetic.

"Couldn't you persuade your wife to—well, go along with you?"

(Mona wouldn't argue, but she travelled as if it were an ordeal. "We don't know those people. They're just being polite and I don't know what to say.")

Marge crawled under the covers.

"Boy, I sure know the problem. My husband! God, his idea of adventure was to polish the car Sunday morning and then drive out to someplace like Richmond Hill—and come home and polish the car again. There we rode—him and me in the front and old dragon lady—his mother—in the back seat scolding because I hadn't gone to church in the morning."

He finally slept on the bed beside Marge. When he woke from a dream and began shaking she soothed him in her arms.

"Marge, you're the one I should be married to."

"Don't say it. It probably wouldn't have worked in the beginning. We're both beat up enough now to be tolerant."

He watched her in the morning transform herself from relaxed blousiness to a girdled, attractive, somewhat matronly womanliness.

"See how you put the pieces together! I wonder how long I can do it, Shane."

She was at the doorway pulling on her gloves, peeking in the mirror.

"Marge, is there any place you really want to go?"

"Sure, I would like to go out that door and catch a plane to New Orleans. Mardi Gras starts in two days."

That, simply, was how they went to Mardi Gras.

It was easy.

"T.A., I've got a case of nerves. I shouldn't have blown up at Anderson. Toronto in February had touched me."

Mona was silent.

"I've got to get away. If I don't, the old booze bit will be back on me. There's work to be done in New Orleans."

She remained stoic even as he left.

"You'll at least let us know where you are?"

The thought of Mona and the children stabbed him all the way to the airport. Marge was waiting.

"It doesn't look very good, does it?"

He picked up the first-class tickets. Toronto to Chicago by Air Canada. Delta from O'Hare to New Orleans.

"Oh, to hell with it."

They were settled and the stewardess brought drinks.

"You don't mind if we—well, bunk together?"

She patted his hand.

"Shane, it's whatever you say. Are you sure it may not hurt you—if somebody—?"

"I'm at that stage where—well, I want you with me."

It was Mardi Gras time and New Orleans was mad and rowdy. When the gala was over, there were days of wandering in the French Quarter. It was an adventure. They met Al Hirt and kept going back to the Original Dixieland Hall. At breakfast at Brennan's on Sunday morning he became intensely aware of Marge.

"My God, woman, something has happened to you. You look like a little girl—at a party."

She blushed.

"You're a good tonic. Maybe in place of all the goo and guck I prescribe for beauty to frustrated females I should simply suggest a good man. You've changed too. Can I say something?"

"Of course."

"Do you know you drink less and less every day here?"

Time flowed without seams. They were together tenderly, and yet one morning he started drinking Sazeracs—as a gag. So he said, but there was a gripping itch inside.

"Shane, it's time to go back."

"What do you mean?"

He knew. The hotel was old and the wallpaper was saggy. The Lenten mood was on the city. There was a drizzle of rain and a raw wind. The television set was broken. A fundamentalist preacher squawked about sin on the radio.

"Shane, let's go back before we spoil it. I don't want to spoil it. You feel better but something is happening. I know."

"How do you know?"

She came to put her hands on his forehead. They were soft and smelled of hand lotion. In a strange and contradictory way they reminded him of Mona.

"The way you looked at that family in Antoine's last night —and—well, I—Shane, you called me Mona—in the night."

Marge helped him buy gifts. A mantilla for Mona—a silver bracelet for Rita—a Dixieland T-shirt for Bill. They were quiet on the way back. He wanted to tell her a lot of things, but the words wouldn't come.

There were tears in her eyes.

"I—I—Shane, dear—please understand—no guilt—and no demands—but just sometime let's—"

She smiled.

"Just let's think about Antoine's—and the beignets and chicory coffee—and the old man playing Dixieland trumpet—"

Shane stood and listened to the whisper of the taxi wheels. A dispatcher tapped him on the arm.

"Are you okay?"

The house was February silent. It seemed vacant but Mona was sitting on a chair in the kitchen like a visitor. She had her hat and coat on. She was a mourner at a strange funeral.

"I was going to go—"

She said it staring down at her clenched gloved hands.

"I packed, this morning, after the children left and I got dressed and I didn't call a taxi because I didn't know where to go."

He wanted to be home. But he was not sorry for going away. And he didn't tell the truth.

"There are times when I can't go on. I didn't want to end

up in another booze session. I had to go away. I wrote a good piece for Peter's magazine."

"That's nice."

They sat on awkwardly.

"I don't know how to explain it to Jackman."

Mona shrugged her shoulders.

"You have nothing to worry about. He called. That's how I knew you were coming home. A crisis—and you know—we need Shane—"

It was an excuse for both of them when he pretended to be concerned. She took off her gloves and started to make coffee. When he came down from changing his clothes, lunch was ready.

"Mona—I wish things were different."

"Do you want to leave us?"

"No," he said, "I don't."

The house reached out to enfold him. He wanted desperately to put his arms around her and make love to her and tell all the things in his heart—but it wouldn't work. So he went to the office.

Jackman was pleased to see him.

The Peabody Food account was giving trouble. Shane worked on it. He had seen a distinguished old man on the street in New Orelans, in a Southern planter costume. Something like the fried chicken man. So—why not have James L. Peabody in costume in all the ads?

The reaction was prompt.

"Shane, take another trip if that's what it does to you."

The gifts were accepted politely. Bill and Rita were somehow remote. He bought a new TV set for the recreation room and a record player for Rita. Mona was quiet. She now slept in the spare room. There was an atmosphere at home he couldn't break through. On a Saturday night, he sat in St.

Peter's and tried to exorcise himself. It didn't work, so he went to his cold and empty office; finally he went to see Marge.

"Shane, am I glad to see you."

She was in what she called her New Orleans nightie. There was an urgent need in their love-making.

Marge was far from a philosopher but she clasped her hand over his.

"Surely human beings deserve to be happy like this sometimes. Shane, for those few days I would pay anything. I never knew before I could be just—well, joyous."

He went home but in the early morning light he came awake and saw that Mona was sitting in a chair by the window. He wanted to go to her but he was powerless to move— and finally he went back into a troubled dream about Olga, who hadn't crossed his mind in years. Next morning he felt the old stirring impatience, and although he didn't intend to, he started drinking at noon with the public relations man of the steamship company.

He came home late for dinner and found that Mona had gone to a Sodality meeting. Rita and Bill were studying, so he went to his den and drank a half bottle of scotch and fell asleep on the couch.

Next morning Mona was silent. She barely spoke, and while he ate breakfast, he heard her going out the front door and down the street to Mass at St. Peter's.

There was nothing he could do about it.

12

Shane found he gravitated to Peter O'Hare, a big dynamo of a man with restless energy. O'Hare believed in doing things and worrying later. His attitude kept him moving from job to job—columnist, TV interviewer, author—but, there were always jobs and experiences. And O'Hare could pull him out of his introspection.

"Christ, Donovan, stop the crucifixion scene. That was done well two thousand years ago. Now, we are homeless, shamelessly thrown from this middle-class place of snobbery and will attempt to rectify some of the pain the world has inflicted on Jake."

Four A.M., and they were driving Jake Piloski, the chef, home from the Dunston Club. That was after the maitre d' pleaded with them to leave. Now, half terrified and thrilled, the pale man with the blue pallor and the tattoo of Dachau still on him insisted they come up the stairs of the Spadina Avenue building.

"Momma—for mine friends—the best."

A sleepy peasant-jowled woman in a grey flannel bathrobe shuffled around the tiny kitchen producing enormous quantities of food. Jake made his own vodka. It was fiery. There were many toasts.

"Look at the little Jew," said O'Hare as they drove home against the commuters coming to work. "Bloody death all around him and he comes through it and he cooks for drunks and snobs and goes home to his little flat and drinks his own vodka and eats the good food his wife makes—and God, did you see the number stamped on his arm—concentration camp number. That, old cock, is what the world and drama is all about. Write a play about that."

Eight A.M. His mind blazing. There was a story to be told of Belsen, Dachau and Treblinka—and what Jake and Martha Piloski thought of the Dunston Club. Mona was in the kitchen. Silent. This was the time to show her. There was an abyss between creative and non-creative people that had to be spanned.

"God, Mona, I've got an idea—a smasher—about this old Jewish couple—and they're from a concentration camp—and it's really terrific—"

Rita came down for breakfast.

"Hi, Dad. You up early?"

There was a doubletake and "Oh." It was unmistakeable, and Shane went up the stairs to shower and change. He fell asleep on the bed and when he woke at ten-thirty the house was silent and empty.

He could try but it was almost impossible at these times

to go back to the office. Making an excuse, he would go to a bar in some remote corner of the city. Forget the office—and yet, he couldn't. He must call.

"Can't get back. Any messages?"

Important or non-important, he gave the same answer.

"Remind me first thing in the morning. They'll hold."

Back to the bar. Snatches of conversation with working men—shift workers—local merchants in for a quick nip.

Finally calling Mona.

"Mona?"

"Yes."

"Is there anything you need?"

"No."

"Mona?"

"Yes, what is it?"

"I'm sorry."

No response.

"Oh, Shane, please—"

Long silence and finally she would hang up the telephone. He usually went to the Ambassador but this time he went to the Flamingo. Flashing lights and frothy illustrations of nudes with long shimmering hair and a multitude of accents.

This was off Spadina Avenue, which had once been Jewish and was now a point of entry for thousands of middle Europeans. Butchers in blood-spotted white coats, and milky white women with bulging breasts under black clothes, and an Irish band trying to play Greek music at the insistence of a tousled, black-haired merchant seaman.

Marge came in. He knew he had been expecting to see her. She worked for a Jewish tailoring concern nearby. He was arguing philosophy—St. Thomas Aquinas—but the Bulgarian tailor was just as ignorant and happy as himself. He had a roomful of friends and there was an argument to make him go home, and someone wanted him to stay. It was confusing, but Marge was there. He felt himself falling.

"He's a good man, lady. He is only happy. So, we not let him buy more drinks."

The bartender gave Marge Shane's wallet as evidence of good faith. Shane tried to avoid her. She sat on, obviously concerned. His coat was torn. His shirt was stained. When he fell from his chair and scratched his forehead, a dozen boozily friendly patrons took him to a spare room behind the bar. He knew Marge was going to call someone and at the moment it didn't seem to matter.

He could recall coming hazily out of black sleep. There were voices. All frighteningly clear, but he couldn't see faces or bodies.

"If we had any idea of how much alcohol he has in his system, we could treat him better."

"The man who brought him in and the girl said he had been drinking almost steadily for a week."

"Well, if he doesn't rally in the next few minutes, we'll have to try something else. I've seen worse, but his liver is pretty badly enlarged."

"Hello—"

A grey-haired woman in a nurse's uniform was holding his wrist. She smiled.

"Welcome back, Mr. Donovan."

"Have I been away?"

"Well, it all depends how you look at it. You talked a lot last night but I'm not sure you realized what you were talking about."

"Where am I?"

"This is the Crestwood Clinic. Your friends brought you

228

in last night, about midnight. We've called your wife. And Mr. Jackman called and said to take all the time you needed. So all you have to do is get better."

"Oh, God—"

After that he was sick.

He was trembling and sick, able only to form hazy ideas of the place. The shame faded beside his physical suffering. In one instant he would be aware of the hospital-like room and in the next moment he could see the dock of the summer place in Muskoka and Rita falling into the water. He couldn't move to help her and she kept falling . . .

"Mr. Donovan, here's something to help you."

Deep sleep and then thin lassitude. A puckish-faced elf of a man was sitting on a bed next to him.

"Boy, you sure been goin' good."

Shane struggled up.

"Lie down, fella. You'll just start them old hammers in your head. I'll get you some fruit juice."

The walls were pale green and the curtains were ivory. The elf was his roommate.

"I'm Joe Casey. Train horses. My fourth time in the clinic. You'll meet the best people in the world here—"

"People are very kind."

"Drunks are good natured. Maybe that's what makes us kind. Have a smoke."

He coughed himself into bringing up the orange juice.

"Take it easy, Shane. I'm Dr. Crest."

"What is this place?"

The doctor was a chubby-faced man of medium height in a hospital smock. He nudged a hip on the edge of the bed.

"A place to get better. Get your system in good shape. You see, it isn't really the harm of alcohol as much as what it makes you do without that hurts you."

"I've got to get out of here. When can I get out?"

The doctor smiled.

"Have you tried standing up?"

Shane nodded.

"Well, get your sea legs back and we'll see then."

"But—I—who knows I'm here?"

"Your family—your friends who brought you in. Your boss —who by the way called me. He wants you to know he thinks it's a great idea. Says he has been worried about you. Please remember that. A lot of people will be pleased you are here. That's important to remember."

His melancholy was like the inner chill when he was a small boy alone in the house on a cold rainy day in fall.

"Feeling blue?"

A lean man with stiffly brushed grey hair and the blue face of a heavy beard came to sit beside him.

"I'm Father Ted. American from Detroit."

"A priest?"

The man inhaled deeply and blew the smoke into patterned rings.

"Yes, I am. Also a drunk. Surprise you? Let me tell you there are no distinctions. You met your roommate. He spent twenty-four hours here last week in a coma driving horses all around his bed."

"Is that the normal thing—raving like that?"

"Not exactly. We have an actress upstairs who insisted they give a bed to her pet python—imaginary, of course."

"Oh, my God."

"Well, strange as it seems we are still His children. Be thankful at least you arrived here in place of somewhere else. Two nights ago they brought a lawyer in here who insisted on his rights. Got a fellow lawyer, a drunk also, to get him out. He drove his car into the harbour last night and drowned."

There were twenty-four patients in Crestwood. When Shane managed shakily to make his way down to breakfast there were eleven at the table. No one paid attention when he dropped his orange juice. There was a not unpleasant form of "shop" gossip.

"There's a real live one in 9A. Came in after midnight. Came a week early from Vancouver for the Grey Cup and missed it. He stayed three weeks in his hotel room."

"Yeah, and he had over three dozen tooth brushes. Sent the bellhops out for booze and tooth brushes."

He sat in the solarium and listened as the patients told stories about drinking. Everyone had a compulsion to talk about their drinking. At first it appeared like defensive boasting. Then he realized it was something else.

The realization that you were different. People here regarded you differently. Joe with the shaking hands. They still trembled violently after seven weeks.

"When I get out of here I'm going to open a mixed drinks bar. Won't need a Mixmaster."

The timid little man who hated his wife and nephew for bringing him in. Protesting he was not an alcoholic, day by day, and finally in a rare disclosure saying, "Things weren't too bad until the night I got up and used my wife's dresser drawer in the spare bedroom. Crapped all over her best underwear and her grandmother's Irish lace tablecloth."

There was the hellish first days. Happy Valley they called the admitting rooms where the shaking, nervous wrecks were shivering and sweating—and the de-toxified ones from the upper floors would come to administer hope, as they expressed it—but secretly to glory a bit that this phase was over for them. Above all there was a need for a public confessional.

231

"I was sober for eight months and then got stranded in St. John's in Newfoundland. Fellow took me over to the Crow's Nest. Hadn't been in it since the war. Two hot rums and I started and the next thing I knew I was in Boston. Don't know how the hell I got there, but I called Dr. Crest and one of his former inmates came to see me. A doctor at the hospital there. He got me on a plane to Toronto. Thought I was going to die until I got here. My fifth time."

He tired easily, as if he had been physically working. Mona came with his shaving kit and pajamas and he came awake to find her sitting beside his bed. Conversation was awkward and stilted.

"How do you feel?"

"Terribly tired."

"You can get a good rest in here."

"I'm getting out of this place as fast as I can."

There were many pauses.

"The kids—they're okay?"

"Oh, fine. Bill has been talking about quitting school."

"That's bloody nonsense. Let him get his degree then he can do what he wants."

They gnawed at the subject of Bill and school. It was a device to keep off other subjects. Finally there was no way of avoiding it.

"I'm sorry, Mona. I just don't seem to know—well, I can't seem to help myself."

"I—I—"

He braced himself for the familiar distressed words.

"What can I do? I try, Shane. I try, but we don't seem to have anything. My world is so simple. It's you and the children and that satisfies me. You—you seem to fight against it."

It swept over him again. Mona's shoulders slumped, the edge of a sob in her voice.

"Don't, Mona, please, I'll try."

232

"Maybe this place—" she said it gingerly, "they seem to be so kind and understanding. Perhaps if you tried here you could find some answers."

And in the moment, because he was ashamed and tired and his body was still suffering he agreed. He even told the doctor he was tired of living without answers. He would try.

"Mr. Donovan, that's the most important thing."

Dr. Crest was enthusiastic.

"Just try. You have a sickness. A kind of chemical imbalance. You've probably lost your tolerance for alcohol. If you try, you'll find a good and satisfactory way to live without it. Look around you. Get out of your mind that it's a sickness of the gutter. Talk to these people. They've probably got one of the highest proportionate rates of intelligence you could find in a single group anywhere."

He dressed and sat through a lecture next morning on nutritional deficiency caused by extended drinking. There was a bar filled with non-alcoholic liquids of all kinds and they were encouraged to help themselves.

"Shane," said the elderly man with the shock of silvery hair, "I'm a judge. I drank all through law school and practice. My practice was getting weaker and then I was appointed to the bench. Didn't drink for a year and then one hot day at the golf course—well, the gin rickeys looked good."

He downed his glass of apple juice.

"My friends covered up for me. I was half stoned one day and made a stupid judgement. Took a vacation and ran away. Went to New Orleans."

Shane winced.

"A former partner, former drinking partner as well, came after me. Brought me in here three weeks ago. I don't know whether I'm going to make it or not. I'm going to try, however."

Mabel was a housewife.

"My husband took the children and kicked me out. Me, a Ph.D., sleeping in a flophouse. How did I get here? I was broke one night, and believe it or not, I was thinking, really thinking about picking up a man on Jarvis Street—just for the price of a drink. My God, a man came along who knew my husband and me and he took me into a bar and bought me a martini—and I wanted another so badly. He said I could have it if I could come up and see this friend of his—a doctor. I thought—what the hell—and I came—and I was tired of it all—and I stayed."

That morning she was a tired, wan woman wearing old bedroom slippers, with her hair hanging in stringy strands. At noon she was transformed; she wore a lemon-coloured linen dress with buckskin pumps and her hair was done.

"My husband is bringing the children to see me this afternoon. Do I look okay?"

Shane saw the neat man with the blue suit, white shirt and plain tie. He wore glasses and fussed over the two small children. They screamed and ran to their mother. Shane found he couldn't hold back the tears and went to his room.

He spent three weeks at Crestwood. There came a moment about ten days after he entered the place when he felt better.

"God, Mona, I feel wonderful. I must have needed this rest."

The tension had gone. She came every day and once a week at night when there was open house. This was the most amazing experience of all. On open house nights former patients came back with their families to experience the therapy.

"Look, Shane," Mona nudged him, "there's Larry Peters, the television actor, and his wife. What's he doing here?"

He didn't have to answer because Peters came over to shake hands.

"Good to see you, Shane, Mrs. Donovan. You know my wife, Alice. I've been coming for four years now. Haven't had a drink in five years, two weeks, and one day. Not since I lost that outdoors series."

There was a litany—a credo—the nurses said it—the patients said it—you heard it all the time.

"Don't promise the impossible. Just get up in the morning and say—today I won't take a drink."

"Today I won't take a drink—not another drink."

Shane repeated it. He slumped into the bed and the electrical rustling whispering sound started.

"Take it easy," he told himself.

It was better to sit up and concentrate.

"I could write about Crestwood."

He spoke aloud. The thing to do was concentrate.

There was an amazing camaraderie at the clinic. In the days when he felt better there was less and less of a compulsion to leave. The building was a refuge. There was comfort in the routine. Meals and lectures, walks and naps and special exercises to relax. A patient going home. Some afraid and nervous with their families who came self-consciously to take them home. Others aggressive about the whole affair. Some left reluctantly, postponing the moment as if the world was something alien and hostile.

"Boy, have I learned a lesson."

Moonfaced Jackie was built like a wrestler. He pathetically wanted to be liked. In his two weeks at the clinic, none of his family had appeared.

"My wife is working. I told her not to bother coming up."

But each night Jackie paced the reception hall. Talking, laughing, joking—but always searching for his family. He made the rounds, shaking hands with everyone.

"Boy, only way I'll come back here will be to visit. Great place to visit. Wouldn't want to live here."

He left, cured.

Two nights later, he arrived back. He was boisterously drunk, and it took four attendants to cajole him to bed.

"The old pattern," the doctor said, a trifle wearily. "He went home looking for someone to bolster his courage. No one understood or else they were tired of that kind of bolstering. So he's back here."

Just remembering could flare Shane into temper. If booze is a sickness and people want to help, why do they always crowd you at the wrong time? The silence in the house when your nerves are screaming. The chasms that yawn when all you need is some form of affection.

Why was it the people like Marge who knew by instinct? Jackie's wife loved him but she always punished him when he was down. Of course, she loved him, but as she explained it, "I've got to take care of myself."

Squirrels in a cage—roll around the ring. Try and explain it to Mona and you come out merely dizzy.

The telephone rang. He hadn't been answering it all day. It was an intruder in his hotel-room cave. On impulse he undressed and crawled into bed. The sheets were clammy and rumpled. Pull the covers up. Now, maybe he could sleep.

This was the ritual of a man trying, although he's not quite certain why, to go "cold turkey." The water cure. A vague urge for purification and recognition that another drink will produce almost a shock. Trying to calm nerves and sore muscles with sleep and stay away from temptation and get some rest and escape the scratching sounds and the 3-D horrors.

Shane was on a plateau.

"I am going to spend tomorrow writing a speech about advertising that will knock them off their asses. Ladies and gentlemen, we who make the world of advertising our occupation are about to be dethroned. For it is a new world, with new people and new ways—and we have to change."

But the mood slipped and he was back in despair.

Call Dr. Crest! There would be no harm. He had done it before. Just to talk to him. They called it a life line. Something to hang onto when you're down. It was a life line, but when the voice came on the line, sleepy, he hung up. They encouraged you to call them. But then they talked to you about being reasonable.

He was hiding in an almost frightened way—half aware of people at his door—the bell ringing—conversations with the chambermaid—but she was bribed—and then he dimly realized that hours had gone by and there was probably someone else on shift.

The buzzer went on the door. Shane didn't respond. He sensed that an envelope was being pushed under the door. He waited and then struggled to the door and picked it up. The envelope was marked *Personal and Confidential.*

Dear Shane:

Tried to reach you but gather you are mustering armament for Saturday night. Wanted to tell you the idea we discussed has been bought. All I need is the attached release form. To all intents the idea and name will come from the sponsor, in fact you will note the attached check comes from him. I appreciate this very much, for reasons I needn't elaborate on now, but you may count on me to reciprocate if the occasion ever arises. Regards. J.L.F.

P.S.—I know you will treat the matter as confidential.

He had a new purpose and he must organize himself. He felt sober. There was the cheque and he must organize. He was calm. He must be calm. Purpose made the difference.

"Christ, what would my people think. Twenty thousand dollars for a name!"

A litany of procedure.

"Send a note to Fathingham and send him the release papers. Get something to eat. No excuses. No bloody excuses. Not like raising money. Found money."

Shave and shower. First send the note to Fathingham: *Thanks J.L. Here are the papers. Mum's the word and I hope middle-aged romance flourishes. Getting down to the speech.*

He had to write and rewrite it to conquer the spidery handwriting. Five dollars for the bellhop to deliver the note marked *Personal and Confidential.*

Now call Mona.

"I want to place a call to 925-7736 in Toronto, Canada."

He sat back in the chair. Better calling from the desk. Funny the difference in your attitude depending on where you are calling from. More vulnerable on the side of a bed. He must enunicate properly. No trouble.

"Yes, Shane Donovan calling. Room 502. The number—KEnnedy—oh, yes, the President."

There were clicking noises and then he began to feel as if he were slipping. His confidence was oozing away. He poured vodka into the orange juice. He was swallowing when Mona came on the line.

"Yes, who is it please?"

Gagging and confused, he put his hand over the receiver and coughed until the pressure seemed to be bursting his eyeballs.

"M-Mona, it's Shane."

The concern was gone from her voice.

"At it so early?"

Icy cold.

"Don't be silly, Mona. Just had to call you. Damned coffee went down the wrong way and nearly choked me."

"Uhhuh."

"Well, darling, I got the name for a man's lotion. Leonine! Isn't it great?"

There was a pause that seemed to hang like a cloud.

"Aren't you pleased, honey?"

"I suppose you're celebrating?"

Her words were distinct and clear.

"Well, J.L. is quite excited about it. Says it's just what he has been looking for. You know, Mona honey, this is what we wanted. We can to to Europe this summer!"

Donovan could recognize the weary resignation in her voice.

"Sure, Shane. Last year we were going to Ireland; and the year before it was—where was it?"

The fluid persuasive salesmanship of the idea man started now.

"But, darling, you know I was busy. This one is the clincher. I've really made it this time. J.L. was ecstatic. I've really coined a new one that will go down in history."

The mechanism of his talking was running down and the last words trailed off.

"Mona?"

There was a dull "Yes."

"What's the matter, darling?"

It came like an icicle.

"I'm sure Bonnie appreciated your genius even if I don't seem to be able to."

He had to say something.

"Mona."

There was a note of hurt in his voice as he fumbled with the vodka bottle. He had to think of something to say. Gulp! The vodka stung his chin.

"Can't you talk now?"

She suspected that Bonnie was in the room.

"Of course I can talk now. Fathingham sent me a cheque for twenty thousand—at least it's Castelli's cheque."

He was fumbling for the envelope.

"Oh, Shane—really!"

She didn't believe him and there was the cheque in his hand—mauve and green with the raised red letters etched in—"Twenty thousand dollars"—and he couldn't say anything. He heard the receiver click.

He wasn't angry. How else could she be expected to respond?

13

The restless stirring was in him, and sitting around in the hotel room was no good. There was no damned way he could work. His place was outside, walking around and moving. Get out in the street. Just swim in the mass of people going in and out of shops and buying things.

Silly bloody people!

You there—nature gave you a scent—a natural erotic scent to attract males. But we've convinced you it's nasty—so you must douse it and buy a synthetic one to arouse a man. And he douses himself with another scent, and the world gets dirtier and smellier all the time.

You there, lady, we made you buy crotch-length clothes and now you must cover everything up to your ankles—and you'll look like a perambulating potato sack.

Silly bloody people in a silly bloody world. What's his name paying twenty thousand dollars for scented alcohol to make middle-aged men feel erotic.

"Mr. Donovan, yes you—my father, listen. I was given twenty thousand dollars for naming stuff for men to rub on—like the bottle of Florida water you nursed for years—only this stuff is supposed to make someone feel horny."

Madness . . . plain, bloody madness! Twenty thousand dollars would be an obscenity to a man who desperately wanted to work for forty cents an hour, and couldn't even get that. Divide forty cents an hour into twenty thousand dollars and how many years . . . oh, hell . . . a lifetime of trying to get work at wrestling ties and grading roadbed, sweating in the sun and freezing your ass off in the bitter winter . . . and, worse, sitting at the kitchen window and seeing the jigger go out with the foreman and his brother-in-law and his cousin and you not working and the only heat in the house coming from bootleg coal.

Two worlds. Mona, Bill, and Rita in the big house had all the things he never had or his family never had. The other world of being paid for an idea . . . an idea every time you absobloodylutely had to think one up—and getting paid for it.

He was somewhere between . . . a man and a boy, a man who was never a boy, wanting and aching for things he couldn't find. Music and dark nights and peace and quiet and no pressure. That's what he had to find, but how do you find it when your wife won't believe you and you are alone in New York? And there is no loneliness like New York.

The thing to do was walk. Walk until he was hungry. Eat something. Concentrate on his speech. Concentrate on being rational.

The speech must be significant. Protest if you like about advertising and agencies and sales and production, but how could you find another system as efficient? There were valid reasons.

"Bullshit!"

Most people ignored him.

"Got a quarter for something to eat?"

Hunched shoulders, neck chords standing out, hands in pocket.

"Sir, here's a buck—buy a quart."

The talon fingers snatched the dollar, but there was hate in the eyes.

Bloody city!

He came to a phone booth. He should call Bonnie. She was concerned about him. Just go and talk. No booze but a talk and then go back and sleep and write the speech. Maybe talk to O'Hare as well.

Busy.

There was a confusing answer the first time he called Tina. Sounded like a wrong number. Try again.

"Yes?"

"Tina?"

"Yes."

Her voice was dull, almost sleepy.

"It's Shane. How are you?"

"Fine. Want to come over?"

"If you don't mind."

"Not at all. There are some people here but you come."

"Swell."

There was a pause.

"Is that you, Shane?"

"Sure it's me."

"Oh, you sound funny."

"I'm in a phone booth."

She laughed. It was a puzzling sound.

"In a phone booth. Poor dear."

"Tina, are you okay?"

"I'm splendid. Just walk in when you come."

The door of Tina's apartment was open. The stereo blared a raga-rock number. The fat man was sitting on a chair in the tiny foyer, and he made a sweeping motion of his hand to Shane.

"Lock the door, old boy. Don't want the fuzz."

Tommy was sitting on the floor with his back to the wall beside the white angular stone cat.

"Shane. Meet Isis. Isis meet Shane. You are a goddess and he is a genius."

There were people all over the apartment but they were isolated from each other. Sitting and staring. They moved and gestured like performers in an underwater tableau.

"Mister, join the protest everything group. Climb aboard."

A skinny young man with a blond beard who wore a purple robe gestured Shane to lean over. He dumped several capsules in his hand.

"There's plenty No-Cal in the fridge."

Four youths were sitting around the glass-topped table in the dining alcove.

"Where's Tina?"

A girl in a mini-dress, which clung to her body like a wet jersey, stood up and dreamily took his hand. No one spoke. She stopped in the kitchen and opened the refrigerator door. There was a bottle with a red fluid.

"Try this, George," she said, facing him but with her eyes focussed in the distance.

"I'm Shane."

"Yes, George. It's very good."

244

"What is it?"

He swallowed a tablespoonful that tasted like wild cherry. She poured one for herself.

"Dexy—"

"Dixy?"

She giggled. Her eyes were strange. She was like a witch.

"Dexedrine, silly. That's the sweet stuff. Here, look."

She opened the door again and pointed to a second bottle. "That's Dexamyl. It's too bitter. You don't look like a bitter man."

When he dropped the pills from his hand, the girl stopped and picked them up with a slow, gliding motion. She selected two blue ones and put the others in the breast pocket of her dress.

"Here, man. Try these."

For a fraction of time he hesitated. He swallowed them because he had always responded to dares such as this. A new drink. Let's drive to Quebec City. Tell the difference in the rum. It didn't matter. What he really wanted was a drink. Bloody pills didn't matter. He had seen a silver cocktail-shaker beaded with moisture in the refrigerator and while the sad-eyed girl looked on dully and somewhat reproachfully, he poured a drink. The martini was ice cold.

"Naughty boy."

It made him feel better for a moment. There was a death-like stillness in the apartment, until the stereo began again.

"Come and meet Tina."

Tina was propped up like a priestess on pillows on the white bed. She wore a black Nehru jacket over white lace pants that ballooned at her ankles. Her hair was combed straight back from a pale face. Her eyelids were open. Her eyes were very black.

"Is she all right?"

The girl was gone. When Shane leaned close, he could see a faint jewel-like glitter in Tina's eyes.

"Please kiss me."

Her lips were yielding, but cold.

"What's the matter, Tina?"

One arm came up like a signal from the bed as she gestured. He sat down on the edge of the bed, aware of a constricting feeling on his chest.

"Shane, I am so glad you are here."

"What the hell's going on?"

"Ssh—listen—Ravi Shankar. It makes my soul feel cool and misty."

The bedroom, only faintly lit when he came in, appeared to be changing as luminous colours crept in from the partially opened bathroom door. The window overlooking the balcony was a screen of pastels that moved, shifted and changed.

"Shane, you are my very good friend. You are the one who knows all about me. I am close to you."

Her hand on his shoulder urged him back on the bed where he lay passively. The urgent pounding was gone from his system.

"Tina?"

"Yes, Shane."

"What's all this in aid of?"

Her laughter was mechanical. He was reminded of a disc used in radio commercials. "Laughter A-1—Mirthless."

"We talked about the strange and useless quality of life. Tommy—you—myself. Fighting for survival. No satisfaction."

She paused. Her speech was interrupted by pauses as if she were constructing phrases.

"Strange people in a strange place. War and bombs. Fighting on the streets. Black men and white men."

Her hand on his forehead was as cool as ivory—and as smooth.

"Join me, Shane. I am going to a plateau of peacefulness. That's what my guests are all doing. We are finding peace . . . just peace. No trouble."

She offered him a crystal dish, like a serving piece for bon-bons, except that it contained dozens of capsules. They were all colours.

"What have you had?"

"Blues."

"That's very good to begin."

He wanted to disagree and go to the kitchen for a martini but Tina was gentle in her persuasion and he took a capsule. It lodged in his throat when half dissolved and she made no protest as he left. He drank another martini to wash it down and ease his throat.

"Hi—"

A very slim Negro girl wearing bra and panties lay on a rug in the second bedroom. She was leafing through a book of prints.

"Like man, I got sixty-sixty vision. If I ever made a commercial in living color like this, I'd be just the greatest thing in the business."

She raised a shapely brown leg as if in greeting. It was completely sexless. On the bed he saw the married couple who had been at the brunch. The man blinked.

"How are you, Johnny Canuck? I hope—high. Write me a song for Johnny Cash—I hope—high—high—"

His voice trailed off. He scarcely moved but his eyes were bright. Tommy seemed to be asleep with his arms around the stone cat.

The only sound, except for the muted one of traffic from

247

the street below, came from the sitar music—the record repeating over and over.

"You like that?"

"Yes. It's like making love—over and over—"

"Tina—"

There was no use in talking. The rooms were quiet except for the music. It was monastery-like. There was a smell of incense or perfume and he felt relaxed. He didn't want to move. Tina was smiling at him.

This was peace! God, it was the chapel during the all-night vigil of the Passion. Then it all changed.

Shane was on the edge of an enormous precipice. He felt the exhilaration of death—the flesh-like plunge into unconsciousness when pain has been numbed. But inside him there was also a glow like a blanket-wrapped lantern against his belly on a very cold night when he rode in a sleigh and the million piercing arrows of cold rained on his cheeks, and his feet were warm. He tried to steady himself.

Time was there and there was no time, and when he spoke it was a very long time until he heard the words. He tried to muster anger at himself for taking the pills, but his emotions were in a dim, far-away cavern inside himself—and he listened to his own words.

Tina was a princess, a priestess, and her movements as she lit a cigarette were regal. The flare of the match was a greater spectacle than any sunrise in his life.

"My darling Shane. I am so glad you came back to me."

He was sitting on the top of a flat rock in the mesaland of Zane Grey, with the colours spilling in all directions.

"I was never away."

There was fog drifting on the harbour mouth. It was Canso or Digby or Seldom Come By—or Ferrydale and the cod fishermen were coming in—or the morning he saw the clam diggers—or the Newfoundland priest blessing the Portuguese fleet in St. John's harbour.

"Love me gentle, Shane. I'm a vase of Persia—a Grecian urn—"

Those lips—lips—lips—and they were soft but unresponsive and the pillows were hills and he didn't want to love Tina.

"Shane, you are my entire life. Say sweet things to me— God—you are a god and I am a goddess." For the first time there was a fire in her voice. "Speak poetry to me, Shane. I need poetry more than blood itself. My people are Greek— and we are a people of poetry."

She laughed in his ear—a deafening sound absorbed in his body until it echoed in his stomach.

"If I were educated like you I would be happy—and I would sing poetic things—"

To Shane they were now planets floating in a universe of indescribably beautiful colours—rainbows of strange hues arching ceremoniously as they glided on and on . . .

Tina said, "I wish I were a Persian."

It came from somewhere—a fragment at first—remembered and stored and almost forgotten . . .

"I passed by a—I passed by where a potter kneaded earth and I beheld what he did not behold, that it was my father's dust which lay in the palm of that potter."

Tina's hand was on his body.

"Just to know that I lie with a potter—a poet—is enough. Shane, I want to go with you and live in a whitewashed stone cottage in Hydra. Then you can write songs for me the way Leonard Cohen wrote for his girl. That's what I want to hear, Leonard Cohen—I'll put on a record."

But she didn't move.

Shane was quiet. There were colours and music, and now he could speak.

"I came not hither of my own free will.
And go against my wish, a puppet still.
Cup bearer! gird thy loins and fetch some wine.
To purge the world's respite, my goblet fill."

"Oh my darling Leonard, I knew you would come to me.
Take me to Hydra—take me—oh, Leonard."

Tina raised up and stretched and finally slumped back.

"Oh, God, my darling Leonard, you have made me a full
woman—I feel you—feel you—"

Shane tried to touch her but the colours closed in and he
was too tired to swim any more.

14

It was an enormous wombed hall. As he walked on the pink sand he could feel the impact of his feet, like steel on steel, but there was no sound. The walls began to vanish and he was alone in an infinity.

Then he was awake. Where the hell was he? Tina's. He was in the enormous white bed with the white shaggy cover. For a few seconds he wanted desperately to be at home. The tree outside the bedroom window would be in bloom.

Five A.M. Bending brought pain but he wasn't sick. Her clothes were neatly stacked on the bench of the dressing table.

"Tina?"

No answer. In the living room a strange couple huddled

on a rug. The Tiger was curled up asleep on a chaise longue
—but no sign of Tina. He pushed the door of the second bedroom open. There she was, half-propped against the headboard with Tommy cradled in her arms. Shane eased back.
In the elevator he thought of a stop-action scene in a movie.
If he had snapped his fingers, they might all have come back
to life.

He sat on the bench in the foyer and lit a cigarette. It tasted
strange.

Then the feeling started. At first it was only the beginnings
of a depression. A let down, like the slump after exhilaration
or excitement. No, this was more than that. It surged up inside and he had an almost uncontrollable desire to cry.

"God, I can't do this."

The tears came anyhow. He sat there on the carved oak
bench and wept until his handkerchief was soaking. This was
more than loneliness. It was like waiting on a lonely road at
night for a ride in the cold rain—and being left alone by a
passing car.

It was like waking at 3:00 A.M. when Mona was in the hospital having Bill. It was not fair to always blame Mona and he
didn't really want to . . .

Coming awake, fuzzily, with Bill shaking him. Trying to
orient himself as the boy kept saying, "Dad, please, Dad. Rita
is sick."

Mona was at a Catholic Women's League convention in
Montreal. It was one of the few times and Rita, a very small
child, had woken up feverish and croupy. He had been
drinking.

"I want my Mummy."

The small half-delirious cry in the room.

"Your mother will be back soon."

She cried as if she hadn't heard.

"I want my Mummy."

The sight of Mona at the airport and the agonizing trip to the hospital. The vigil in the waiting room, while Mona sat, pale-faced, and grasping her rosary like a life line.

The doorman appeared and looked at him curiously.

"You okay, sir?"

"Sure—sure. Just tired and a bit cold."

"Nippy this morning."

The streets were almost deserted and grey with cats stalking around garbage on the sidewalks. An occasional taxi passed, the drivers ignoring his signal.

Shane turned into a narrow street and was suddenly accosted by a pair of men. He hadn't seen them. When the skinny one made a move, Shane backed against the wall of the building. The short one in the knitted cap flicked a knife in his hand and said, "Look, man, we don't want any trouble. We just need bread, man."

It was all part of the strange night.

"Beat it, you bastards."

Both lunged. He ducked the skinny one, and in jumping slammed into the runt with the knife. The knife clattered on the street.

"Get him, Johnny."

Shane felt the stale breath. He was being hugged.

"Get the knife, Bronco, and let him have it."

Shane went limp; taking his assailant off guard, he elbowed him sharply.

"Jesus, Johnny, fuzz."

They were off then. Shane had fallen against the fence. There were shots, and a beefy policeman was helping him up.

"You okay, fella?"

"Yes, sure."

A Negro policeman came back holstering his gun.

"It was Johnny Silora and Little Bronco. We'll pick them up later. They can't get far. They need money for a fix."

"I've heard about this, but—"

"Christ, fella, ya must be nuts to go wanderin' around alone at this time of the night. What the hellya doin'?"

He explained about being with friends and expecting to be able to hail a cab.

"Some friends, lettin' ya out without callin' a cab."

When he said he was from Canada, it explained matters. He was not expected to understand the violence of New York.

He couldn't face the hotel and gave them Bonnie's address. His legs were beginning to tremble. He felt ill.

The sense of what might have happened overwhelmed him when Bonnie appeared at the doorway. Her hair streamed over the flannel bathrobe and he smelled sleep on her. For a time she just held him very close and the shaking eased.

"My God, Shane. I've been worried sick. What happened? You look beat up."

He was aware then of his appearance. His coat pocket was turned out. There was a rip in one sleeve. One lapel was torn. His tie was askew.

"I've got to sit down."

"Do you want a drink?"

Shane shook his head.

"No, Bonnie."

When he tried to speak, his teeth chattered. His hands were shaking.

"I'm cold."

She led him to the bedroom.

254

"Here, take off your clothes and get in there. I'll turn the electric blanket on."

She went to the kitchen. The warmth started but it didn't seem to help. He was cold, and his teeth chattered. When she brought hot bouillon he drank it, but it didn't warm him.

"Shane, now please tell me."

He couldn't tell her about Tina.

"I had to go and visit Tommy Smith. You see, I fixed up an account for the agency and it was a—well, kind of a personal deal, so they paid me separately—and there was a lot to drink."

Lying again. There was no sense in lying to her.

"Bonnie."

"Yes, Shane."

"Bonnie, please get in here with me."

Without a word she moved in beside him. His head nestled against the soft warmth of her breasts. In time the shivering stopped.

"I'm lost, Bonnie."

"Never mind now. You're here and you're warm."

"But, Bonnie, I took something at that place."

"Drinks?"

"No, some purple gunk and some pills, not all of them, and I passed out and then two guys tried to hold me up and the cops came along."

She was incredulous as he explained.

"The cops came?"

"Oh, I didn't know what I was doing when I came out on the street. Thought I could pick up a taxi. None would stop. So I started walking. Got a bit mixed up, I guess, and turned into an alley. One guy grabbed me and the second guy was going for his knife when the police arrived. They scrammed but the cops know them and say they'll pick them up. They're junkies, I guess."

Bonnie held him close.

He talked—talked—scarcely aware of the words—it poured out.

He, Shane Donovan, transplanted from childhood, carried with him some power in his genes. It came from an ancestor victim of the famine years, who had gathered his family from a black stinking hovel of the Irish countryside and mustered them, in defiance of plague and pestilence, in the squalid hold of a sea vessel that was battered in the North Atlantic gales for weeks on their tortured way to Canada.

Unlettered, ignorant of the harsh winters and the fierce seasons, that man had triumphed in clearing a holding in the forest. In cabin and field he had held up his spirits and those of his dependents to found a Canadian strain; and at night by the fire, the stories and songs rang out to make the place and the people live.

But the song had ended in dour Uncle Matt on the Ontario farm and in the desperate defeat of his father in the section man's house by the railroad in Western Canada. Now things had come full circle and he was the throwback who, not content to simply accept his fate, had struck out on his own.

Like the people who called themselves "depression casualties," Shane Donovan felt the scars. The depression was a conspiracy against him. While he was still in Nonsuch, he had a vague impression that his parents were to blame. It never occurred to him that his parents were the real depression victims.

You learned to look out for yourself.

"Flesh it out a bit. Get some spice in it. God, man, people

don't buy newspapers to read pleasant things. They want to see the troubles other people got."

"But that's the way it was," Shane had replied to the night editor, turning in his assignment on a common-law wife murdering her drunken husband.

Blackman was a heavy-set man, with greying hair like a projecting thatch over his eye-shade and enormous pouches under his eyes.

"Kid, she must have been in a negligee—a torn housecoat—exposed breasts or flesh—booze around the place—get something sexy in it."

Shane was still perplexed.

"We got competition. Another newspaper. Get something in this they haven't got."

This was newspaper morality. The four tombstones toppled by a drunken party of youths became forty vandalized by unknown marauders. The newspaper was a freewheeling entertainment source that depended on circulation.

At the agency, there was never any doubt.

"This," said the account executive, "is approximately three ounces of bicarbonate of soda, a touch of sugar, a whiff of essence of peppermint in a two and a half cent container and it sells for ninety-nine cents. Your job is to persuade people they need it every time they get a bellyache or think they have one. Is that clear?"

This was advertising morality before public concern brought in regulations. The copy chief used to drink large quantities of a tonic that he got from the manufacturers.

"Here, Shane," he said thickly one night, "take a belt. Cheapest booze in town."

"You mean you have liquor in there?"

"No, I've got old Colonel's Whatsisname tonic. Try it."

It had a taste of maraschino cherries but Shane could feel his stomach warming.

"You must have put rye in it."

The copy chief roared.

"Of course not. Bloody stuff is almost sixty percent alcohol. I save myself a fortune in booze. That's what you're selling, boy. Little old ladies who wouldn't be caught dead drinking belt themselves up on this and totter off to bed, splashed, every night."

Shane had preserved one dream, to remain untouched.

"Mona, as soon as we get enough money, we're going to a farm, or maybe to Ireland, and I've got to write all this. It's not for real. It has to be said. I've gotta write."

Mona agreed, but there was always the suspicion she hadn't really heard. How could anyone want another life than the one they enjoyed? The home and money to spend, and the children doing so well in school, and the church so close.

"The world, Mona, is all going to hell and people who feel about it should do something. I get so damned discouraged because all the people I'm with just see their jobs and a bonus at the end of the year. There's more than that in life —and—"

It was no use.

"If you're unhappy, why don't you talk to the priest about it?"

Shane belonged to a group who came from depression backgrounds, homes where either the romantic after-life concepts of Catholicism or the fundamentalism of Protestantism had shaped them in ways that were challenged all the time. Because they were too young, or for health reasons, they had been excused from the tie-shattering experience of World War II; but they had nevertheless migrated to the alien cities.

They eased themselves into a form of living immeasurably better than what they had known in their childhood.

But there were a lot of things he didn't understand about this life, like buying the groceries.

"Mona, why do you drive so far away to buy stuff when there's a perfectly good store just three blocks away—and they deliver?"

Mona was shocked.

"But they're more expensive."

Shane was angry.

"Look, when I was a kid the only store that would sell us groceries—and on tick—was a little fellow. Bloody chain had to have cash for everything. Oh, yes, they'd honour relief vouchers, but never give you a loaf of bread the day before, when you were starving. Not likely, and the damned chain finally put the little fellow, Thomson, out of business."

He was nearly shouting. Mona, Bill, and Rita were staring at him in a form of shock.

"Oh, Dad, that's ancient history."

The explanations were useless. It shocked him to be yanked back in his subconscious to the childhood that he rejected.

Thomson's was a long boxy building with a false front and two large windows made up of small panes of glass, under a sagging veranda-like roof. It was a frame weather-beaten building showing remnants of a sign that had once adorned a whole side. Now it showed only faintly visible evidence of the yellow and brown paint that had once admonished customers to *CHEW STAG TOBACCO*. Closer scrutiny also disclosed that there had once been a very large animal outlined in brown paint as well, but you had to use vivid imagination to trace the lordly creature.

"Well, Shane, and how's our budding author?"

He liked going in when Mr. Thomson, looking like a bespectacled gnome, would be reading by the light which filtered through the dusty skylight at the back. It was a long trip back past the grocery counter on the one side, and the yard goods and draperies and big pot-bellied stove with the ring of nail keg seats around it. Mr. Thomson would be sitting in the old arm chair, with the cross bars beneath the seat to keep the legs from spreading out.

"Mr. Thomson."

"Sit down, boy. Have you read *Riders of the Purple Sage?*"

Mr. Thomson was known in Nonsuch as a reader. He also wrote items for the Regina newspaper whenever something of major interest happened, such as a railway accident or a fire. There were many who felt he would be a better businessman if he didn't read so much.

From Ike Thomson, Shane received groceries on "tick" and books he hid away and read in secret.

"You read, boy. Best education in the world."

"Miss Loomis is against Western stories."

"Bah," the little man exclaimed, "what does that dried up old fart know. Never been married—never been kissed—never been—" Mr. Thomson checked himself. "Never been married myself, for that matter, but—well, I know reading is one way you can get yourself out of this Godforsaken town. Words, boy—and learn about places and then get out and go visit them."

His father was angry when he discovered the books.

"I'm going to tell that old fool not to give you books like that—"

His mother interceded.

"Shane does his homework—and he likes to read—and besides there's the bill—"

The overdue grocery bill saved him.

"God, Bonnie," he muttered, finally exhausted, "how do you explain that to your family—that's just one thing—"

When he woke up at noon sweating under the blanket, Bonnie was gone. There was a note telling him she felt better because he had talked, and explaining where she could be reached by telephone. There was orange juice in the refrigerator.

He had things to do and he must do them. His head was light but it was nothing compared to an average hangover. The bank manager wanted to talk about Montreal, where he was born. Shane found it an effort. The manager didn't like New York, but he was worried about separatist problems if he asked for a transfer back. Shane wanted half the money to go to Mona, and how difficult was it to go to Mexico?

The bank manager was offering him a drink because he seemed pale. When Shane left he was convinced the arrangements were complete and Mona would be notified—but how would she get to New York, or was that the money? It was being sent to the hotel. Something about a visa and San Miguel de Allende sounded familiar.

He intended to call Mona when he arrived back in the room but there was a new IBM electric typewriter sitting on a stand. Courtesy of the agency. Fathingham had sent it with a note.

"Glad to see you are getting down to work. After all, this is Friday. We're counting on you for Saturday night. Thanks again for the other matter."

Shane's hands were shaky. He had gone through the ritual of taking a shower, shaving, clean pajamas. Now he sat poised over the typewriter.

"May I clean up now, suh?"

Black woman with grey hair and a blue-grey tinge on her

face. Moving slowly to pick up what he had been flinging around the room.

"Sorry for the mess."

"That's all right, suh." She chuckled, straightened up to lean on the handle of the carpet sweeper. "You should see some places. They just toss everything every which way. Women's worse than men."

He could hear her chuckling while doing the ritual of the bathroom. Wipe and polish, flush the toilet. Take out the dirty clothes.

"Here—please."

She smiled and tucked the bill in her pocket.

"Thank you, suh. I'll be back later and finish up so's I won't disturb you. You a writer, suh?"

Shane nodded. "In a way."

The maid nodded wisely.

"I see. We get lots of writers here. Had a man doing a TV play here—never left his room for ten days—wouldn't let us in."

She paused with one hand on the door.

"He cut his wrists finally. Near to died."

He was alone again in the room.

"Ladies and gentlemen."

Type and tear out the paper. His head ached. When he tried to write in longhand the words came out scrawled, shaky and illegible.

"I am a Canadian. That is different from being an American —oh, yes, it is much different."

But how? How could he express it to this group? There were no differences in cars, soft drinks, pet foods, toiletries and all the garbage of this system. That audience didn't recognize differences. They just assumed that everyone in the world wanted all their products.

"I think some of our people are shortsighted!" J.L. had said. "Our agencies are going multi-national just like our industrial corporations. Arabian sheiks want Cadillacs, so why won't the bloody Arabs want cleaners? See what's happening in Israel and France and it's a hell of a lot more than Coca-Cola. The American way is becoming the international way."

There must be a way to tell this audience they were off base.

"In an age of so-called communications and global village dimensions, there has never been such a lack of communications. Poverty is a common, if neglected, factor of North America, to say nothing of South America. Wars spread like heat rash—bloody wars of ideology, where people are unable to communicate, to see each other's point of view."

It was no use. Sweating and uncomfortable, he wanted a drink. In a kind of desperation, he lay down on the bed after taking some 222s. That was America for you. Almost every drugstore in Times Square would sell you amphetamines or a hundred variations, but if you asked for aspirin with codeine the druggist looked at you as if you were demented.

He had a hazy half sleep, but then drove himself back to the typewriter.

Ladies and gentlemen:

It's strange for a Canadian advertising man to be in this position. First of all, in Canada we are never quite sure that America recognizes the fact there is a country north of it— sovereign—independent—or at least as independent as you allow—

The smoke scratched his throat. Shane's hand hovered over the bottle of rye. He finally opened a split of soda, and made an elaborate ritual out of getting ice. No booze.

Ladies and gentlemen:

Why am I an advertising agency man?

Why?

I suppose because I never had confidence enough in myself to try anything else. I began with a dream of becoming a creative artist. The laugh in the whole thing is that now I'm supposed to be a creative vice-president. Whoever really believed in the self-delusion of advertising agencies about creativity?

That would make them sit up!

He felt a wave of energy. He must get up and get away and move around with people. Change all his clothes.

The speech?

"Simple. I'll go down tomorrow and dictate it to a secretary at the office."

The words came as the energizing force drove him.

Ladies and gentlemen:

I am an advertising man. I am amongst my peers. In this, the age of anxiety, we who make possible the merchandising forces of the massive productivity of the North American continent are often misinterpreted. We have been named hucksters.

Well, if to be a huckster is to keep our mighty nations in the forefront of development—to keep them—

The words trailed off. The high pitch was gone and he barely made it to the chair.

"Crap."

His heart was pounding wildly. Sweat oozed on his forehead and he could feel it drenching his armpits. It wasn't weakness. It was a deep, deep blue feeling inside him. It wasn't illness. It was a blue grotto.

A drink, someone said, was rebirth at a certain time. To slide into it and away and let it go down and feel the warmth of it and forget the problems. They drifted away when you reached a certain point.

Switch on the automatic pilot—let the whole geezly thing

go—and no regrets. He was good to Mona and the kids. Not a goddam thing they wanted they didn't somehow get.

The agency was no bed of roses. Dip into the old reservoir and get a new idea. The only way you survive—easier ways than making money for Jackman and Bates—wouldn't it skin their arses if they knew about Leonine—might know he had been saving that for a tight squeeze.

Jackman wouldn't mind, but Bates! Ptui!

"Shane, you and I have never hit if off too well, but—"

Alf Bates was a small, intense man. He was methodical about sorting out the objects on his desk. Clock, pen stand, copper cup for paper clips, he moved them precisely—like a robot.

"I have nothing against you, Alf."

The flicker on Bates's face could be either a smile or pain.

"I know, but I'm a routine man. A day to day plodder. You're a brilliant man. No doubt of that."

He held his hand up to stop Shane's interruption.

"No, Shane, please let me finish. I have a heart and feelings. I admire your work. I see you wrestle with yourself and you've proven over and over again that you have ideas."

"Well, I'm just that way."

Bates nodded.

"I know, and don't take what I have to say in a wrong way. I—think—well, you should really take better care of yourself."

The little man went to stare out the window.

"You're wearing yourself down physically and mentally. You simply must have—well, some kind of spiritual help or something—"

Shane blazed. Somehow some restraint kept him from exploding into hot bitter retorts. Bates subsided into a helpless silence. They were both appreciative of a telephone interruption.

Why hadn't he said what he felt now?

"Alf, you're a louse by instinct, petty and timid. You should be beating the drum in a revival tent in a hillbilly town where their idea of faith is to kiss rattlesnake asses."

No, that was silly. But nothing was too silly for that bastard. But how do you explain the repugnance of having to work with someone like that?

He said it aloud.

"Why did Michelangelo paint the Sistine Chapel, or Maugham roam the world looking into the sex life of British planters and their virginal English brides, and Graham Greene search his soul?"

And he knew what Mona would say because she treasured stories about Brendan Behan, Dylan Thomas and Hemingway . . . and their torments.

"Is it always tragic? Aren't there nice things and peaceful things to write about?"

Shane would drop the subject. He couldn't answer. In the wakeful hours, smoking in the den while Mona slept, he knew the bitterness of not being certain about his ability.

He was loaded with the memory of his attempts to go beyond the superficial in his writing. There was always Nonsuch. Bloody awful poverty on earth and the railroad not caring and his father so bitter and his mother being ground away and it was hell and down the road there was a vision of heaven on Sundays—and the only way to avoid the purgatorial bit between was to be independent.

That's where he was, between heaven and hell. His knees were shaking now at the thought of two thugs with knives after him, and yet he had been strangely unafraid when it happened. He could face life the same way as he faced the hop heads.

He was finally going to do something. Half the twenty thousand was on its way to their joint account in Toronto. The tickets to Mexico City and the rest of the money—he must call the bank manager and straighten it out. There was some misunderstanding. All the bastard did was talk about Montreal.

Why in the name of God had he dialled the number? That's why the operator had asked his name and room number.

"Yes, this is the Donovan house."

For a few seconds he couldn't speak.

"Dad?"

Bill repeated it.

"Yes, Bill. How are you?"

His son's voice was neutral. No anger. A flat voice.

"Oh, I'm okay, but how are you?"

"I'm good. I was out all day—working on my speech."

"Well—we were kind of worried. Mr. Jackman called and said you weren't at the agency. By the way, he and Mr. Bates left today for New York. Dad?"

"Yes, Bill."

"You're sure everything's okay?"

"Fine—fine. Is your mother there?"

There was a hesitation.

"Mother's in bed. The doctor gave her a sedative."

"Is she—is your mother sick?"

The conversation tensed.

"Her nerves were bad so Rita and I thought we should send for the doctor."

"Oh, I see."

Bill was waiting on the line. Shane scrambled for something to say.

"I don't suppose she feels like coming down tomorrow night?"

It was lame.

"Well, she's sleeping now and I hate to wake her up. Where will you be, Dad?"

"Oh—oh—I'll be here at the hotel. Just polishing up the speech now and I—well, maybe I could call later. I thought maybe we could—for a trip . . ."

"Okay—"

"You're sure your mother's all right?"

The answer was patient.

"Yes, Dad. The doctor said she had to get some rest. She hasn't been sleeping well all week."

"Goodbye, Bill."

"Bye."

He sat and felt a numbing, as if he were exposed to a severe freezing cold, and drank and knew he was back at the point where there was no self-torture—not even thinking—and to hell with it all. Who was he to think of writing, or creating, or anything? He was a hack, pure and simple—and the hell with it.

15

It was a pretty good go at that. Drinking wasn't so bad.

Peculiar, how you missed many of the better aspects when you were uptight. Great guys who drank—and good times too. A bank president winning a bet by walking out of the Park Plaza Hotel around the parking lot and back to the suite at 3 A.M., wearing only his shorts. There was a fraternal feeling amongst drinkers.

The announcer from the CBC who called the Kremlin and got it—

"Hello Kremlin—this is Comrade Charles. I wish to speak to Comrade Stalin."

Telephoning was a hotel disease. A hotel was quite an institution. Perfect refuge, the President, but God, was there ever a place like the Frontier?

A womb-like room. There was one in the Frontier Hotel he liked especially. The corner one on the twelfth floor—southeast corner—where the bed was close to the window. Beer on the floor. Beer on the dresser. Beer on the window sill. To spend the long day in bed sucking at beer bottles and forgetting about the whispering people outside the door and watching the sky and feeling secure with only the staggering, swaying movement from the bed to the bathroom as a trial, when you absolutely had to make the trip.

George, the clerk who could convince anyone you were not in the hotel.

"A man wants to take a little time out for serious drinking," reasoned George, "it's no one else's business but his own."

Watching the winos on the street in the morning, panhandling, converging and counting the take. Then they headed for the wine store. They came back like gaunt vultures with their prey, bottles in plain brown paper bags. They hurried or shuffled faster and then, with the dreadful urge on, they moved into alleyways between buildings. Roll the paper bag down and leave only the neck exposed. Pass it back and forth. Tilt it up and then down. Kill it and leave the husk. They moved back into the street, with a subtle difference. Now they were monarchs.

The battered winos bothered him. Jensen, the City Hall reporter, tried to ease his mind.

"Never mind. They're not the only ones. Just watch the court where I work. The judge has brandy in his coffee, to get the juices moving. The prosecuting attorney has a bitchy ambitious wife who wants him in private practice, and he uses vodka and smells of Listerine. Most of the older defense attorneys keep a Plimsoll line of rye. The younger ones smoke pot and get mad as hell when their young clients get heavy sentences for mary-jane. Don't let it worry you. The sergeant has a mickey in his locker which he says he needs for war wounds—although he never left Canada."

When you started unravelling there was no end to it. The world was a bloody mess. That's what laid you if you were at all sensitive. But he was in a mood of resolve now.

There were things to be done, powerful things to write and say about Canada. There was a way to make politicians wake up to the realization that people were Canadians because of circumstance and environment, and the silly bastards who wrote in the press questioning it weren't questioning anything except their own inability to break away and go to the United States or England and make a lot of money.

Shane hated the ones who stayed home and harped less than the ones who sucked awards and scholarships out of colonial-minded cultural bureaucrats, so that they could retreat to England or the Continent and, on the basis of their own meagre, ghetto childhoods, make a living out of criticizing a society they were no longer a part of—and probably had never understood.

Sons of writing bitches!

Aided and abetted by flower-like creatures in the CBC, whose faces would always be turned to the backsides of the expatriates.

Write a book and call it—

Hell, why the hang-up . . .

Earle Birney was good and he roamed and randied all over and—maybe that was because he dealt with people and had never had to really bathe in the Montreal or Toronto incestuous baths—taking in each other's wash—and finding a way to fake it in the complexities of TV and radio. They were all secretly ready and willing to sell their souls to get to the United States.

Lord God!

There must be a reason he could never join the group—a reason to believe Canada deserved something better—or a reason why he wanted to escape—or live—or some . . . The glass fell from his hand. Now he could sleep. But it was a good idea to put the vodka and orange juice on the table and to prepare himself like a man going on a long journey.

"Miss, please take callsh, gonna sleep."

He hadn't meant to hurt the old man in the park.

"What would you do if you had twenty thousand dollars?"

The old man had pale blue eyes and a face on the edge of bleeding. Shane could imagine him carefully unwrinkling the skin and scraping his face with a straight edged razor—probably an old King Kutter. He stared at Shane for a few minutes, raised his hat and brushed at his wispy grey hair.

"You ain't foolin', are you, mister? Oh sure, you must be. Jesus, if I had twenty thousand dollars I'd go back—back to where I should never have come from. Married a woman who itched—and wanted a big place. She died here—and I never had the gumption to go back. A little place in the Tetons— Red Lodge—outside Yellowstone. Get a cabin and fish and hunt and look at the mountains—and drink that fresh air that's like cool wine in the morning."

He got up and walked away. It was abrupt. Shane felt guilty for intruding on his dreams. But the old man without a thumb on his left hand had also invoked for Shane dreams of *Big Sky* and A. B. Guthrie, and he had to get up and move.

He had squeezed an old man's heart by suggesting an impossible dream. His own heart was always squeezed—had always been squeezed.

Trying to reach his mother.

"But, Ma, don't you feel as if something were going to hap-

272

pen? The world may turn over and go upside down. There will be a big volcano come up behind Mr. McTaggart's hardware store from that knoll."

There was a look of shock in the tired face that for the moment was all chalk with no features. But the hurt came when he heard the betrayal as he listened at night in the house of no privacy.

"I tell you the boy frightens me. He does. He has such imaginings. Such talk about the way the wind whispers and the world may turn over."

His father answering in his normal voice of dull defeat.

"That goddam kid will be the death of me yet. He says goddam stupid things."

She persisted.

"But think of a volcano coming up from that mud hill behind McTaggart's store!"

She said it in a voice that was frightening.

"Well, I don't think you should listen to that kind of talk. Only makes him worse."

There was implicit blame in the statement.

"What can I do? He talks on so at times and I feel it's at least better to listen."

Shane was in the half-world of alcoholic justification. Fragmented and jumbled thoughts came to him, but always in terms of betrayal.

Jackman, Mona—

"Shane, are you sure you explain yourself to Mr. Jackman? Surely he can understand your desire to be creative. Couldn't there be an arrangement?"

"Shane, there seems to be some kind of barrier between

273

you and Mona. Do you make yourself clear to her? She seems like a sensitive woman."

He was trying to explain—only this time slowly and distinctly—what he meant to Mona—only he kept slipping.

He slipped down, and when he came back the whirly-go-gig of colours kept rolling in on him and going back out. Sometimes they were smothering waves of cloudy pinks, reds, and greens that swept in like great breakers. It was suffocating until they began to sort themselves out into shapes. The squares, parallels, and triangles were like measured hieroglyphics that boxed him into a steamy world of riotous colours, but when he moved they ran into a Niagara of colour.

Shane was swimming. He was trying to swim, but the colours had dried into chalky dust now. It was a spraying, polluted compartment of riotous dust. It started to choke him. His mouth had the taste of a chalk brush that old Nelly Loomis had once struck him with. "Old Nelly has a yellow belly." She was there dancing and prancing in her extravagant yellow nakedness, and then she wasn't there.

"Stand still, Old Nelly."

Somebody said it, but the words were a little way from him, as if he had wanted to say it but the words had come from somebody else. When he said it, she shimmered into colours, but she was pink, green, and red and she should be yellow.

That was silly. He wanted to laugh. He did laugh, or at least it seemed to him he had laughed, but somebody else had actually done the laughing. It was hollow and just far enough away that you couldn't catch the words, but there they were, coloured miles of words.

Stalactites, or was it stalagmites?

Coloured icicles of pink, green, and red all pointed at him and they were stabbing down and down and down—and somebody was screaming, but it was a wind tunnel of a sound.

That was good, and in the splashy black blood of the moment he wondered why he couldn't write words like that.

There was the passacaglia of mood. Was that right? It didn't matter because passacaglia was a cool, dark passing of something all around him that was like the way the underside of a dark rotted log smelled. The woods were dense, and black, and you could swim in them without striking the trees. It was soft and lazy and the air was like the feel of a soft slug on your skin. It was rubber soft and that voice was crooning.

"Come, Shane—come, Shane."

He was drowning in black soft flesh. It tasted like a strip of inner tire tube—hard, gummy, and bouncy on the teeth.

"Shane, Shane—Sheen—shon—sheeny—shive—shon—shot!"

There was a stabbing shot and something loomed before his eyes. The blood poured over him, trembling and falling and, separating back into the rainbow of the prism held by Old Nelly, and she was laughing loudly in his ears. No, she was singing. This was the sound of music in the night of the dark red blood, but he had never heard the sound of a thundering harp that was a harpsichord but had the sweetness of a piccolo with the power of a mighty organ.

There was the great organ in all its shimmery, rainbow colours and all the people were applauding, but they were clapping in another room. They were in a cloudburst of sound and each big hand was pink or red or green, and they looked like broken tiles on a green beach. When the yellow waves came in the hands flowed out on a stage.

The chaise came rolling across the stage and the scene faded and now it was an upturned bowl on wheels with transparent sides and "La Goulue" was really a man smoking a cigar, whining at him, and his single eye detached itself and flew straight at him.

He screamed and the scream was in another room, but the sound kept up and the voice was still there.

"Mr. Donovan—Mr. Donovan."

The voice was persistent. Somebody was thumping on the door.

"Mr. Donovan."

Blood anger came up.

"Fuck off. I'm okay. Do you hear me? You woke me up."

"Okay, only you were yelling pretty loud."

Now he had to gather up the shreds of his shattered campaign. First, off with the shoes and socks. Why was it that such fluent wording could come when he was half wet? There was a saying about it at the agency.

"That Donovan is a mad Irishman, but by God, when the chips are down, he always comes through. Good old Shane."

Bromo-Seltzer.

Uh! The thought of the sweet salts made a hot lumpishness in his throat. Open the medicine cabinet.

"Good old Shane."

At this moment Shane was striving to regain momentum. Gripped by a sense of unreality he shaved, spilling a bottle of pre-shaving lotion in the process. A gulp or two of the vodka, tomato juice and egg mixture propelled him into the shower. It was a time of sweaty prickliness. He slipped and went skithering down the tiled side of the shower, his elbow smashing on a faucet.

"Oooh—must watch out. Get killed that way."

In the shower, a drip-drip of water on his head, he started to shiver. Those bastards with their knives—the pills—God Almighty! He felt like a man who had just narrowly escaped a fatal car crash.

The matter of dressing. Everything must be clean. Tying

shoelaces was a monumental job. Then he sat back to try and stop the pounding of blood in his head.

Where the room had been refuge-like shelter from the crush of people in the street, it was now oppressive.

In the mirror he saw that he was wearing a blue suit, and a blue and white tie he couldn't remember even owning. He poured a martini and sipped it.

The telephone rang in the bedroom. He started to move towards it and then stopped. He felt a warning. Danger sign.

"My God, Bates and Jackman!"

He went out of the door and took the elevator to the mezzanine. It was an old-fashioned balcony affair with large pillars and clusters of chairs and occasional writing desks. Shaded by a pillar, he looked down on the main desk.

Bates was waiting, a plump guard over the pile of luggage, as if he didn't trust the bellman swinging a key impatiently around his finger. Jackman walked into sight from under the mezzanine balcony. He shook his head. Bates motioned to the bellman who picked up the bags. They were swallowed up by the elevator doors before Shane walked down the stairs, through the lobby, and into the street.

He had to write a speech. The recipient of the Hiram Aldred Award must respond. In an industry aware of its public image, it was vital to stress how advertising worked to keep up creative standards while advancing the Gross National Product. Advertising was constantly being bombarded by critics. Left-wingers harped on how agencies were parasitical, advancing materialism while abdicating all sense of social responsibility. These were the ingrates. Pariahs, resigned to adopting so-called Thoreauesque attitudes and living off the profits of criticizing the industry.

That's the kind of speech they would love.

277

Why not tell them the truth? America was a nation that lived on waste and obsolescence. Perhaps it, like the containers it was now throwing away, was itself a disposable country?

The New Romans!

Romans controlling an expanding empire, clawing in an ever-increasing share of the natural resources of underdeveloped countries. The empire was swelling itself to a state of satiation, like the liver of a Strasbourg goose—and all the while it was starving the people who lived in the supply countries.

Award night!

A Canadian winning an international award. It was strange how all American awards seem to be international. "Time" would cover it, giving it a hallmark for Canada. Of course, it would be spread all over the Canadian section—that handily disposable three or four pages not carried in the U.S.A. editions.

Would the TV networks be blackmailed into covering it? News? In the carefully rationed time available for dispensing vital information about world and domestic affairs, could someone apply enough pressure on behalf of the advertising industry to get good old Shane Donovan, world supporter of causes through new designs on toilet paper, into the glare of TV's flickering light?

"Another, mister?"

When the bar girl leaned over, her breasts were pushed up so prominently he had to smile at the memory of a joke about bunny girls wearing their knees in the tops of their blouses. It was dreadful gin, so he ordered a Heineken.

A polite speech?

Something about the honour. A few ringing phrases about how advertising helped the economy. It was easy. Everyone would be half-stoned. The trade magazines would run a picture of him clutching the repulsive gold statuette that looked like Stubby Kaye posing for Rodin's *The Thinker.*

"Fifty years—goddam award—and what about tomorrow?"

Shane knew he was not a phenomenon. Middle age was a depressing period, when actuarial tables bothered you.

"Yes, we are going to try advertising on TV," the advertising manager of the life insurance company told him. "Too many people drifting into mutual funds. Gotta get 'em back in insurance. Of course, you know and I know that this enjoying life after sixty-five for most men isn't true. Actual figures show they live about two years and some odd months and they die."

He was simply trapped!

He had a speech to write and both Jackman and Bates were waiting at the hotel. Fathingham would be coming. Great meetings, and then "Where is Donovan?" But Good Old Shane would come through. He was like that guy pursued on TV by Barry Morse—The Fugitive.

Jackman explaining. Telling a favorite story about Donovan.

"Three o'clock in the morning and he's on a garbage pail on Portage Avenue in Winnipeg reciting limericks. Bates, of course, has spent the last fifteen years of his life waiting for Donovan to not show up! But right as rain—a bit hung over, but sharp—he's at the meeting at the Fort Garry at nine o'clock. Hands are shaky. He doesn't say a word and then when the client has turned every idea down, he speaks up. He's got this farm lingo down pat. He knows about John Deere and Massey-Harris—and the prejudice against Eastern manufacturers—and that's when that slogan about machinery 'Made by your Manitoba neighbours' came up."

Oh, he knew about the West.

Pete Kaska, whose Ukrainian father had gone screaming to

his death one night when he slipped in 40 below zero weather under the grain car he was braking on the siding. Pete's mother was a Stoney Mountain Indian from Alberta, a silent dark woman who wouldn't go back to the reservation.

"Come on, Shane, let's go poison gophers."

They slid down the mud banks of the slough in the spring season, combed the village dump, tried to shoot jackrabbits with a bow and arrow, and at night sat still and small in the great amphitheatre of the skyed world when the setting sun splotched the clouds.

"I miss my old man." The squared tanned face topped by the jet black hair gave Pete the appearance of being a diminutive version of the portraits of Indians hanging in the pool hall. He looked more Indian than a full blood.

Shane was too young to respond.

"It's kinda tough," he said, and felt the inadequacy of his words.

"If my old man was here they wouldn't pester my mother."

"Pester your mother?"

"Yeah, guys like the teller in the bank and Joe Landers in the garage come down liquored up and they try to get her to go out."

Shane was mystified.

"They shouldn't do that."

He could see tears in Pete's eyes. He had never seen him cry, even when he broke his arm.

"Shane, my old lady may only be an Indian but she's good to me. I like my old lady. She works, and you know something, my grandfather is a chief—a real Indian chief out in Alberta—and those guys come trying to get her to drink— and I went to the town constable and told him and he musta said something to them because one night a car went by and somebody heaved a rock in the window and it almost hit me where I was sitting. Every time my mother took washing to the lawyer's place, that guy in the garage would come out the door and try and get her to go in."

Shane tried to absorb it. The darkness came and the breeze was cooler and he knew he should hurry home, but he waited. Finally Pete said, "I'll tell you something because outside my old lady, you're the only friend I got. You gotta swear never to mention it. Swear."

It was an elaborate oath, of earth and water and sky, which frightened Shane a little because of its pagan note.

"Now you remember when Joe Landers almost got burned up in that garage fire?"

Shane nodded.

"I remember. He had to go to Winnipeg to hospital."

Pete leaned closer.

"I set it."

"You did?"

"Yes, and you can't break the Stoney promise or you'll die."

"No, I won't tell."

They were walking back along the tracks when Pete said: "I only wanted to frighten him. You see, he stopped my old lady on the street and said if she didn't do as he wanted and not tell Jeff the constable, he was going to tell the lawyer's wife she kept them overnight at our place and did nasty things for them."

"Gosh!"

"Shane, I love my old lady and nobody's going to do things against her. I'll kill them first."

Now, in New York, he remembered how Peter Kaska loved his mother. He had joined the Army and taken the veterans courses and graduated as a lawyer. Shane had heard the story in Regina of how Peter had taken his mother home to be buried by her people, proud of the fact, and wanting his own children to know.

A sense of longing? Was it homesickness or was it something else? Why had he never gone to see Pete or even returned his call that day when Pete was on his way through Toronto to Ottawa to present the petition for the Indian Brotherhood?

"Why?"

Why did the memory of Pete Kaska come to him?
What was love?
Had he ever loved anyone, really loved anyone?
Success?
Shane, like so many others of his age, was a man who felt robbed. His self-analysis always ended in self-pity, and increasingly, he was becoming aware that destroying the emotion by alcohol was self-defeating.

He was of a generation that had been born in rural surroundings, but was without any Thoreau-like inclination to go back. Impaled by the memory of hardship, accompanied by the almost relentless presence of his mother's attachment to religion, which had been her only means of survival, Shane was more deeply sensitive to right and wrong than he ever dared admit. He had even mentioned it to Jackman.

"T.A., when I pull a trick like that, I feel kind of cheap," he admitted.

Jackman guffawed.

"Not a bit of it. That gimmick with the box of detergent was a masterpiece. Showed those smart bastards up. I know, you don't have to tell me. It's the phoney part that gets you."

"Yeah, it sure is. Put some yellow crap in the stuff and do commercials and it'll sell like hell, and it won't be a damned bit better than any of the others. It seems such a hell of a waste of effort and time."

"It keeps us in groceries. You don't mind eating."

"But a lot of other people aren't."

Jackman kept staring out the window. Shane finally added, "And, T.A., don't tell me it doesn't affect you, too. You're a sensitive man. You know what I mean."

Jackman nodded.

"I know. There was a time a few years ago when I—well, I was going to get out."

"Bask in the sun?"

"No. Don't laugh at this, but I spent Christmas in Jamaica. They were going independent and I met Bustamente, a politician, but an amazing man. We spent quite a bit of time together and he kept telling me how they needed teachers. Well, I seriously thought about it. The being useful bit. You see, I taught school for three years when I first came out of college."

"I'll be damned!"

"Yeah, then I came back and there was a crisis of some kind and time went on—and here I am and I'm going to have to retire in a year or so."

"Teach then?"

Jackman's snort was startling.

"Can you imagine Trixie being married to a teacher for black kids in some place like Ghana, or the Congo or God knows where?"

Shane laughed, but Jackman continued: "The worst years are when you begin to see the end. It's like looking down a long street and you get busy as hell working on the side of the street but you're on that old moving belt and no matter what you do it's taking you closer. Ever feel like that, Shane?"

No matter how he regarded it, the award was some kind of symbol. Deep in his consciousness he knew that acceptance represented capitulation.

He had to talk to someone. Keep away from agency types. Try Tom Hamilton. He was in the Village. A fugitive from the National Film Board, obsessed by Canada's indifference to building ties with Mexico and South America to counterbalance the United States.

"Drop me at the smoke shop on Eighth Street," he told the driver.

Eighth Street bustled like the Kensington area in Toronto. He couldn't just barge in—so he took Tom cigars.

"Shane, good God! Aren't you getting some kind of gong for something? Come in—come in—"

Hamilton was a small wiry man with tousled wiry grey hair and a drooping moustache that gave his tanned face the look of a bandit. He wore black slacks, black turtle neck and a peace symbol on a string around his neck.

"Sorry to barge in, Tom. I'm plagued at the hotel and I need some place to think."

"My friend, you are welcome. I'm going out to do some shooting and my humble hacienda is all yours. Sorry I'll be away, but maybe solitude is what you need. Have a drink?"

Shane shook his head.

"No, I got fed some drugs at a pill party and I'm woozy. Can't get down to earth."

Hamilton was solicitous.

"Know what they were? Is it like a bum trip? This town is lousy with bad stuff."

"No, under the circumstances, they were probably good. Slept and now I'm just restless. Can't seem to light."

"I know—I know. Things don't seem useful any more. You know my hang-up—greatest potential in the world for film and I was making things like how to deep-fry frozen cod. I had to cut out."

"How goes it?"

Hamilton was happy.

"Great, man. I'm free anyhow. Get enough work, like documentaries that aren't too bad. Mind you, on the American networks, you don't exactly show the U.S.A. in a nasty role—and in that exploding South American country you don't picture the CIA men standing behind the benevolent dictators as provocateurs. But I'm building footage of my own—great stuff I could never afford on my own—and then one day, you'll see Tom J. Hamilton's feature on South America. That's it. Hey, are you sure you're okay?"

Shane felt as if his insides were shaking against his rib cage.

"Here, drink this. It's fruit juice. Won't hurt you."

"That's good."

Hamilton sat down and lit a cigarette.

"Look, is there anything I can do for you?"

Shane made a motion to get up.

"Now, Shane, don't worry about it. You were a real friend to me during Expo when I wanted to kick the Film Board. I have to go out, but that doesn't matter."

Shane looked at the red-tiled floor, the pottery figures, the straw mobiles, and the fiercely coloured hangings.

"No, you go ahead. You see, I have to give that speech here on Saturday—tomorrow."

Hamilton snapped his fingers.

"I remember. You're getting an award. I was going to send you a wire—but—" He shrugged his shoulders. "You know how it is. Best intentions and all that—"

"You're really heavy on Mexico."

"Yeah. I like all South America but I dig Mexico. Mexico will be the clincher in my film. You know, they're the only country in this hemisphere—well, outside of Cuba—but they did it peacefully—that can cope with Big Brother here—"

"Mustn't make you too popular here."

"Oh, you'd be surprised how many Americans there are who are really concerned about the way they are exploiting the world. In Mexico they come in—on Mexican terms—and they do it. Some beat the ownership rap with dummies—but, in essence, they have to live as guests—not like conquerors, which is pretty much how they treat Canada."

"I'm trying to say some of that—but I've had a hell of a time getting anything done—damned telephone and—"

"Stay here."

"Oh, I couldn't."

Hamilton insisted.

"Of course you can. I'm going to be out all day and tonight I'll go to my girl friend's. The place is yours. Let me show you."

In the plain white bedroom, a large bed was covered by a fur throw. The walls were undecorated except for a collection of what appeared to be crude wooden and iron crucifixes.

In the studio there were stacks of colour films. On an easel Tom had a collection of paintings and sketches.

"That's stuff from students at the Instituto in San Miguel de Allende. Bloody marvellous place."

"God, that reminds me. I'm a little hazy but I think that's the place the bank manager suggested I go. I was there the other day."

Tom laughed.

"That would be Bateman. He hates running a Canadian bank in New York, is afraid to go back to Montreal and keeps trying to get head office to open a branch in San Miguel. You still writing on the side?"

"Some—like to do more but can't seem to find the time or place."

"Go to San Miguel. You'll find your soul there. Seriously. Now look, there's a bar here with anything you want. The kitchen is a bit untidy but there's lots of food if you're hungry. Bathroom right here and look—"

He showed him the roof.

"My rough but serviceable patio. Looks over what the goddam developers have left of the village. Now how about it? No one will disturb you. There's a portable typewriter under all that crap on the desk—paper—anything you want."

"Well, Tom, it's the best offer I've had in New York."

Hamilton had only one admonition.

"You're more than welcome to stay all night. Stereo machine—TV—booze—food—use anything you want. But make sure the spring lock is on the door and the same thing downstairs if you go out. Keys are on the mantel."

Tom left and he was alone again.

Open rooms above trees and people and cars—another New York. From the parapet of the roof he watched the people moving—into bars and out of bars—in sidewalk restaurants—by art exhibits that were splashy, vivid rambles of minds extended to breaking point.

In other places, lofts and cramped attics, rooms and makeshift apartments, dingy basements and old, grease-spotted garages and husk-like former factories, an assortment of people were striving to, or working to, or pretending to create. Creation was the name they all used.

There was a mass of papers on the desk. Scribbled notes and typed fragments. In red pencil on a pad, Hamilton had written words: *I want in my work to have people show sympathy for me as I demonstrate how important I am.* Below it were the typed words, "At forty I left a steady job, my wife

287

and family to start over again, because I had to either give up my creative urgings and subscribe to the process or else find out before it was too late, what I could do—"

The paper had been pulled from the typewriter and half crumpled.

He moved curiously about the penthouse. The stereo flooded the room with the sound of mariachis. Mexico! Shane Donovan, from the day he left Nonsuch, had always had an urge to go and wander. Now he was fifty years old and driven to do something besides thinking up advertising ideas and copy.

"The new nude look in pantyhose. Deterge the world into a wonderful wasteland. Fly to those far-away romantic places."

Shane sniffed at the bottle of tequila. He tilted it up. Sweet balls of fire. Try it with a mix. Tonic water. Squeeze a lemon in it. He took the drink out to the roof.

"Fear, boy—fear, boy."

The drink walloped. He remembered.

"Mona, I was talking to a fellow who says you can rent a really nice place year round in Ibiza for fifty dollars a month. I was thinking—you know, I showed that outline of a novel to one of the editors at the publishers—we handled their book club advertising. He thought it was pretty good."

Her face tightened as he spoke. He stopped talking.

"Go on, Shane. I'm listening."

He was getting angry. She was preparing an answer.

"Oh, God, what's the use? There's the school for the kids. How do I know I can write? I'm just fooling myself. I'd be drunk all the time. I know what you're going to say."

Mona had protested.

"Shane, how do you know I was going to say that? Maybe

288

there are schools there. After all, a lot of Canadians and Americans go to schools—I mean, live there and must have their children in schools."

It had gone on that way for an hour until neither knew which side they were speaking on.

Now, he had to work. Go inside and really work. He pushed the papers away and sat down at the desk. The bits and pieces he had compiled at the hotel wouldn't work. He made several false starts, paced out on the terrace and back in again and finally began.

"I intended to give a polite speech of appreciation for the award which you are giving me. I do appreciate it. Thank you very much.

"Having said that, I am moved to go beyond it and express and share some of the torturings of my soul at this time—for all of us who live and work in North America must feel some unusual twinges about the circumstance of the time, of the place, and of the emotions we have, not only as citizens but more essentially as human beings.

"It may come as a shock to you that Harold Innis was a forerunner of McLuhan. Innis, also a Canadian, studied communication going back to clay tablets. He said as a result that writing which requires tools and training preserves traditional ideas and perspectives. Broadcasting is instant and requires no training to perceive. If you accept the Innis contention that the use of a medium of communications over a long period determines the character of the knowledge to be communicated, it is not difficult to assume that we have a revolutionary change in society after each revolutionary change in the means of communication.

"Radio and television revolutionized communications. You must know of the consequent revolution in our societies."

Shane was a traveller who finally departs on a long-postponed journey.

"And what do we find? These instruments of change and revolution are still dominated by few of us—and if not alone by the members of the advertising industry, at least by a claque of individuals who refuse to regard media—in particular, radio and television, as anything more than instruments of profit.

"They persist in the neutering process. Their kingdom is the kingdom of banality—where originality is truly a sin: and, in the final analysis, omission will be their sin rather than commission.

"We, who are in the middle age, desperately hang on to the familiar—much as we earnestly despise it and ourselves—and all because we hate to admit that it takes courage to face the unknown.

"Someone has called the generation we have sired—the children of the Apocalypse. Our credo seems to have been 'never let our children be exposed to hardship—cradle them in the comforting arms of consumerism for commercial sakes —for if obsolescence be the rod—the G.N.P. shall be thy staff all the days of thy life at all costs.'

"But our gospel is being rejected. Our children are cynics who look on much of our efforts as the products of dishonesty. They laugh at our distortions. If the truth were truly known, they may be crying, not in the panic of their chemicals—but shedding tears for our lies . . . for they know, for instance, that our market research is a tool of manipulation—and the education that we offer them so freely is booby-trapped to keep them in our system."

He stood up and stretched, half-reached for the tequila, but went back instead to the typewriter.

"I am convinced we have brutalized the senses. In our concern about manipulating the masses—not always selfishly, but often with a careless feeling that we are doing good—we have forgotten the individual. The assembly line process of production has robbed the producer of the dignity of skill and pride in his work. Manipulative merchandising has taken away our dignity as consumers.

"America is sad. From being a benefactor of mankind in the post 1939–45 years, it has moved to where it is regarded as an oppressor. While it writhes in social and economic chaos at home, its pervasive influence, economically and militarily, sows discord as it disrupts in all corners of the world—on behalf of causes that most Americans can't identify or don't want to remember—

"Sad, too—is *my* country. Because while it has the opportunity like a younger brother to avoid the mistakes of an older one, it is often traumatized and fascinated either into easy acquiescence or imitation. Instead of developing those unique qualities with which heritage and environment have endowed us, we are too often passive and defeatist.

"We are spoiled by the proximity of a country that has squandered an abundance, ignores us, and somehow feels we are similar in nature. We are, in the words of President Dias of Mexico, 'So near the United States and so far from God.'

"The hurt is in being ignored. That hurt, by the way, is not unlike the hurt felt by consumers who are coming to the realization that their needs and desires have all but been ignored by advertisers, and by merchandisers, and by producers.

"If we, as advertisers, are important in the scheme of living —as we like to suggest—then we must recognize our responsibilities to consumers as well as to producers. Aren't we all consumers with interests and needs? And skepticism, just like the skepticism and cynicism in the emerging life style of the generation we reared embraced more strongly by a television set than by our own arms and emotions.

"We must recognize that we do not have much time. Our democratic system is fragile—and further abuse may well leave it—democracy—as a frail memory in a world of intellectual slavery."

He ached.

He was finished. There was nothing more he could say.

16

The mariachi music was still playing when he came awake. My God, the recording had been going on and on . . . a repeater device of some kind. And the place was stark and there were gourds and hangings and splashes of colours . . . Hamilton's! The speech!

The speech was okay. That he remembered. There it was, messy with something like blood that was more likely catsup spilled on the first page. He must have been eating something. Good God, a splash of red on the white, goatskin rug. Hamilton would murder him. It rubbed out . . . almost.

Anyhow the speech was finished. Call Jackman? Hell with it. Bates would be buck toothing around and Bates he could do without. The orange juice cramped his stomach and he spent time straining in the bathroom trying to remember when his bowels had last moved. That was probably causing the headache.

He had to get back to the hotel and let the typist work the speech into a clean copy. There was the old pull about leaving a place like this . . . these rooms, like so many hotel rooms, became protective after a time. He sipped gingerly at a drink, poured the remainder out and rinsed the glass. Just enough to start the old machine!

"President Hotel."

The cabby slammed on the meter and made a sudden turn in the street, grazing an old man with a pushcart. Driver and pushcart operator yelled ritualistic insults at each other.

Shane felt better than he had expected. On an impulse he redirected the driver to Tina's address. There was a vague reasoning about checking the speech out with Tommy . . . or was it really to show Tina . . . And even if Tommy wasn't there, Tina would know where he was . . . could talk to her about that drug business. God, how stupid it was for a girl like that.

She needed affection. Tommy was a cold, little fish in a way. Tina was a stainless-steel girl but she was warm underneath. She did respond to him . . .

The encounter in the alley came back to send a flood of fear washing inside him. He mustn't think about it. But there was an excitement—perhaps danger—in Tina.

There were occasions when Shane felt as if he had missed a great deal in his life. He had never been quite able to obliterate the feelings about not going to war. His life had been marked by that one reckless, dangerous trip from Nonsuch. But after that there was a void. Cheated? Perhaps.

The newspaper, the agency—a steady, slow path and the

dreams were always secondary. The job—the money—and then the writing. An old familiar treadmill.

But Tina! Behind that façade—oh hell! He had mentioned Mexico to her. She would go with him. Days in Mexico with Mona would be simply—hell, there was no sense in going on and he was tired.

Sleep tonight. He would lay off the drinking, eat dinner and surely Tina would have a Valium or Librium stashed away. In that private pharmacy, there must be some ordinary old-fashioned sedatives.

He was smiling as he went in the lobby of the apartment. A different attendant was on duty.

"Shane Donovan—Miss Bond's apartment?"

The man looked at him gravely.

"Are you police or a newspaperman?"

"No—I'm just a friend."

The doorman shook his head.

"Sorry, but no one is allowed up."

It was all confusing. Shane turned away. The cab driver was still in front, writing something by the dome light of the cab. He could still catch him for the ride back. No, he must see Tina. He passed the doorman a five-dollar bill.

"Is there anything wrong?"

The doorman palmed the money but continued to look solemn.

He removed his uniform cap and wiped his forehead.

"Perhaps you would like to go up and see the gentleman, sir. You being a friend and all, you might help him."

"What do you mean?"

The doorman held the elevator open.

"I would prefer if the gentleman told you."

A concerned doorman, but he had no reluctance about taking the money. What the hell could be going on? Busted for drugs! God, that's all he would need. Better not get involved; but he went on anyhow. Hell, he was clean. Maybe he could help.

Tina in jail! Why not Tommy? He might have been arrested himself. Ad executive in jail on eve of award! How many times after a memory blackout he had worried about where he might have been—what he might have done.

The bell rang several times before the door opened. Tommy looked smaller and older. His clothes were uncharacteristically rumpled. He stared at Shane as if he didn't recognize him.

"Good God, Tommy, what's the matter?"

Tommy's voice was a monotone, but his expression was unchanged.

"It was good of you to come, Shane. I guess you heard it on the radio. Tried to get you at hotel. Didn't tell the police you had been here. Didn't want to complicate you—is that the word? No involvement. Didn't know what to do. Called a doctor I know at the club. He came. Could tell he bloody well didn't think much of me. Didn't know what to do! Funny, I don't even know how to contact her parents. You might know. Live in some place up in Canada. Must tell them. Don't even know if she wrote them. I've been trying to find a letter or something—"

Shane interrupted.

"For God's sake, Tommy, what the hell are you talking about? What happened? Where's Tina?"

"You don't know?"

"I don't know *anything*. The doorman was all mysterious until I gave him five bucks, and now *you're* raving."

Tommy hadn't been listening.

"What are you doing here?"

296

"Tommy, I came to show you what I wrote for tomorrow night and see what you think of it."

Smith sat down.

"I see. I see."

The plastic chair squeaked rudely under his weight. He ran his hands through his hair.

"I hate plastic. Always hated it. She liked it. Shane, she was really a grand girl—but she did like some tacky things. But I guess that doesn't matter. Not any more. Strange how little the matter of taste means now."

"For God's sake, Tommy, what's wrong. You really haven't told me anything."

Again Smith appeared surprised.

"Oh, Shane? Yes, I'm sorry, but Tina is dead."

Donovan grabbed for the mantel. He felt dizzy.

"She's not!"

Tommy's head went up and down mechanically.

"She is, Shane. She is dead. She is. Just like that."

"I don't believe it."

"I know. I can't but I saw her—oh God, Shane, the poor creature was almost purple. She was—she was—"

The tears came. Shane went to the kitchen. He could remember her showing him the hidden bottle of brandy.

Metaxa's! Greek brandy. He poured two drinks. Tommy swallowed his, meticulously wiped and dried his eyes and seemed to regain his composure.

"Tommy, now can you tell me what happened?"

"Sorry, old boy. It's been a bit of a strain. She was in bed with me. I woke up and the old ticker was unsteady and I called her. She came in from her room. She gave me brandy and held me—and said some very strange things—but I was half in and out—and I knew she had been popping pills—that fat eunuch Tiger had started her—and she would get very

297

high—and I fell asleep. All very hazy. I woke up about eleven and chased Tiger out. The others were gone. Made some coffee and went in and she was bunched up—clothes rumpled and my God, she wasn't breathing. As I say, I finally got the doctor—he said she was dead but had her taken to the hospital—and it was too late. Maybe if I had called the police, they would have given her oxygen—or pumped her or something—but I didn't know what to do—and the police were —well, it's old stuff to them—and they look around—and said —really—so what—and I stayed here, trying to find an address for her parents."

Tommy had a half smile on his face.

"You realize how unimportant you are. Police were only concerned about foul play. The hospital gave my doctor friend hell for bringing her in and said they had to be paid cash. The undertaker has to be given money in advance or he won't look after her. Do you know there was actually a call a few minutes ago to see if the apartment would be vacant?"

Pop art—mod art and a Tiffany lamp—white walls—white rug and plastic furniture. Ché Guevara on a poster. Ché Guevara dead. Tina dead and a stone cat dead. Tina was ivory. Ivory girl with black eyes—now white faced—black-gowned widow in Zorba—stoned to death by angry villagers —and Tommy was weeping in a plastic chair that could float down the East River.

"God—oh, God—oh, God."

He half-whispered the question.

"Tommy—did she—I mean?"

The little man nodded.

"The bottle was beside the bed. Nembutal. The doctor gave it to me because I had a bad back—slipped disc. I kept them here—should have kept them at home. Why didn't I? Why didn't I?"

"Oh, Tommy, when a person—hell, when a person makes up their mind—they'll find a way. Look at how they tried to keep Hemingway away from guns."

He stopped. It was stupid. Hemingway had nothing to do with it.

"Sorry—sorry—sorry."

He whispered the words. Death wasn't such a shock. Bill Edmond, the fat copywriter, had slumped in Shane's office and contorted and died with a puff of froth, like an overweight youngster blowing a soap bubble.

But Tina! He had felt the pull of her all week. There had been an element of suspense about her—perhaps danger. It was risk! Of what, he didn't know, but there was an understanding between them—perhaps a sympathetic knowledge of each other.

"I shouldn't ask this, Tommy. It's a rough time for you and—"

"Oh, Shane, what's the difference? What do you want to know?"

"Why?"

Tommy got up and went to the windows. He pulled back the drapes and stood looking out. He went to the kitchen and poured more brandy, ignoring Shane.

Tommy, I know it's none of my business."

The older man turned quickly. He plucked a cigarette from a dish on the table and lit it.

"What do you mean—not your business? God, man, you were in her bed when I called her."

"But, dammit, I just—well, somebody poured me something—or gave me pills or something—and I crawled in there and passed out—and Tommy, before God, Tina was on Cloud 9."

Tommy's anger subsided.

"Sorry, Shane, sorry."

"Tommy, it's understandable. Of course, I was attracted to her—she was attractive—"

Smith didn't seem to have heard him.

"Oh, it's not blame. I don't mean that. I'm to blame. She was pretty badly hurt and I tried to be good to her. I didn't make demands on her—we drifted along—together—and not together. She had—she told you, I think—she had a pretty rough initiation into sex . . . but, even that worked between us—I'm not actually a very great lover."

He paused.

"There was my mother. Domineering and certain no girl was good enough. No, goddamit, that's not right. My mother wanted me to be a bachelor because she couldn't bear to think of some day being infirm and not having someone to look after her. That meant no wife for me—and the ridiculous part is she'll probably outlive me."

"Did she know Tina?"

Tommy nodded.

"Had private detectives follow me. Then she lowered the boom. It was all very well to have a relationship—but no marriage. If I married a Greek restaurant owner's daughter she would sell her stock in the agency and cut me off. You know damned well how long I would have lasted in that case."

He seemed reluctant to go on.

"But, Tommy, how did—"

The agency man squashed his cigarette.

"I thought Tina was perfectly—well—she understood. I tried to be good to her. We drank too much, but who doesn't? Then the pills started. A year ago she got something and it was a bad, bad trip. The doctor warned her. Since then, it wasn't too bad—not good—I guess. Always people around—

300

too many people—God—but I was sick of them—every weekend and Tina—I thought Tina wanted them—I was so stupid."

His voice was choked. He stopped. After a time, Tommy continued: "Last night Tina was strange. I know she had a strange mixture of pills. She said she was going away unless I wanted to marry her. Said her career was a bust, and she didn't want to end up—as a—well, whore, because she didn't have any talent."

Tommy's hands were clutching at the plastic of the chair.

"Well, what could I do?"

Then, as if remembering, he paused to stare at Shane in a way that made him uncomfortable.

"And you, you bastard, made it worse."

"Me—what do you mean?"

"She liked you, and all your goddam talk about taking her to Mexico and writing a book. That set her off. She said she was more tempted by that than by anything in her life, and told me to get the hell out and stay out."

Tommy's voice cracked and he swallowed deeply.

"I went to bed—no, I guess I wasn't in bed when you came. Oh, it doesn't matter. I started to go and went to bed. When I woke up I called her and she came in—actually, Tiger heard me and called her. He was the one said you were in bed with her. She was very sweet—very kind. As I say, I went to sleep and . . . oh hell, I told you that about finding her . . . and what more is there to say . . . except that an hour ago I wanted to kill you."

"Why?"

"Because you . . . you started her thinking about . . . about an escape I guess."

The realization came then. Tommy really blamed him.

"But, Tommy, sure I was boozing it up . . . and this old dream about getting away to Mexico and writing . . ."

Tommy's face set into a hard, small mask.

"About the twenty thousand dollars you had and the tickets to Mexico . . . and how you were going to write the book . . . Jesus God, even that old chestnut about the Great Canadian Novel and the fact that Canada had to be defined and you were the one to do it."

"Goddamit, Tommy, I was talking, but . . ."

"Listen, as I said I was mad but . . ." His face softened . . . "Shane, she was attractive. I was no good for her. That girl wanted love and consolation and to get above all this crappy life and you had . . . I could hear you in her words . . . 'been tested in the crucible' and you wanted to turn the unhappiness into something positive and let the fire burn out of your soul and on to paper and redeem yourself . . ."

He stopped talking. Shane couldn't bring a word to his tongue. He *had* talked about Mexico, but it was all so vague. When he left he didn't say anything. Tommy, sitting with his head in his hands didn't look up, but Shane heard his words distinctly.

"What's Mother going to say?"

He was reciting it over and over as the elevator doors closed.

"Get you a cab, sir?"

"I think I'll walk a bit."

"It's raining, sir. Light, but it's really not wise to walk down here alone at night."

Shane nodded. The doorman had to shriek his whistle at least a dozen times before he flagged a taxi.

"Where to?"

It was the voice of the New York cabby. Not polite. Not angry. A fine point of surliness on the edge of rudeness.

"Just drive."

The driver shrugged his shoulders.

"Okay by me, bud, I'd just as soon get out of this neighbourhood."

Shane scarcely heard him.

"Used to be a nice neighbourhood. Ain't that way now. People gotta watch every step. I been in N'Yawk all my life. Somethin's happened. Everybody for himself. I think people has gone mad."

There was no response from Shane. The driver stopped talking.

In Nonsuch, old people died, but they were wrinkled, yellowed leaves that clung precariously to the connection of their lives in a family. Finally, racked by coughing or convulsed by some strange force, as fall leaves are by wind, they fluttered down, and died. Unlike the leaves left on the ground, or raked to burn, or whirled away in fall gales, the old dead were cosmetized into an overdrawn image of younger times, draped and placed in coffins and finally transported in a hearse, an oversize hearse with windows draped in flounced grey silk to give a view of the coffin, to the cemetery, wind-blown and dusty, where men lowered it into the dry yellow earth. The priest or the minister, depending on the chance of how the person was born, would say words. The priest would be in a white surplice, and after taking the sprinkler which Shane had carried handle down from the church, he would dispense holy water on the coffin. Then the earth closed in as the Edson brothers, the gravediggers, who received a dollar each, shovelled in the raw earth and everyone went back for a community lunch, a necessary bridge to the normality of living disturbed by death.

It had never seemed anything but natural to Shane until it

was George Humphrey. George was a veteran. He had come home in 1918, gassed and unable to work.

George Humphrey was a man with time on his hands, and he was one of the rare men in Nonsuch who spoke to youngsters as if they were grown-ups. In the kitchen with the yellow scrubbed wooden floor, he talked of Vimy Ridge and of the gas. He spoke of men, now dead, who seemed to be present, and he let them handle his rifle and his revolver.

Once they went shooting gophers with him, but he walked slowly and stopped for breath, and when he finally killed a gopher on the edge of the town dump, he told them harshly to leave it alone.

"I've seen enough blood, any kind of blood, to last me all my life."

He was driven by the doctor in an old open McLaughlin Buick with flapping sides to Regina Hospital one November day. In the way of children, they had almost forgotten him until he came back in May. Then, on spring days, he sat on a chair on the back stoop, wrapped like a mummy. He spoke in a hoarse voice, his face shrunken and his eyes dark in black-rimmed sockets. He didn't say much, and he had an old baking powder tin he used when he hawked and coughed.

They heard the news on a Friday afternoon on the way from school.

"George Humphrey shot himself."

His wife had gone up to see the doctor because he couldn't sleep.

"Had to sleep in a chair."

"Couldn't sleep finally."

"Going to die anyway, so he killed himself with that revolver he took from a dead German."

"Blew half his head off."

"Did it in the kitchen and his brains were all over the ceiling and the wall."

Shane started home but when his stomach started to retch, he had gone to the privy behind the station house. When he came out the stationmaster saw him.

"Too bad, boy—too bad. You kids all liked George. Everybody liked George. Too bad, but maybe it's all for the better. George had nothing to live for."

Shane nodded. The stationmaster looked away.

"He couldn't face going back in the hospital. I saw him last night. He was cheerful but last thing he said was how he wouldn't go back in that hospital. Don't take on, boy, too much. When you get older, you'll understand. Soldiers learn about dying. You will too. Now you better run home before your mother starts worrying."

The stationmaster, the Edson brothers, the lawyer, the doctor, and the scarecrow figure who cleaned out privies and drove the "honey" wagon, were pallbearers. They all wore their old uniforms and they seemed to look alike on that day when the hearse, without a cross because Humphrey was a Protestant, took the coffin to the cemetery a mile down the road from the Catholic one. The coffin was never opened, and Shane shivered when the taller Edson blew the old trumpet. That day the whole town was different and the lunch was in the community hall because the doctor's wife said the Humphrey house had to be cleaned, and death felt close to Shane Donovan.

How would Tina's father respond, and would Tommy attend and . . .

"Driver, take me to the President Hotel."

The envelope was at the desk with the tickets. Two visas. One had his name. The other was blank. The letter said it was unorthodox, but he could fill in the name; Señor May-cotte of the Mexican Consulate understood. Nine thousand dollars in traveller's cheques, loose Mexican and American money. The receipt for the money in his joint account with Mona stabbed him, but he stuffed it all in his pocket. Bateman had scribbled a note saying he hoped to see him in San Miguel de Allende. There was an excellent railway from Mexico City to San Miguel.

His packing was a diversion. It would make it easier to leave on Saturday night after the awards dinner. It was essential for him not to stay around. There would be parties.

He scrabbled through the mail. Originals of the messages poked under the door. A letter. Mona had written.

Dear Shane:

I didn't know whether you would want me to write or not. There isn't much to say. It has been cold here and old Mrs. Herbert has been in her garden. Wonder she doesn't catch her death of cold. I guess she just wants to be first to garden ahead of Tom Dooley. He was over asking all kinds of questions because he heard on the radio you were getting an award. Bill finishes school next Friday. Says he wants to work his way to Europe on a cattle boat. Rita is still talking about the convent, but I talked to Sister Veronica and she is not convinced it is a vocation. She would like to talk to you when you come home. I am feeling better. We all miss you.

Love,
Mona

The tentacles reached out for you and brought you back into the world of home and the old lady and her petty rivalry with her neighbour. Sister Veronica would tell him Rita wanted to run away to a convent to escape. Bill was determined not to be caught in an everyday work-a-day world and he wanted a year of bumming in Europe—and there would be Mona and himself alone.

Mona had written that letter on purpose. It was a reminder of his duty. Dr. Leddy would know.

"Shane," Leddy said once when he had gone to the doctor's home after a lost week in Chicago, "do something. I can shoot you full of B1 and get you in some kind of physical shape, but I can't really do anything about your emotional problems."

The poor, it seemed, were too busy staying alive to indulge in emotion. The rich could afford any kind of arrangement they desired, from psychiatrists to mistresses to lovers and divorce or even annulments if they were powerful enough Catholics. Leddy sympathized with the poor bastards in the newly affluent middle class—especially the highly moral ones. As he explained it:

"Shane, they come into affluence with the puritan standards of peasants. Like wearing all your clothes during intercourse. Well, they have consciences stuffed with all kinds of things—especially sex fantasies. It's bloody good fun if it's healthy. But the moralists have been trying to make it dirty for a long time. They stuff the heads of their kids with all kinds of taboos and never tell them the to-doos."

Leddy was vehement.

"You want to write and tell the truth as you see it. You want to share what you know about the world—good and bad—but you can't even tell your wife or your own family. In some ways, you are just as hung up as Mona, with her visions of angels and purity and first communions and all that—"

Pacing the floor, he stopped, and his face gentled.

"Oh, well, look, see if you can get Mona to come and see me. I'm no psychiatrist, but I'll try. I hate to see good people like you two wasting precious lives. I'll see if I can get some sense into her head. And try and bust your own locks. Get writing and get out of that whore's house of an agency."

Under a pretext, he had Mona see Leddy. That night she didn't mention the visit. Later, when the children were in bed, he introduced the subject as casually as possible.

"You saw Jim?"

"I saw him."

The clock ticked loudly.

"How is he?"

She was sewing. Her shoulders shrugged.

"I don't think he's very well. I couldn't make head nor tail of what he was trying to say. It was baffling. Does he drink?"

He packed carefully. The effort made him weak, but he resisted having a drink.

Tina?

Poor, bloody bird—like one of those creatures that dash against a lighted window. He couldn't be responsible. Simply talking about Mexico couldn't have been the reason.

What it must take to do that!

He stuffed the tickets, traveller's cheques and pesos in the suitcase and locked it. Would it work if he went home sober and took Mona to Mexico? Get away entirely. Quit the agency.

Going down in the elevator he began thinking of a play. The old Scotsman outside of Handrich who wouldn't give control of his farm to his sons. Staunch old non-drinking Presbyterian who took his grown son out of the bootleggers' hut by the scruff of the neck—tough and dedicated, who finally had to give in—a proud, old chieftain who finally yielded control.

308

There were ideas galore.

The girl on the train who was crying. He had lain awake in his compartment and imagined where she was going and plotted scene on scene—and let his mind wander back to Tom Wolfe's ride back to the death of the older Gant and the pounding rollicking way young Gant was on a screaming train to college—or Carol and her doctor husband in the dirty, smelly day coach going to her new home on the drab prairies in *Main Street*—and wondered how he could ever possibly write—and tormented himself finally to sleep.

Sometimes he tried. Sometimes it worked. There was the radio play he did in a white heat of creation about *The Girl in Compartment C*, which had been used by CBC and the BBC and had been repeated on NBC in the days when American networks used radio drama.

Shane walked on. He could go to a show. A girl at a doorway stepped out and touched his arm.

"Gotta light, sir?"

Her hand rested on his while she drew in on the cigarette. Dark eyes, in a heavily made-up face under dyed blond bouffant hair, looked into his. He shook his head. She shrugged her shoulders and walked into a bar.

It was a cold, damp shroud of a night and he had to physically restrain himself from going into a bar. Instead he called a cab. He gave the driver Bonnie's address.

It was 1:45 A.M. when he pushed the buzzer of Bonnie's walk-up. After what seemed a lengthy wait, she opened the door, keeping the chain on.

"Shane, where on earth have you been?"

She opened the door. There was a small light over the TV set. She was wearing a housecoat.

"Where haven't I been?"

Bonnie caught his arm in her fingers.

"Ssshhh. Peter is asleep."

"Peter. What the hell's he doing here?"

"He worked right through last night and all day on revisions of the play and he just flaked out here." Then, as if sensing his question, she added, "Oh, now listen, don't get any ideas. I was typing and he was in no condition to go out so I made him go in and lie down—I'm sleeping on the daybed."

Shane was caught in a strange mixture of rage and embarrassment.

"You don't have to explain."

She caught the tone of his voice.

"I know I don't but I wish you would. I've been half crazy worrying about you. Not at the hotel and I took a cab up and wondered if you were sick and when the bellman let me in, it looked as if you hadn't been there—"

His mind flooded with anger.

"Jesus Christ, you sound like Mona."

Bonnie pulled away.

"I was just concerned—and so was Peter—"

"Peter, God, you just met him."

Her voice was a shaft that went deep inside him.

"Well, I just met you, too, the other night—remember?"

He had no answers.

He turned and walked out. Before closing the door he remembered; taking the two keys from his pocket, he threw them back into the apartment. Going down the stairs he thought he heard Mona saying something, but his head was full as if it was ready to burst.

Alone again, utterly alone. He walked and his legs were stilts. New York flowed around him and he was unaware of anyone. A bartender was a blurred face, and he yelled back at a cab driver who protested taking a Canadian quarter as a tip.

"Oh shut up, you miserable bastard. You're like all the

other stupid Americans who think there's nothing in the world but this crazy country. It's money . . . good money . . . so if you don't like it, shove it."

He remembered drinking and checking out and almost missing the plane at the airport. There was something about a girl on the next stool in the cocktail lounge who slapped his face when he offered her a free ticket . . . and he had been protesting when the attendants steered him on the plane.

He had remembered to get the speech typed.

No sign of Jackman or Bates at the hotel. He had been somewhat disappointed when they were not there . . . but he must have sent a note to Fathingham. He must have. Drunk or not, he would surely let Fathingham know—but the hell of it was, he just wasn't certain.

17

His departure from Mexico was solemn. Felipe had taken charge from the moment Shane told him he was leaving. There were no recriminations; in fact, it hadn't seemed to be a surprise.

"My cousin will come for you."

It was a ceremonial, a ritual of dignity, apparent in the way the ancient black Dodge was clean—and even more evident in their apparel. They could have been hauling mourners for a funeral.

There were elaborate farewells. Drinks for Miguel and Pablo. Then Roncalli handed him a bundle of cigars tied in a ribbon and called him professor. He had wanted to pay Shane for the typewriter.

"The señorita will be welcome for whatever she needs. This is my promise, Professor Donovan."

Felipe was sweating and dabbing at his forehead with his bar apron.

"I wish to say something, Dr. Donovan."

The title was a form of the respect he wished to show.

"I am a simple man, and unable to make words in the way of you."

Shane put his hand on Felipe's arm.

"Don't worry, my friend, you have been very good to me."

"There are great thoughts in your head. I knew that, even while you were in my cantina and talking a great deal and some said it was only the tequila, but you have a . . . how can I say it . . . *machismo* . . . for your country, just as a Mexican has and it is a great thing for a man. You are a man of honour, señor. You will always be welcome here, and it is my promise that Marguerita will be protected, for she has been lucky to be with you, and . . ."

Words failing him, he turned back into the cantina. The two cousins stood solemnly by the car. Shane had his hand on the door handle and then he went back to the house of Miguel.

Marguerita was sitting on the cot holding the tissue-papered clothes. It was almost as if she had been waiting for him to ask her to go.

"Maggie."

She put the dress aside, stood up and walked across the tiles. There were no tears. Her hands came up to his shoulders and softly caressed his beard. She silently looked at him, and in the instant all shreds of reproach vanished. Her eyes were strong and steady, and he glimpsed a love deeper than he had ever known in his life. He kissed her on the forehead and went back out to the car and made a silent trip to Mexico City.

It was uncomfortable. The seats were covered with a hot, unyielding armour plate of plastic. A sudden stop for a wandering donkey, a stopped peasant bus with its amazing load of animals and people, or simply for someone walking in the middle of the road with a studied unconcern for the fact that it was a part of the north-south Pan American Highway sent him sliding off the seat. The drivers didn't look back. They didn't speak. Silence showed their responsibilities. In Mexico two men are required to drive on such a trip. Shane was amused. Engineer and fireman?

The rains had come. The land was just beginning to green. In a way he would be sorry to miss the resurrection of flowers, grass, and leaves. But there could be no delays, although it was harder than ever to maintain resolve in the Mexico City airport. The difference between Latin America and North America begins to take shape in this place.

Planes arrive and take off and the mechanical ritual is the same as at any international airport. But the atmosphere is a shock. It has a distinctive feel, smell, and sound, and there are smiling girls dispersing free rum and tequila. It is a part of North America, but a proud part that resists deadening conformity. It is Mexican.

Here were Americans and Canadians not able to assimilate it all because it was so different from John F. Kennedy or Dorval. They looked disbelieving, as if they had been hijacked to some mysterious place, more Spanish than American.

Shane waited. The returning tourists swarmed through the shops, changed money and chattered.

"This is such a fantastic place. So picturesque but I just said to George it makes me appreciate Philadelphia all the more."

"Oh, my husband was so sick. The idiot drank the water—and talk about the Aztec two-step—it would have been funny if it hadn't been so tragic."

"We were so careful. Ate tinned foods and drank only bottled water—and you know what happened?"

"No, what happened?"

"We forgot about the ice in the drinks. We were both just so sick—dear me, I don't know how these people live."

"I'll be so glad to get home."

There were other things Shane must face. The speech he had mailed to Fathingham—left at the desk. The other copy he had left for Jackman along with a note:

Read this for your dear departed brother or shove it. I don't really care. Better still, let Alf read it.

Why worry? The agencies were capable of handling difficult situations. The speech had probably been rewritten. Must save the mystic order. "Mr. Donovan was called away but he asked me to tell you how overwhelmed he was by this great honour bestowed on a Canadian."

Subservient crap!

But there was no sense in getting angry. The whole thing was an abstraction in a sense. That was one thing he had learned in Mexico; the problem would be to retain that reaction.

But how do you retain a mystery? Drinking time and blurry days and the greasy, earthy smells and the haze of sunlight and the nights of sitting in the cantina—just taking pleasure from being with people, talking and not having to be bothered listening to them because you didn't understand the language.

The mystery happened with the desire to work and not drink. The feeling of Marguerita. A sense of warmth and affection for a—simple—what other word—woman! That was it!

Good, bloody days!

Words spilling out on page after page—a lifetime—hate and love—and suddenly it was finished. Packed up and sent off. Exorcism. But as he had walked back from the post office he had again become an alien. Marguerita annoyed him— and when he was angry she would cower like a frightened puppy. And the fleas bit him. And why did they put that bloody, hot tabasco in everything?

His stomach hurt with gas pains, and in the mornings his legs ached. He wasn't drinking. Why should he suffer? A man could expect it from drinking, but to suffer while you were sober was bloody—and he began pacing alone, knowing that he was hurting the girl. He would come back late and go to bed on the cot and later she would creep in beside him and he would ignore her; but coming awake and feeling her warmth, he would be punishing enough to make her cry out in pain at times.

The real mystery was in the simple matter of perseverance. His life for a good many years had alternated between drinking and sobriety. But there was always a canker of knowledge —an inner nerve that pulsed like the light in the corner of the TV screen warning for a commercial—a certainty that on a certain day the steady drinking would all begin again.

It wasn't simply bad luck or misfortune. That had worked as an explanation for a time but it was no longer valid.

It just happened. A dark cloud, the way Mona spoke, a traffic snarl-up, a sudden urge to order a double before lunch —and going on without lunch. The awesome clutching inside —the despair of a world of trouble and tragedy—or the sheer weight of pressure release when an account was firmed up after a plugging campaign. Or sometimes a loin pain on a night when he walked in a distant city and looked at hotel and apartment window lights and imagined the warmth—and felt chilled. That was enough to do it.

Perseverance would be the problem!

"You get restless, señor," said Roncalli, "you are a Northerner and it is all the same here. Too much all the same with the sun—and the heat—and you miss the cold."

He was going to miss them, the unaffected people who accepted him, protected him and had been tolerant of his drinking moods. He remembered the bullfight, where he sat with the natives, avoiding the seats sold to tourists. He was scarcely aware of drinking tequila again until he was suddenly sick.

The man in the rumpled white suit handed him a handkerchief that smelled faintly of disinfectant.

"Here, señor."

He was slim and dark with a thin straight moustache. His eyes, very dark, were set in deep sockets. A ridged scar marked his chin. The black hair with the white traces looked sculptured.

"Thank you. Sorry. Must be the heat."

"Yes, señor, too much heat is not good."

Shane noticed the slim elegant hands and fingers.

"I'm afraid I made a mess of your handkerchief."

"Not to worry, señor. It is trifling—but you must take care of yourself."

He hadn't said any more but in the night when his stomach felt as if he had been butted severely, Marguerita had brought the stranger. He was Dr. Berrendo—but the locals called him Captain.

He was very sick. When he lay down, the pain and pressure swelled up and tried to force an opening at his breastbone. The dark man examined him carefully.

318

"A sedative, señor, to relax you and a liquid to try and soothe your stomach. Better, señor, to sit for a time."

It was easier sitting. The doctor lit a cigarette and sat by the doorway on the stool.

"Would you like a drink, Doctor?"

"Oh, no—I may go and have a cold *cerveza*."

Marguerita brought one from the bar.

"Mexican beer is excellent, don't you think so, señor? The only one I remember like it is the Pilsen of Prague."

"You are not a Mexican doctor. I thought there were only native—I mean Mexican—doctors here."

"Oh, no, I am Spanish. Very strange for you, señor, because as you may observe, Spaniards are not too—how do you say—high regarded by many of the people of Mexico."

Dr. Carlos Berrendo, physician and surgeon of San Miguel, former captain of the Loyalist Forces of Spain. Formerly of Paris, Prague, and London, now a general practitioner to the poor.

"I came as a refugee many years ago. It was my wish to be useful and there was no doctor here. I came to work for the liberation of Spain and return some day to a free country. But —Spain has never been freed—there is perhaps a price on my head—I haven't worried for a long time. I am useful here, and a man can ask for no more."

In time the sedative took effect and Shane fell asleep. In the morning he was sore. His withdrawal pains were severe, but nothing to match the force of what Berrendo described as an internal hernia—an occlusion between stomach and intestine.

Marguerita took him to the doctor's office. The waiting room even at 10:00 A.M. was packed with patients. Women holding infants, a man from the jute mill, patiently holding a crushed hand in a bloody wrap.

319

"Come in, Señor Donovan. Come in."

Shane had been ashamed to pass the injured man.

"But that man is seriously hurt—"

Berrendo shrugged his shoulders.

"He will live, and go back to the mill and maybe next time not be so fortunate."

He would miss Dr. Berrendo. At night when he was exhausted from writing or trying to write, he used to call on the doctor. Not often, but occasionally, Berrendo told him about Spain—of the war—and even of contacts with Canadian volunteers in the Mackenzie-Papineau Battalion.

But he never mentioned drinking.

Until the disastrous night when Shane had fallen into the old pattern. Drinking until Marguerita helped him back to bed, where he came screaming awake into a world of snakes and coiling monsters.

Berrendo had given him an injection. He waited, sipping black coffee brewed by Marguerita until Shane had quietened. Next evening, he had come to sit and smoke.

"Señor Shane, you know—you are an intelligent man, you must stop or you will die."

"Is death so bad?"

"My friend, I have seen very much death. It is to be avoided. I know. When I left Spain, I would, perhaps, have welcomed death. But then, it passed and now I—I shall fight it, as long as I can."

They talked half the night about death. To Berrendo death was to be accepted when it came, but only a fool welcomed it.

"Pablo, who was in my office the first day you came, Señor Shane. He was discharged by the mill for being clumsy because they did not want to pay damages. Pablo has nine children, but when I dressed his hand Pablo worried about none of these things. Pablo plays in the concert orchestra in the plaza. He plays the bass, and he worried in the fear his hand might keep him from playing his bass violin. Señor, these are brave men—tomorrow is an abstraction, as is death —while there are things to be enjoyed today."

That night Shane dreamt he was dying. He was dying alone in a Mexican hill town and Mona and Bonnie were laughing. There were many men around the grave and they were arguing about placing him in the grave. They were so busy they scarcely noticed him crawling over the raw earth and, when he looked down, Tina was lying there. She opened her eyes and extended her arms to him and he came awake screaming.

Marguerita nursed him. He tried to stay awake and when he finally slept he was again a small boy trying to keep awake at Midnight Mass. Marguerita must have told the doctor about his nightmare because he arrived next morning.

"Señor Donovan, I have come to see if you will accompany me to visit a patient. Perhaps, because you are a North American, you can tell me the nature of this man's illness. It is something of the mind."

They drove in the battered Volkswagen to a casa on the mountain.

"I must tell you a man's principles erode in facing practical things. I swore when I left Spain I would never use anything German. No more *Liebfraumilch*—no good sausage—and here I am with a German car. But Señor Shane, I did not get it until they were defeated."

The house was surrounded by a pink stone wall. It was white adobe and gardeners worked amongst the profusion of flowers while sprinklers whirled. Outside the land was desert-like with clumps of cactus and Spanish bayonet and an occasional greasewood tree. The Casa Sardo was an oasis.

The woman was of indeterminate age, tall and dressed in a brilliantly striped caftan. Her blond, almost ashen, hair was bound with a bright scarf. Her face was obviously constantly cared for, but the eyes betrayed the mask.

"Mrs. Engle, I brought a Canadian man of business who is also a writer. I felt it might do your husband good to speak with him. They may know things and places of common interest. I hope you do not mind?"

"Oh, no, Doctor. I'm very pleased you could come, Mr. Donovan. Doctor, he just sits there—sits and won't speak and I don't know what to do."

"Has he eaten?"

"He tries—milk—orange juice—even rum and coconut juice—and it all comes up."

Herman Engle was a heavy man, once muscular, now gone to fat. There was loose skin on his jowls and neck, and his stomach wrinkled through the sports shirt. He wore shorts and sat with his grey wiry hair bristling like that of a middle-aged squat Japanese wrestler. He barely acknowledged the introductions and began talking.

"I suppose you are also working for one of those great corporations like the one that mailed me my last cheque. Thirty-eight years from puddler to president and the sons of bitches buy the place out and close it down to kill our competition because it was the only way they could lick us, and they let 4,156 men and women go and they haven't the guts to face me. So they mail me my last cheque and twenty-five thousand dollars. What the hell do I want the money for? I just want my job and to work, and they took that away from me. Well, get out, because that's what they'll do to you. Buy up all the companies and have only one left and then where will you be at?"

"Perhaps, Señor Engle, you could tell my friend the kind of business you were in."

Engle didn't appear to hear him.

"Doctor, you've got to do something about my nerve ends."

He rubbed his hand over his chest.

"They're all raw right here. I can feel a pain in the end of every one of them and there must be thousands."

Berrendo prepared the hypodermic.

"Yes, Señor Engle, this will ease the pain, but you must rest and concentrate on other things. Take a drive with the señora and try bathing in the *tabuada*. It is very good to stop pain such as you have."

Engle nodded.

"I'm going back as soon as these pains stop, and I'm going to fight them. I didn't cash those cheques and I'm going to fight them. Elsie, you have those cheques?"

"Yes, dear, they are in your dispatch box."

"Good."

His head dropped forward and he put his hands across his chest. Mrs. Engle nodded to them and they went out to the patio.

"He probably won't say any more now all day except to try —you know—juices or drink or something. Doctor, what can I do? I'm desperate."

"Mrs. Engle, I have consulted Dr. Juan O'Hara of Mexico City, a psychiatrist, and he will come to see your husband. If he finds he can do something, he will expect you to take your husband to his clinic in Mexico City."

"Oh, I'll do anything. Don't you think you can do some-thing—I know somehow, I know you can help him."

Berrendo acknowledged her statement with a mere nod.

"You are very kind, but I am a simple doctor of the people.

I patch wounds and inoculate babies and ease death, I hope, for the old; but your husband needs a man of deeper skills."

"He's not—I mean—"

"No, but he is convinced he is very sick and that is often more dangerous than to be truly sick. He has had a great shock. A very great shock to his pride—and I am afraid he does not find anything to make him want to live."

The woman stiffened with shock. But she braced her shoulders to go on and tell them without rancour of her husband's promotion from being a helper in pouring steel to foreman, to superintendent, to manager and ultimately to the presidency of the Illinois plant.

"He was very good to us. Our daughter graduated from Bryn Mawr and is married to a naval captain in Los Angeles. Our son went to Northwestern. That was a disappointment. He wouldn't go near the steel plant and he's a magazine editor—well, a sub-editor—in Chicago. Herman worked seven days a week. One year the only day he didn't work was Christmas. We have a beautiful home, a summer place on the lake—which he didn't use—and—well, I would think he has everything to live for. And he could travel now—and get the education he said he never could get because he went to work so early in his life—"

Shane went out to the car and the doctor stayed. They were both quiet in the car going down the mountain. The doctor threaded the car down the narrow streets to Shane's place.

"I don't suppose you want a drink, Doctor?"

Berrendo smiled.

"No, but I would enjoy a cup of Marguerita's coffee."

When they were sipping the coffee, the doctor said, "You know he will die."

"Will the man from Mexico City help him?"

"No. There is no will there. Besides, I have lived with death all my life and I can smell it. Don't ask me why. I just know. Juan is an excellent doctor. It will be a great help to Mrs. Engle, a very patient woman who I think deserves some attention—for this is a very bad time for her."

"Did you really think I could help him?"

The doctor smiled enigmatically.

"My dear Señor Shane Donovan, I perhaps thought he could help you."

"Hmm. Devious, aren't you?"

"Not so. We have spoken in great frankness between ourselves. This place is not—"

He stopped, aware that Marguerita, poking at the charcoal, was absorbing their conversation.

"One should not form too deep friendships under certain circumstances. Perhaps that is a clumsy way of saying it. Look at these people, people with so little—hanging on. Watch them at the bullfight—the fiesta—in the cathedral even, although, as you know, I have reservations about that. But take Pablo—his hand crushed and worried about playing music—and that man on the mountain—worrying about his nerve ends and killing himself because of his pride—and a narrow selfish life."

He told also of his own pride. Disaffection for the Loyalist direction, never for the cause and hatred for the fascists. He had been too visible in Mexico City and came to San Miguel because it reminded him of his home. He had sat and got drunk and ignored the need until a very old man whose son was dying of pneumonia threatened to kill him if he didn't respond to the call.

"I cured that boy. I had to. Sixteen hours and I know my will had as much to do with it as medicine—and when I came back there was a line-up at my house—and there has been one

325

every day since. And I am a doctor and I am of use. What else can there be in life? I am Dr. Berrendo and I cannot be in Spain, and I who say there is no God, I wonder at what power sent me here. I go on, and I will go on and do what I can."

Berrendo paused.

"There is a die cast—or perhaps a form in which we are conceived and grow. Something happens to us when we are young—and we live with it—in it—in the shadow of it, all our lives. It is our individual mystery—and no matter how we try to escape, we cannot."

"I wish I knew mine."

"But, señor, you do. Somewhere it is an inner feeling of wanting to be of help—of wanting to protest against those things you do not like in your society—and perhaps you have avoided it. It is not that you are afraid—it is more that you have not found a direction. But, señor, that direction becomes apparent in what you write—you have found many things in Mexico, but you who do not have to be a stranger at home must go back, and I must go on."

Berrendo had refused further comment.

Shane was on his way home but he knew he was closer to the heart of the mystery that had pursued him all his life. It was not solved, perhaps never would be solved. Yet this progress was a relief, and more would unravel in the days to come.

18

There was really no sense in attempting to coax sleep. He was tired, but it wasn't enough to counter the restless urge. He could recognize the symptoms. They had not been bothering him in the latter days of his stay in San Miguel but they were back . . . just as Leddy and Berréndo had warned.

A cool beer?

God, just to feel the coldness and dampness of the bottle in his hands. That first sip. Running, tart over his tongue and down his gullet and easing into his stomach. The minute feelings of strength and the easing of the edge of pain in his legs and the relaxation of the bar and . . . goddamit, he had to get up and walk.

Bloody sirens of the rocks. Scotch . . . tequila . . . fire and

water . . . and as sure as God made little kittens a session in
the bar would mean missing the plane, and then another,
and he would crawl back into the room in San Miguel and
Marguerita would be there and no one would fuss him and
. . . good God, every direction of argument led to the same
thing . . .

"I must go back."

The long vigil of San Miguel de Allende was over and the
manuscript had been dispatched to McMaster. For once in
his life Shane had accomplished what he planned to do. It
was no quick and easy solution to a problem, produced like
a conjurer's trick to stave off trouble. It wasn't an appease-
ment gift to his family for real or fancied neglect.

"It's bloody well finished."

But the voices were always clamouring. He could stay in
Mexico forever, writing. There was that guy who had written
from Mexico, a mysterious figure whose anonymity produced
publicity and questioning . . . And if he used a pen name
and Eric would protect it, he could go back to San Miguel
. . . and Marguerita . . . there was no doubt about missing
the girl.

"No, I must go back."

A cleric reading a breviary looked up at him curiously.
Shane shrugged his shoulders. The priest smiled apologetically and went back to his breviary, but Shane noticed him
eyeing him.

Surely going back was the real test of it. There was no escape, because Nonsuch had become more real in the mountains of Mexico than even in the downtown canyons of
Toronto. Just as Tina carried the Soo . . . and Tommy . . .
well, hell, Shane had to go back.

And his book would enter the little world of Canadian letters! Smothered by parochial criticism and drowned by the

waves of American and British books, what the hell chance could a book have? Published in New York, with the copy writers frantically trying to find some references to America . . . "an author who has been honoured by the American advertising industry for ideas . . ." God, you had to work to get a notice in *Time*. They'd bury the review in the flimsy Canadian section, which was conveniently deleted from all other editions, and if it were a Book Club choice, it would be a choice only in Canada . . . but some of them made it. Some Canadian authors somehow managed to get exposed to the American public without actually packing up and moving.

"You're Hugh MacLennan."

Shane had introduced himself in the washroom of the Toronto Arts and Letters Club and they were zipping up at the urinals. There was an elaborate ballet ritual of handwashing, towel rubbing, and hand shaking.

"Mr. Donovan . . . oh yes?"

The tall man with the sideways-held head and the sonorous voice still ringing with the accents of his Highland ancestors was obviously trying to figure out who he was and what the hell he was talking about. There was a mumbling and muttering and by mutual consent they parted and lost each other in the cathedral-like dining room.

Shane had been polite. He had wanted to say, "So you wrote a good book about the Halifax explosion and a pretty good one about the Quebec thing. But that latest is for the birds, and how the hell did it ever get on the lists? You must have really worked to intrigue the Americans enough, or who did you pay?"

Sour, sour, sour.

And there were others as well. Mowat, with his beard and his absurd kilt and all that crap about wolves and deer. Drinking rum as if it would go out of style and acting like an extravagant bohemian . . .

They were all wrong. Callaghan was dated. Richler was an expatriate who couldn't stand the country and spent his time excoriating it because he was trying to scourge the memory of his Montreal ghetto childhood.

The only one he enjoyed was Buckler—*Ox-bells and Fireflies*. Why? Somehow he had to face it now, before he went to New York. There was no competition in Buckler because only a few people, like Claude Bissell of the University of Toronto, had discernment enough to see that it was a classic. A truly contemporary Thoreau.

Why? Why? Why?

Why did he dismiss Canadian poets, contemporary ones, as a bunch of randy, old darlings pursuing their diminishing sexual powers?

Yet why was he haunted by Bill Mitchell's *Who Has Seen the Wind*? Why did he abhor most of the dramatic efforts on CBC? Why couldn't they be as good as some of their documentaries?

It was tearing at his gut. He had never consciously thought of it before. He had spent much of his time defending Canadian consciousness, but had never accepted what was Canadian. Goddamit, those characters of Mitchell's were as Canadian as the people around him on the Street of the Goats were Mexican.

MacLennan was far more real than O'Hara with his sleek, cardboard creatures manipulated in Gibbsville. That puzzled priest of Callaghan's was a man, better than Bascom Hawke.

David was a distillation of Birney from Banff to—and even Duddy Kravitz smelled of salami from Montreal's Main Street and not from Broadway.

Shane had come to a conclusion. His mental meanderings had stopped. He was a Canadian and that meant he had been conceiving and feeling in foreign images while thumping for a realization of what he imagined to be his own. Nonsuch was Nonsuch because of John A. MacDonald, downing his whisky and teetering into Parliament and driving the bloody railway through by hook or by crook—and it wasn't Fargo or North Minot.

He was a petty—no—selfish—maybe—but self-pitying man who had absorbed a British education in the shadow of an American presence and had fought against those of his own people who made it!

Morley Callaghan! What the hell else was he but Canadian, and Paris and New York hadn't taken it away.

Who then had been the foreigner in his own land? Who had been selling his soul in the pseudo existence of the agency, pretending to be Canadian when each and every idea was in effect an imitation? Who had walked through Quebec and failed to see that it was as real and as different as Mexico, and had gone along with the play-acting of translating the untranslatable and retailing it in Quebec?

He looked at his watch. An hour to go. If it were late . . . he took out the letter from McMaster:

My dear Shane,

I've read it . . . The Great Canadian Novel? Don't laugh. It's good. It's different. Even my editorial associates have shivered a bit over some of it.

The firm will publish it.

Now, what I have to say is going to be most difficult. This is a lacerated, painful thing you have written. It will probably sell. I am afraid it will, and probably for the wrong reasons.

It is not a formula book. We are of course flooded with formula books. They pose as answers to the di-

331

lemma of modern living, exploit the raw, connective tissues of sex, conceal personalities, dead and alive, just below the libel line and some . . . well, some are launched like new detergents or floor wax. They are merchandised along with the items people buy because they somehow think they must have them.

Our promotion people will launch your book as the middle-aged man's dilemma. *What every middle-aged man should know about his dilemma* . . . or even worse, a smart allusion to his libido or lack of it.

It may also sell because it catches the emptiness of our lives. I again say I think it will sell. Is it the book you want to write?

I have a feeling you have started on a long journey, at last, and you have turned something around in yourself. Who really cares about another exposé of empty lives?

I care about the shaping of Nonsuch and St. Gerald's and the way a generation in your country have been exposed to the combination of subtle shaping of British manners and colonial attitudes and the unthinking exploitation of Americans. The Great Canadian Novel, no matter what you call it, is the story of the generation that is coming to realize the natural qualities of environment and justice and love and hatred and sweep and power that all belong to the kind of existence you spoke of that night when we talked. You had me spellbound.

We need, and I mean international readers need, a book without self-consciousness. It should be done with pride and without a sense of martyrdom.

You can do it.

By the way, Peter gave up and went back to be host of a TV show in Canada. Bonnie is here now and is working well as a reader. Tends to children's books. Well, too! She often mentions you. I think you haunt her as someone she somehow failed.

So, we will publish this book, but we will look as well for another. That choice is up to you. I'll be here for two years and your book would probably be my swan song. I would like to be here for the next one as well. I've bought a small book store in a New England town and am going to operate it. Can't get away from books, you see, and in spite of McLuhan, I have faith they'll be around. I even have faith that books of integrity, of heart and fortitude will even triumph over the present infection.

Do let me know when you are coming and we'll try to meet you at the airport.

Most sincerely,
Eric.

Berrendo had said: "Life must have a *raison d'être*. Here it may be survival. For my brother it was the church. For you— you must learn, but, señor, you live in a dangerous society. I do not know America or Canada too well, but we see two kinds—the men like Engle who places everything on success —and when it vanishes, he is lost. The others are escaping. They look for pleasure. Mexico is full of these women, lonely widows of men who kill themselves and divorcées of men who seek pleasure. I watch the bus tours in the plaza, women like sheep being herded from place to place by guides. It is perhaps some of these things that you protest. You are an artist, señor, who has avoided it. But being an artist is lonely. It is like being a doctor—in some ways—at least like being a doctor who cannot go home. But you will do what you have to."

He put the letter away and went to the desk.
"Miss, I'm booked on Flight 1114 to New York City."

She was dark with slightly protruding, very white teeth.

"Yes, sir, it leaves in eighteen minutes."

"Do you have a Toronto, Canada, flight?"

"Yes, 1207 leaves in thirty minutes."

"Do you have space?"

"I think so."

She punched a card and inserted it in a machine.

"Yes, sir, I can book you. What name shall I say?"

"I am Shane Donovan."

She fussed over the exchange of tickets and Shane thought of an old film, a Saroyan story, that had a small boy crawling through a fence and a large black man waving as he clutched the ladder of a tank car and yelling, "Going home, boy. Going home."

There were so many things to do. They were calling the Toronto flight. He went on board. The stewardess smiled, mechanical, doll-like, and offered him a newspaper.

The New York Times!

The pattern came back in a mosaic of headlines. Threatened strike! Middle East! Unemployment! Racial disturbance! Bombing! Pollution in Lake Erie! Mercury poisoning! Increase in prices predicted! Flood and famine in India!

He rested the newspaper and looked down on the vanishing city. Marguerita would be watching every plane that went across. He must arrange to get her a shortwave radio. She was curious about Canadian shortwave. No, not a radio. Send her a record player. What San Miguel didn't need was a flood of communications. Save it from the global village as long as possible.

He was sleeping when the stewardess came back.

"The bearded fellow who is sleeping looks familiar."

But he wasn't sleeping when she came back to ask if he would have a drink.

"No thanks."

He said it, but added almost apologetically, "Not just now."

Dr. Crest had said something about that at the clinic . . . finding it strange to refuse a drink. Thinking it set him apart. The plane droned on and he was going back. Toronto. The act of booking had been impulsive. In New York there would have been time to get adjusted, make some calls . . . but Toronto was a different matter. He wanted to go back. Almost as if it were time.

His mind combed over possibilities. Stay in a hotel. Have a chat with Jackman; he could persuade him, in spite of Bates. Send the carbon of the book to Mona. It was proof.

"This is what I had to do."

Yet, there was no real answer in either. Escape into the agency. Go back home and try and pick up the ravelled ends of life.

"At fifty I had to prove I could do it, Mona."

God, he was almost fifty-one now, and it was only a numeral. San Miguel de Allende. What had it proved? The real satisfaction was in the effort, and it was the first real satisfaction . . . and when the effort ended . . . strange, wasn't it? He had to leave or drift back into . . . What had Berrendo said about Pablo losing his job and playing that night in the orchestra?

"For Pablo today is reality and tomorrow is an abstraction . . ."

His stomach contracted and he pushed the call button.

"Could I have something to eat, please?"

The girl smiled.

"Of course, Father. We have steak or chicken and would you like red or white wine?"

"Steak? It'll be good to have a decent steak again. No wine, please."

"It's tenderloin, Father. We'll pick you out a nice one. It must be really difficult down here . . . were you in South America, or Mexico, Father?"

He kept from laughing with an effort.

"Mexico, my child. It was . . . well, rewarding."

She tripped off beaming, obviously proud of herself.

Rewarding? In a sense . . . but was life rewarding for Marguerita?

He had often wondered about his mother. Particularly that one shining time when she had broken her own silence. He had asked her simply:

"Maw."

The light from the kerosene lamp cast her face in yellow bronze. Her eyes squinted as the thin restless fingers moved shuttle-like—to and fro—mechanical extensions of the blue-veined hands that pushed and pulled the needle through the cloth.

"Yes, Sean."

She never called him Shane. Her head was still, as if the effort of raising the grey-streaked, once yellow, hair was too much effort.

"Did you like composition, when you were in school?"

They were alone in the house. There was only the sound of insects scrabbling on the screen door. His father and brothers hadn't come back from the softball game played on the dusty ground behind the hardware store. His father would be talking, Pat and Mike making themselves obscure in the darkness surrounding the patch of light from the single bulb at the back entrance of McTaggart's.

"Composition?"

She said it softly—then, like a bird, looked up. He saw her eyes. They were red-rimmed from strain. Two dull jewels in the cross-hatched veined pockets sunk beneath the furrowed brow so taut against the bone of her forehead. It was a timid question. But they were alone; and sensing there would not be a contradiction as there always seemed to be when her husband sat in the rocker, waiting gloomily to drop assertions over all coversation, she smiled and let her hands fall with the patching to her lap.

"Why, Sean—composition. I never thought much about it."

He caught a flash, as if the tiny fragments of blue in her eyes came into form and gave expression. Then she smiled, and, forgetting to put her hand up to cover the three missing teeth of her lower plate, she nodded.

"Oh, yes, I did."

He didn't interrupt. A moth noisily fluttered itself into a stunned death on the lamp chimney.

"Miss Grierson, once when I was in the third book, made me read my composition—she called it an essay—right out to the whole class."

"She must've liked it, Maw."

His mother closed her eyes and leaned back. With the strain gone from her face and the neck drawn back to obscure the way it seemed to hang in loose flaps on the cords, Shane realized for the first time that his mother really looked like the brownish-tinted picture in the oval art glass that hung in the tiny front parlor with the fading flat straw of palm they brought from church on Palm Sunday. If she had a ribbon in her hair and if the tan faded . . .

"We drove to Handrich one Sunday. My father had a double rig—that was like a double buggy—and he had a team of three-year-old sorrel drivers. My, they could step along so high

337

spirited and father drove well—said they needed a run to get the oats out of their system."

Her hands lay like peaceful doves on the nest of patching.

"It was the Sunday before the first of July. Jim sat up front with your grandfather, just itching to get hold of the lines. He was going on for fourteen. Clare—she's the one I told you died of the erysipelas—poor Clare, her first baby and her only eighteen."

A pain, a shadow passed over his mother's face, the same way a light cloud blotted out the sun for a few seconds.

"There was Ma, Clare, and myself in the back seat and we had a parasol. Oh, it was a red and yellow one. Uncle Ned brought it back the time he went to work in Michigan at the lumber woods near Bay City. Ma always said it was too gaudy but we begged her that day—"

She was looking at him now. Only seconds and the moment of love, it must have been love, because it warmed him—the moment was gone. When she was silent, Shane urged her on.

"We had a picnic lunch under the seat. Lemonade from spring water wrapped in a wet cloth and—oh, but it was a good feeling. The horses' hooves just went clip-clop and the dust was rolling away behind us—and father would pull out and pass someone and try to keep from smiling when he passed them and he'd say, 'No need to take any dust from anybody when you're behind Bess and Bob.' That was his names for the drivers."

Shane exclaimed.

"Did they go fast?"

His mother laughed. The unrestrained laugh startled him.

"Oh my, they just seemed to coast along, and the woven wire fences were shimmery, and people waved at us and when we got to Handrich Poppa—"

She had changed from calling him Father.

338

"Poppa drove us around the square. There was, you see, a park in the centre—"

Her hands moved to illustrate and for a moment he thought of buds fluttering.

"Like this—the park was the hub of the wheel and the street ran around where the spokes would be and the stores were all along the rim facing into the hub—and, of course, there were streets running off in six, maybe eight ways through the town, and one of them went down to the harbour."

"Like with ships and stuff, Maw?"

His mother nodded.

"My yes! There were boats there that brought grain to the big elevators and the flour mills there—"

"Where from?"

"From here—the West."

"Gosh!"

He had never consciously thought before of the links between the open wide prairie land and the East of little farms and towns that he read about.

"There was a big steam yacht—like a palace, it was. Some Detroit folks sailed it up and they spent the summer in Handrich. We walked by and they were sitting under a kind of awning on the back eating a meal and a coloured fellow in a white uniform was serving them."

His breath expanded in his chest.

"Were you in the water? Did you go in the water?"

"Oh, yes, off to one side was a nice sandy beach. Ma sat in the shade on a bench by a bathhouse where people could go and change to bathing clothes."

"Did you?"

"No, we splashed and paddled. Poppa put the horses away. The water would roll in on the sand and catch you if you didn't watch out. We could see the town up on the bluffs and we walked out—away out on a long pier into the water and there were some men fishing there. Ma made us hold hands because at one point you just believed the pier was sailing along through the water."

"Gosh."

"There were sea gulls whirling around and little boats sailing in and out and they would get away out to be just like white specks on the far edge of the blue water. We played with some other children."

She sighed.

"They were from town and they teased us but there was one nice boy. His father was a jeweller and he took our side and he came back and met Ma and—"

His mother broke off.

"Did you like him?"

She was startled into placing a hand in front of her mouth.

"What a question! We were only children—well, in a way."

There were traces of a pinkish flush on her face.

"He was a nice boy. He's a member of Parliament now. His name comes up in the papers sometimes—the farm papers, because he speaks a lot about farming. I think he has a farm."

"Did you eat your lunch down there?"

"Oh my, yes, it was grand. The water and feeding crusts to the birds and it got dark and we went home."

Remembering now, Shane could feel his disappointment. "Is that all?"

"Clare fell asleep. I was too excited."

"And you wrote that for the teacher?"

"I wrote it and for once, I didn't seem to have no trouble finding words. I just—"

That's when they heard his father and the boys coming

up the gravelled walk. His mother picked up the garments and the needle.

"You two plotting something?"

His father's face was flushed. He could tell by the way his brothers grinned that someone had provided moonshine or white lightning at the game. They were chewing licorice. That was a tell-tale. They were bribed, but his father couldn't conceal his own evidence.

Shane remembered saying, "Maw was just telling me about a composition she wrote about going to the lake one time."

Why had he said it? Was it because his father was always prodding him about wasting his time at writing? He had an ally in his mother. *She* had written.

"Well now, tell us all, eh, boys?"

He sat down, still wearing the battered old railroad cap he persisted in wearing long after his lay off, when they were allowed to go on living in the section hand's house on the off chance that work might come back.

"Did you tell him or did you tell the teacher about your paw getting liquored up on his way to get the team, and how you had to sit down there shivering by the water until your brother went finally and got him?"

Pat and Mike stopped smiling. His mother's shoulders bent over and over as the words came like whiplashes. Her head was finally down at the level of the edge of the table. He stood up and ran out, slamming the screen door. When his brothers came to find him he would have been safe, except that Old Peek betrayed him. They were gentler than usual.

"Maw wants us to go to bed."

"I'll be along."

"Don't take too long."

They went and he was alone in the black night beside the track, his hand clinging to the cold iron rail, hoping it might somehow take him away. Finally when the light was gone from the kitchen and he saw it in his parents' bedroom he crept through the weeds and up to the stoop.

"You always get britchety about me."

He hadn't seen his father sitting there and the voice seemed to come out of the night.

"No."

"Well, I didn't mean no harm but she's always telling it like as if everything was great back there. Just a regular heaven and that makes all this a plain kind of a hell, which I guess it is—but everything wasn't."

Shane eased in so as not to let the screen door creak.

"—and I've tried, boy. I've tried every goddam way a man knows how. Country isn't fit for people."

Shane left him talking, and in a way it sounded as if he were crying. His brothers were asleep when he came in, with the covers bunched up at the foot of the bed, so he sneaked them off and padded them up and lay on them as a pallet until after a very long time he fell asleep.

"But she loved him—goddamit, she loved him."

He muttered it. It would be the puzzle of his life, how this faded shrivelled woman who opened tentatively like a flower and then shrank back into a shrivelled pod from the intense heat of rage or scorn from her husband could still love him.

He was scarcely aware when the stewardess brought the tray and fussed over him. Perhaps he should start back in Nonsuch and discover what had kept the slender thread from breaking all these years, and look for more than a litany of alibis. All his life he had been searching for possession or to be possessed.

What in the name of God made that stewardess single him

out as a missionary? Perhaps that's what he was, a celibate, in spite of everything that had happened.

But he had been touched and of the flesh and a part of the flesh and a phrase from R. D. Symons skittered across his mind. The book? *The Broken Snare.* God, the phrase was so close. Now, that was it. "But perhaps the happiness was in the doing and not in the having."

PaperJacks

MOSTLY IN CLOVER
by Harry J. Boyle

An open door to an era full of warm nostalgia, this is a collection of articles that Harry Boyle contributed to *The Telegram*, edited for book publication, and rescued for a wider immortality than the yellowed newsprint clippings pinned to kitchen walls in rural Ontario. *Harry Boyle* has "a marvellous power to evoke the sounds and sights and smells and feelings of a boyhood gone . . . commands the eye and the heart of the reader in every page".
– Burton T. Richardson in the foreword. $1.50

A SUMMER BURNING
by Harry J. Boyle

A Canadian farm boy learns the hard facts of life from a young hoodlum fresh out of the slums of Toronto in this piquant novel about a lad's two worlds.

At fifteen, Joey Doyle knew only the world that surrounded the Ontario farm on which he lived – a world of nature and simplicity. But in his sixteenth summer – when Sammy Adams, a tough city boy, came to live at the farm for a few months – Joey was suddenly exposed to a world he had never imagined, in which tobacco and liquor, sex and prostitution, crime . . . and death, played principal roles. $1.50

PaperJacks

WITH A PINCH OF SIN
by Harry J. Boyle

It's the turn of the century and a young boy is growing up in the small rural town of Clover. It's a vibrant life, only one or two generations removed from the Frontier, where the Methodists and the Catholics eternally feud and the church-going people work hard for a living. The town characters and amusing events from the author's childhood seem so vaguely familiar, you're likely to think you're reliving your own childhood – or wish you were. *With a Pinch of Sin* is a delightful reminiscence by an author with a startling ability to recall the past. $1.50

HOMEBREW AND PATCHES
by Harry J. Boyle

Crowding around the wood stove with the rest of the family on a bitter January night in the Hungry Thirties brought an indescribable feeling of comfort and security. Full of touching and sometimes hilarious episodes, this book brings to life fiercely fought elections, Valentine's Day box socials and the amazing effects of grandfather's patent medicines. The author has the gift to draw laughter and tears with his memories of growing up in the country. $1.25

PaperJacks

STRAWS IN THE WIND
by Harry J. Boyle

A collection of musings about pussywillows, garbagemen, real fireplaces, farm barns, twilight, Easter hats, spring thaw, vacant lots, women shoppers, owls, picking berries, treehouses, noise, June, fig leaf fashions, mud, autumn mists, squirrels, crickets, Christmas trees, and everything else that makes up an escape-fantasy for the generation that's too old for pot and protest but too young for the rocking chair. $1.50